Summer at Tiffany's

Karen Swan was previously a fashion editor and lives in East Sussex with her husband and three children.

Visit Karen's website at www.karenswan.com or you can find Karen Swan's author page on Facebook or follow her on Twitter @KarenSwan1

Also by Karen Swan

Players
Prima Donna
Christmas at Tiffany's
The Perfect Present
Christmas at Claridge's
The Summer Without You
Christmas in the Snow

Summer at
TIFFANY'S

KAREN SWAN

PAN BOOKS

First published 2015 by Macmillan

This edition published 2015 by Pan Books
an imprint of Pan Macmillan
20 New Wharf Road, London N1 9RR
Associated companies throughout the world
www.panmacmillan.com

ISBN 978-1-4472-8019-4

3 5 7 9 8 6 4 2

A CIP catalogue record for this book is available from the British Library.

Typeset by Ellipsis Digital Limited, Glasgow
Printed and bound by CPI Group (UK) Ltd, Croydon, CR0 4YY

Visit **www.panmacmillan.com** to read more about all our books
and to buy them. You will also find features, author interviews and
news of any author events, and you can sign up for e-newsletters
so that you're always first to hear about our new releases.

For Plum.
Bunny. Off-piste polar bear.
Never apart. Always in my heart.

Chapter One

End of March, New York City

Cassie stared back at the polar bear. Standing on its hind legs, forepaws raised like a boxer's fists at her head, black lips pulled back in a snarl, she couldn't tear her eyes away from that unseeing glare, which still carried so much menace. It stood eight feet tall – its intimidating majesty undiminished by the fact that it had been frozen in this warrior stance for over eighty years already – and there was no question the bear commanded the room. Everyone revolved around it like satellites, eyes sliding back to it with silent respect over the tops of cut-crystal glasses, the opulent crush of velvet and rustle of taffeta nothing compared to its plush, snowy fur, which saw several of the finer-boned, sapphire-ringed hands discreetly brush it lightly as they passed.

The light oozed from chandeliers like liquid amber, candles flickering against the burr-wood-panelled walls and throwing shadows across the barrelled ceiling, faded rugs still soft underfoot as feet that were more often dressed in crampons, muck boots or desert boots and waterproof socks tonight trod with a lighter step in polished leather.

Cassie looked over at Henry again. After the polar bear,

he was the second most magnetic presence in the room, everyone glad-handing and back-slapping, head-nodding and brow-furrowing as they pressed for details of the trekking expedition to the Qurama mountains in Uzbekistan, which had won him his fellowship to this, New York's hallowed Explorers Club and brought them all out here on an icy March night.

Sleet slanted past the mullioned windows, the muffled roar of life outside on East 70th Street at odds with the room's steady murmurings, the trophies all around them – elephant tusks arranged either side of the fireplace, a stalking cheetah positioned mid-stride on a table – now old-world relics when they had themselves once heralded a new world, new frontiers. The irony wasn't lost on Cassie – they were memento mori, proof you had to keep moving. Life wouldn't wait for anyone. Nothing and no one got to stay new for long. The people gathered here in this room perhaps knew that better than the rest of the city combined. A door downstairs must have opened, for a breeze wrinkled the large flag that was hanging like a tapestry on the wall opposite. A striking blue, white and red diagonal design with a compass rose in the middle and the initials E and C either side, Cassie knew it well.

'Did you know that that flag was flown by the very first explorers to both poles, the deepest point in the ocean, the top of Everest *and* the moon?' Brett asked her, following her line of sight, as he returned with their drinks.

'Well, not that actual flag,' she clarified, taking her champagne from him with a smile. 'But yes, of course. What kind of fiancée would I be if I didn't know that? Henry wouldn't love me nearly as much if I didn't know the capital of Tajikistan or the currency of Peru or the date of the first moon landing or the dietary preferences of the Kombai tribe in New Guinea. *Or* the history of that flag.'

Kelly chuckled. 'He'd love you even if you didn't recognize the Union Jack, just so long as you promised to wear that dress.' She nodded towards the red Valentino dress Cassie was wearing – full-length, pillarbox taffeta with no sleeves and a trail of neat bows running down the centre of the bodice. Cassie still couldn't believe how Henry had grabbed her hand and marched straight into the boutique on Madison when he saw it in the window. He never did things like that; they couldn't afford him to. An explorer's salary didn't get paid into one's bank account with monthly regularity, but ran on the 'feast or famine' business model, and while tonight's event was a huge honour, it wasn't going to pay the rent – not unless he could secure the $120,000 shortfall for his next project, an underwater filming expedition to unexplored areas of the Arctic. The United Nations Environment Programme looked poised to come on board if the resulting documentary could premiere at the UN Conference on Climate Change – they were waiting on a call back on that – and Henry was hopeful that their involvement, combined with the ground-breaking footage and data they'd compile, would qualify the project as a flag-worthy expedition for the Explorers Club and bring in the grant that would mean it could finally go ahead.

'Oh, thanks. I never usually wear red.'

'Always wear red. It's your colour,' said Kelly with characteristic emphasis. Her colour was black. She rarely wore any shade but – graphite and navy being occasional exceptions – and tonight she was an exemplar of urban chic in a jet Alexander Wang column dress and cuffed heels. Her long dark hair was always styled ultra-straight, and her only concession to colour was the slash of scarlet on her lips. No woman in the world – be she from Osaka, Ottawa, Oman or Ohio – could doubt that New York was Kelly's home town: she wore the city in the way she spoke, moved, laughed even.

Not that she had laughed much tonight. In fact, both she and Brett – her husband of two years – were wearing sombre expressions that only disappeared when they sensed someone's gaze, and Cassie was aware of a small knot gathering in the pit of her stomach. As a box-fresh divorcee herself, she recognized the tension that pulled at the corners of their mouths, the slightly too-wide eyes as they overcompensated every time they made eye contact, the lavish focus on others instead of themselves.

Cassie just hadn't had time to talk to Kelly about it, though. In the three days that Cassie and Henry had been in the city, they had been to two lunches, five parties and this was their third dinner out. Cassie was dropping, even with the enlivening effect of wearing a $4,000 dress and having her blonde hair styled, backcombed and groomed into a slick ponytail thanks to her best friend Bas's extraordinary – and professional – skills with a comb and hairdryer. Cassie's jet lag had been brutal and had shown no mercy in the face of the back-to-back social arrangements that Brett and Kelly had organized, and Henry's itinerary which was just as gruelling, as he met up with acquaintances and contacts, forever on the lookout for potential sponsors. They were flying back to London tomorrow and Cassie – instead of following through on her plan to watch back-to-back films – already knew she was going to spend the entire flight sleeping.

'You look tired,' Kelly said, watching as Cassie tried her best to suppress a yawn.

'Me? No, I'm fine,' Cassie refuted. She knew from her four-month stint living here two years earlier that tiredness was practically a capital offence.

'Well, I sure am beat. I don't reckon I can stand in these shoes for another thirty minutes.'

Cassie – and Brett – looked at her in amazement. Tiredness? Sore feet? Brett couldn't have looked more surprised if his wife had turned to him and asked him to please address her as Bob.

'Well . . .' Brett looked flummoxed.

'Listen, if you guys are tired, please do go. Don't stay on my account. I'm perfectly happy waiting here for Henry, honestly. He won't be much longer, and I've got to finish my conversation with the chap I sat next to at dinner, anyway. Apparently he's just back from touring all eight of the earth's poles.'

'There are eight?' Brett looked even more surprised.

Cassie shrugged. 'Who knew, right?' She put a hand on Kelly's arm. 'Are you OK?'

'Of course. It's just been a long week.' She did look pale, the strain of her smile telling in her eyes.

'Ah, the man of the hour,' Brett said brightly.

'Hey!' Henry slid an arm round Cassie's narrow waist, bending down to kiss her on the cheek before straightening up with a suspicious expression as he took in their over-eager smiles. 'What's wrong? Oh God, are you all bored rigid? Did Old Mayhew corner you on his expedition to Chimborazo? I know precious few people actually care about whether or not that's the furthest point from the centre of the earth . . .'

'Absolutely not!' Kelly rebutted firmly. 'I've met more interesting people here tonight than I could meet in a decade in my industry. They only want to talk about the new Aman resort. Your crowd's so much cooler, Henry boy,' she winked.

But Henry wasn't fooled. 'So then you're all looking as shifty as a skulk of foxes in a hen house because . . . ?'

Brett laughed. 'Tell us how it's going with the flag pitch. Any luck?'

Henry's smile grew and Cassie felt herself loosen. The sight of him undid her – his muddy-blond hair curled gently over his ears and collar, stray cowlicks kicking out roguishly by his temples, his unfairly long lashes highlighting air-force-blue eyes that had the power to read her mind, and his skin was permanently tanned from a life lived outdoors . . . Combine those raw materials with a smile that always seemed reserved for her alone and a midnight-blue velvet smoking jacket, and it was a wonder she was able to breathe unassisted.

Her hand found his, burrowing into it like a hibernating dormouse, and she felt his grip tighten as he squeezed her in a non-verbal communication of adoration, affection and promise.

'Well, we've tabled a meeting in London for June. There's another submission already in that's worthy of the flag, but they've let it be known between friends, seeing as I am their newest fellow . . .' His voice had lowered to almost a whisper and the discreet look he gave them all from beneath his lashes made it clear that it was a shoo-in.

'Damn, that's great,' Brett beamed, looking genuinely pleased. As a trader for Cantor's, he earned four times what Henry could make in a year and yet he inhaled every anecdote and dastardly tale of Henry's daredevil job like it was pure oxygen.

Kelly put a hand on her husband's arm as though holding him back. 'I'm half expecting Brett to quit his job and volunteer to explore the Arctic depths with you. If he makes any noises about that, you tell me pronto, right?' she grinned. 'We. Have. A. Mortgage,' she said to her husband, sounding out each word as though communicating with him through bulletproof glass.

'Hey! I know where my limitations lie. Henry might be able to make a career out of this Indiana Jones stuff, but frankly, I lack the charisma. If I told anyone I wanted to go to the deepest point in the ocean, they'd put a ball and chain round my leg and give me a big push, not over a hundred grand!'

They all laughed.

'It's not everything it's cracked up to be, mate,' Henry replied with usual modesty. 'Frankly, a bit of job security would go a long way. It was great when I was younger – I could afford to live on toast and bunk at Suze and Arch's flat between jobs. But now . . .'

'Now that you've got a beautiful fiancée who's accustomed to only the best . . .' Kelly said, looking at Cassie with a wink. 'Talking of which, any news yet on a date, or are you still keeping us all hangin'?'

Cassie groaned. 'Oh God! Not you too!'

'What?' Kelly laughed. 'I need a new dress, OK?'

'Well, trust me, when we know, you'll know.'

Kelly looked at Henry with arched eyebrows. 'Unbelievable. She's engaged to you and yet *still* playing hard to get.'

'Tell me about it,' Henry said with a wry look.

Cassie turned to him. 'So, is there anyone else you need to talk to?'

'You're not changing the subject there, are you, missy?' Kelly asked devilishly.

'No! I was just finding out whether we can go. After all, you're the one dead on your feet!'

Kelly gave a melodramatic wince, as though Cassie had dropped her in it.

'I knew it! You *are* having a terrible time,' Henry said, deadpan and shaking his head.

A chorus of 'No's came back at him.

'I'll bet it was Cornell banging on about the biomes near lakes Geneva and Baikal that did you in, wasn't it? No, be honest.'

Yet more 'No's.

'We are crazy proud of you,' Kelly said, leaning over and patting his shoulder. 'I intend to dine out on this evening for months.'

He sighed, looking bashful. 'Well, you'll be happy to learn my work here is done, anyway. I have a fancy new tie' – he slid out the Explorers Club tie from his jacket pocket – 'dinner in my stomach and a fat grant poised to drop into my bank account. What say you all to going on somewhere for a nightcap? I know a great little place in the Village that keeps fifty-year-old single malts behind the bar.'

'Great,' Kelly said with an easy shrug, her earlier tiredness gone.

Cassie looked down at her and Kelly's sumptuous floor-length dresses, wondering how their uptown dress code would be received in a downtown bar and already knowing there was no point in worrying about it – Henry had once talked down a man who had pointed an Uzi automatic at him in Yemen.

'Super,' Cassie smiled, squeezing his arm and leaning into him tiredly.

Brett went ahead in the hope of hailing a passing cab, as Henry retrieved their coats. Kelly had lent Cassie a tiny black faux-fur bolero, which did practically nothing to combat the temperature, but they would only be outside for a few moments as they moved from kerb to car, and at least it covered her arms.

'OK, guys!' they heard Brett call, as they stood just inside the doors of the Jacobean townhouse, looking out into the white-speckled night.

Henry pushed open the door, a gust of wind skirmishing around them as Kelly led the way down the steps towards the waiting cab. The slick pavements shimmered in the street lights, yellow taxis speeding past with their roof lights off and droplets spinning from the wheels. It was more shockingly cold in the bitter night air than she had braced herself for and Cassie wrapped her arms tightly around herself, shivering, as she waited for Kelly to slide across the back seat in her narrow dress. A gusty wind had picked up while they'd been at the dinner and she half laughed, half gasped as the skirt of her dress was blown back against her legs, billowing behind like a scarlet sail.

'Oh my God! This weather!' she squealed.

In the next moment, as though heaven sent, sudden warmth settled upon her shoulders and her fingertips found the soft splay of velvet as Henry tucked his jacket around her. She angled her head happily as he stood behind her and kissed her neck, a small sigh escaping her as she reflexively closed her eyes.

'There's no such thing as bad weather . . .' he murmured, his breath hot on her exposed neck.

'Just the wrong clothes,' she finished for him, easily recognizing the quote from his lifelong idol, Sir Ranulph Fiennes. She was a *very* good fiancée.

He laughed, impressed, and she carelessly arched an eyebrow – pleased with herself too. She turned to get into the car just as a cab slowly sluiced past, a pale face behind the rain-mottled window fixed upon them – her.

Cassie stiffened in shock as the cab glided past into the night. *No.* There were more than nineteen million people in this city. *Not possible.* There was no way that could have been the one person she didn't want to see. *No way.* The rain was too hard, the night too dark to see properly; she hadn't even caught a glimpse, just garnered an impression really.

And yet . . . she had been known to recognize friends in her peripheral vision just by their walk.

'Cass? You OK?'

She looked back at Henry, who was watching her with quiet calm, his hand by her elbow. She realized she had paused, mid-step into the car.

'Of course,' she said weakly, trying to laugh off his concern and sliding in beside Kelly.

The door closed behind Henry with a *thunk*, his thighs warm as they pressed against hers, but the cold had already seeped into her bones and she gave a big shiver.

'Ooh, someone just walk over your grave?' Kelly winked.

She couldn't know how right she was.

Chapter Two

Three months later

Morning had broken – the tuneful din of two hundred coal tits chirruping in the crab apple tree outside the open window told her so. She stirred fractionally, heavy-limbed and rested, as the breeze rippled over her bare skin like a breath, Henry's hand in the nook of her waist; she felt his fingers spread as she stretched, her body firming beneath his inert fingertips before relaxing back into the softness he adored.

Her eyelids fluttered open and closed several times like a basking butterfly's wings, blinking the busy blossomed tree into focus. They never drew the curtains, and she didn't need to be standing at the sash window to know that somewhere Breezy, Mrs Jenkins's cat from the flat below, would be sitting watching and waiting for just one of the tiny spirited birds to linger a moment too long on the shaded grass.

She could see the sky was already a promising blue, narrow drifts of clouds spinning into airy thinness as the sun began to get into its stride, and the dull roar of traffic on Embankment was already beginning to build. She sighed sleepily, used to it now.

Another zephyr blew in, unsettling a sheaf of papers stacked loosely on a tower of books on the floor, several pages blowing free and settling on the coir matting like stepping stones. Her eyes wandered the room with bleary indolence. Heaps of clothes were piled along the footboard of the iron bedstead so that nothing could be seen of it; a picture they'd bought at the Affordable Art Fair in Battersea Park was still propped against the far wall, ready to be hung whenever Henry remembered to buy nails; the whisper-pink roses he'd bought for her the week before were still luscious and dewy on the chest of drawers; the powder-blue walls colour-matched the sky, at this early hour at least. Her eyes stopped at the photo on her bedside table, taken of her and Henry at Kelly and Brett's wedding almost two years ago, the very hour they'd finally got together; it was their favourite photograph – her arms wrapped tightly round his neck, both of them laughing, eyes bright as tigers' so that to the casual observer, it would have seemed it had been *their* wedding.

She closed her eyes again, a smile on her lips. Home.

That wasn't to say it was perfect. The flat was far too small – even she would admit that now – but after a decade of being the chatelaine in a grand Scottish country house, she had fallen hard for the intimate charm of somewhere 'cosy' – her buzzword for everything good: log fires, Henry's jumpers, a bubbling pot of chilli con carne – and when they'd first viewed it, she'd sworn to be the queen of edits. They would live minimally, she had declared; she didn't want 'things' anyway; her divorce from Gil had shown her just how little comfort they provided when your world was dismantled bit by bit – *my* chair, *my* lamp, *your* mirror, *my* silver . . . And Henry proudly considered himself someone who prioritized experiences over possessions in any event (although that wasn't to say he wasn't dearly fond of his PS4 and the plasma that took up almost one wall in the sitting room and made her feel on Saturday afternoons that their flat was actually a box at his beloved Twickers).

Their intentions had been sincere and well meant at the time, but it's hard for two people to build a life together in only 800 square feet of prime London property, not to mention their mutual careers which came with unwieldy accoutrements. Henry's, as a professional explorer, meant ice axes and crampons were stored beneath the sofa, and metres of fluorescent climbing ropes were loosely looped on nails tapped in along the picture rails round the tops of the walls. Cassie's career, meanwhile, as co-owner of Eat 'n' Mess, a vintage picnic company that put together old-school hampers for high-end society events, meant – in a reversal of Kelly's Manhattan bachelorette apartment, where cashmere jumpers had been kept in the unused oven – there were baking trays in the shelving unit where her jeans should be, cake boxes instead of hatboxes; her make-up was kept in the cutlery drawer, and the kitchen had no table as such but a carefully stacked arrangement of wicker baskets that held Eat 'n' Mess's vast collection of mis-matched porcelain tea sets and Welsh rugs, resulting in their 'dinner parties' – which actually meant plates on laps, sitting on upturned terracotta flowerpots (or, most prized of all, an upside-down large yellow bucket) on the fire escape – becoming as famous with the neighbours as with their friends.

So yes, it was a tiny flat, but she still maintained it was a gorgeous tiny flat. The clotted-cream sitting room caught the evening sun, and on every one of their four windowsills there was a herb garden: Henry liked to have the basil outside their bedroom, as he said it reminded him of Italy and the time they'd almost, but not quite, got it on; he said he never wanted to forget how excruciating it had been to have her in his life but still just out of reach; The lavender, which reminded him of his mother's garden, where they *had* got it on, was outside the bathroom; the camomile, which she used for tea and was one of their earliest love tokens, was outside the sitting room; and the thyme and rosemary were outside the kitchen.

She loved it here. She loved him. Their messy, spilling-out-at-the-edges life was everything she wanted. Henry shifted beside her, his arm easily drawing her in tighter so that the small gap between their bodies closed and they touched from tip to toe again so that nothing – not even the breeze – could slip between them.

Her eyes were just closing again when she caught sight of the time on her alarm clock beside the bed.

'Oh *crap*!' she shouted, sitting bolt upright. 'Henry, we've overslept!'

'Wha—' he groaned sleepily as she threw back the duvet and ran starkers across the room towards the hall console, where her knickers were kept.

How could this have happened again? It was the third time in five days. They *had* to start going to bed earlier. They were in their early thirties now, not twenties. They weren't bright young things anymore. If either one of them had office jobs, they'd have been sacked ten times over by now.

'Get up! You're late!' she yelled over her shoulder, wishing she had a chest of drawers like most normal people. It'd be easier to access in emergencies.

Henry sat up, the white duvet falling back to reveal his beautifully cut shoulders and smooth stomach, although his face was hazy with sleep. Then he saw the time on the clock and wide-awake horror crossed his face too.

'Oh shit!' he hollered, leaping out of bed and almost immediately going flying on a stray sheet of paper that had drifted to his side of the bed. He grabbed the door for support, but that only swung under his weight, leaving him in an undignified half-crab pose above the bedside table. 'Bloody buggery hell!' he shouted crossly, righting himself and wondering if he'd pulled a muscle in his hip.

'Here!' Cassie said, throwing him a clean pair of boxers from across the room. Luckily, he'd already hung out his suit and shirt the night before and he was in those and straightening his tie before Cassie had found her clean shirt – the red lumberjack one – to go with her jeans.

'Cass, come *on*,' he said impatiently, snapping on the clasp of his watch. 'I'll have to go without you. You know I can't wait.'

'It's OK. I'm done. I'm coming,' she panted, tightening the double knots on her Converses and standing up. They both jogged across the room then to the front door.

'You mean like last night?' Henry grinned, with a wink, as he held the door open for her and she sprinted down the four flights of stairs. 'Because that really was something . . .'

'Shut up!' she laughed.

Everyone was waiting for them when they arrived eleven minutes later, with ninety seconds to spare.

'Jesus Christ, you cut it fine!' Archie said, wild-eyed, his red hair leaping like a lord – he badly needed a haircut – as Cassie and Henry shot into view on the westbound District Line platform at Victoria, the agreed meeting place. There must have been thirty or forty other men just like them – in suits and trainers – clustered around, waiting for the four minutes past eight. 'Give a guy a heart attack why don't you? I thought I was going to have to do this thing on my own.'

'You'll never walk alone, mate,' Henry winked, patting him heartily on the shoulder.

'It's not the walking I'm worried about,' Archie said, checking the tension on his red braces and loosening his tie. 'I didn't fancy asking Suze to be my running buddy.'

Henry laughed, not least because his sister, Suzy – Archie's wife – was wearing a face like thunder as she tried to hold on to her wriggling two-year-old daughter, Velvet, who was unfortunately in the throes of a biting phase and was eyeing the legs around her with particular appetite.

The train pulled in to the station with a squeal of brakes, the doors hissing open as everyone spilled in, the carriages blessedly relatively empty as they went against the rush-hour traffic and headed out instead towards the suburbs.

Cassie greeted Suzy with a kiss, easily taking Velvet from her as the toddler spied 'Auntie Kiss-Kiss' and settled peacefully on her lap.

'Oversleep again, did you?' Suzy asked wryly. She knew perfectly well why Cassie and Henry were forever sleeping past their alarm.

Cassie mouthed a sarcastic 'Ha, ha' back to her as the train pulled out. It was carnage in the carriage as the panoply of men in suits and trainers dominated – some, led by Archie, began singing sea shanties (quite why, she didn't know); others were jogging lightly on the spot, stretching their arms and necks – as the regular commuters looked on in puzzled but persistent silence.

'God, it's like the last train to Brighton in here,' Suzy said, wrinkling her nose as the aroma of a McDonald's breakfast drifted over. 'Honestly, every year it's the same and every year I swear never again . . .'

Cassie tilted her head sympathetically. 'Arch is so determined to make it, though. He tries *so* hard and it'd be terrible for you to miss it.'

'He's *never* going to make it, Cass,' Suzy said in a low tone. 'His idea of a training session is jogging down to the pub.'

Cassie shook her head resolutely. 'Nope. This is his year. I can feel it.'

'Well, that's one of us.'

Cassie jigged her legs lightly, softly singing the theme tune to *Sleeping Beauty* to Velvet – her emerging favourite film – as the train rattled along the tunnel, rocking side to side in the blackness until the gradual whine of the brakes was heard, the iconic London Underground sign whizzing past the windows, indecipherable at speed, but gradually slowing like a roulette wheel so that she could make out 'South Kensington' in red letters.

The doors opened again and most of the passengers on the platform took one look at the assorted bunch in shirtsleeves and trainers – some of whom were trying to raise a haka – and opted for the neighbouring carriages.

'Right, well, nearly there,' Archie said as the train started moving again. He put himself through some dubious stretching exercises before bounding over, his freckled hand gently rustling Velvet's white-blonde hair. 'Kiss Daddy for luck, Velvet?' he asked, bending down, lips pursed in an impressive trout pout as he waited – and waited – for his toddler to comply.

Suzy was just as reluctant, fussing with Archie's bike clips instead, which he had attached to his trousers to minimize 'wind resistance', then adjusting his braces and checking he'd put Vaseline on his nipples. 'We don't want a repeat of last year, do we?' she asked, before giving him a firm peck on the lips.

'Ready, mate?' Henry asked, rolling up his shirtsleeves and handing his jacket and briefcase to Cassie with a kiss. He pushed his index finger against the tip of her nose, his eyes lingering on her mouth, just as the train jolted to a complete stop. 'Don't move,' he said with a wink, before turning and slipping through the mass of City-shirted backs to the doors.

'As if,' she sighed to herself, hugging his jacket tighter.

With their customary hiss, the doors opened and the pack set off with a roar, sprinting onto the platform, arms pumping and ties flying. Cassie couldn't help but get up with Velvet and watch them go. Henry was in the lead group, of course, racing up the stairs, which were positioned bang outside their carriage; Arch was bringing up the rear and looking like he'd got a stitch before he'd even reached the top. Within a minute they were out of sight, although not earshot.

Cassie ducked back into the carriage. Having been overcrowded only seconds before, it was now empty and quiet, the remaining passengers settling back down with relief to their newspapers and smartphones, the new ones boarding hastily as the station attendant held up his paddle and blew the whistle.

Suzy lifted the massive nappy bag, which was significantly larger than the toddler it served, off the seat she had 'reserved' and Cassie sat down again, handing over Velvet and carefully folding Henry's jacket over her lap as the train pulled away. She checked his briefcase to make sure he'd remembered, in all the rush, his iPad, which contained his notes.

'When's the meeting?' Suzy asked.

'Nine.'

'*Nine?* How's he going to get back into town in time for that?'

'He's not. They're doing it over breakfast at the Hurling-ham.' The private club was based on the outer boundary of Fulham, the Thames flanking it on one side, and was only two Tube stops further on from where this daft interlude was supposed to end.

Suzy shook her head. 'You are completely stark raving bollocksy-mad. I thought you said this meeting was the make or break for the Arctic expedition?'

'It is,' Cassie murmured, checking the iPad was actually charged.

'And yet he thought it was a good idea to do his best *Chariots of Fire* impression half an hour beforehand?'

Cassie smiled. They both knew this event was run to mark the anniversary of Bannister breaking the four-minute mile. It was usually scheduled for the date of the actual anniversary – 6 May – but Henry, as the organizer, had had to push it back a few weeks as he'd been travelling so much, pulling the team together and schmoozing the great and good of the political and environmental worlds who liked what he was doing. He couldn't afford to cancel again on account of a meeting, especially with the expedition just around the corner now, which would take him out of the country again. 'He reckons they'd understand if he's late.'

'He'd better hope they do. Isn't someone else in the running for the grant?'

'Yes, but it's fine. This is just about being seen to be following correct procedure; the fact is, the whole thing's been all but agreed.'

Suzy paused, only slightly mollified. 'Well, I personally think you're loons.'

'I know.' Cassie instinctively reached across and stroked Velvet's round cheek again. She really was a dreamy-looking child, inheriting her father's dimples and her mother's distinctive blonde hair and dark brown eyes. (It was on account of her rich, velvety eyes that she was known by her middle name and not her first, Clemency, or even her beloved antenatal nickname, Cupcake.)

'You're dead broody,' Suzy smirked.

Cassie whipped her hand away smartly. 'I am not!' she retorted, as though Suzy had said, 'You're dead ugly,' instead.

'So then . . . ?'

'I'm simply hatching a plan to kidnap your delicious daughter and sell her to Vera Wang as a professional flower girl.'

'Ha! Don't think I haven't considered it!' Suzy gave a sharp laugh, but something in her tone vibrated in Cassie's head like a tuning fork.

'How *is* work?'

Suzy's wedding-planning consultancy in Pimlico netted all the chicest, most cosmopolitan brides in one of London's smartest quarters, although that also meant their demands were off the scale and Suzy was often run ragged in her quest to deliver them the perfection they sought. Yet she had seemed uncharacteristically mellow recently.

There was a protracted silence as Suzy's eyes roamed the carriage as though looking for spies. 'Houston, we have a problem,' she said finally, her eyes meek, for once, as they met Cassie's.

'What kind of problem?'

'A problem that I hadn't realized is as bad as it is.' Suzy shook her head, distractedly playing with one of Velvet's cowlicks. 'You remember Archie's last bonus at Christmas was pants?'

'Yes.' How could they ever forget? Suzy had rampaged like a wounded bull at the bank's very clear message for her husband to push off, as Henry had taken Archie down to the pub to drown his sorrows.

'Well, I thought it was just a matter of him making a few phone calls, you know? But I kid you not, he has more meetings with headhunters than he does with clients, and still nothing. The market's dead and he's stressed to the eyeballs.'

Cassie couldn't pretend she knew anything about the world of finance or what a risk-weighted asset was. 'But people are still getting married, right? I mean, things are still good for you work-wise?'

Cassie realized the train had stopped, the carriage emptying dramatically, and she glanced round to see where they were. Earls Court. Already? They had sailed through Gloucester Road without her even noticing.

'Listen, I didn't realize the scale of things with Arch. He's been trying to keep it from me, and I've been so wrapped up in Velvet . . .' She kissed her daughter's head again, her eyes instinctively closing at the scent of her. 'Well . . . I've been turning jobs down, trying to strike that famous work–life balance.' She looked across at Cassie, her big brown eyes doe-like as Cassie saw fear in them. 'I was trying to learn from my mistakes, for once. I didn't want to be all strung out like I was before she was born, you know?'

Cassie rubbed her friend's arm lightly as the train pulled away again. 'Of course you didn't. You've done exactly the right thing, putting Velvet first.' Suzy's mania in the run-up to Kelly's wedding had led to Velvet being born several weeks early.

'Have I, though? Cass, the phone's barely rung with any new enquiries for weeks now. I think word went out that I wasn't taking on any new jobs, as opposed to I wasn't taking on *too many* jobs. I've got Marie colour-coding the magazines, and my last bride gets married a week Saturday. There's nothing in after that.'

'Nothing?' Cassie couldn't keep the surprise out of her voice.

Suzy shook her head, swallowing hard. 'That's not all. We're . . .' Her voice faltered. 'We're struggling with the mortgage. Arch thinks we might have to sell.'

Cassie grasped her friend by the wrist. 'Oh, Suze, no!'

'But you mustn't say a word about it – not to Arch, not to Henry either,' Suzy said urgently. 'If Arch wants to talk about it, then he will. You've got to let him bring it up. He'd kill me for telling you.'

'Of course not. I won't say a word.'

They sat in silence for a bit, both rocking to the motion of the train.

'So what are you going to do?' Cassie asked.

'Not sure. Hang out at the London Eye and hand my card to anyone coming off with a red rose and an empty bottle of fizz?'

'Surely your contacts and suppliers can put the word out for you?'

'Listen, by the time someone gets to a caterer or a florist, they've already got the wedding planner.'

'Oh, right, yes, I guess.' Cassie bit her lip. 'Well, I mean, I can keep an eye out for you. I've got the Ascot gig tomorrow and then the Gold Cup polo. I bet loads of proposals happen there! I could keep a load of your cards on one of the tables.'

Suzy arched an eyebrow. 'Or you could just hurry up and marry my brother? Now that's a wedding I'm dying to organize.'

'We're too busy to get down to the nitty-gritty of organizing something like that at the moment. Henry's about to swan off to the Arctic, and I'm booked for the next five years of Ascots already.'

It was Suzy's turn to place a hand on Cassie's arm. 'And that is precisely why people like you hire people like me.'

Cassie had to grin. 'Suze, I promise you that there will be no one organizing my wedding other than you. Not me. Not even my mother.' Cassie frowned. 'Actually, especially not my mother – she'd have me in gold.'

'Well, I don't know, Cass,' Suzy sighed despondently. 'What hope do I have of landing other brides, if I can't get you to marry my own freakin' stud-muffin brother?'

Cassie shrugged. 'It's not because I don't love him, you know.'

'Oh, I know that! We all know exactly how much you two love each other, thanks to the almost-permanent snogging going on between you.'

The train stopped again. West Brompton. They were overground now and Cassie looked out over the London rooftops, pigeons roosting on chimney pots, inflated white clouds billowing across the sky like flyaway sheets.

The carriage was almost theirs alone now, save for a couple of teenagers with their feet on the seats at the end – they were lucky Suzy hadn't pounced on them: she was to dirty shoes what Kirstie Allsopp was to litter – and a man in a suit two seats along, engrossed in a level of Candy Crush on his iPad. Cassie wondered whether he'd missed his stop. The area they were travelling into was becoming more and more residential.

Velvet was beginning to wriggle on Suzy's lap now, the amusement factor of travelling on public transport diminishing with the crowds. Suzy reached into her bag and pulled out a small Tupperware of carrot sticks, handing one to her eager child.

The doors closed and the train pulled away again, Cassie still lost in thought about her friend's problems.

'So, are you all set for Ascot? You said it was a big gig,' Suzy asked.

'Oh . . . yes. We've got sixty covers and three separate sittings to cater for: champagne breakfast, lunch and high tea. I've got to bake a hundred and eighty eclairs today, once I've picked the car up after this.'

Her cream Morris Minor was back in the garage again. Henry had warned her about the unreliability of the alternator and radiator, but she'd been so adamant it looked right (much as the teeny-tiny flat had looked right) – so shiny! so post-war! – parked beside the bell tent on their big-set, yesteryear picnics that she'd gone ahead and bought it instead of a new Golf. Now it was in for 'touch-ups' every other month and she knew Jim, the mechanic, so well she took him tins of home-made rainbow-coloured macaroons for his wife's birthday.

'How is Jim?'

'Really pleased. Kayla got her first-choice school.'

'Yeah? That's great,' Suzy murmured distractedly about the family she'd never met.

The train was already slowing again and they were pulling into the platform at Fulham Broadway, their destination.

'We're here,' Cassie said, getting up and walking over to the doors.

'Yes, but are they?' Suzy asked as the train slowed almost to a stop.

'Hmm, I can't see them,' Cassie said, pressing her face as close to the glass as she dared. 'Oh, wait!' Cassie laughed suddenly as she caught sight of Henry racing into view like he'd been catapulted, his blond-brown scruffy hair flying behind him, his tie flapping like a windsock by his shoulder as he ran over the bridge and descended the stairs three at a time, coming to a stop *just* as the doors opened. Jammy devil.

They stared at each other for a beat, him panting hard, before he grinned. 'What took you so long?' he asked, kissing her on the mouth and straightening his tie as he stepped back onto the very carriage he had disembarked from four stations earlier. Mission accomplished. Winner of the Annual Tube Dash six years running.

A gaggle of other sprinters, all racing for second place, hove into view moments later, jumping down the stairs like grasshoppers – missing four at a time – and flying into the carriage with roars of delight, slapping each other and high-fiving, as they too had successfully negotiated twenty-seven roads, four Tube stations and thousands of pedestrians to sprint the 1.5-mile course and beat the train.

'Oh Jeez, where's Arch?' Suzy asked, resignedly throwing the nappy bag over her shoulder and lifting Velvet as she stood up. The runners seemed more in need of her seat than she did. 'Anyone seen him?'

Henry shrugged. 'Sorry, Suze. I wasn't looking behind me,' he grinned.

Suzy swatted him about the head – as his big sister by thirteen months, it was her prerogative.

'I overtook him at the hospital if that helps,' one of the other guys laughed, holding his arms up protectively in case she came and walloped him too.

'It's OK – I can see him, Suze,' Cassie said, pointing to the bridge.

Archie and a couple of the other runners were not so much running as lurching their way across, their eyes on the train already at the platform.

'Come on, Arch!' Suzy bellowed, leaning out from the carriage. She had the lungs of a pufferfish. 'You can do it!' She turned to Cassie. 'Oh, please, God, let him do it. If he can just do it this one time, then he can give it up.'

Henry sucked on his teeth. 'I don't know, sis,' he teased. 'Look, the station guard's got his paddle up. It's not looking good.' Cassie marvelled that Henry's breathing had already returned to normal. Henry leaned back out through the doors again. 'Come on, Arch! One last push!'

'He's not having a bloody baby!' Suzy protested as Archie began descending the stairs, holding the handrail as he staggered down them.

The warning beeps that the doors were about to close

sounded and Suzy automatically leaned against one of them, holding it open.

'Come on, Arch!' she hollered again.

'I don't think so!' Henry said, spotting her trickery and pulling her away, allowing the doors to close.

'Henry!'

'No, no cheating. It's not fair, and it's not what Arch would want. You either win or lose on merit alone – he knows that.'

As if to prove the point, an exhausted runner got to the doors, two seconds too late, pressing his palms to the glass windows as the train slowly began to roll towards the river and Putney beyond. The other guys began to jeer at the poor fellow; Henry gave an apologetic shrug and a 'never mind' thumbs-up.

'Well, that's all very well for you to say when you're six foot four with legs as long as ladders,' Suzy argued, exasperated that this would mean another year of listening to Arch moan about having to 'train for the train'.

'Wait . . .' Cassie gasped, her tone like a blade through the siblings' spat. Suzy and Henry looked back out of the window. Archie was near the bottom of the stairs, but he had stopped running – not because the train was pulling away. His eyes were wide, but he didn't even appear to be seeing the train. He was holding on to the handrail with one hand, seemingly frozen on the spot.

'Arch?' Suzy whispered, taking in his grey pallor compared to everyone else's florid pink cheeks, watching as the freeze in his features gave way to a silent splitting spasm, which wracked his face and shocked his body back and then forwards, sending him flying down the last steps onto the platform.

He was only feet away from where they had been, but the train was moving faster now, and as she was whisked out of sight of her dying husband, Suzy began to scream.

Chapter Three

Midnight had been and gone by the time Henry eased open the spare bedroom door and peered in. Cassie, who had been staring at the wedding photo of her two closest friends in the world – wholly unable to sleep – propped herself up on her elbow and blinked back at him, trying to read the news in his face. All she could see was his exhaustion.

'Just say it quickly,' she said, before he could open his mouth.

'There's nothing *to* say,' Henry said, sinking onto the side of the bed beside her. She was still in her clothes – not sure if she would be summoned to bring Velvet to the hospital at a moment's notice – and lying on top of the duvet. It had seemed easier to stay at Suzy and Archie's rather than in their tiny flat, not least because all of Velvet's toys and nappies and bottles were here, but the tragedy seemed amplified in the house of its victims – photographs on every surface, memories at every turn – and she hadn't been able to close her eyes long enough to doze.

Henry absently reached for the raspberry-pink wool blanket at the bottom of the bed and draped it over her while he talked, trying to stay busy, keep occupied as he said the words. 'He's not out of the woods yet. He's still in the CCU. His heart rhythms are too erratic for him to be moved anywhere else at this point.' His eyes flicked to hers. 'He had another heart attack two hours after being admitted, so they're not taking any chances.'

Cassie's hands flew to her mouth. Another one? He had been completely grey by the time Cassie and Suzy had got to him. Henry had run all the way back from Parson's Green, the next stop, beating the cab the girls had frantically hailed on the street and, no doubt, all the trains too.

'And how's Suze?' Cassie's big blue eyes were as wide as the sky was dark. She knew that behind her friend's straight-talking, don't-mess demeanour was a heart as fragile as a bird's egg.

'Being invincible. She's watching over him like a bodyguard, wanting to know what every tube is for, and she didn't let go of his hand once the whole time I was there. She bawled out one nurse because she got the date wrong. She said if she wasn't even sure of the day's date, how could she trust her on anything more serious?' He shrugged, rubbing his face in his hands. 'How's Velvet?'

'Oh, she's fine,' Cassie nodded. She had been looking after the child from the second Suzy had clambered into the ambulance with Archie. 'Oblivious, really. The only wobble was when she wanted Suzy at bedtime, but she was fine as soon as she had her bottle. I thought she might want to sleep in here with me, but she went down in her cot, no problem.'

'Sweet thing,' Henry murmured, but a fault line ran through his voice, close to cracking it in two. 'She's too young to—'

'Shh, I know,' Cassie said, scrambling up onto her knees and wrapping her arms around him. She knew what he had been going to say – that Velvet was too young to be without a father, that she'd be too young to remember him if Archie did die.

'No. All this is my fault,' Henry said, pulling away from her and, resting his elbow on his knees, pinching the bridge of his nose as agonies ran over his features.

'Henry, how can you think that? Of course it isn't!'

He whipped up his head. 'Cass, I physically stopped Suzy from keeping the doors open. *I* kept her from getting to him.'

She remembered how he'd moved Suzy out of the way of the doors to let them close, how, as they'd pulled out of the station, he'd had to stop Suzy from tugging the emergency cord – *his* logic wrestling with *her* instinct, as he'd tried to explain it was, counter-intuitively, quicker for them to get to the next station than stop in a tunnel outside that one, even though her husband was lying on the platform and beginning to die.

'You did the right thing, at every point,' Cassie said quietly.

He shook his head irritably. 'I set the pace too fast.'

'No. The train set the pace too fast. You had nine and a half minutes to make it; the train wasn't waiting for anyone. That's the whole point.'

Henry got up and paced across the floor, raking his hands through his hair. 'I shouldn't have talked him into it. He didn't even want to do it. *I* made him do it.'

Cassie watched him. 'The only person who makes Arch do anything is Suzy. We all know that.'

Henry laughed, but it came out like a bark – joyless and hard – and he continued pacing. 'I shouldn't have—'

'Henry, stop this! Archie is unfit and stressed to the eyeballs. Suze told me on the train while you were gone – his job's on the line. They might lose the house. She's been worried about him for weeks.'

Henry stopped moving. 'What are you talking about? He hasn't said anything about it to me.'

'He hasn't talked about it to anyone.'

Henry stared back at her, his eyes unseeing upon her face for once as the news sank in, before he collapsed back down onto the bed again, dropping his head into his hands.

Cassie crawled over to him and began kneading his shoulders. They were practically sewn together by the tension in his body. 'Listen, he'll be OK now. He's in the safest place he could be, and it's been nearly twenty-four hours since it happened. That's the most dangerous time, right?'

Actually, it had only been fifteen hours, but neither one of them made the correction. They both wanted to believe . . .

Henry groaned as she worked on a particularly hard knot in one of the muscles.

'You're exhausted,' she said quietly, reaching over and kissing the side of his neck. 'Lie down. You're no good to anyone without sleep, and Suzy's going to need us to keep the wheels on for her tomorrow.'

Without resistance or complaint, but guilt still written all over his face, Henry rolled down onto his side. Cassie covered him with the blanket. He was still wearing his suit trousers with the trainers, his meeting with the Explorers Club completely forgotten in the aftermath of Archie's collapse. Cassie pulled his trainers off for him, the laces still tied.

The slow rise and fall of his ribs told her he was already almost asleep and she spooned herself around him, her hand resting on his hip, his tight body slackening with incipient sleep. But there was no crab apple tree outside this bedroom window, no birds singing, and she wondered how she could have felt so safe and bulletproof in her world yesterday when today it felt made of glass.

The blue hulk of the Chelsea & Westminster Hospital towered over them and Cassie held Velvet closer to her as she walked through the doors, half a step behind Henry. It was the hospital where Velvet was supposed to have been born, had she not come early, and Cassie's only visits here had been happy ones – accompanying Suzy on some of her antenatal appointments and laughing at Suzy's lively facial expressions as she jumped on the scales or had blood taken, before linking arms and splurging on coffees and cake in the Starbucks outside. They, neither one of them, could have foreseen that two years later they'd be back here in such terrible circumstances.

Henry, after only an hour and a half of utter oblivion, had slept badly and he jabbed the lift button impatiently, his jaw thrust forward, hands on his hips. They hadn't showered or had breakfast, and Cassie watched his foot tap before she broke her gaze to stroke Velvet's hair as the child asked for Mummy and Daddy again.

'Just one more minute, darling,' Cassie whispered, kissing her head, before repositioning her on her hip. 'We're on our way to see her right now.'

The lift opened and Henry tutted as he stepped out of the way of a porter pushing a man in a wheelchair. He pressed the button too hard again to the right floor, shaking his head irritably as the doors closed at a sedate pace.

'It'll be OK. They would have rung us if there'd been any change,' Cassie said, touching his shirtsleeve lightly.

Henry glanced down at her with ashen skin and blood-shot eyes, and she swallowed at the sight of him so cut up. She'd never seen him like this before. Henry was always the fixer, the calm eye at the centre of every storm, the beating heart of every party. He knew everyone and everything (the temperature of the sun? The velocity of a speeding bullet shot in a vacuum? The speed of sound when measured at sea level? Cassie had flung all these questions at him and he'd known the answers off the top of his head), and his happy-go-lucky smile and energy for life saw him make friends, contacts and alliances wherever he went.

She was the weak link in the relationship – the flapper, the panicker, the worrier, the hider, the one who couldn't change a wheel, mix a Martini or cope in a crisis. But he needed her now. Archie wasn't just a brother-in-law; he wasn't just a friend. He was the guy who had hopped into his beaten-up Golf and driven 800 miles when seventeen-year-old Henry got lost on the wilds of Rannoch Moor and had only enough phone battery to make one ten-second call; he was the guy who not only dug the grave for Henry's beloved childhood Labrador, Rover, but bought and planted a rosebush above it too; he was the guy who still held the world record for Pac-Man (but was pitiful at *FIFA*), who laughed like a goose, had never knowingly worn matching socks and had married his wife on account of her rich lasagne and even richer eyes. He was Henry's blood, his brother. There was simply no question of him dying.

The doors opened and Henry was off again, arms swinging like a soldier's as he marched directly to the CCU, from which he'd come – at the nurse's insistence – only six hours before. Cassie and Velvet caught him up just as a nurse in blue trousers and tunic buzzed open the door. She must have been on the night shift, as she obviously recognized Henry, letting them all in with a nod and a bright smile.

Inside the unit, everything felt different – the air was solid and thick like a slow-moving cloud, the light blue-tinted, and behind drawn floral curtains twenty different cardiac monitors beeped out of time with one another. Cassie closed her eyes, trying to brace herself for the sight of Archie on one of the beds, clad in a gown with tubes coming out of him; but all she could conjure was him this time yesterday, puckering up for a kiss from Velvet as Suzy adjusted his braces so that they didn't rub his nipples when he ran – something Henry had been teasing him about ever since they'd bled on last year's run and stained his shirt.

Velvet dropped her favourite toy – a ragamuffin pig – on the floor and Cassie bent down to scoop him up.

'How's he been?' she heard Henry ask the nurse in a low voice.

'Quieter.'

Quieter? It was hardly the answer they'd been hoping for, and as she stood again, Cassie saw a muscle clench in the ball of Henry's jaw. Henry crossed the room in four strides, but Cassie saw how he paused before he stepped round the curtain; she clocked the slight rise in his shoulders as he took a deep breath, steeling himself for the horrific sight of his best mate flattened and barely alive on the bed.

She turned back to Velvet and handed the child her beloved toy. 'Here you go, darling.'

'Can I help you?'

She turned to find the nurse now looking at her, although her smile was brisk and considerably less warm than the one she'd given to Henry.

'Uh, yes . . . I'm here to see Archie too.'

'Archie . . . ?'

How many Archies did they have in here? 'Archie McLintlock.'

'Are you family?'

'Well, sort of . . .' Cassie hesitated. 'I mean, not strictly, not in a blood sense. But in a legal sense – well, one day, anyway.'

The nurse stared back at her, baffled and cool.

'He's married to my fiancé's sister,' she said by way of explanation, jerking her head in the direction of where Henry had disappeared. 'He's my fiancé.'

'Who is?'

Cassie blinked. Was this woman being deliberately obtuse? Was she the nurse who'd got the date wrong yesterday and was out for revenge on Suzy's nearest and dearest?

'Henry. The man you were just talking to.'

'I'm afraid only family is allowed in the CCU. I'm going to have to ask you to leave.'

'But . . .' Cassie protested as the nurse shepherded her towards the door again, 'I just explained.'

'Your status does not qualify as family. I'm afraid you cannot stay in here.'

'But surely I can at least say hello?'

It was precisely the wrong thing to have said.

'This is the Cardiac Care Unit. Mr McLintlock is in no state to "say hello".'

Cassie stared at her, a hot blush of indignation washing

over her otherwise peaches complexion. 'This child here is his daughter,' she said, planting her feet firmly and hoisting Velvet higher onto her hip.

'Children are not allowed on the ward.'

'I understand that, but perhaps her mother would appreciate a few moments with her child, after what has undoubtedly been the roughest twenty-four hours of her life?'

The nurse, who was standing by the door, hand poised over the entrance buzzer, looked back at her and Cassie tried to arrange her expression into something less combative. This was about Suzy and Arch and Velvet, not her having a battle with the nurse who was furtively flirting with her fiancé.

The nurse relented. 'Bay three. But only for a moment. If Mrs McLintlock wants to spend time with her daughter, she will have to do it off the ward. I can't have any of the other patients being disturbed.'

'Of course,' Cassie nodded, before adding magnanimously, 'Thank you.'

She walked slowly across the room, already oblivious to the nurse's eyes on her back, trying to brace herself for the image she already knew would be waiting for her behind the brown floral curtain. She peered round cautiously; she didn't want to risk frightening Velvet and needed to see how bad things looked first.

Suzy was asleep on a small camp bed that had been set up against the wall, with only a thin blanket over her, although she didn't need it – it was so warm in here. And Archie . . . Archie looked like a dystopian warrior, his pale body covered in tubes and wires so that he looked more machine than man.

She recoiled. It was every bit as brutal and mechanical-looking as she'd feared – her own father had died from a heart attack six years earlier, and although he had been in Hong Kong and she in Scotland at the time, this was the very image that had haunted her dreams. She stepped away from the curtain, shaking her head and trying to smile as Velvet frowned.

'Kiss-Kiss,' the child squawked, reacting to her unfamiliar expression.

Cassie clasped her head and kissed her firm, chubby cheek again at the sound of the pet name her god-daughter had bestowed upon her. Velvet was too young to be able to say Cassie yet, and besides, Cassie never, ever stopped kissing her.

'Velvet?' The sound made them look up, as Suzy – wide-eyed but still shrouded in sleep – suddenly appeared round the curtain with a gasp of joy to see her daughter. 'Oh, Velvy,' Suzy whispered, taking her child from Cassie's arms and covering her face in kisses. 'Mummy's missed you so much.'

'Mum-my. Dad-dy.'

'He's sleeping, my sweet thing. But you can see him very soon, I promise. Did you have fun with Auntie Kiss-Kiss?' Suzy looked across at Cassie and squeezed her arm hard. 'Thank you,' she mouthed.

'I didn't know whether you wanted her to see Arch or not,' Cassie said in a quiet voice.

'No. No. He looks . . . He looks . . .' Suzy bit her lip as huge, swollen tears raced down her cheeks.

Cassie threw her arms around her, around both mother and daughter, as Suzy's shoulders began to heave. 'Come on. Why don't we go downstairs for a coffee? It'll do you good to have a break from this place, and you can play with Velvet more easily. We've not had breakfast yet, anyway, so she's probably starving.'

'But—'

'No buts. Henry's here and we'll only be a short while. I promise you'll feel so much better for having a break.'

Suzy nodded, frankly too exhausted to argue further. Her skin was almost bone-white, and even her famously chocolatey dark brown eyes had lost their richness. Cassie peered round the curtain – taking care not to look at Archie this time – but Henry had overheard and nodded in reply, without either one of them opening their mouths. He was leaning against the wall, arms folded over his chest, staring down at his closest friend and feeling – Cassie knew – help-less. And if there was one thing he wasn't, it was that. He could cope with anything but that.

Cassie ordered briskly – and too much – at the Starbucks counter as Suzy and Velvet bagged the leather sofas in the far corner, the two of them engrossed in a clapping game. She set down the tray of lattes, foamy milk for Velvet, croissants, pain au chocolat, pain au raisin, two muffins (double-chocolate and a 'breakfast' blueberry one), fruit salad and a muesli-yoghurt pot.

Suzy arched her eyebrows.

'You need to keep your strength up,' Cassie said weakly, before Suzy could get a word out.

'Clearly.' Suzy reached forward and handed the fruit salad to Velvet, who instantly started sucking on a slice of mango and within seconds set off a bright yellow river of juice running down her chin.

Cassie handed over a napkin, before grabbing the double-chocolate muffin and peeling back the case, slicing it in half and handing it over to Suzy on a plate. Suzy was famous for her sweet tooth, but she just looked down at it like it was made of chipboard.

'Suze, you have to eat,' Cassie scolded, bringing her chair closer.

'I know. And I will.' She set the plate back down on the table. 'I just need to . . .' She inhaled deeply. 'Take a minute. Everything happened so quickly yesterday – the train pulling away as Arch fell, being trapped until the next stop . . . It was like being in one of those dreams where you can't run, can't throw a punch . . . you know?' Her head dropped down, her legs shaking.

Cassie squeezed her knee, remembering it all too clearly: Suzy's screams, the way she'd pounded at the windows so hard Cassie had thought they would shatter, how Henry had had to hold her back from pulling the emergency stop as she wrestled with him, reaching for the red handle.

'I keep thinking I'm dreaming. Last night, when I was lying in that bed and all I could hear were these *machines*, keeping everyone alive, keeping Arch alive . . . ! I mean, how is it even possible that this is happening? Yesterday I had to kick him out of bed for snoring like a train, and now he's in here.'

'You're in shock yourself, Suze.'

Suzy's eyes lifted to hers and a long moment passed between them. 'What will I do if he doesn't . . . ?' She couldn't articulate the thought, as though to give it voice were to give it life, as though the words would be comprehensible to Velvet even if she weren't involved in a suck-to-the-death on an orange segment. 'No one else would put up with me the way he does, as you're always telling me,' she muttered with a wry, hollow laugh.

'Well, it's true. You're a nightmare – far too bossy and always right. Which is why Arch *is* going to survive this.' Cassie smiled kindly. 'There's no way he'll leave you and Velvet. There's not a man on this planet who has got more to fight for than him. You two are his world.'

Tears began to fall from Suzy's eyes again, her lips drawn thin as she struggled for self-control. 'God, the irony. Just when you think things can't get any worse, they go and do.' She shook her head. 'I thought the past few months had been so hard on us – Archie's barely been around, and I've been a snappy cow, knowing I should have been doing more than I was but not wanting to burst my bubble with Veevs. I thought *that* was our hard-luck story, you know? A piffling little bonus was our karmic retribution for . . . whatever. But what does any of it matter now he's lying in a bed up there on a ventilator? Who gives a stuffed cow about some job? He always hated it anyway. Said the blokes on his desk were losers who—'

Cassie interrupted her with another squeeze of her knee. 'You will get past this, Suze. Archie isn't going to die. He wouldn't bloody dare, not till you give him the OK at a hundred and six, once his arthritis means he's stopped being able to open bottles of cava for you.'

Suzy sniffed. 'You think?'

'I know. But I also know that it's going to be a while before he's back on his feet, so you're going to be spending a lot of time around here for the foreseeable. What can I do to pick up the slack? Didn't you say your last bride's getting married next Saturday?'

Suzy nodded. 'Texted me at eleven thirty last night wanting to know if the scented candle wax had been poured into the garden urns yet because she'd changed her mind on the patchouli.'

Cassie grimaced. 'What did you do?'

'I didn't reply. I didn't trust myself not to tell her where to go. Who gives a fig about—'

'She doesn't know what you're going through. It's not her fault. Listen, I'll speak to Marie, OK? She can take the reins, and anything she can't deal with, she can come to me and I'll deal with it, yes?'

'Are you sure?' Suzy asked, without protest for once, as she handed over the phone.

'You need to put your time and energy into helping Arch get better. Nothing else matters for the moment.' Cassie had become well versed in the dramas of Suzy's business after she'd worked for her during her first summer in London while the divorce was going through. She knew the contacts, protocols and drills for dealing with stressed brides and their mothers, and Suzy passed as many catering jobs over to Eat 'n' Mess as she could, so they often still worked together. 'And what about Velvet? Do you want me to carry on staying at yours with her till Arch is discharged?'

'If you can just carry on holding the fort till Mum gets here? She's already on the way. She was in Scotland doing some, I dunno, herbaceous borders convention or something, but she should be here mid-morning. She might take Velvet back home to West Meadows with her for a bit. Or not. It depends on how long the docs think Arch will be in for.' Her lower lip trembled. 'It was so horrible in there last night.'

'I bet it was.' Cassie rubbed her hand soothingly.

'Did you know I've never spent a night apart from Velvet before?'

'I didn't,' Cassie smiled. 'But you both got through it. And she looks OK, doesn't she?'

'Actually, it's depressing how unbothered she appears to be,' Suzy replied with a sniff, a glimmer of her old fire flickering in her voice. 'I think you could just take over from me and she wouldn't much notice.'

'That's not true. I can only buy her love and attention with food.'

The doors opened and they watched as a few nurses walked in – either on their coffee break or at the end of a shift. Suzy stiffened as though their watch may be over but hers wasn't. 'We should get back.'

Cassie glanced at the untouched food on the tray. 'Sure.'

They took the stairs. 'The lifts take too long,' Suzy said, as she walked straight past them, carrying Velvet in her arms, her body vibrating to the same nervous energy as Henry's. Cassie hurried to keep up, already dreading the smothering synthetic quiet that was contained by the CCU's locked glass doors.

The same nurse who'd buzzed them in earlier came to the door again and Cassie knew from her surprised look at the fact that Cassie had actually come back that she wasn't going to be setting a foot over the threshold this time.

'I'd better, uh, leave you here,' Cassie said quietly, not wanting to alert Suzy to her 'persona non grata' status; the poor woman had bigger things to worry about. 'It's probably better not to take Velvet in there. All the machines bleeping, you know . . .'

'Oh yes. Good thinking.' Suzy squeezed her daughter

tightly to her, sniffing her hair and savouring the feel of her skin against her own. 'If I can't get out—'

'I can be here anytime you need. Just say the word. We can be here in fifteen minutes.'

'You're an angel.'

'No. Just your friend.' Cassie smiled, wishing she could see Henry, but she knew he wouldn't want to be called away without good reason.

She watched as Suzy walked back into the unit and the nurse closed the glass door on her with a resolute click. Cassie waited for a few minutes, wondering if Henry might come out to see her when Suzy reappeared, but not a single curtain flickered and eventually – Velvet growing restless in her arms – she had to turn and walk away.

Chapter Four

'Come on. Pick up. Pick up,' Cassie murmured to herself, chewing on her thumbnail as she paced Suzy's narrow dog-leg hallway, one ear still straining for the diminishing chunters behind the nursery door. The lights on the baby monitor in the kitchen were a soothing green now, at least, indicating sleep wasn't far away.

''Allo? Cass?' Anouk's refined Parisian accent was so delicate, yet husky, it almost came with its own scent – a blend of amber, jasmine and musk. 'How are you?'

'Nook—'

'What has happened?' Anouk asked, quick as a flash. With old friends, one syllable was enough.

'It's Arch,' Cassie said, one hand clutching at her throat, as though she was trying to squeeze the words out – or keep them in. 'He had a heart attack yesterday.'

There was a shocked pause.

'But he is OK, yes?'

'He seems to be stable, at the moment.'

There was another long, stunned silence. And then: 'Yesterday, you say?'

Cassie picked up on the rebuke immediately. 'I'm sorry. There was so much going on it was impossible to call. Suzy was in pieces and I had to look after Velvet. Henry only came back last night to sleep, and he's still with Suzy at the hospital now.' She swallowed, the words almost a slur as a silent tear slid down her cheek.

'What can I do? I can be there in a few hours.'

'No, no. I honestly don't think there's anything you can do over here. Not yet, anyway. Hattie's due any minute to take Velvet, and until Arch is discharged . . . they're only letting family stay.'

She was still smarting from the bitter blow that engagement to the patient's wife's brother wasn't a strong enough bond to admit her to the CCU's inner sanctum. Hospitals didn't care about bonds that were thicker than blood, friendships that had spanned their lifetimes; fact was fact and she wasn't family. Not yet.

'I just wanted you to know, that's all.'

'Have you told Kelly?'

'Not yet. I'll wait till it's a decent hour over there.'

'She would want to be woken for this, Cass.'

'I know, but what would it achieve? It's not like she can do anything from there.'

'No.'

Neither of them said anything for a few beats. They didn't need to.

'How is Henry?'

'Not great.'

'No. I bet . . .'

There was another pause.

'Guillaume?'

They were the same words but it was a different question. Guillaume wasn't tied in to this tragedy like Henry. He wasn't struggling to keep it together. The words, framed around him, amounted to a nicety, an automatic social more that meant nothing in the circumstances. Anouk, as though recognizing this, paused before replying and Cassie could just picture her friend dragging slowly on her cigarette. 'Fine.' Anouk's voice had that bored insouciance only Frenchwomen could pull off when talking about their lovers. 'He is in Cap Ferrat. Back next week. You are sure I should not come over?'

'At the moment, no, but I'll let you know if his condition changes.'

'OK. Well, you give that man a kiss from me.'

'That might give him another heart attack, Nooks.'

They disconnected just as the sound of keys scratched in the lock. Cassie turned. Through the frosted glass she could make out the hatted, billowing silhouette of Henry and Suzy's mother, and a moment later the door opened, Hattie's tall, wiry frame filling the doorway. She was wearing her usual uniform of black Nicole Farhi apron dress, draped taupe openwork cardigan and plimsolls, and her frizzy ash-blonde hair was contained by a bashed straw hat that was fraying in so many places it looked like it had been nibbled by a donkey. Battered holdalls dangled from each brown hand, but at the sight of Cassie – pale-faced, moon-eyed – staring back at her, she dropped both bags on the spot and wrapped her arms around her, rocking her gently from side to side.

For a split moment Cassie felt herself go limp – a 'grown-up' had arrived: she didn't have to pretend to be brave now – but as they stood there, swaying slightly in the open hallway, she realized it wasn't Hattie who was comforting her: stoic, no-nonsense Harriet Sallyford, the renowned garden designer and four-times gold-medal-winner at Chelsea, the woman who'd shown Suzy exactly how strong and imposing a woman could be . . . Her. *She* was the one trembling, holding on too tight as she tried not to cry, as broken down by the rest of them at the flattened sight of her happy-go-lucky son-in-law, who still looked at her daughter, every day, like she was a dream come true.

'He's going to be fine, Hats. You know Arch,' Cassie said weakly.

Hattie pulled away, drying her damp eyes with a quick one-two motion of her hands, before clapping them together loudly. 'Of course he is. You're quite right. He wouldn't dare leave my two girls. It's not his time. It simply isn't.' She inhaled sharply, pulling herself together. 'Tea?'

Cassie watched as Hattie swept into the kitchen behind, busily choosing two mugs and sniffing the milk. Cassie picked up the abandoned bags from the doorway and closed the door softly, so as not to waken Velvet. 'You've come from the hospital, I take it?' she asked, stepping into the kitchen.

'Yes.'

'Any change?'

'Not this morning apparently, although since *I* saw him last – what, two, three weeks ago . . . ?' Her blue eyes flicked up to Cassie's. 'He looks like he's been steamrollered. I mean, his skin is *actually* grey. Roger and Emma had arrived only minutes before me and they looked like they needed oxygen themselves, poor things. No parent should ever have to see their child like that.' She paused, a look of genuine puzzlement crossing her features as she was drawn back into the tragedy again. 'I just don't understand it, Cassie. He's such a young man, so vigorous—'

'He'd been under a lot of stress, apparently, at work.'

Hattie gave a sceptical frown.

'I know – he hid it from everyone. No one knew. Suzy barely realized the severity of it herself.'

'But . . . there must have been warning signs, surely? Men of thirty-three don't drop down half dead after a quick run just because they've got a lot on at work. Surely he must have been looking unwell or complaining of aches or pains beforehand. I mean, we all know how *stricken* Archie is by the man-flu every winter.'

Cassie shrugged. 'He really did look totally normal. I saw him and his colour was as good as ever, and he was leading the other runners in a round of songs just before the race.'

'Well, that does sound like him. Let me guess: "Sweet Chariot"?'

Cassie smiled. Arch had played prop for Harlequins's youth team and had been gunning for a place in the senior squad after university, when an ill-advised tackle in the bar broke his collarbone so badly he not only had to wave goodbye to his ambition of going pro, but any contact sport at all. Touch rugby in Battersea Park was as good as it got for him now, although Suzy – who had met him six months after the injury – had consoled him, saying he couldn't afford cauliflower ears anyway, 'not with his nose'.

They sipped their tea quietly for a while, Cassie leaning lightly against one of the Heals bar stools and warming her hands, which were unaccountably cold, Hattie distractedly dead-heading a begonia that still had the red reduced label on the pot and clearly hadn't been watered since it had been bought. For a mother and daughter who were so alike in every other way, it was a source of constant despair for

Hattie that the one thing her daughter hadn't inherited from her had been her green fingers.

'Listen, if you'd prefer to get back to the hospital, I'm more than happy looking after Velvet,' Cassie said.

'I know you are. You're such a natural. I can't wait till you and Henry crack on and have some of your own. Then I really will be spoilt rotten.'

Cassie gave an abashed laugh. Having children was on the 'One Day' shelf, along with a few other things that she preferred not to dwell on. Like setting a date.

'It's just that it can feel more difficult to be stuck back here, rather than at the hospital. At least there you feel like you're doing something.'

'Oh, there's nothing any of us can do for that poor boy right now,' Hattie sighed. 'I'm as much use being a good grandmother as anything right now. What about you, though? You've been stuck here a day and a half baby-sitting? You must be desperate to go in and see darling Arch. Henry said you haven't been in yet.'

Cassie looked away. 'Well, if Roger and Emma are there . . . it may be a little crowded,' she murmured, not wanting to elucidate on her 'outcast' status. It felt humiliating and belittling somehow, to have been left stranded behind glass doors as one of the most beloved people in her life fought to save his own life – all because the lack of a ring and a piece of paper kept her at one remove too far.

She suddenly remembered her car, her shiny, malingering car, which had been repaired again – for the time being – and was waiting for her at the garage. She had been on her way to pick it up when Archie had collapsed. 'Actually, though, there is something I need to do. If you're sure you're happy to man the fort here . . . ?'

'Absolutely. You go on and do what needs to be done. I thought I'd take Velvet down to the flower stalls at the farmers' market after her sleep. They should have some marvellous agapanthus now and it's about time I started introducing her to the Alliaceae family. You can never start them too young, you know.'

Cassie drained her tea and set down the cup with a smile. 'I've got my mobile with me. You will ring if anything changes?'

'Of course. Now go, go.'

'See you later, then.' Cassie grabbed her cardigan from the stair banister and closed the front door quietly, glad to be out of the stifling quiet and suspended atmosphere of the house, glad to be doing something other than waiting. It wasn't until she was on the train to Putney Bridge that she remembered something else that had been forgotten in yesterday's events.

She struck gold at the Travellers Club in London's Pall Mall – the heart of Clubland – a white wedding cake of a building, winking opulent and gilded interiors through its street-facing windows. Unlike the colonial style of the Explorers Club in New York, this club boasted the kind of grandeur that was standard for hosting royalty, aristocracy and eminent diplomats and luminaries, with silk walls and marble floors and shimmering chandeliers that would bring down the roof of an average London terrace house.

Not that Cassie got to see much of it. The lobby was as far as she was permitted, and to save both herself and the concierge the embarrassment of staring at each other politely, she was busily occupying herself by reading the club housekeeping notices on the walls while Bob

Kentucky and Derek Mitzenhof, the president and chair of the Flag Expedition Grant Board, were called from their rooms.

She had been lucky to have made it this far (although she was going to pay through the nose for it when her mobile bill came in – half-hour calls to New York didn't come cheap), but there had been no other way to get the names and London addresses of the men Henry had been en route to meeting yesterday. The Explorers Club had been reluctant to impart their details, even after she had lengthily explained her relationship to Henry and yesterday's disaster; they had much preferred the option of getting the board to contact Cassie, but she had stood firm, for once. This had to be sorted today. She had called them, standing outside Jimmy's garage in Putney as he hunted for her car keys, and it had taken her another hour to get back into town and find a parking space.

'Miss Fraser?' Cassie turned to find a tall, white-haired man with a lean face and neat moustache standing before her. 'Bob Kentucky.' He held out his hand. He was wearing a dark grey suit and a tie that she recognized as being Explorers Club – Henry had been given the same one when he was made a fellow back in March – and she wished she was wearing something smarter than her blue-and-white-striped sundress, Converses and navy moth-nibbled cashmere cardigan.

She saw Bob Kentucky wish it too and he discreetly looked over at the doorman, who, after a moment, gave a nod as subtle as the Mona Lisa's smile.

'We'll take coffee in the reading room,' Kentucky said – whether to Cassie or the doorman, she wasn't sure – holding one arm out in an open hook and inviting her to step into the gilded sanctuary.

It was immediately apparent the walls must be as deep as Afghan caves, as the rush of London traffic speeding along to St James in one direction and Admiralty Arch and Trafalgar Square in the other was instantly muted when the inner door closed behind them.

'I'm afraid Derek can't join us,' Bob said with an apologetic smile. 'He's engaged in a fight-to-the-death rackets game with an old acquaintance.'

'Oh, no, of course. I'm just so grateful you could see me at such short notice. I'm really sorry for turning up unannounced like this,' she said, as they climbed the elegant winding staircase, which was set at such a gentle pitch it seemed almost embarrassed to turn.

Kentucky smiled. 'On the contrary – I was delighted when the club rang to tell me you were on your way. We were so baffled by Henry's no-show yesterday.'

'I'm also sorry for looking so scruffy. I hadn't planned on coming here when I left the house today.' She tried rolling the cuff of her cardigan to hide the fact it had a thumb-sized hole through it.

'Well, I admit jeans would have been harder to get around, but I think Mr Stanley at the door was also of the opinion that with a face as pretty as yours, nobody's going to be looking at your feet.'

'Oh . . . Thank you.' Cassie blushed. 'You're very kind.'

'We can talk in here,' he said, stopping outside the door to a large and sunny room. Inside, groups of leather chairs were arranged at intervals beneath the solemn and lavishly gilded portraits of illustrious former members. It took her straight back to her days in Scotland, living in one of the country's great houses. This was another level again, but she didn't feel out of her depth here. This was a world she knew and understood.

They settled themselves in a pair of wine velvet wing chairs by the window – she could see the buses sitting in traffic outside – as Kentucky ordered some coffees.

He sat back in the chair, fingers interlaced, an interested smile on his face as he waited.

'Um, so I don't know how much they told you on the phone . . .' she began.

He shrugged. 'Not much, but once they said you were Henry's fiancée, I knew you'd be coming with an explanation of sorts.'

'Well, yes, exactly. Because, you see, none of it was Henry's fault yesterday. He was en route to see you and everything was tickety-boo.'

He chuckled at her choice of words and she grinned back nervously.

She started again. 'There's this annual event, you see, that Henry organizes. It's called the Annual Tube Dash, or Beat the Train, as the runners call it.'

'Runners?' Kentucky sounded as amused as he was intrigued.

'Yes. It commemorates the anniversary of Roger Bannister breaking the four-minute mile' – Kentucky's smile turned into a low, rumbling laugh as he began to get the gist – 'At least it's supposed to; we're a bit late with it this year. Anyway, all the runners have to jump off the same carriage of the train at South Kensington and run a set route through the streets, getting back on the exact same train and carriage at Fulham Broadway.'

'How wonderful!'

'Yes, well . . . Henry's unbeaten at it.' Cassie rolled her eyes. 'It's pretty gruelling. Basically a nine-and-a-half-minute sprint in the middle of rush hour. You can imagine all the people they've got to dodge, the cars and bikes crossing the roads . . . Only about ten per cent actually finish it.'

'And Henry was doing this *on the way* to our meeting?' he laughed.

'I know, it's mad, isn't it?' She shook her head. 'I kept telling him it was crazy, but well, I think he feels honour-bound, as the organizer, to do it himself. And truthfully, he's so fit he could run it and you'd never know five minutes later, whereas I bet all the others have to take the rest of the day off.'

Kentucky smiled, sitting further back in the chair as their coffees, in porcelain cups, were set down on the table between them.

'Anyway, yesterday . . .' She took a deep breath, willing her voice not to break. 'Yesterday the worst thing happened. Everything was fine to begin with – Henry had finished the race and was back on the train. We were pulling out of the station when Archie, his brother-in-law, who was doing the race too, had a heart attack on the platform.'

Kentucky's bemused expression changed to one of immediate horror. 'Dear God!'

'I know. It was terrible,' she said, her voice cracking slightly as she remembered it all too clearly, yet again. She wasn't sure she'd ever get over the sight of Archie's face in the split second before he fell. 'We couldn't stop the train, because then we'd have been stuck in the tunnel and unable to get off, so we had to go all the way to the next station, knowing what was happening behind us, that he had only strangers looking after him.' She bit her lip and reached for her coffee, needing a break from the words and images, but it was still too hot to drink and she had to replace it, untouched, on the table. She noticed her hand had begun to shake.

'What happened?' Kentucky asked gently.

'Well, Suzy, Archie's wife, who is Henry's sister and my best friend' – her eyes flickered up to him, as she worried she was bombarding him with too much information – 'she was there with their little girl; she's only two.' She sighed. 'So you can probably imagine the state everyone was in.'

Kentucky murmured his agreement.

'When we got to the next station, Henry jumped off and ran *back* to Fulham while Suzy and I got a cab. She couldn't run carrying Velvet too,' Cassie mumbled. 'Anyway, the ambulance had arrived by then, so Suzy went to hospital with the paramedics and Henry caught a cab after them and basically stayed there all night. He's still there now.'

'What a truly terrible story. Is Henry's brother OK now?'

'Well, he's hanging on,' she said after a moment. 'He's still in the Cardiac Care Unit. He had another heart attack soon after getting to the hospital, apparently.'

'I'm truly sorry to hear that. What a dreadful thing.' He shook his head as he picked up his coffee, cradling the saucer in his palm, and stared out of the window for several long moments. 'Well, that certainly accounts for things. We knew something drastic must have happened for Henry not to have shown, or even sent word. We just couldn't understand it, sitting there as the minutes ticked past and no word.'

'No, I'm sure. It was just so crazy, you see – everyone panicking and screaming, Henry running all over London,

56

CPR . . . And he's not allowed to have his phone on in the hospital, obviously.'

'No, no, of course not,' Kentucky agreed, taking another sip of his coffee. He sighed heavily. 'I just wish we had known this yesterday morning.'

Cassie swallowed. 'It's not too late, though, is it? It was only yesterday, and in the circumstances—' She was stopped by his sympathetic smile.

'My dear, I wish it were that straightforward, I honestly do. But you see, the nature of our profession means we're rarely all in one country – much less one room – at the same time. A decision had to be made there and then.' He gave another sigh. 'It's all the more frustrating because, in truth, the flag was his. Henry's a great ambassador for the exploring community and we're very proud to have him as one of our fellows. This expedition he's pitching appeals to us on many different levels, and the meeting yesterday, really, was just a formality. But when he didn't show and there was no explanation . . . Well, I'm sure you can appreciate we can't afford to lay ourselves open to claims of favouritism or, worse, nepotism. It would have seemed, at the very least, curious, if not downright suspicious to the others if we had tried to accommodate the proposal outside of the formal process.'

'So then the grant's been awarded to . . . someone else?'

'I'm afraid so. We really had no other choice.' He sipped from his coffee again before returning it to the table and looking back at her with a kind smile. 'But it's by no means the end of the road for Henry's quest. *We're* desperately disappointed not to have the club's name and flag associated with the trip, of course, but with a reputation like his, he should have no problem securing the rest of the funds.'

'Well, it's more of a timing issue than anything,' she said quietly, bitterly wishing Henry hadn't been all but promised the grant in New York: it had meant he'd stopped looking for the funding elsewhere and had focused on nailing the itinerary and booking the rest of the crew instead. How was she going to tell him it was over? How would he tell all of them? There was no way that they could raise that kind of money in the time they had left. They were leveraged to the hilt . . . She thought suddenly of the divorce settlement sitting untouched in her bank account but dismissed the idea as quickly as it had come. Besides, Henry would never want to use Gil's money to bankroll his work, she was sure of it. She sighed. 'This was pushing it as it was,' she said quietly, the flat tone of defeat hammering down her words. They had fallen into every cliché – put their eggs in one basket, counted their chickens before they'd hatched, run before they could walk – and with less than a fortnight until departure, it had come back to bite them. 'Obviously he can only travel there during the summer months. Once the sea freezes . . .' It was professional humiliation, the entire thing a shambles . . .

'Ah yes, yes, of course. I hadn't thought of the small matter of being iced in.' He tutted pensively, one finger tapping his lips. 'Hmm.'

Cassie took heart from the gesture. Was there still a chink of hope after all? 'This was simply the final round of funding needed to make it happen, you see – obviously if he'd had any inkling things would fall through with you, he'd have lobbied elsewhere, but as you said, it was pretty much just a formality. Everything else is in place,' she said, a pleading note sounding in her voice. 'UNEP, the UN Conference on Climate Change – it's taken months to get them all on board and signed up, and the National Geographic Channel was really interested in running it as a series afterwards . . .' She looked at him hopefully.

He looked back at her through focused eyes, as though reading her mind. 'Well, you know . . .' he said, stretching out the words thoughtfully, 'maybe this thing isn't dead in the water yet.'

She sat straighter, feeling like her heart was doing shuttle runs in her chest.

'There's always next year's grant, and I have no doubt that everything I've just said about Henry will still apply – possibly even more so – twelve months from now.'

No. Cassie visibly deflated, giving a polite but weak smile in return as he beckoned the waiter over for more coffees. He didn't get it. Assurances about next year were no good to her when she and Henry were already worrying about next month's rent. They'd been planning their finances around this expedition since the spring; they'd been banking on it setting them up to Christmas and a bit beyond. Now what were they supposed to do? The salary she drew at Eat 'n' Mess was barely enough to cover their food and the repair bills for the car; and C et C, the restaurant in Paris where she retained a minority stake, may have a four-month-long waiting list for a table, but with significant start-up costs still to cover, the company wasn't issuing any dividends yet. The divorce settlement flashed like a red light in the back of her mind again.

'A top-up?' He held up the coffee pot.

She gave an abject shake of her head, feeling suddenly uncomfortable to be sitting in this grand salon in her market clothes like a modern-day Pygmalion. She watched as the other members shook out their papers, brows furrowed as they studied the business and sports pages. If the grant was completely out of the picture, surely there must be a few high-net-worth individuals in the club – in this room, even – who could be persuaded to part with the outstanding sum? Exploring was and always would be the pursuit of rich men's whims, and $120,000 was mere pennies to the billionaires who played these adventurous games.

The question was, how to find them without having to beg?

The light was fading by the time she got home, pulling into Denbigh Place with a weary sigh. After leaving Bob Kentucky, she had driven over to Zara's flat in Stockwell to apologize and give her the lowdown on Archie – her poor business partner had had to go it alone at Ascot today, sans eclairs – and they had gone through the menus and shopping lists for their next job, an all-day affair at the Gold Cup polo at Cowdray Park this weekend.

She rested her head against the steering wheel for a moment, worn out and wondering how she was going to break the bad news to Henry. She could see the light on in their little flat and wished she could teleport herself into his arms up there, on the top floor; she loved their little flat but sometimes wished it wasn't nestled in the grey-tiled eaves of the roof. The building itself was a junior version of the grand club she had left only hours before – cream Regency with porticoed windows, four floors and an elaborate balcony that wrapped round all the French doors on the first floor; but whereas the club was palatial inside, the flats within this building – which themselves sold for millions – were furnished in a stealth-wealth style, with antique wooden floors, Moroccan Beni Ourain rugs, over-sized linen sofas and crushed-velvet bedspreads.

Their flat was the shabbiest, as behoved the attic rooms really, but even at that the rent was exorbitant and more than they could afford; Henry had suggested numerous times that they buy somewhere together instead – 'Rent money is dead money,' he was fond of saying – but they could never afford to buy somewhere like this, and Cassie so loved the central location and quiet street and, of course, the ancient and bowed crab apple by the rear window.

She saw the back of Henry's head first as she let herself in. The rugby was on the telly, and he was sitting with one foot on the coffee table, his other leg bent with one arm lolling on his knee, a beer in his hand, his head resting against the sofa cushions.

'Hey,' she said softly, kissing his hair before she walked round the sofa, ready to snuggle into his lap. A bath and a glass of wine and they could—

'Where have you been?'

The ice that veined his words brought her up short, stopping her feet and her heart simultaneously.

'What?'

'You heard me.'

She blinked in astonishment, unable to process the hostility she saw in his eyes. 'I . . . I was at Zara's. We had to go over the last bits for the job this weekend.'

'*All* day?'

'No. Of course not.'

'So where were you, then?'

'Henry, what is this?' she asked in bafflement, dropping her bag to the floor and sinking onto the edge of the sofa beside him.

'What is this?' he repeated with incredulity. 'Mum's down, Archie's half dead, and you're nowhere to be found and you ask me, "What is this?" Christ, I can't believe you. You had every opportunity to be there. I needed you there. Suzy needed you.'

This was because she hadn't been to the hospital? 'Henry, look, just calm down. I can explain.' She took a breath. 'I wanted to be there, more than anything, but . . .' She didn't want to say it. It was like letting the genie out of the bottle.

'But what?' he prompted impatiently. Had he slept at all today? He looked rough and worn out.

'They wouldn't let me in, OK?' she said. 'They said only family could go in. I explained to the nurse that I was your fiancée, but she said it didn't count.'

He blinked at her, sliding his lower jaw to the side and nodding in silence as he processed the words, his anger filling the room like smoke in a jar.

He didn't reply immediately, instead taking a deep swig from the beer bottle, draining it, and she wondered how many others he'd had. 'Well, she's absolutely right, of course. It doesn't. Engagement isn't anything. It's just a nice idea, a promise you can make with your fingers crossed behind your back. It's only one level up from a suggestion of something you might possibly choose to do someday. Or maybe not.'

'Henry, stop.' She could feel it beginning again.

'Why? It's true, isn't it? A year and a half ago I gave you a ring and you said, "Yes," but that doesn't *actually* commit us to anything. It certainly doesn't make us family. It certainly doesn't mean that you can be there at the moments that count! Either one of us could change our mind at any given point and the whole arrangement would just come down as easily as a house of cards. Poof! Gone.' He clicked his fingers hard, the gesture making her jump.

She blinked at him, feeling the first smarting of tears behind her eyes. There they were – back to their age-old argument, their only one. 'This isn't about us.'

'Of course it's about us!' he scoffed. 'It's about you refusing to commit to anything beyond the next meal. We can't buy a flat together because that would mean using your divorce settlement, and that's your fallback, right? I mean, God knows after you caught Gil in the act, I might turn out to be just as big a bastard as him, and then where will you be?'

'Henr—' It wasn't like that, and he knew it. How many times had she tried to explain that the divorce money felt tainted to her? How could she get across her fear to him that using the money would feel, somehow, like she was letting Gil back into their lives? But he wasn't listening.

'You won't let us buy a flat, talk about having kids, set a date – all the great unmentionables that must never be brought up, the fucking elephants that fill this flat more than any of our junk.'

'Just stop it!' she cried, standing up. 'You have no right to throw these things back at me like they're not important!'

'Of course they're important! But you won't ever discuss them. I'm the only one in this relationship who seems to have any kind of hope that there's a certain future in it.'

'That's not true.'

'No? Where do you see us living five years from now?'

She threw her hands up in the air in exasperation. 'Well, how would *I* know?'

'How about ten? What are we going to be doing?'

'I don't know!' she cried, bringing her hands down into fists and stamping her foot on the floor. 'That's not how I think anymore. I like just—'

'Living in the moment. I know! My God, do I know!' Henry rolled his eyes, on his feet now. 'The thing is, Cass, that doesn't work for me – not now. If what's happened to Arch proves anything, it's that we don't have a bloody clue what's round the corner, and I don't want to live with vague promises. I want you to be my wife, not my fiancée, not my girlfriend – my wife. I want us to belong to each other in every way possible. I don't want there to be grey areas when it comes to *us*. I want to know you're mine in good and bad, sickness and health. You may have been married for ten years, but *I* wasn't and I'm not going into it expecting it to fail. I fully believe I'm going to spend the rest of my life with you. There isn't a doubt in my mind.'

He stopped – so suddenly that she double-blinked as she realized he was waiting for her to respond. This was her cue to chime in that there were no doubts in her mind either.

She opened her mouth, but no sound came out. His surety was a luxury she just couldn't afford. If they could just have a little more time without adding extra pressures on themselves, without needing contracts or titles . . .

He looked away, a mirthless laugh on his lips. 'And there we have it. That old chestnut – once bitten, twice shy. I guess it's a cliché for a reason, right?'

'Henry—'

'Forget it. I'm staying at Suze's tonight with Mum.'

'Henry, this is ridiculous!' she said, turning to watch as

64

he crossed the room in two strides and picked up a small khaki duffel bag, already packed, from the foot of the sofa. 'You can't just run out like this! We have to talk. Look, you're stressed about Arch. I get it—'

'Oh, do you? Well, that's good to hear. Nice to know you're so *in tune* with how I feel.' She flinched at the scorn in his words. 'Tell you what I don't understand, though – if you didn't want to marry me, why did you say, "Yes"?'

Words fled her yet again – her silence damning her – and Henry inhaled sharply, his hands on his hips as he stared up at the ceiling. Cassie reached for his arm, but he brushed past her, his head dropped low, and a moment later she heard the front door click shut, separating them like a sea.

Chapter Five

She was just pulling the third batch of almond macaroons – Archie's favourite – from the oven when the doorbell buzzed. Cassie frowned as she took off her oven gloves and lay them on the counter beside the hot tray. Henry had a key, obviously, as did Suzy.

She peered through the spyhole. 'Yes?' she called through the door, seeing two dark heads – one significantly higher up than the other, one distinctly glossier than the other. She gave a gasp, throwing open the door.

'Oh my God! You came!' she cried as two of the faces she loved most in the world turned to her with pleased smiles.

'Of course we did,' Anouk said, hugging her hard. As ever, she smelt of nappa leather, her beige linen jumpsuit and panama putting Cassie's pyjama ensemble of Henry's tartan baggies – rolled low on the hips – and a khaki vest in the shade. It was barely nine in the morning, meaning the two of them must have been up at five to make it here from Paris, and yet still Anouk looked box-fresh from the Isabel Marant store.

Bas, Cassie's best friend in New York, swooped down second. At six foot five, thin as a noodle and with skin the colour of a walnut, he was her sounding board and partner in crime, the man who'd understood the therapeutic effects of a head massage and a greasy fry-up when a girl was on a no-carbs diet and going through a divorce. Bas released her from his bear hug so that her toes touched the floor again. 'How is he?'

'Still critical, but stable, at least. I was just on my way over to Suzy's to get the latest.'

Bas looked her up and down. 'You sure it's only Arch who's sick? You look like hell.'

'Thanks!' she half laughed, half wailed. She had yet to look in a mirror, but she knew it wouldn't be pretty. 'I'd like to see how good you look on three hours' sleep,' she said, hoping they wouldn't notice her puffy, reddened eyes. 'Come in, come in.' She stepped back into the tiny hall, aware that Henry's sailing jacket – newly waxed – on the pegs behind, stank like burnt rubber and the coir matting, which had cost £99 per metre in the store, now looked like a cat basket. 'Coffee?'

'Like you need to ask,' Anouk replied, taking off her hat and tousling her hair lightly. Anouk was famously hard core about her drinks, only ever choosing knock-you-out black coffee, cognac or, at the other end of the spectrum, purer-than-thou mint tea; she refused to believe that water that came from taps was drinkable and would argue to the death that anything with milk in it was an abomination.

Cassie looked over at Bas. 'Tea?'

'Never change, baby.' He winked. 'I don't suppose you've got some—'

'Oh yes, I do. English breakfast or Earlers?'

'Full English, definitely,' he sighed with an elaborate hand flourish.

She grinned. She had thoroughly converted him to English tea during her stint in New York and they had long ago moved on from bog-standard PG Tips to the more delicate and rarefied strains of boutique tea companies – Prince & Sons was their new favourite and Cassie sent regular batches over to him, as it wasn't yet available in the US.

They walked into the kitchen, her visitors staring in amazement at the racks of cakes – madeleines, eclairs, macaroons, millefeuilles – stacked high on the worktops.

'So *someone* was up early,' Bas said with an arched eyebrow.

Cassie reached for the espresso caplet and dropped it into the coffee machine. 'Just getting ahead for a big job we've got on Saturday,' she said, avoiding his eye. She knew that he knew she baked when she was stressed.

'But these pastries won't keep,' Anouk argued, finger-pinching a flake of millefeuille.

'They freeze well.'

Bas's hand reached for a warm macaroon.

'Enough. Those are for Arch.'

'Really?' Bas said. 'You honestly think that's what the doctor's going to order for him after a major heart attack? Sugar and fats?'

'Oh.' Cassie sagged dispiritedly. She hadn't thought of that. 'Well, just a couple. I don't want anything happening to you too.'

'To me? Ol' snake hips?' Bas grinned, biting into one of them and closing his eyes in pleasure. 'Ugh! I'm *starving*.'

'If I'd known you were coming, I'd have got in some bacon and black pudding.' Another acquired taste they had bonded over.

'There's always elevenses,' he grinned, shrugging his eyebrows hopefully.

The kettle boiled and Cassie turned away, aware of looks

being passed behind her back as she reached for the cups. 'Stop that.'

'We're worried about you,' Bas said, advancing with concern.

'It's Arch you should be worried about.'

'Of course! And we are. It's why we're here. But is that all that's really going on in your life right now?' His eyes flicked over to the half-empty bottle of vodka she'd forgotten to return to the freezer last night, the spoon still in the empty tub of Phish Food ice cream. 'Where's Henry?'

Cassie's hand hovered above the kettle for a moment before she began to pour. 'He's at Suzy's. Hattie's down looking after Velvet, so he's keeping her company, what with Suze staying overnight at the hospital.'

'Why didn't you go too?' Anouk's voice was direct, as ever, and Cassie knew if she turned, she'd see that all-knowing look in her friend's eyes.

'Because Hattie's in the spare room, so Henry was sleeping on the sofa. It doesn't seem right to sleep in Suze and Arch's room when . . .' Her voice trailed away as she tried not to remember the image of Archie wired up like a circuit board. She turned round with the cups in her hands, keeping her eyes down. 'Anyway, it was only for the night, and I saw Hattie yesterday morning when she arrived.'

Her eyes met Anouk's fleetingly as she handed over the cup of coffee, but that was all it took for Cassie to know Anouk had already guessed at their fight. 'Smells good,' was all she said.

'You must have been up while it was still dark to get over here,' Cassie said, changing the subject and walking the four paces across the small, glossy white Ikea kitchen and heaving the recycling box of empties out of the way.

She opened the back door, letting in the riotous birdsong that was only ten feet away, and they all settled themselves on the various steps of the fire escape, both Cassie and Bas automatically leaving the prized upturned bucket for Anouk. 'I'm assuming you came in from Paris together?'

She looked at Bas, who had rested his head against the whitewashed wall and was enjoying the feel of the sun on his face – his favourite feeling, in fact. 'Couture run-throughs. Finished yesterday. Almost killed me.' He looked at Cassie through one open eye. '*Plenty* of gossip. Want to hear it?'

'I don't know. Do I?'

Bas regarded her for a moment – pale, puffy eyes – and shook his head. 'Later maybe. Now's not the time. We all know you're not the best in the mornings.'

She swatted his arm playfully, but wondered what he had to share with her. She had walked through his world for only a short time in that brief, exciting 'gap year', as her friends called it, when her marriage to Gil had blown up in her face and she'd lived in each of their cities for a season. Kelly had looked after her in New York, introducing her to Bas and giving her a job at her fashion PR firm, which hadn't gone *that* well, but there had been flashes of fun and first dabs of happiness again on her vastly altered land-scape. She had tasted freedom and independence, been made over in the image of the butter-blonde, ultra-toned Manhattanite and fallen madly in lust, conducting a highly inappropriate affair that was off plan and out of character – and exactly what she'd needed.

She blinked the thoughts away. She never let herself think about *him* anymore. The way things had ended . . . it had felt almost more toxic than the end of her marriage.

Anouk had lit up and was staring out over her neighbours' gardens with slitted, interested eyes and Cassie wondered whether the German man at number 24 was gardening nude again.

'How's Guillaume?'

Anouk sucked a little harder on her cigarette. 'Didn't you ask me that yesterday?'

'Yes, but that was on the phone. This is face to face. Now you have to give me a proper answer.'

'I think you would much rather hear about Bas's *divertissement* with his new man.'

Cassie frowned, her curiosity really piqued now. 'I do, of course, want to hear about that, everything. All the gory details,' she said, squeezing Bas's skinny calf. 'But I was asking about *you*. What's happened? What's wrong?'

'Nothing is wrong.' She paused before giving a weary sigh. 'Everything is right. That is the problem.'

Cassie's face fell, understanding the problem immediately. Men just fell too deeply in love with her, which was a problem for a woman who craved a little danger. 'You're bored.'

'It's not his fault.'

'No, of course not,' Cassie said loyally; she had always liked Guillaume.

'And it's not mine either.' Anouk was typically unapologetic, frank about what she did and didn't want. In some ways, Cassie was surprised they had lasted as long as they had, although Anouk had been so bruised by the end of her long-term great love affair it had been no surprise that even she had needed to retreat to a place of safety for a while.

'Have you met someone else?'

'Not yet.'

'But you'll tell him before it gets to that.'

'*Bien sûr.* I am very fond of him.'

Bas met Cassie's eyes and she gave a small shrug. Her friend's Gallic insouciance could be hard to relate to sometimes, and she knew Bas's soft-heartedness often translated it as coldness.

A sound behind made them all turn and Cassie bit her lip anxiously as she heard the sound of keys being dropped onto the kitchen counter. Henry came and stood in the doorway, a surprised look and then a bemused smile growing on his lips. He looked like a fallen angel, all stubble and piercing eyes that seemed to see more than anyone else. 'Well, well, well, what's this? The naughty kids sneaking fags on the stairs and spying on the neighbours?'

He bent down to Anouk – his eyes well away from Cassie – and she kissed him on the cheek, her cigarette held away from her. 'That man down there – his ass is disgusting,' she said, shaking her head despairingly and sitting back on the bucket again.

'I know. We've tried everything – pea-shooters, accidentally on purpose watering him instead of the herbs . . .' Henry said, his tone jokey, but he was pale beneath his tan and Cassie could tell he hadn't slept much either.

'How's Archie?' Anouk asked, intensity in her eyes, and Cassie felt a rush of love for the emotionally cool friend who had still dropped everything to be here.

'A lot better. Stable at last. They're moving him to a general ward later today.'

Cassie's mouth opened with happy surprise and she clapped her hands together, keeping her steepled fingers by her mouth, but still Henry didn't look at her. Her heart rate began to rev. How long was he going to be able to keep this up for – the happy-go-lucky routine while cold-shouldering her?

'Now that's the news we've been waiting for,' Bas said with a grin as he held up his hand for a fist-bump and the two men affectionately shoulder-barged. It was like watching puppies wrestle.

'He'll be made up to see you guys. I can't believe you came,' Henry said, his hands on his hips, finally running out of people to greet. Except her.

Their eyes met – apology, sorrow and so many other things besides in his grey-blue eyes. He was making light of the strain of the past couple of days for their friends' benefit, but Cassie could clearly see the toll it had taken on him: he hadn't shaved for days, and his cheeks were drawn – she realized she hadn't seen him eat for two days. For the first time in their history together, he'd fallen apart. Without a word she got up and threw her arms around him, nuzzling her face in his neck as she felt the heat of his palm across her back.

'Wow. Really? Only a night apart?' Bas chuckled, reaching over for a drag on Anouk's cigarette. 'True love's dream.'

Henry clasped her head in his hands, pulling back to gaze down at her. 'I'm a stupid arse.'

'Maybe. But you're my stupid arse.'

'Your arse is gorgeous,' he grinned, grabbing a handful of her bottom and squeezing it hard.

'I think it's an English thing,' they heard Bas whisper below them.

He kissed her lightly. 'You know Arch won't be allowed the macaroons?'

'I know. Bas has already enlightened me – and scoffed half of them.'

His finger traced her cheek. 'It was deeply adorable of you, though, to make them for him.'

'You think?'

He nodded, before kissing her again.

'Oh Jeez,' Bas sighed, closing his eyes and topping up his tan.

Walking down Sloane Street with Anouk was like dragging a toddler to the dentist and taking a shortcut via Disneyworld. She wanted to look at *everything* – the dress on this mannequin, the shoes just beyond that door, the flowers framing the windows at Cartier, just a few minutes to chat to her friends (and colleagues of sorts) at Dior, for as one of the most sought-after and elusive jewellers in Paris she had collaborated with their couture atelier for almost a decade now.

Cassie was patient. So long as Henry remained in eyeshot, his straight back and easy, long-legged stride within view as he marched with Bas down the famous shopping street, she didn't care. Her eyes were feasting on him, anticipating already the make-up sex they'd be having the second they dropped Bas and Nooks back at their hotel. The foreplay had already begun in fact. He had swooped on her from behind a beech tree earlier in Cadogan Square – today was an open day for all the usually private and locked garden squares of London – his hands all over her, the hunger in his eyes leaving her breathless as Nooks and Bas got teas for them all from the café. The horror of last night was gone already, it was a blip, an anomaly that didn't count. They were back to their best.

She turned, realizing she was alone again and saw she had lost Anouk to the Marni window display. 'Ugh, Nooks!' she scolded, marching back fifty steps and dragging her away.

'But the bag. Do you see the bag?' Anouk protested, arms thrown in the direction of the window as Cassie began leading her down the street.

'You have thousands of bags,' Cassie said, grabbing the small ocelot-printed, across-the-body pouch she was currently sporting. 'See? That's new isn't it?'

'Jerome Dreyfuss.' Anouk winked.

'Incorrigible. Henry and I would need to move house if I had as many bags as you.'

'You need to move house anyway. I cannot spend another night eating dinner on that yellow bucket.'

Cassie laughed, throwing her head back and feeling the sun on her face as they walked. She loved the yellow bucket. When it was just her and Henry, eating supper on the fire escape, watching the birds and their naked German neighbour, he always gave her the bucket. It was one of his many, small signs of chivalry that she loved – along with walking on the road-side of the kerb and having a bath ready for her when she came in from jobs.

'Come on missy, faster. Look, the boys are almost out of sight.'

'They should not walk so fast. They are too tall, that is the problem. Who can keep up with their legs?'

'Well, they're on a mission, aren't they? Bas is clearly going to go into shock if he doesn't have black pudding and brown sauce immediately.' She looped her arm through Anouk's and they picked up the pace.

The street was alive with colour, glossy black and gilded

Royal Borough of Kensington and Chelsea flower-boxes filled with heavy-headed tulips that nodded as the buses passed by; women in silk playsuits and linen dresses looking lean and tanned and very rich as they made five-metre dashes to Gucci, Prada, and Dolce and Gabbana, for something to wear that night.

Anouk's phone rang and she pulled it from her pocket, eyeing it carelessly before replacing it, unanswered.

'You're not taking it?' Cassie asked. She had glimpsed the caller ID.

Anouk didn't reply but her small sideways glance was dismissive enough.

There was a small pause as they stopped at the lights on Pont Street. 'You won't break his heart, will you?' Cassie asked. But it was more of a statement than a question.

'It won't come to that. He already knows we are fading. Besides, I have a new friend I think he would like. I plan to introduce them soon.'

Cassie tutted. She would never understand her friend's mindset on this. Anouk genuinely believed love was like a game of musical chairs: you just had to make sure you were never left without a seat; that way, you were still in the game. It never seemed to occur to her that her men wanted her and only her, not just 'any woman'.

'How about you? Are you going to break Henry's?' Anouk batted back quietly as she squeezed Cassie's arm tighter. The lights changed and they began to cross the road.

'Of course not!' Cassie gasped, so horrified by the suggestion that she forgot to walk and Anouk had to drag *her* onwards.

'So then what was the fight about – or can I guess?'

They had reached the other side and Cassie stopped again. 'You're just about the only person who understands, Nooks,' she said in a low voice. 'You actually remember that I was married for ten years before this. Half the time I feel like people have forgotten that I've already spent a third of my life in a marriage. But I love how our life is now. Everything's just perfect. Why change?'

'You are preaching to the converted, mon amie.' Anouk prompted them into a walk again.

'There's just so much pressure, you know? The same questions, all the time . . . Sometimes I think they must all be right and I'm wrong. Like maybe I'm mad.'

'Hey, you think that's bad? Try telling people you don't want kids. Then they look at you like you're disgusting, not just half woman, but half human.'

Cassie patted her arm sympathetically. She couldn't begin to imagine the grief her friend received on that score. Rejecting marriage was one thing, rejecting having kids was a whole new level of taboo.

'It's the way they're all so superior about it that drives me mad – as though I'll come to my senses,' Cassie muttered, giving full rein to her indignation and getting into her stride now.

'And you will. You want to marry Henry, just in your own time, right?'

' . . . Exactly.'

They were at the lower end of Sloane Street now, where the labels were younger, cooler and edgier. Anouk's antennae started twitching again as they passed the Stella McCartney boutique and Cassie tightened her hold on her friend. She could see Bas just ahead on the corner of Sloane Square. He appeared to be standing there alone.

'Hey. Where's Henry?' Cassie asked.

'He said he just had to get something. He'll only be a minute.' He held out his arms and she smiled, walking into his friendly embrace.

'So, tell me, how long have I got you for?' she asked as he looped one of his long Mr Spaghetti arms around her shoulders and squeezed.

'Only till tomorrow. I'm flying back in the morning.'

'Oh Bas.' She pouted sadly, gently smacking his chest in protest. 'Would you have even come to see me if you hadn't heard about Arch?'

'I would have *wanted* to come to see you,' Bas grinned.

'But he wouldn't have been able to tear himself away from Luis,' Anouk said mischievously. 'It has been hard enough for me to see him and we have been in the same city. I think it is love.'

'Luis? That's his name?' Cassie asked, stepping back to look and talk to him properly. Come to think of it, he did seem a little different – he'd lost a bit of weight from his already lean frame, and his eyes had a brightness that was usually dimmed by crazy working hours and too many international flights.

'Luis Rodolfo,' Bas said, his fingers reaching for her hair and checking for split ends. He couldn't help himself. 'He's the manager of the Jerome Dreyfuss boutique in Saint-Germain.'

'Oh. So then he gives good . . . bag,' Cassie said wickedly.

Bas laughed, delighted to be on his favourite subject. 'Exactly.'

'Well have you got a pic of the fellow? I get to vet anyone who lasts longer than a weekend, remember. If I think he looks mean or –'

Bas showed her a photo on his phone: Bas was head-to-head with a dark-haired, olive-skinned man with ultra-white, even teeth, and straight black hair that was undercut-shaved below the ears, the longer upper sections pulled back in a short ponytail. The happiness was evident in both their faces.

'Oh Bas,' Cassie said, her hand above her heart. 'It really *is* love.'

Bas shrugged; he was famously unlucky in matters of the heart, always falling for the unavailable or the un-gay. 'We'll see,' was all he said, but Cassie could see by the way he lingered on the image a second, before closing down his phone, that he had already fallen hard.

'When are you seeing him next?'

'He's coming out to New York next month.'

Cassie nodded but her heart filled with dread. How many people could sustain long-distance relationships, especially after such a short 'courtship'?

'So out with it then, how did you meet?' Cassie asked, wanting all the gossip.

'I was doing the Isabel Marant show,' he said. 'And obviously Jerome Dreyfuss is Isabel Marant's partner so he was around at the castings and stuff.'

'I want to meet him.'

'You will.'

'Henry and I could come over one weekend.'

'Great.' Bas frowned suddenly as his tummy rumbled loudly. 'Hey, now where'd Nooks go? Don't tell me we've lost her too. I'll never get fed at this rate.'

Anouk, left unattended for half a minute, had already wandered off again. Cassie saw her peering into one of the Tiffany's windows behind them.

'Honestly, Nooks!' Cassie said, walking over with Bas and joining her. Thick sprays of white orchids were arranged in each window, every one of which was enclosed like a tiny, private theatre with jet backdrops and pinprick cones of light. The scene for this display seemed to be an enchanted forest as animal silhouettes were cut out from the pages of books and diamonds twinkled like dew in the grass or stars in the night sky.

'I love that bracelet, you see it?' Anouk murmured, pointing to a floral diamond design draped over the branches of a tree.

But Cassie didn't see it. She straightened up, realizing where they were. She and Henry had history with Tiffany's. They had *form*. He'd bought her engagement ring here . . . 'Hang on. Where did Henry have to get something from?' she asked, feeling suddenly chilly in the sunshine.

'In here,' Bas said, jerking his head towards the vast girder-strapped Art Deco building that was the Tiffany flagship in London. 'Why?' Bas asked.

Cassie felt her heart drop to her feet. No. No no no.

She rushed over to the door, standing between the two potted bays and the security guards flanking them like a matching pair. Henry was standing within, in profile to her, smiling as he chatted to the sales assistant at the desk and she handed him a receipt. Oh God. Cassie felt gripped by sudden panic. Had he . . . had he misconstrued their make up? Had he taken their reconciliation as evidence of her capitulation on the issue?

Everything felt wobbly suddenly. Her legs, her heart, her future. He was moving too fast. Why couldn't they just *be*?

She caught her breath as he turned, his smile brightening as he caught sight of her, illuminated and unmoving in the sunny doorway. He walked over, looking indecently good in his scruffy jeans and T-shirt, the distinctive blue bag swinging in his hand.

'Hey.' He kissed her on the lips, that light in his eyes that was reserved for her alone, flickering on a low flame, ready for later. 'You took your time.'

'Nooks,' she whispered, hoping that would suffice as an explanation. It was all she was capable of right now. What was in that bag?

'What's in the bag?'

'This?' He held it up. 'Something for you, of course. I should have given it to you ages ago.'

'Really?' Her voice was a croak and she felt alternately cold then hot, prickles of anger, rushes of panic that he was putting her in this position, beginning to ignite in her bloodstream.

'But you can't open it yet. Wait till we get to the pub. Poor Bas is going to keel over if we don't get him caffeinated and carbed up.'

'Well can I hold it?' she asked, trying to reach for the bag. If she could gauge the weight of it, if she could glimpse the size of the box inside . . . But Henry shook his head, his long arms easily keeping it out of her reach as he fondly tapped the end of her nose with his finger. He was completely oblivious to the maelstrom of emotions raging inside her right this very moment.

'Let's go.'

*

Ten minutes later, they were in the Builder's Arms, just behind the King's Road. Henry's bright mood had been soured slightly by the fact that its dark timbered confines had been overhauled in favour of a Farrow and Ball make-over so that the interior was now all battleship grey panel-ling with trendy wallpaper and black and white photos. Bas didn't care. They had placed their orders and his food was coming. He would live to fight another day.

Cassie wasn't saying much. Her heart had been banging repeatedly against her ribs all the way for the rest of the walk, wanting to know what was in the bag whilst desper-ately not wanting to know either. She didn't want another fight.

'So come on then,' Anouk drawled, drumming her mani-cured nails on the table impatiently. 'Let's see what's in the blue bag. Cassie may be able to stand it but I cannot.'

Henry winked at Cassie as he finally slid it over the table towards her.

'Nice to see someone got lucky – *again*,' Bas said in mock complaint as he rolled his eyes.

Cassie checked her hands weren't shaking before she placed them on the bag, but she didn't notice she was holding her breath. Warily, she peered in – only to be hit by a wave of relief. She pulled out the flat, rectangular box that couldn't in any way have been used for what she'd feared.

An enormous smile enlivened her face. 'Oh!' she said excitedly, as intrigued now as she had been terrified a moment ago, biting her lip as she gently tugged on the satin ribbon and lifted the lid.

'Passport cover,' Henry said triumphantly as she pulled out a soft Tiffany blue leather jacket. 'I've been telling you for ages that you need one. It's never looked right since you put it through the wash in your jeans.'

'You bought me a passport cover,' she whispered, clutching it to her chest.

'I did,' he grinned, delighted by her response. 'So you like?'

'I love it, *love* it,' she replied, leaning forwards on her elbows to kiss him on the lips. 'You're always so amazing to me.'

'I wanted to treat you,' he murmured, his eyes on her lips.

'Although you know we can't afford –' She stopped, as she realized suddenly that he didn't know. Not yet.

'Listen, there's going to be no more worrying about the rent or eating jacket potatoes for dinner for at least six months. This expedition's going to mean we can relax for a little while, at least –'

He stopped suddenly, growing pale, and Cassie knew he'd finally remembered the missed meeting. The grant had been a promise for so long now, he had stopped thinking about it as a variable at all; all he'd had to do was turn up at the meeting and turn on the charm – he could do that in his sleep. Only . . . 'Oh *shit*.'

'What's up?' Bas asked, taking in their stilted body language.

'. . . Uh,' Henry stalled, his mind whirring as he took in the ramifications of the missed meeting. The expedition was supposed to be leaving in a fortnight. Everything was in place – sponsors, team, the weather even; the grant was just the final instalment needed to actually cross the t's and get everything kicked off at last. 'I was on my way to pitch for the grant when Arch collapsed,' he said slowly, his voice quiet.

'Oh *merde*!' Anouk exclaimed sympathetically.

Henry shook his head, distractedly. 'Christ, it went right out of my head.' He winced, raking a hand through his hair and looking more ill by the moment. 'How could I have . . .' he looked at Cassie. 'How could I have *forgotten*?'

'There's been so much going on,' she said quickly, pained by the expression in his face. 'Of course you haven't had time to think about it. You've been completely focused on Arch.' And her. He'd been distracted by her last night.

'I'm sure when you explain to them what happened, they will understand,' Anouk offered.

He looked over at her, a glimmer of hope in his eyes. 'Yeah?'

'Of course,' she shrugged with utter conviction. Cassie widened her eyes, desperately trying to message her to shut up, but Anouk just gazed back quizzically.

'You're right.' Henry stood up from the table, reaching for his phone in his jeans pocket. 'I'll call them now. I've left it too long as it is.'

'No!'

He fell still, looking back at Cassie.

She swallowed. How could she tell him, in front of everyone, that that dream was dead? Well, for this year anyway.

But she didn't need to tell him. He read it all in her face, slumping back into his seat, the phone still turned to 'off' in his hand. '. . . Oh, right.'

Bas and Anouk looked over at her quizzically but Cassie couldn't take her eyes from Henry's face – the way his lower lip had pulled down slightly, the way his Adam's apple bobbed in his throat as he swallowed the disappointment. For this wasn't just any lost deal – the arcane world of exploring was becoming more and more difficult to pursue. The hidden world was shrinking as cities spread and satellites peered into the most remote uninhabitable reaches of the planet from space. Even the final frontiers, the polar caps, were commonly visited now, with tourists travelling to see the aurora borealis, charity groups making ever more elaborate and obscure sponsored expeditions and every financial superpower in the world muscling in for fishing, mineral and drilling rights.

When he spoke, it was slowly. 'Did they leave a message at the flat then?'

'No. I met up with Bob Kentucky yesterday,' she said in a quiet voice, her hand reaching for his.

Henry looked surprised that she even knew Bob Kentucky's name. 'I called the Explorers in New York,' she said. 'They told me he was staying at the Travellers Club so I went up to see him yesterday afternoon.'

Yesterday afternoon? Henry's eyebrow lifted faintly as he registered what she'd been doing instead of waiting around at the hospital and guilt creased his brow at the accusations he'd thrown her way last night. He shook his head, dropping it into his hands, his fingers pulling tight against his hair. Cassie wanted to cry. She wanted to cross the table and sit on his lap and tell him everything was going to be OK. But she couldn't, because she didn't know that it was.

'He *wanted* to give the grant to you. You were right, they were completely on board with it. But . . . they had to make a decision there and then. The other committee members were all flying out again that afternoon and with the other applicants there and you not . . .' She shrugged. It didn't need to be spelled out.

Henry nodded but was silent, his eyes studying the grain of the table, her hand in his as he absorbed the ramifications of what this meant – it was over. £120,000 was too big a hole to breach. He was going to have to let go of the team he'd cherry-picked, explain to UNEP they now had a gap in their conference schedule, apologize to National Geographic who'd been making noises about branding him as the thinking man's Bear Grylls . . . It wasn't just a personal disaster, it was a career catastrophe.

Bas shot Anouk an aghast 'OMG' look as silence covered them all like a cloak. He'd never seen Henry at a loss before. No one had. What could any of them possibly say?

'Well I wouldn't change any of it,' Henry said, trying to be positive. 'Arch comes before any job.'

'Exactly,' Cassie murmured, still gripping his hand. 'And you can regroup for next year. The Explorers are still desperate for you to take the flag with you.'

Henry shrugged, the movement seemingly painful for he winced a little.

'Christ, I can't believe you tracked him down,' Henry mumbled after another pause, forcing a grin that couldn't quite get to his eyes. He was putting on a brave face in front of their friends, but Cassie could see the worry in his bones. 'Who's the explorer in this relationship, me or you?'

'What's meant for you won't go past you, mister,' she smiled back, eyes shining with fierce love as she squeezed his hand this time.

'And don't I just know it!' he replied, picking up her hand and kissing the back of it. She knew from the way his eyes locked on hers that he was referring to the small issue of having 'waited' for her decade-long marriage to end before he could make her his. They would weather this, somehow . . . He looked back at the others who were rolling their eyes at each other again. 'Don't worry, I'm not going to kiss her.'

'Thank God for tha—' Bas began.

'Gah, who am I kidding? Of course I am!' Henry grinned, tugging on Cassie's hand and pulling her towards him for a kiss.

Everyone laughed, the sombre mood broken – or at least postponed for a private moment later.

'So what shall we do tonight?' Anouk asked, moving the conversation onto happier ground as their drinks were brought over. 'Do you think Suzy will come home? We could cook her a special meal. She must be dropping, after spending so long in the hospital. The food in those places is always so bad.'

'Yeah, she's shattered,' Henry said, reaching thirstily for his pint of Harvey's. 'But now Arch is going onto the general ward, I think she'll just have a quiet night in with Velvet. She's missed her like mad.'

'Poor thing,' Cassie murmured. 'I think a quiet night's in order for everyone isn't it? You've barely slept or eaten since Wednesday either,' she said, tenderly pushing his hair back from his face as he drank deeply. 'How about takeaway and a film?'

'Sounds great,' he part-sighed, part-groaned as he placed the pint glass, half empty already, back on the table. 'But we'll have to wait a day.'

'Why?'

'We've got a welcome-home party to go to at the Cross Keys tonight. My little cousin's back in town.'

Cassie, who had been about to open a packet of crisps, dropped her hands down. 'Henry, we *can't* go to a party when Arch is so ill! That's tactless.'

'No, it's actually a kindness. If we don't go, Mum will feel like she has to and she's stretched thin enough at the moment trying to keep the balls in the air with Suzy and Velvet. Clearly Suze can't go and someone from the family's got to turn up.' He raked his fingers through his hair, looking worn out and battered. 'Trust me, you don't want to see Gem in a sulk.'

'Gem . . . ?'

'Gemma. Her dad was Mum's big brother. Uncle Pip.'

'Oh, right . . . I don't think I've ever met her, though, have I?' Cassie asked. She'd heard plenty of anecdotes from Suzy about Uncle Pip over the years but she didn't recollect ever hearing Gemma's name before now.

'Probably not. She's a lot younger and she's been back-packing around the world for the past two years or so. Mum's her legal guardian. Gem's parents died in a house fire when she was twelve.'

'Oh God, the poor girl!' Cassie exclaimed, her forearm falling flat to the table like a dead thing.

'Yeah, she took it pretty badly. As if adolescence isn't hard enough . . .' He took another swig, manifesting his stress that way. 'Mum says she's settled down now though. They've been emailing and she's a lot calmer apparently.'

'Calmer?' Anouk echoed with eyes slitted in suspicion.

'The fire really messed her up for a bit. She was expelled from something like six schools? Ended up at some arty-farty place in Dorset eventually, went to Sussex uni, dropped out and then went travelling.'

'So then . . . she's only about twenty?' Cassie had an

antenna for people living bigger lives than she had dared to do and it already sounded like this girl had done more living in twenty years than she had in thirty.

'Yeah. Twenty-one this summer. You'll love her anyway – she's a blast. Talks twelve to the dozen, loves *everyone*, believes grass has a soul.' He shrugged. 'What's not to like, right?'

Cassie and Anouk swapped alarmed looks. They were on guard already.

Chapter Six

'Henry, you've got to get a bigger car, man,' Bas said, unfolding himself from the Flying Tomato, Henry's faded-red old-school Mini, with a groan. Cassie always found it hysterical how oversized Henry looked driving it, but Bas had another three inches on him and had cruised the Kings Road with his chin on his knees, leaving both girls crying with laughter on the back seat.

Henry reached for Cassie's hand to pull her out and Anouk hopped easily from the back seat, looking up at the red-brick mansion blocks surrounding them on all sides. They were in the heart of Chelsea, a hop, skip and a jump from the prestigious Cheyne Walk, home to rock stars, top-flight designers and aristos wise enough to live on interest, not capital.

The river slipped silently past only metres away, and mature trees cast dappled shadows on the pavements. Nothing went for under five million in this area – not a garage, not a studio, not even a broom cupboard with a pull-down bed – and there was a moneyed hush to these backstreets, which sat nestled between the river and the Kings Road, the narrow facades belying cavernous homes with dug-out, subterranean levels and meticulously land-scaped back gardens with Japanese or modernist themes.

At first glance, the crowd outside the pub seemed anomalous with SW3's groomed vibe – girls were in denim cut-offs and baggy dungarees worn, bra-less, over vests, fluoro bracelets stacked up their arms and hair piled up in scruffy topknots; the guys looked like they belonged in Shoreditch, not Chelsea, wearing skinny rolled-up chinos, tatty linen espadrilles with the heels crushed underfoot and narrow check shirts. But their tans were expensively layered – Christmas in Mustique, followed by Easter in Verbier – and their accents betrayed expensive educations that no amount of roll-up cigarettes and prolific swearing could hide.

Cassie looked down at her chambray minidress and ankle boots, feeling caught between worlds – not cool enough for this crowd, but too casual for Gem's party? Anouk, of course, fitted in perfectly, effortlessly drawing admiring glances from the hipster girls in her slate silk harem pants and a grey linen T-shirt, with gladiator sandals and some of her own-design leather lariats, having pulled the outfit from her overnight bag like it was a bad smell but would 'have to do'.

They all walked into the pub together, each of them pausing momentarily as they were hit by the wall of noise. It was rammed in there – every table taken, barely standing room at the bar – and Henry found Cassie's hand, pulling her through the crowd towards the staircase to the left. The bass beat of music thumped louder as they squeezed past people standing on the stairs, all drinking and laughing above the din.

Cassie wondered where the usual pub crowd ended and Gem's party began. Everyone in here seemed so young. Or was that just a sign that she was getting old? She frowned.

Her marriage to Gil had prematurely aged her, as she settled down throughout her twenties to a life of shoot dinners and Highland balls, but since being with Henry, she'd felt her youthfulness blossom again, as she caught up on all the things she'd missed out on: going to concerts, wild swimming, creeping onto the roof with a duvet and pillows and sleeping under the stars, drinking a whole bottle of wine and not caring about the hangover the next day . . .

She wasn't ready to move over for the younger kids. Not yet. This was her time, her moment, when life was exactly as she wanted it, exactly as she'd dreamed – young, free and living with the man she loved in a set of rooftop rooms they'd managed to make into a home.

Balloons were clustered on the wall lights, and a huge banner made from a bed sheet was strung above the windows at the front and spray-painted to read, 'Welcome home, Gem!'

'So where is she, then?' Cassie called up to Henry, taking in the sea of dewy complexions, gap-year tans and effortlessly firm flesh.

'Do you really need to ask?' Henry laughed, his eyes on a petite brunette dancing on a table in the far corner. Her dark hair had been woven into tight cornrows, her face and palms upturned to the ceiling – but notionally the sky, Cassie suspected – as she swayed, eyes closed, to the ambient strains of London Grammar.

'Ew,' Bas said, wincing at the sight of Gem's cornrows. To a hairdresser of his international standing, cornrows were to hair what braces were to teeth.

Cassie rubbed his arm consolingly as they made their way over, Henry eagerly ploughing through the crowd ahead of them.

'Hey, you!' he shouted, stopping in front of Gem's table and pointing up to her aggressively.

Gem opened her eyes and looked down, her eyes lighting up with delight as she saw her tall, handsome cousin looking back at her.

'Henners!' she yelled, a smile of utter delight on her face at the sight of him.

'Who said you could start dancing on tables before I got here?' he shouted up to her, making her throw her head back in laughter.

'You're so right! Geronimo!' she yelled, and in the next moment she had flung her arms out and propelled herself forward through the air, towering above the crowd that separated them, before toppling onto their outstretched arms and surfing her way over them. Henry grabbed her hand as she was passed back towards him, lifting her slightly – his height gave him enough advantage to get her to a more vertical position – and as the hands accordingly fell away, she was standing in front of him.

'Hating being back, then?' he grinned, before hugging her tightly so that her feet came off the ground. She really was tiny – no more than five foot three, with a heart-shaped face, snub nose and small dark, nearly black eyes. Her smile seemed elastic, like it was on strings, and apart from the clear addiction to adrenalin, Cassie couldn't see the family resemblance.

Gem reached up, her hands solemn upon Henry's shoulders, her bright smile of seconds before suddenly completely gone. 'Tell me, how is he?' she asked, her face so utterly solemn Cassie wasn't quite sure whether she was taking the mickey or not.

'Improving all the time. On a general ward now. You

know Arch – he couldn't understand why he couldn't come here tonight!'

Gem laughed – a sudden high squeal of delight and surprise that made Cassie jump and Anouk take a half-step back, her left eyebrow already in its customary arch. 'I love him so much!'

'I know. He's mad about you too. And Suzy's gutted not to be here, but she said if she doesn't set a good example for him . . .' Henry rolled his eyes.

'Love it! Love it! Good old Suze. It doesn't sound like she's changed, then.'

'I think we can say her ways are fairly set now. Besides, you've only been gone a couple of years! Not that much has changed.'

'Well, *you've* gone and got engaged again!' She slapped him lovingly on the arm, quite hard.

Cassie winced – not at the slap but at Gem's choice of words; wishing she hadn't brought up the memory of his previous engagement.

'I got lucky.'

'*She* did, you mean! Is she here?' Gem seemed oblivious to their small crowd, gathered politely at Henry's shoulder, waiting to break into the cosy reunion. Her eyes hadn't left his, once. 'I want to see the woman who's ensnared my slippery, enigmatic, elusive cousin.'

Cassie felt her stomach tighten. Well, when it was put like that . . .

Henry pulled Cassie forward and she tucked her hair behind her ear as she smiled nervously at this tiny girl who was clearly way more important to Henry than he had let on.

'*Cassie?*' Gem asked, her eyes so wide Cassie thought she might overbalance.

Had they met before?

'Hi,' Cassie smiled, holding out her hand.

'I can't believe it! *You're* marrying Henry?'

'Uh, yes. Yes, I am,' Cassie faltered, tucking her hair behind the other ear as it became clear Gem wasn't going to shake her hand. No doubt she was supposed to have fist-bumped.

Gem nodded, her hands on her hips and grinning at her. 'You don't remember me, do you?'

'Um . . .' Cassie bit her lip apologetically.

'*Years* ago,' Gem said, swaying to the side like a Weeble as she spoke. 'You were back from boarding school with Suze and the two of you made me be your Girls' World.' She watched Cassie's face remain blank. 'You know, like one of those styling heads – blue eyeshadow, lip gloss, little plaits?' She pulled one of her cornrows. 'Not that you could do that to me now, right?'

'Gosh, I'm sorry. I don't . . . I don't remember that at all.'

There was a tiny pause. 'Agh, that's OK.' Gem made a dismissive gesture with her hand. 'It made more impact on me because you two were the cool big girls and I was just the little-squirt cousin, over for the night while my folks went to some hunt ball or something.'

'Oh . . . Did we . . . did we give you a good hairstyle?'

Beside her, Henry laughed. Cassie imagined Anouk was scowling.

'Hey, where d'you think my love of braids comes from?' Gem laughed, twirling another of her cornrows like it was a cancan dancer's leg.

Cassie felt embarrassed that she had no recollection of

the event at all. 'Well, you really should meet my friends Bas and Anouk.' She stepped back to widen the circle. 'Bas is one of the top hairstylists in New York. He's just on a stopover from Paris.'

'Hey, Bas, you like? Pretty rad, right?' Gem beamed, leaning in slightly so he could see the masterful precision of the cornrows across her scalp. Not a hair was out of alignment.

'Impressive,' he nodded politely, looking like a sunflower in a field of daisies.

'And I *love* your lariats. I didn't see any like that in Ibiza,' Gem continued, looking at Anouk with something approaching reverence (although to be fair, Anouk got that a lot).

'*Non?*'

Gem's eyes narrowed as she took in Anouk's accent. 'Oh hey, wait! You're not . . . you're not the French one, are you?'

'The French one?' Anouk didn't look happy with the label.

'Oh God, you are! Do you guys *still* see each other?' Gem asked, eyes wide again as she clapped her hands and looked between the two women. 'What was the other girl called? American.'

'Kelly,' Bas said.

'That's it! Kelly! Oh God, you know her too, Bas.' Her hands folded over her heart, and her head tipped to the side. 'You're all still together, like a little family.' She placed a hand on Anouk's arm. 'Do you have any idea how much I idolized you guys when I was growing up? I wanted all of you to be my best friends. I wanted to be just like you. Actually, who am I kidding?' she laughed. 'I wanted to *be* you. I wanted Cassie's eyes, Kelly's hair, Suzy's bosoms' – Gem cupped her own, but they were resolutely flat – 'and your skin,' she said, gazing at Anouk reverentially.

Anouk merely blinked. 'We don't have drinks,' she said bluntly, throwing out her incomprehensibly empty hands to make the point.

'Allow me,' Bas said with a nod of his head, turning on his heels towards the bar.

'I'll help,' Anouk said, following after, which was notable, as she never usually helped. Cassie watched them go enviously.

'Isn't she great?' Henry whispered in her ear, before kissing her on the cheek. Cassie nodded, but in truth, she'd never met someone who spoke so quickly before. It was like being machine-gunned.

'So, Gem, give me the virtual tour. What was your route? Where've you been?' Henry asked, looping an arm over Cassie's shoulder, keeping her by his side.

Gem took a deep breath. 'Well, we did the first summer in Ibiza. I mean, nowhere near San Antonio – *obvs*. I just can't take that touristy, clubbing crowd, you know? They're all just so young and immature, and they act like they're the first people who've ever had drugs, you know?' She rolled her eyes. 'No, we were up in the mountains at this great little hostel where they grew all their own food and there were freaking goats everywhere. It was just really . . . humble. More like a kibbutz really, except not, you know . . . Jewish.'

'Right.' Henry frowned, clearly a little puzzled. 'And then?'

'So then we moved on to India, went to Jaipur and Kerala and met some amazing spiritualists. I got so into

Ayurveda it's not even funny. And in Braj, we were there in time for the Holi festival – you know, when everyone throws paint powder all over each other and dances in the Ganges?'

Cassie was instantly grateful to realize Anouk would miss this comment. As someone who bathed in coconut milk and honey, the thought of bathing in the Ganges would no doubt elicit a violent physical reaction more akin to an enema.

'Although, my skin was blue-tinted for about a fortnight afterwards,' she laughed.

'Funny, I've never done India,' Henry said, clearly riveted. 'But everyone raves about it.'

'Apart from those who get Delhi belly,' Cassie joked, but her words must have been swallowed up by the crowd as neither Henry nor Gem laughed.

'You could go on your honeymoon!' Gem said excitedly. 'You so should! I know this guy who owns this uh-mazing palace that he rents out to friends and friends of friends. It's really exclusive and word of mouth only. Honestly, you'd love it – the views are to die for.'

Cassie smiled, nodding politely every time Gem glanced at her, which wasn't often.

'It's a definite possibility, isn't it?' Henry asked, giving her a loving squeeze.

Cassie nodded again. Last night's argument – although triggered by the stress of Archie's predicament and already forgiven – remained as unresolved as ever. 'Where else did you go?' she asked quickly.

'Well, then we shimmied over to Bali for a bit. Don't you just love gamelan?' Gem's eyes were on Henry again.

Henry nodded. He travelled for a living. He knew

exactly what gamelan was without having to look it up on Wikipedia.

'I did some yoga out there and really got into it, so I took my teacher training qualification.' She said the words with undisguised pride. 'Ah! Ah! You see? You're surprised, aren't you? You thought I was just swanning about the world and putting off getting a job, but I've come back with a qualification. You weren't expecting that, were you?'

Henry shook his head indulgently. 'You're right. I wasn't.'

'No. Aunt Hats couldn't believe it either. But I just thought it was important to come back with something to show for my time off, right? I mean, it's not all just watching sunsets on the beach. Although, ohmigod, doing yoga? On a beach? At sunset?' She closed her eyes, her middle fingers and thumbs pinched together in an 'om' position. 'Di. Vine.'

'I bet,' Henry grinned, joshing Cassie lightly with his elbow.

'Do you do yoga, Cassie?'

Cassie was startled. Being in Gem's sights was like having a lighthouse lamp shone right at you. 'Uh, well, not really, no. I'm more of a runner.'

Gem shook her head. 'Running makes you so tight.' She scrunched her face and hands up tightly, as though her words could only be true if she followed them through bodily. 'We should do some yoga together sometime. I'll take you through some om shantis.'

'Oh, OK. Yes, groovy. Thanks.'

Groovy? *Groovy?* Who said that? Why had she said that? She never said that! Cassie scanned the room, wondering whether everyone else in there was looking at her like she was old. She felt old – and very tired – in Gem's company.

'Anyway, after, like, five months, I was done. Done I tell you. There's only so many pink sunsets you can take, you know?'

'So where'd you go then?' Henry's eyes were alive with curiosity.

'Oceania. Isn't that just the best name?' She wrinkled her cute snub nose. 'Went to New Zealand first because I wasn't ready to . . . immerse myself in city life again so soon, you know? I just felt so pure after all those months of living on fish and stretching my body and rubbing salt on my skin. I needed a halfway house to get me back to civilization again. I had to retox!' she laughed.

'I totally get that,' Henry shrugged. He was often quiet for a few days on returning from a trip, wanting nothing more than to hole up in the flat with Cassie for four days at a stretch, speaking to no one but each other.

'I knew you would,' Gem grinned, looking at him intently and jabbing him affectionately in the chest with her finger. 'So we spent a couple of months there before going on to Oz.'

'We?' Cassie asked, pleased that she could see Bas and Anouk on their way back with the drinks.

'Me and Laird.'

'Aye-aye,' Henry said with a wink, as Bas reached over and put a pint into his hand. 'Anything we need to discuss?'

'Funny you should ask . . .' Gem beamed, clapping her hands together.

'Drink that – it'll make you feel better,' Anouk instructed, handing Cass her gin and tonic. 'What are you all talking about?'

'Gem's fella in Oz,' Henry said. 'I was just finding out whether he's worthy of my little cuz.'

'Oh, he totally is. Wait till you meet him.'

'He is here too?' Anouk asked, looking languidly around the room.

'Well, I wasn't going to leave *him* behind. Wait till you see him. He's a total keeper.'

'Where is he?' Cassie asked, intrigued.

'Over there.' They all followed Gem's point to a sun-bleached-blond guy by the bar. He had pecs that looked like they were inflated and a tan that only Bas had copyright on. 'He's a surfer.'

'No shit,' Henry quipped, one eyebrow cocked as his eyes met Cassie's.

'You should see him catch a wave. Honestly, it's almost a spiritual experience.' She reached inside her top and pulled out a roll-up, quickly cupping a hand as she lit it, her eyes closed as she inhaled the first drag. 'Damn, that's good . . . Got to be careful he doesn't catch me. He's very anti.' She took another deep, deep drag, just as Henry took it from her with a sympathetic tut.

'That's illegal over here now.'

'What? My little rollie?' she pouted.

'Smoking indoors,' Henry said, wetting his fingers and quickly extinguishing the cigarette. He handed it back to her with a stern expression. '*Not* that you should be smoking anything anywhere.'

'What are you? My dad?'

'As good a substitute as you'll get,' Henry smiled with a wink.

Gem sighed, staring at the roll-up sadly. 'I've promised to give up anyway. You know, in time for the wedding.'

'What wedding?' Henry asked, taking a swig of his beer.

'Mine! Whose do you think, bozo?' she cried, holding her arms wide. 'And seeing as you're the nearest I'm going to get to a dad – your words! – will you walk me down the aisle?'

Henry coughed, spluttering on his drink and spilling most of it down his poplin shirt. 'Will I *what*?'

Gem laughed, delighted at his response. She clearly had a love of dramatics. 'I said, will you walk me down the aisle?'

Henry gawped at her as he wiped his chin, plainly searching for a sign or a clue that she was joking. 'But . . . but . . .' He looked back at Laird with a less friendly look. 'Does Mum know?'

'Not yet. I'm telling her tomorrow when we go to see Arch.' She pulled an 'Oh Lawd!' expression. 'Wish me luck.'

'Christ, I wouldn't, Gem. You'll give her a heart attack and all.'

'Why?' Gem asked. 'This is exactly the kind of good news Aunt Hats needs.'

Henry hesitated. It was clear he did not think his mother was going to receive this as good news. 'Yes, but . . . well, it's a bit bloody swift, isn't it? How long have you even been with the guy?'

'Long enough.' Gem pulled a stern face similar to the one she'd pulled when asking about Arch earlier. 'Besides, what does that matter? Didn't you always tell me that when you know, you know?'

Henry shifted his weight uneasily. 'Yes, but . . .'

'What? It was different for you? Listen, I'm nearly twenty-one, which is the age you were when you told me that Cassie had gone and married that old bloke—'

Anouk spluttered with surprised laughter, and Henry cast a sly, happy look to hear his old rival described as such. Cassie scowled, not so much in defence of Gil but from her own hurt pride to have married such a man.

'But you still said you *knew* she'd be yours. I mean, that's a properly mad thing to go and say, you've got to admit. Besides, I'm twenty going on forty. I'm an old soul, me. I know what I want, and I want him.'

'But what's the rush, Gem?' His eyes fell to her stomach, but she just laughed and shook her head. 'What did you have to get engaged for? Why can't you just wait a bit?'

'Wait for what? Tomorrow may never come. All we have is now. This day. This moment. My parents went to bed one night and never woke up. I *know* how capricious life can be. Everything's fine and boring and planned out, and then – wham! – the rug's pulled out from under you. Life can change in a day; it can fall apart in a moment. We have to grab our happiness when we find it and not assume that we're entitled to the light.' She shook his arm gently as she dropped her voice. 'I know you understand it. You always got me. You were the only one who ever did.'

Henry sighed deeply as Gem finally lapsed into silence, her dark eyes hopeful and still upon him. Somehow, Cassie found her silence more unnerving than her mile-a-minute chatter. He gave a slow smile, reaching for her and hugging her tightly round the shoulders. 'Yes, and I still do. And you've always got me,' he said quietly, kissing the top of her head. 'Of course I'll walk you down the aisle.'

Chapter Seven

'He said what?' Suzy screeched, losing her voice midway through and almost falling off the bed. Velvet was sitting between them all, playing with her favourite doll as Cassie and Suzy sat cross-legged on the pillows, Anouk draped decoratively along the footboard and inspecting her manicure. Henry was downstairs with Hattie and Bas in the kitchen.

A bunch of sweet peas in a milk jug, picked by Hattie that morning from the garden, was gently scenting the room, and the blue check Jane Churchill curtains billowed in the strong breeze. Every window in the house was open. Suzy had read 'something, somewhere' about the air quality in houses being significantly more toxic when the windows were left shut and accordingly was trying to blow the house through before Archie's eventual return. Could stale air cause heart attacks? It wasn't worth taking the risk.

'I know. It's crazy,' Cassie shrugged, unfolding her legs and recrossing them the other way. 'No one should be allowed to get married at twenty-one. Honestly, I think there should be a law against it. I mean, who really knows what they want at that age?'

'Well, you didn't, that's for sure,' Anouk said, her arm

outstretched as Velvet patted at the stacked and twisted gold bangles she was wearing, the doll all but forgotten.

'No. Thanks for that,' Cassie groaned, rolling her eyes.

'What? I am agreeing with you. You are the case in point for why this wedding should not go ahead.'

'Nooks is right,' Suzy said solemnly, staring into the middle distance. 'We let you make the biggest mistake of your life because we were all as young and stupid as you were. Are we just going to sit by and watch history repeat itself? Mum's in a right state – Germ's nowhere near as sorted as she's trying to make out. She was the proverbial wild child when we were growing up – don't you remember? I used to read Mum's letters out to you. I thought Mum was going to lose her hair worrying about all her antics.'

Cassie frowned at the nickname Suzy had used. Gem was *Germ*? Why had no one said? Of course she remembered the girl! Suzy had never stopped moaning about her when they were at school.

'She was expelled from *everywhere*, dropped out of uni, disappeared round the world for nearly two years, and now she's come back saying she wants to settle down for the rest of her life? Ha!' Suzy gave a contemptuous snort and wagged her finger. 'I don't think so.'

'Is Hattie very close to her, then?' Cassie asked.

'Incredibly. It's not just that Mum became her legal guardian. Mum was so close to Uncle Pip, and when he died, I think she felt a responsibility to give his little girl a happy life. I mean, it was obvious why she was playing up – everyone could see it. Even the headmasters – when they'd call Mum in to tell her they couldn't have Germ at the school anymore, very often they'd end up crying more than she did! And Mum never threw the book at her. She'd just hug her and say that she was loved and everything would be OK.' Suzy narrowed her eyes. 'Honestly, if ever there was an argument for tough love . . .'

'You can't keep calling her Germ,' Cassie said disapprovingly, hugging a scatter cushion to her and staring past the billowing curtains to a couple of pigeons sitting on the telephone wire.

'Well, not to her face, maybe,' Suzy grumbled. 'What? My poor mum was run ragged by her. She was a brat, I'm telling you.'

'Yeah – because her parents died. Cut the girl some slack,' Cassie said, her hand automatically reaching to stroke Velvet's hair as she came within touching distance on the bed.

Suzy huffed crossly but didn't try to defend her position further.

'Besides, she talks about you with a lot of fondness. Isn't that right, Nooks?'

Anouk shook her head, inspecting a rogue hangnail on her right index finger. 'She wants your bosom,' she murmured.

There was a momentary silence as Suzy looked, puzzled, from Anouk to Cassie.

Cassie soothed her friend with a reassuring pat on the arm. 'Your bosom, Kelly's hair, Nooks's skin . . . She idolized the lot of us, apparently. Thought we were this tight-knit gang of cool big girls.'

'I am not big,' Anouk said with a prickle of defiance.

Cassie laughed. 'I meant big as in older.'

Anouk frowned. 'I am not old either.'

Suzy slumped back into the pillows with a short laugh,

her eyes on her daughter. 'Well, I'm not having her come back and stressing Mum out again. The last thing Mum needs is Germ—' Suzy caught herself, biting her lip as Cassie shot her a scolding look, 'I mean *Gem* marrying some total stranger when Archie's still in hospital. A wedding's the absolute last thing she needs.'

'Or maybe a happy event like a wedding is exactly what Hattie does need,' Anouk said, playing devil's advocate, as ever. 'Who knows? Perhaps they are love's young dream.' The words were laced with particular irony, coming, as they were, from Anouk – hardly the proponent of enduring love.

'Poppycock!' Suzy spluttered. 'The girl is lost, that's all. She's come back from this big global adventure to what? What's she going to do? She's got no qualifications—'

'She's a qualified yoga instructor,' Cassie interrupted with a finger in the air.

Suzy inhaled slowly, patiently, refusing to be derailed. 'No education to speak of. Of course she wants to get married! I see it all the time with my brides – it's a big, exciting project, something to do while she gets used to being back in Blighty again. But then what, huh? Six months, a year down the line, when that's all done and she realizes she's shackled herself to this surf bum for the rest of her life . . . ?' Suzy shook her head. 'Nope. We have got to stop this from going any further. My daft brother may be too soft-hearted to refuse her, but I'm not. I repeat – Mum does not need this kind of stress.'

'Well, there's not much you can do about it,' Cassie said wearily, twisting slightly on the pillow so that she was angled in to the bed, her head resting in her hand. She had to resist closing her eyes. The bed felt so clean and soft she was sure she could fall asleep in an instant. She was shattered; the past few days had really knocked it out of her and she needed to get a solid night's sleep, which was almost impossible with Henry in bed beside her.

'On the contrary,' Suzy replied with bright eyes. 'There's everything I can do. Weddings are my business, after all.'

'So then you're going to *plan* the wedding?' Anouk asked. 'Isn't that the opposite of what you just said?'

Suzy nodded back happily.

Anouk looked at Cassie in bafflement. 'Is my English failing? Did that make any more sense to you than it did to me?'

'None whatsoever,' Cassie mumbled with a frown.

'It makes perfect sense,' Suzy beamed. 'There's no point trying to talk her out of it. Germ— Gem!' she cried before Cassie could admonish her. 'Gem's never been talked out of anything she wanted to do. Trying to stop her getting married will only make her the more determined to do it. That's what Mum doesn't understand. There's no reasoning with the girl. So, we do this the smart way.'

'We?' Cassie echoed nervously.

'I'll be the big sister she was looking for all those years ago. I'll make like I'm on her side and then spend the time we're supposedly planning the wedding actually talking her out of it.'

'Oh Jeez.' Cassie collapsed into the pillow with a groan. Suzy's 'plans' were invariably well intended but disastrous.

'That will never work. She will be on to you immediately,' Anouk said firmly. '*Non.*'

Suzy looked pensive. 'Mmm. You're absolutely right, Nooks – she would be on to me straight away. I mean, what kind of advert for unhappy marriage would I be, anyway? I'd be useless. She'd only need to take one look at me and Arch together and she'd be straight down the register office.'

'Exactly,' Anouk shrugged.

'Which is why Cassie should do it.'

'*Me?*' Cassie spluttered, whipping her head out of the lovely cloud-soft pillows. 'Now just hang on a minute! She's your cousin!'

'And yours too, soon, if you'd ever actually marry my poor brother.' Suzy rolled her eyes and exhaled with a dramatic tut. 'Cass, of course it has to be you! You're the poster girl for doomed young marriage.'

'Could you stop saying that, please? It wasn't like I was desperately unhappy for *all* of the ten years, you know.'

'Yeah, but it wasn't like it is with you and Henry now, though, either, was it?'

It was a rhetorical question and they all knew it. Cassie sighed, catching Velvet as she wobbled on the mattress and pulling her down onto the duvet for a cuddle. She kissed the top of the child's head, inhaling that sweet scent that could never be bottled.

Suzy turned her legs inwards so that she was facing Cassie too and Cassie knew from a lifetime's experience that her best friend was cutting to the chase. She assumed the brace position.

'Listen, Gem thinks you're *so* pretty and sweet, and you know she idolizes Henry – I'm sure part of the reason she took off on her adventures was just to try to impress him. So, with you marrying him, she's going to be dead keen to get to know you better and be on your good side. And you're the obvious candidate for warning her about the mistakes you made. You don't have to have any kind of agenda; just spend time with her and chat . . . I dunno, about all that time you lost, how you lost contact with your mates and grew old before your time.' Cassie watched Suzy's hand spin in circles in the air as she reeled off the long list of Cassie's inadequacies when married. 'I mean, you knew nothing about fashion; you could barely even dress yourself. It was like you'd been dead for ten years, not married.'

'Worse than dead,' Anouk muttered, rolling onto her back and inspecting her hair for split ends.

'Christ, and you wonder why I'm in no hurry to march down the aisle again,' Cassie cried indignantly.

'But you see, you can *use* all that misadventure to do some good,' Suzy ploughed on, oblivious to or just ignoring her sarcasm. 'Gem'll hear your stories and she'll see quickly enough what a massive mistake she's making.'

Cassie kissed Velvet's head again. Was it possible, she wondered, to recreate this smell? Anouk probably knew someone, some famous nose in Paris, who could do it. Now, that would be a birthday present . . . She realized Suzy had stopped campaigning and was staring at her. 'Look, I am not going to hijack someone else's happiness, even if it is well intentioned. I love Hattie too. I don't want to see her stressed and upset, but what if it's like Nooks said? What if he really is her great love?'

'This isn't great love!' Suzy sneered. 'This is distraction, life displacement . . . Call it what you will, but we are saving her from herself.' Suzy slapped a hand across her heart. 'Don't you want to save the poor girl from the heartache you've only just come through yourself? Weddings are no picnic, but divorce . . . ? Horrific!'

Cassie plucked non-existent lint from the duvet with a trembling hand. Gil had drawn out their divorce as long as he possibly could, instructing his lawyers to negotiate on every last asset as her lawyers trawled through the old family's complicated and meandering trusts.

'Listen, if I thought I'd be half as effective as you, I'd do it myself,' Suzy said in a quieter voice, patting her knee. 'But what with looking after Arch, we've both got to scale things down and keep any stresses to a minimum . . .'

'Oh, you did not just do that!' Cassie laughed, reaching over and swatting her arm away.

Suzy's eyes were wide and innocent. 'What?'

'I can't believe you! Using your husband's near-death experience to cajole me into doing your dirty work!'

Suzy grinned back at her slyly. 'Does that mean you're in?'

'No, it doesn't!' Cassie refuted. She looked across at Anouk. 'Can't you help me out here, please? You're supposed to be on my side.'

'Well, it's a stupid idea – of course I agree.' She gave a Gallic shrug. 'But there is perhaps some sense in it. You have been there and bought the T-shirt. Where's the harm in just talking to her, I guess? Check the relationship is real.'

Cassie groaned, outnumbered. 'Well, I'm not making any promises,' she said finally. 'I will simply try to suss her out, and if I think she's doing this for the wrong reasons, or if I have any doubts, then I'll stage a modest intervention and offer up my history as a cautionary tale. But I'm not making any promises.'

'I wouldn't ask you to,' Suzy replied. 'All I'm asking for is just a heart-to-heart chat and a metaphorical takedown.'

Her hand slammed down on the bed as she made the point, making Cassie jump.

'But you have to behave yourself,' Cassie said, holding up a finger warningly. 'I know what you're like. Don't start putting pressure on me. I could have a heart attack too, you know. I get very stressed.'

Suzy's mouth dropped open and she kicked Cassie's legs. 'I can't *believe* you just used my husband's near-death experience to get out of doing my dirty work.'

Anouk laughed. 'You two will never change.'

Velvet reached out for her mother's arms and Suzy leaned forward to take her. Cassie watched as the little girl nuzzled into her mother's neck, seeming to fit into the nooks so perfectly. A sigh escaped her. She had wanted a baby once, before Gil had destroyed her idea of family life as well as marriage.

'I suppose you are going to say Cassie has to keep this a secret from Henry?' Anouk said, watching the tender scene with more remove.

Cassie's head whipped round. 'Why?'

'Well, like Suzy said, he's too soft-hearted; they are clearly very close – he has agreed to walk her down the aisle.' Anouk shrugged. 'Do you really think he will approve of you both trying to break up her relationship?'

'He'll understand when I explain why we're doing it,' Cassie said quickly. 'There's no malice behind our actions. In fact, just the opposite – we're trying to help her.'

'Nooks is right, Cass. Henry's a romantic. Look at him – he's finally got you, the only girl he ever wanted, and that's after you were married to someone else for ten years! He believes in true love and happy endings. He'll never understand. You've got to keep him out of the loop.'

'No. I'm not comfortable with that,' Cassie protested. 'Henry and I don't keep secrets from each other.'

'Listen, all you're going to do is open Germ's eyes and ears to the brutal realities of marrying too young to the wrong person. It'll be her decision to break off the relationship. It's not like you're going to have Laird exported or—' Suzy's eyes widened. 'Hey, we should check his visas.'

Anouk laughed, rolling over onto her side, in a mirror image of Cassie's pose. 'You are incorrigible.'

'No, no, you're right. Keep it simple,' Suzy said, getting back on track as she rubbed Velvet's back. 'Germ will dump him and then she'll tell Henry it's over and he won't think twice about it. In fact, deep down, I'd expect he'll be pretty relieved. I bet right now he's beginning to get an idea of how stressed Mum is about this . . .'

'Gem. Her name is Gem.'

'That's right. Just what I said,' Suzy agreed solemnly.

There was a knock and Bas's mahogany face appeared round the door. 'Is this discussion only for people with ovaries, or can anyone join in?' he asked, advancing towards the bed as Cassie motioned gratefully for him to join them. He would be on her side, at least.

'Say you don't have to go,' she implored as he lay down, sardine-style, next to Anouk, but where her feet dangled off the side of the mattress, his long legs meant his feet were planted flat on the floor. Velvet immediately wriggled from Suzy's grasp and began crawling over him, like he was a giant climbing frame. 'Just stay a few more days. It's been so long since we had a stretch of time together.'

'No can do, sweet cheeks,' he said apologetically, reaching overhead and grabbing one of her hands, kissing it affectionately. 'I'm booked for Bazaar on Monday. Cara and Jourdan. New sports luxe.' He rolled his eyes as he said the words. 'Ergo, swishy ponytails and headbands.'

Anouk sat up, instantly more animated. 'Tell me the truth. What are her eyebrows *really* like? Mannish? They are *de trop, non*?'

'She's as pretty as a doll. The whole thing, it just works,' he shrugged. 'Sorry.'

Anouk slid back into her previous position, a slight sulk on her face.

Bas looked across at Cassie. 'So what were you all talking about, anyway, before I came in? We could hear you squealing and laughing from downstairs and you know I can't bear to be left out of the gossip.'

'Gem,' Suzy said solemnly.

'Gah. That's all they're talking about downstairs too,' he sighed. He turned his head towards Cassie. 'Promise me one thing – if that girl is going to take out those cornrows, you call me and I'll be on the next plane over and do 'em myself.' He stretched his fingers as he gave a little shiver. 'They make me OCD, those things.'

'Mmm.' Cassie wrinkled her nose. 'And they must be so uncomfortable to sleep in, don't you think?'

'I *don't* want to think about it. Chanel suits are woven, not hair.'

'You can take the boy out of fashion . . .' Suzy chortled.

'When have you got to leave for the airport?' Cassie asked.

'Now, really.'

She pulled a sad face. Their twenty-four hours had flown by too soon, everyone losing precious time together by sleeping late this morning in an attempt to recover from the tequila shots that Gem had insisted upon last night. 'Are you missing Luis?'

'What makes you think that?' Bas asked, before gnawing on his fist and making them laugh again.

'Oh, it's horrible you being separated,' Cassie sympathized, laying her head on his chest so that he could stroke her hair. He had always loved her hair. 'When did you say you'll see him next?'

'He's coming over to New York at the end of the month.'

'That's grim. I know how hard it is trying to keep a long-distance relationship going. I hate it when Henry goes away.'

'Do you?' Anouk seemed genuinely surprised. 'In my opinion, absence is the best thing for desire. More people should try it.'

'Oh Christ, don't tell Arch that!' Suzy said urgently. 'I'm forever trying to tell him the longer he goes without sex, the less he'll want it.'

Bas and Cassie spluttered with laughter.

'What? It's not funny,' Suzy said, but chuckling herself. 'I've not slept in two bloody years. I keep a packet of pregnancy sticks on the bathroom shelf just to put the fear into him and stop him getting any ideas.'

'Well, he's not going to be bothering you for a while, at least,' Bas said cheekily. 'That's the last thing his ticker needs.'

Suzy's eyes brightened. 'Oooh, I hadn't thought of that. Silver lining!'

Everyone laughed, feeling guilty and yet relieved at the same time – joking about Archie's heart attack would have seemed unthinkable even yesterday, but now he was out of danger and had come out the other side, they all had.

It was official – life was back on the straight and narrow again.

Chapter Eight

The sky was as pink as a sleeping child's cheek when they set off, the cream Morris Minor pulling noisily out of the quiet, immaculate, tree-dotted street and heading west towards the M4. Henry was driving, his head bowed low to keep from knocking against the roof as Cassie struggled with reading the map before her car sickness kicked in. A thermos of tea was propped between her knees, and some bacon baps wrapped in tin foil steamed temptingly beside them.

Henry turned on the radio – Radio 4 on account of the soft-spoken programme presenters; Cassie wasn't renowned for coping well with mornings – his hand automatically coming to rest on her knee and squeezing it gently. Cassie shifted position slightly and stroked the curve of his cheek, remembering their athletics from the previous evening – so much for that early night!

It was impossible to hold hands driving a manual car, but they listened in easy silence as they motored through a slumbering London – enjoying its Saturday-morning lie-in – to the motorways and the countryside beyond. Cassie fell asleep again, the Radio 4 presenters doing their jobs rather too well, dozing through most of the suburbs and missing the stunning vistas of the North Downs. But as the roads grew smaller and more winding, she blinked slowly back to alertness again, far preferring being woken by the sight of heavy-headed oaks and lush wheat fields speeding past the window than the angry red numbers on her alarm clock, shouting '5.15 a.m.' at her.

'Tea?' she asked, weakly reaching for the thermos as they passed the village sign for Midhurst.

'I think we may as well wait till we park now,' Henry smiled, patting her hand before changing gear and swinging the car through the imposing gates of Cowdray Park, flashing their hospitality pass to the security guard. It was on the nose of eight o'clock and barely anyone else had arrived. In the distance, the castellated ruins of the original great house dominated the outline of the present property where the Cowdray family lived. The two giant polo pitches ran ahead of them, perfectly flat, pristinely striped, as groundsmen buzzed up and down on their specially adapted red machines, scarifying the turf before the thunder of hooves decimated the lawn later on. The grandstands stood empty, the hard green plastic seats folded closed against the strengthening sun, but there were plenty of horseboxes in the competitors' area and Cassie could see some of the ponies being walked by the grooms, others tethered to the posts, their faces in nosebags. The distinctive smell of leather and manure that Cassie had always loved carried on the air, filtering through the old car's basic radiator system, and she unwound the window to stick her head out like a happy dog, inhaling deeply.

Zara had beaten them to it, her tall, skinny olive-green Mark II Land Rover bagging the plum spot of the first parking space in the corner – hence the dawn call – meaning pedestrians coming from either the north or west sides would have to walk right past them.

'Hey!' she beamed, even that one word clipped with her South African accent, as they parked alongside. She looked very awake and very beautiful as she scampered along the foot rails; her skin was the colour of almonds; big, splodgy freckles peppered her nose and cheeks, and her pale brown eyes always seemed to be sparkling. Anouk thought she could be the most beautiful woman she knew, if only she'd 'consider her nails'. She was already wearing her usual working uniform of Land Girl baggy dungarees and Peter Pan-collared blouse with boots, her afro kept back from her face with a headscarf knotted at the front. The two of them had decided early on that they would back up the company's retro branding by dressing in vintage themselves and Cassie's look was a prim floral tea dress and pinny, her hair rolled at the front, and red cupid's-bow lips.

Zara was unzipping a safari tent that was tightly rolled to the side of the roof rack so that it looked more like a telescope. 'What do you think? Good spot, huh?' she called through their open window.

'For as long as I've known you, you've always been the first to arrive and last to leave any party, Za,' Henry smiled, jumping out of the car and playfully swatting her off the foot rail to deal with the tent himself. 'Off. Let me, missus.'

Zara laughed gratefully and wandered over to Cassie, who was still sitting in the passenger seat, now munching hungrily on her bacon butty. A smudge of ketchup was smeared on her chin, her eyes closed with satisfaction as the carbs began to work their magic on her tired body.

'Worn out, are you?' Zara cackled, peering in through the open window.

'Ugh. I am never waking up in any hour that has a five in it ever again,' Cassie moaned, taking another bite. 'I bet Jude can't have been pleased having you roll out of bed so early on the weekend either.'

'She didn't notice. She's like you – she doesn't so much sleep as die for eight hours every night.'

Cassie chuckled, taking another heavenly bite of the bap. 'Arch OK?'

Cassie nodded – her mouth full – and gave a thumbs-up sign, accompanied with much relieved head-nodding.

'Great stuff.' Zara patted the open window frame with one hand. 'I'll start hulling the strawbs. Come and find me when you're a fully functioning human again.'

'OK,' Cassie mumbled with a mouth still full of food, watching with a different sort of hunger as Henry pulled the tent tight over the collapsible aluminium frame, his athletic physique thinly veiled in his faded black T-shirt and jeans as he set to work with the energy of a child on a six-pack of Coke.

She loved it when he helped out at weekends – if nothing else, he was a whizz at popping the champagne corks – but today his presence felt somehow . . . pitiful. Arch was being assessed in a series of tests, so Henry couldn't 'fruitfully' spend his day sitting by his bed and cracking jokes, and it wouldn't even occur to him to spend the day on the sofa, but there really was nothing for him to do at the moment. The expedition was done, gone, over for this year at least. Henry was trying to be philosophical about it, agreeing with Bob Kentucky's confidence that there was always next year, but Cassie had caught the pensive expression on his face any time he thought he was alone and she knew he was up in the night, unable to sleep. Because being philosophical and 'taking it on the chin' didn't resolve the pressing – and alarming – issue of what they were going to do for money until then.

She thought of the lump sum sitting in a bank account in her name. It would solve their problems at a stroke, and yet . . . and yet it felt like blood money, as though in using it – *relying* on it – she was somehow relying on Gil again. Still. And she wouldn't give him either that satisfaction or power. She couldn't.

No. It was better to keep Henry occupied at least. Something would turn up. If nothing else, he'd said he could volunteer to teach at a climbing wall, sailing club . . . She watched as he got the safari tent up in minutes, bashing the pegs into the hard ground with ease. At least it was physical work, manly stuff, better for his ego than hulling strawberries.

As if sensing her scrutiny, he straightened up and turned, flashing her a smile that made her heart pivot. His smile turned into a laugh as he pointed to his chin and she remembered the ketchup on her own. She stuck her tongue out before wiping it off with a Kleenex from the glovebox.

After a quick cup of tea, drunk from the blue lid of the bright green flask, she finally got out of the car, ready to assist in the morning's endeavours. She joined Zara by the back of the Landy, slinging her grass-green ruffled apron on over her dress, and they worked quickly as a team, chatting all the while as they strung up the striped bunting inside and outside the tent, and round the roof rack of the car, set up the champagne-breakfast table, stacked the antique bone-china plates into little towers, bunched the knives, forks and spoons into separate jam jars decorated with ribbons and opened out the antique cream canvas and leather campaign chairs.

When that was done, they took the croissant dough from the cool box and began kneading it into shape, laying the pastries out on trays, ready to bake in half an hour so that they'd still be warm when the first guests started arriving at ten o'clock.

'Hey, slacker,' Zara said, looking up from her duties and finding Henry briefly reading the letters page of *The Times* in one of the chairs. 'We're going to need some crushed ice for the elderflower bubbly. Can you go blag some from one of those hospitality tents?'

'What's it worth?' he asked, folding the newspaper and standing up again. 'Free drink for me? Free bet on Argentina?'

'Free kiss from Cassie,' Zara said, reaching for another tub of dough.

'Done,' he said, sauntering over and kissing his fiancée as she sprinkled almonds over the croissants, smiling at the dusting of icing sugar on the tip of her nose. He kissed the tip of her nose too. 'Won't be long,' he said, grabbing the two large silver ice buckets and wandering off.

Cassie watched him go with a small sigh.

'God, I really hope you two *don't* get married,' Zara muttered with a glint in her eye. 'Your honeymoon period would be insufferable.'

They were lying on the roof of the car, topping up their tans, when Henry came back forty minutes later.

'Hey! When I said get ice, I didn't mean travel to the polar cap to get it!' Zara quipped, rolling onto her side as

Henry pulled the two ice buckets on a trolley behind him. Cassie could barely bring herself to move. The sun, pulsing down on them . . . she was almost asleep again.

He stopped and looked up at them, shielding his eyes from the glare of the sun. He was smiling delightedly. 'Za, you'll never guess who I just ran into.'

'No, I don't suppose I will,' Zara drawled with infinite patience. She had been one of his housemates at university and well knew that he was one of those people who knew someone almost everywhere he went.

Henry paused for a beat, bigging up the reveal. 'Beau Cooper!'

Zara sat upright in surprise. 'No way! I thought he was dead.'

Henry laughed. 'I think he has nearly been, several times.'

'Who's Beau Cooper?' Cassie asked, leaning up on her elbows.

'Hang on. Let me just get this out of the sun,' Henry said, pushing the trolley into the shade of the tent, heaving the filled buckets onto the breakfast table and wedging several bottles of champagne into the ice.

Zara twisted back to face her. 'He was at uni with us. One of the Trust Fund Yahs,' she said in a low voice, her lovely mouth twisted into a sneer. 'Way too handsome for his own good, way too much money. Total junkie – had to be revived twice with adrenalin shots, and that's just the times *I* know about. He was only allowed to stay on account of his father donating millions to the new law library.'

'Sounds charming,' Cassie said wryly, falling back into her sunbathing position. 'I can't believe Henry would be friends with someone like that.'

'Well, I think Henry took a fairly dim view of Beau's lifestyle, but they're alike in lots of ways – both of them free spirits, entrepreneurial mavericks, I guess. Neither one of them conforms to stereotypical expectations; they can't do the suited-and-booted commuter thing. And I think Beau liked the fact that Henry wasn't some sycophantic groupie. If anything, it was Beau who wanted to hang with Henry.'

'Well, I've never even heard of the guy. Henry hasn't ever mentioned him.' But then he'd never mentioned Gem either.

Henry's face appeared at the top of the ladder, his grin growing as he clambered onto the roof and flopped down in front of them, clearly desperate to share. 'So . . .'

'Out with it,' Zara said. 'You're obviously dying to tell us all about him. Does he still look like Byron?'

Henry shook his head. 'The hair's even longer now.'

'Oh my God. Does he still have his own teeth?'

'Well, I think they're his,' Henry laughed. 'He looks really well, actually. Fit, been working out. He's lost that . . .' He strained for the right word.

'Junkie look?'

'Exactly. He's got a tan.'

'Don't tell me – he's just back from Necker,' Zara sighed enviously.

'Oz. He's preparing to sail across the Pacific, all the way to San Fran on a boat made out of recycled bottles.'

'Sounds suitably mad,' Zara said.

'Sounds stupid,' Cassie echoed.

'Actually, he's raising environmental awareness about the amount of plastic floating in the oceans. Did you know there's a confluence of plastic in the middle of the Atlantic that's more than twice the size of France? And most of it is just plastic bags and water bottles. One-use stuff.' He shook his head irritably, his eyes bright, and Cassie watched him with faint sadness. There was a vigour to his movements now that hadn't been there forty minutes earlier. 'Anyway, he's got his own consultancy in San Francisco, mainly doing eco-consciousness camps with the Silicon Valley names, but he thought this would be a great way to really bring attention to such an important and overlooked issue.'

'Cool,' Cassie said, thinking she should probably say something.

'I told him you were here. He's really keen to see you again,' Henry said to Zara.

'Yeah, I bet,' Zara barked drily. 'I hope you told him he's not the so-called cure. He wasn't then and he isn't now.'

Henry rolled his eyes. 'He didn't mean it like that.'

'Yeah, right,' Zara muttered darkly. 'Oh dammit. I need to get those croissants in the oven,' she muttered, crawling on her hands and knees towards the ladder at the back of the car.

Henry waited for her to go before pulling himself over to where Cassie was sitting.

'I said we'd go over. I really want him to meet you.'

'Oh, Henry, *why*?' Cassie scowled. 'I don't like the sound of him. I don't particularly want to meet the guy.'

'Don't let Zara sway you. They had a . . . tempestuous thing going on back then for a while. He's all right.'

'Well, I trust Zara's judgement. He sounds like a complete loser.'

'You trust her judgement over mine?' Henry asked in surprise.

'Of course not, but—'

'Look, he's not the guy he was at university. I don't know what Za's told you, but he's changed. He's an entirely different person now. God forbid we should all remain the people we were ten years ago.'

The words were pointed, directed at her and the version of herself that had said, 'I do,' to another man. Cassie looked away. Her own recent past felt as disconnected from her life now as an amputated limb.

Henry reached for her hand, squeezing it gently. 'Come on, Cass, where's the harm? We're allowed our pasts, aren't we? After all, they're what brought us to here and now.'

She couldn't argue with that. She, of all people, couldn't argue with that.

Chapter Nine

She was saved by the bell – their clients arriving early curtailed any chance of meeting Beau, and the three of them were immediately rushed off their feet. Henry played barman, mixing elderflower-champagne cocktails as an alternative to the Buck's Fizzes, juicing clementines and apples, and brewing up pots of tea. Zara organized the flow of croissants and pastries into and out of the mini oven that had been custom-fitted into the boot of the old Land Rover when it had, apparently, been driven across the Khyber Pass in Afghanistan by the previous owner, back in the 1980s. Cassie played hostess, carrying, pouring, removing and smiling.

She didn't look up for two hours, but when she did, she was astonished by the scene. The quiet industry of the early morning had been replaced by a heaving, buzzing crowd as the occupants of the glossy cars that now cascaded in rows behind them milled past with curious gazes at the Landy, the bunting-festooned safari tent and retro brunch being dished out therein, their mouths turning up into smiles as they clocked the pile of heels strewn at the bottom of the car's ladder and the decorated women who had kicked them off, sitting on the roof with bare pedicured feet, sunbathing and laughing with delight.

A deep male voice was booming incoherently out of the speakers that were set up around the park as ponies cantered over the immaculate grass on the practice pitch, their riders standing in the stirrups and swinging their sticks in warm-up. On the other side of the white posts, spectators sauntered in and out of the shade of the giant sunflower-yellow parasols that had opened like daisies in the sun, as they sipped drinks and delved into their picnics. A few children were running around, playing with miniature polo sticks, which became weapons in their hands, as dogs on leads nosed the ground for dropped bits of burgers.

Henry's back was turned to her as he worked on crushing the fresh ice block with a pick – from experience, Zara and Cassie had found they couldn't keep the crushed ice from melting on day-long events; only solid blocks would last – and Cassie watched as a woman in a pistachio silk minidress came over to take one of their business cards from the table beside him. Cassie noticed more than half the cards had gone.

Henry chatted easily to her, resting the pick in the ice like it was Arthur's sword as the woman tarried, asking questions that Cassie, with growing indignation, was quite sure were just an excuse to flirt with her fiancé.

Henry jerked his head back, indicating towards her and Zara, and both he and the woman turned. Cassie instantly ducked out of sight behind the Land Rover again, not wanting to be caught staring, but of course she had been a vital second too slow and Henry was still chuckling when he ambled over a few moments later.

'She said she was interested,' he grinned, laughter in his eyes.

'Oh, I *know* she was,' Cassie said tartly as she scuffed at the grass with her foot, her cheeks stinging with embarrassment that she'd been caught spying and wishing that she could fight back in something more alluring than her winsome pansy-printed tea dress.

'It's for her mother's sixtieth in September. They're having a garden party for forty people in Dorset.'

She looked up in surprise as he handed over a piece of paper with a name and number scrawled on it. 'Oh.'

He advanced, his hands on her cheeks and his mouth on hers before she could say another word, his point clear through his actions alone. 'Come on. Zara's said she'll do this clear-up if we do the one after tea and she can get away early. Jude's got theatre tickets for tonight. We've got an hour before we need to do the lunches, right? Let's get an ice-cold beer and go watch the nags.'

He pulled her through the crowd, his hand big over hers, not even giving her time to take off her apron. She felt gauche as they wove through the crowds; at least she 'made sense' standing beside the vintage cars and the 1940s 'set' they recreated with their hampers, but this wasn't an arena where old-world charms carried any weight beyond the catering tents; this was the world of the international rich, where anything could be bought – new bodies, new teeth, new wives, new companies, new horses – and the brighter, tighter, shinier, flashier, the better.

Cassie was struck by the uniformity of the event. The men seemed, by silent, osmotic consensus, to have decided on a uniform of navy blazers and chinos, the only variation on the theme being whether their chinos were red, sand or cream. The women were more colourful, of course, but the broad strokes remained similar – a flimsy silk dress, bare arms and legs, strappy heels and wedges, and oversized Tom Ford sunglasses.

The next round of matches had begun and a roar of hooves thundered down the pitch, making the ground tremble beneath their feet as the crowd cheered and the commentator became more excitable at the mic. The onset of action meant the hospitality tents were emptied temporarily – all of them the taut, open-sided Arabian-style marquees – and Henry grabbed them some drinks as Cassie hopped on a bar stool beside one of the standing-up tables and looked out at the action in the sunshine.

Even from here the horses looked expensive, with a salon-rich sheen to their coats, their skinny legs tightly bandaged and bespoke Spanish leather saddles on their backs. Zara had told her earlier 'the Princes' were playing, but Cassie couldn't work out which team was England, much less identify the players themselves.

'We're in the red shirts,' Henry said, kissing her on the cheek as he sat down beside her.

'I knew that,' she protested as he set down her drink. 'Totally.'

He just winked.

She took a sip of her beer, careful not to get a foam moustache, while they sat and watched the match from their cool, quiet vantage point. Henry seemed better able to decipher the match than her, nodding appreciatively at some of the play. Cassie admired the sheer number of Birkins on display today. Just from this spot alone she could see eleven, and there was no doubt in her mind they were all genuine.

'Hey, my man,' she heard Henry say, in a blokey sort of voice.

She turned, just in time to find him standing up and fist-bumping a man who had obviously got the memo (navy linen blazer and narrow red jeans). He was wearing a cream straw panama and silver-tinted aviators too, but even with so much of his face obscured, she could still detect in the Honduras-tanned, lean skin and the black-gold filings of his stubble a rich man ravaged by his indulgences.

Beau slapped Henry on the shoulder, but his attention was entirely on Cassie.

'Mate, this is Cassie, my fiancée,' Henry said proudly.

A moment passed in which no one said anything; Cassie realized she was holding her breath. Then Beau's smile grew even wider and he turned to Henry with a shake of his head.

'You sly dog. How the hell did *you* get a woman like this to even agree to take your number, much less your name?'

Henry laughed, Cassie looking between them both nervously as Beau immediately turned his spotlight back on her. 'It is an absolute pleasure to meet you,' he said, taking her hand and holding it firmly – not in a shake, but as though poised to kiss it instead, though he didn't.

Cassie wished she couldn't see herself reflected in his shades: it was distracting seeing her own frozen expression looking back at her. As if sensing her discomfort, he took off the Ray-Bans, and she found herself, instead, looking into Bahamian-blue eyes that made no attempt to disguise their scrutiny. She realized she still hadn't said a word, but a quick nod of her head was all she could manage.

He let go of her hand with seeming reluctance.

Beau slapped Henry hard on the shoulder again as he barked a sudden laugh. 'You can't imagine how made up I was when I ran into your old man earlier! It's been years. I half thought he was dead.'

'That's funny. He said the same about you,' she said in a quiet voice.

There was a pause. 'Well, we're cut from the same cloth, me and Henry. We both like living on the edge.' Beau looked at her for a moment. 'You know, you look really familiar to me. We haven't met, have we?'

'No.'

'You're sure? Because I'm pretty good with faces. Not much good at anything else, as I'm sure Henry will tell you, but faces . . . I know you from somewhere.'

'It could be from an ad campaign Cass did a couple of years back in New York.' Henry's hand found hers and squeezed gently.

'So you're a *model*?' The light in Beau's eyes told her he was well acquainted with models.

'No.'

'No? Well, what is it you do, then, Cassie?'

She hesitated. 'I run a catering business with a friend.'

Beau's eyes ran slowly up and down her, a wolfish smile on his lips. 'That explains the pinny. I thought maybe it was just a . . . you know, *look*.'

'They do bespoke picnics,' Henry said, elaborating for her. 'Actually, you'd love it, mate. No plastic-wrapped sandwiches and grapes. It's proper old-fashioned, paper-wrapped food, the way picnics used to be, you know?'

'Wicker hampers and Scotch eggs, you mean?' Beau asked, his eyes still on Cassie.

'Bingo. In fact, thinking about it, Cassie's eco message is bang in line with yours.'

'Well, then maybe we should bring Cassie's company in

as sponsors to the trip, huh? You wouldn't feel partial to sparing a hundred thou for our good cause, would you?'

'You jest, but she's also a partner in C et C in Paris,' Henry added proudly, boasting on her behalf.

Beau's eyes narrowed with real interest at that. 'Are you, now? And how the devil did you wangle that? It's my favourite restaurant in Paris and even I can't get past the waiting list.' He patted her hand. 'Although maybe I can now, right? It's all about who you know.'

'I'm a sleeping partner,' Cassie muttered.

'And what a sleeping partner I bet she is, mate,' Beau said with a laugh.

Henry instantly pointed at him warningly, but he was grinning, and Beau put his hands in the air. 'Just joking. No offence intended.'

Cassie didn't reply. She was quite sure offence had been intended, but a small, noisy group of men were walking towards them.

'What's that, Cooper?' one of them called over loudly, even though they were clearly within earshot. 'You? Not intending offence? I don't bloody believe it!'

'Good of you to get the drinks in, mate,' another one said, slapping him heartily on the shoulder, his eyes, along with the others', coming to rest on Cassie and Henry.

One of them recognized Henry. 'All right, mate? Long time.' He held a hand aloft.

'It has been,' Henry grinned, gripping his hand back like they were going to arm-wrestle. 'Fin, this is—'

'Cassie,' one of them said. The voice was American. Male. And stunned.

Even before she saw him, she knew who it was and the hairs on the back of her neck bristled as she remembered the glimpse she'd caught of the face in the taxi in New York, composites of a knowing smile, sure hands, designer stubble and a gently mocking mouth flashing before her eyes.

She looked at Henry quickly, reflexively, but his eyes were already narrowed in concentration, and she felt her own pulse throb in her neck as she watched Henry try to place this man whom he had only ever seen once, via a Skype screen, when he'd been undressing her, the woman who was now his fiancée.

'Luke,' Cassie managed, getting in first and determined to set a civilized tone. She was more than a little worried about what Henry might do when the penny dropped. The last time she'd spoken with Luke, things had descended into a fracas and he'd been laid out by her beloved friend Claude. 'It's nice to see you.'

If he was amused or offended by her use of the word 'nice', he didn't show it. In fact, he seemed nothing but happily surprised to see her, as though he recalled a different ending to their relationship than her. 'What a coincidence seeing you here.'

'Yes.'

'How have you been?'

She nodded, almost wincing at the farce – small talk and platitudes glossing over his betrayal – her face impassive though the humiliation would remain forever fresh from finding the private snapshots he'd taken of her, black-and-white nudes, blown up and exhibited in the name of art at his latest photography exhibition during Paris Fashion Week.

'So you know each other?' Beau asked, with studied interest.

'Yeah. Cassie and I, uh . . .' Luke's eyes kept well away from Henry's, as did Cassie's. 'We knew each other in New York. She lived there for a while, a couple of years back.'

'Is that right?' Beau smiled, clearly smelling a rat.

'Where are you living now?' Luke asked her.

'Here. Well, London.' Couldn't he tell by looking at her? She'd been butter-blonde and black-clad in New York, a bobbed brunette in Paris. Surely her dark roots, almost nude face and Cath Kidston plimmies screamed, 'London'? Then again . . . Her hands fiddled with the cotton of her ruffled apron, itself worn over the flimsy vintage dress. He must be wondering what on earth she was doing dressed as a 1940s waitress.

'Right.'

There was a short pause as they searched for safe ground in front of the small crowd. It wasn't conversation that had been their forte.

'And have you . . . seen Kelly or Bas recently?' he managed.

'Bas was here this week, actually; he popped over after prepping for the couture shows in Paris.'

'Right, right, yes, of course. It's nearly that time of year again.'

'And you? Are you busy?' she asked back politely. As US *Vogue*'s former star photographer, he was on a plane more often than in his apartment.

'You know how it is. Same old. Five different countries in a week.'

'And five different women in a week too, right, Luke?' Beau joked. Something in the way he kept his eyes on Cassie as he said it told her he was testing the waters. Luke shot him a withering look, but didn't reply. Henry, beside Cassie, was ominously still.

'So, how do you two know each other?' Henry asked Beau.

Beau looked across at Luke. 'Us? Oh, we've been kicking around in the same circles for years now, haven't we? Partners in crime. I scarcely remember how we met in the first instance.' He threw his arm round Luke's shoulder. 'This guy's an incredible photographer. I mean really amazing. Have you seen any of his stuff?'

Henry paused. He had, of course, seen the ad campaign of Cassie that Luke had shot. 'Not really.'

'You should try to. I've got several of his pieces – one in my bedroom at home, in fact. I just can't take my eyes off it . . .' His eyes were on Cassie again, a dark shadow falling over the words, and she had to suppress a shiver.

'But hey, if you and Cassie are old mates, you must have known these guys are engaged, right?' Beau asked, turning more towards Luke.

Luke's gaze darted straight back to Cassie. 'No. I didn't.' Another pause, and then he thrust out his hand to Henry. 'Well, congratulations. That's great news. You make a great couple. That's really great.' So great, apparently.

'A reason to celebrate, methinks!' Beau shouted, raising an arm and hailing an order for more glasses.

'Thanks, but we need to get back to work,' Henry said, a new stiffness in his voice.

Beau, who was clearly automatically going to cajole Henry to stay on, hesitated. Something in his old friend's voice seemed to warn him otherwise. 'Sure, sure. Well, listen, it's been so great running into you like this. Stay in touch, yeah? I'll look you up when we get back. Let's get the girls together and go out for dinner. A foursome should be fun.'

Henry laughed, but the sound was hollow. Beau looked back at Cassie. 'You're a great girl, Cass. I can see why my mates are so crazy about you.'

Mates? But before Cassie could correct him, he had stepped towards her and enveloped her in a bear hug, his lips against her ear as he kissed her cheek. 'I *knew* I recognized you,' he whispered. 'Like I said, Luke's damned good with a camera.'

Cassie froze as she realized what he was saying, but he just winked and turned away, leading the group towards a roped-off area that had white leather bench seating and black-suited security guards.

She looked up at Henry, not even sure where to start, but she took one look at his face and knew better than to even try. Together, they walked back to the Eat 'n' Mess bell tent in stony silence.

Chapter Ten

Kelly's long hair, which Gem so admired, swung out of range of the computer screen, falling back perfectly into place as Cassie drained her vodka and tonic.

'It's just a rocky patch,' Kelly said soothingly, sipping her own vodka calmly as Cassie still reeled from her latest revelations. What a month it had been since their last virtual catch-up – Archie's heart attack, Luke's surprise appearance at the polo. Neither she nor Henry had mentioned him once since that day last week, but she sensed the invisible cord that tethered them to each other was vibrating slightly, like a telephone wire as a bird took flight, and it seemed to her that a new mannered tension had slipped into their behaviour as once-lingering kisses on mouths became hurried pecks on the cheek instead. They'd barely seen each other either, which hadn't helped. Henry was spending almost every day by Archie's bedside, and Cassie was in the throes of coming up with a new summer dessert menu for C et C, which entailed hours upon hours in the kitchen, black smoke wafting from the windows, as though a new pope still hadn't been agreed upon. And all the while, in the background, the thorny issue of making this month's rent was becoming harder to ignore.

'What if it's not just a rocky patch, though? We seem to

be bickering all the time at the moment – fine one minute, at each other's throats the next,' Cassie hiccuped, already quite drunk. She and Kelly always got drunk together on this, their designated monthly Skype lock-in – that was the rule; it was how they stayed connected, the boys making themselves scarce so that the girls could talk freely and with abandon. Usually Henry played fives with Arch before they went to the pub, but tonight he was 'doing the late shift' and visiting him on the ward so that Suzy could put Velvet to bed on time. 'What if—'

'Stop right there, lady. A rocky patch is a good thing. You're not a real couple until you've actually survived something together. Hell, it's easy to be lovey-dovey in the good times. It's when the shit hits the fan that you know whether you're meant to be together or not.' She raised an eyebrow. 'Has it crossed your mind at any point to walk away?'

'Don't be daft!' Cassie laughed. The very idea was non-sensical.

'Exactly. My point is proved. You're keepers. Every-thing's good. This is just a bump in the road.'

'But there's been a lot of those recently – that's *my* point.'

'Hey, who ever said the road had to be smooth?' A red-lipsticked smile grew across Kelly's mouth. 'God, Luke must have looked like he wanted to dive under the horses, though, didn't he?'

'He didn't look very comfortable. He was exceedingly . . . polite.'

'No doubt he was worried Henry was going to lamp him,' Kelly chuckled. 'Good. It serves him right after what he did to you.'

Cassie sighed and looked down into her empty glass. She reached out of shot for the bottle and poured herself another drink, the tonic splashing on top messily. 'Cheers,' she said, her voice ever so slightly slurred as she held up the glass.

'Cheers,' Kelly said, matching the movement by holding up her glass and taking a deep swig. Too deep.

Cassie frowned as she drank hers. 'Crikey, you've got a thirst on.'

'Oh. Do I?'

'Is that really vodka in there?'

'Of course. What else would it be?' she laughed.

Cassie stared back at her suspiciously. Was it her imagination or had Kelly's laugh just then sounded forced? And she did seem unusually . . . blank tonight, her voice flat. 'Prove it. Down it in one.'

Kelly arched one eyebrow but did as she was instructed, smacking her lips together triumphantly at the end.

'I knew it!' Cassie exclaimed, peering closer at the screen. 'It's water.'

'It isn't!' Kelly protested with a laugh. 'It's vodka tonic. I always drink this. You know I do.'

'Yeah, and I also know there is no way you would have downed that if it had been vodka. You always pull a little face even after the smallest sip.'

'No I don't.'

'You so do. Look.' Cassie pulled an awkward, slightly strangled look that made Kelly gasp in horror.

'I do not!'

Cassie nodded, laughing. 'That's your vodka face.' She paused. 'So I don't even want to *know* about your sex face,' she spluttered, making herself laugh, before pulling another comical expression that was a cross-eyed, jaw-stretched gurn.

Kelly gave a small shriek. 'Oh yeah? Well, I bet yours is like this,' she cried, distorting her own face to Quasimodo-esque proportions.

Cassie threw herself back on the sofa, her hands over her stomach as she laughed. She had definitely drunk too much, too fast tonight, but frankly, enough had happened in the last fortnight to drive a nun to drink. She hated that Arch was still in hospital, that Henry was unemployed and restless, that Beau Cooper had a picture of her, naked, in his bedroom, that Luke had looked good when she'd looked so ridiculous in her pinny . . . She deserved this night off.

Hang on . . .

She sat upright as she realized she had derailed herself with the sex-face joke. Why was Kelly drinking water? Surely there could only be one reason?

Her eyes scanned her old friend with new critical faculty – looking for bloating around the jaw, a flush in the cheeks, a secret in her eyes. Without saying a word, her hands covered her mouth. She didn't even need to ask.

'What?' Kelly asked, panic in her voice. 'Why are you looking at me like that?'

Cassie just shook her head, her hands still clamped over her mouth.

Kelly shook her head in turn. 'No. I know what you're thinking and you're wrong. Plain wrong.' She picked up her glass again and held it towards the screen. 'This is vodka. Lovely, cold vodka.'

Cassie's hands dropped down. 'How far along are you?'

Kelly rolled her eyes, shaking her head even more fervently as she looked away. She sighed. 'I'm telling you

you're wrong. I'm not . . . I'm not . . .' But the words wouldn't come and Cassie saw the ball of her jaw clench in profile. There was a short silence before Kelly looked back at her. 'I'm not going to be pregnant for long.'

They were the words Cassie had predicted – and yet more besides. Too many. Cassie had been right *and* wrong?

'What do you mean, for long?' The words were whispers as she inched closer to the screen.

Kelly's head dropped down as though she didn't have any strength. 'No, I don't mean . . .' Her words ran out of power again and she rolled her lips together before finally looking back at Cassie. 'This will be my fourth miscarriage.'

Cassie winced. Now it was the tenses that were confusing her. '*Will* be?'

'I can't seem to carry past nine weeks.'

Cassie sat back as though she'd been punched. One of her closest friends had had not one but three miscarriages and Cassie – in spite of their monthly virtual lock-ins – had failed to notice? 'When was the first?' Her voice vibrated with shock.

'Just over a year ago.'

'And the last?'

Kelly took a deep breath. 'The week before you came to New York.'

Kelly's paleness, tiredness and quietness that night came back in a rush; she remembered how Brett had fallen over himself to keep the focus on her and Henry and their exciting new plans – the expedition! The engagement! – and not their own.

'Oh, Kell,' she whispered, tears clouding her eyes. 'Why didn't you say?'

'We've deliberately not told anyone. It seemed easier to just . . . contain it to the two of us.'

Cassie shook her head, hating that she was drunk right now and Kelly wasn't, hating that her friend had carried on as normal when in fact tragedy kept washing into her life like a soiled tide.

'Have the doctors identified why?'

'There's no good reason they can find,' Kelly shrugged. 'Too much stress, maybe. Caffeine? Sugar? Plain old bad luck? Who really knows?'

'Does Nooks know?' Nooks and Kelly shared the sisterly closeness that bound Cassie and Suzy.

Kelly shook her head. 'No one.' There was a small pause as she met Cassie's gaze. 'Not even Brett, with this one.'

'*What?* But—'

'I don't want to get his hopes up. He's found it so hard watching it happen each time and I don't want to keep looking in his eyes and seeing fear. He's so scared of everything for me . . . Thinks I should spend nine months lying on the sofa.'

'Well, maybe he's got a point. Your job is so full-on, and the people you work with are even worse than Suzy's brides.'

Kelly hesitated. 'Well, it's true Bebe has been especially demanding recently.'

Cassie frowned. 'Oh, now I'm really worried! I've worked with you both, remember – I know you do everything at warp speed, and I know what a cow she is. Brett's probably right – you are doing too much.'

Kelly shook her head. 'No, he's just looking for answers. The fact is, stress is all I know. It's relaxation and R&R that my body can't handle. Everything that's happened . . . it's just one of those things.'

'This time will be different,' Cassie said firmly.

'No, it won't.' Kelly shook her head again, her eyes falling to the floor as she shifted position. 'There should have been at least three months between this pregnancy and the last, and my ob-gyn is cross that I'm carrying again so quickly. It was an accident.' Fear brightened her eyes and her hands tightened across her stomach – the protective gesture shrouded in irony given that the danger did, after all, come from her own body. 'It's too soon. After everything my body's been through in the past twelve months . . .' Her voice cracked. 'There's no way I'll be able to carry this baby to term.'

Cassie leaned in closer to the screen, desperate to reach through it and touch her friend, to put an arm round her shoulder and cry with her. 'Kell, you can't go through this alone. You have to tell Brett.'

Kelly looked back at her sharply. 'No. There is no need for both of us to go through this.'

'But you can't *hide* it from him.'

'I can and I will. I've got no intention of ever telling him about any pregnancy unless I get past the twelve-week mark.'

'And when's that for this one?'

Kelly held up one hand, five fingers. Five weeks to go. Five weeks of keeping the biggest secret of her life from the man she loved. She took a deep breath.

'So then the baby's due at the' – she quickly calculated in her head – 'end of January?'

'This baby's *not* due, Cass,' Kelly said forcefully. 'That's exactly the point. I can't afford to think like that. I won't daydream about birthdates or names or any of that . . . I can't.'

Cassie's shoulders sagged at her friend's resolute stance. 'Please, Kelly, tell Brett.'

'*Why?* It won't change the outcome, and what's the point of burdening him with something that's so completely out of our control? It'll just mean there are two hearts broken, instead of one.'

'But if it happens again, you need support to get through it.'

'He's already supporting me anyway. We're still grieving the third loss.' She gave a bleak shrug. 'He'll never know.'

Cassie shook her head despairingly. 'I really wish you'd reconsider, Kelly. I think you're absolutely wrong on this. You should not be going through this alone.'

There was a belligerent silence. 'Well, I guess I'm not. I've got you now. Right?'

'Of course. You know that. I'd do anything for you.'

'Good. So then just promise me one thing.'

'Anything.'

'Don't try to give me hope.'

Cassie's mouth parted, ready to protest, but Kelly stopped her.

'No. I mean it. There's no kindness in trying to get me to believe in something that can never be. I can't battle you as well as myself. If you're going to be here for me, then it means you standing side by side with me in the knowledge that there's no happy ending to this. And if you can't do that, then—'

'I can,' Cassie said quickly. 'And I will.'

Kelly scrutinized her expression. 'You promise?'

Cassie nodded vehemently. 'I promise.'

A tiny smile softened Kelly's battle-ready expression. 'Well, OK, then. And for the record' – she inhaled deeply – 'I do feel a bit better that you know. It's been tough not having anyone to tell.'

'I can't begin to imagine,' Cassie whispered.

Kelly gave a sad smile. 'Bet you're wishing you hadn't been so eagle-eyed now, huh?'

But Cassie didn't think it was funny, and as they hung up, she immediately reached for the diary by the sofa, counting as she flicked through the pages before making three entries in red pen, vividly outlining each day with a decisive circle:

9 July – 9 weeks
30 July – 12 weeks
30 January – baby due

Kelly might not count the days, but she would. She would keep the secret, but she would also, secretly, dare to dream for her friend.

'Hey, stranger,' Henry smiled, closing up the newspaper and getting up from the upturned bucket on the fire escape to plant a kiss in the centre of her forehead as she staggered into the kitchen the next morning, wearing his T-shirt and a hangover. 'You were already asleep when I got back last night. I'm guessing it was a heavy night with Kelly?'

'Something like that,' Cassie groaned, pushing her hair back from her face. A cone of sunlight fell through the open door and she reached for the kettle like she was blindfolded.

'Just sit,' Henry instructed, planting his hands on her

shoulders and steering her towards the yellow bucket, where she sank down gratefully, her head tipped back against the wall as she listened to the birds and let the sun warm her up. 'You look like you could do with a bit of help being revived this morning. And we do need you revived – Arch deserves a wide-awake homecoming, don't you think?'

Cassie's eyes widened in surprise and she looked back into the shaded little kitchen. 'He's coming out today?'

'This morning. In fact' – he checked his watch – 'Suze was hoping to be back in time for *Jeremy Kyle*. She reckons if anything will speed up his recuperation and get him back to work, it's that. Women made pregnant by their sons-in-law on today's show, apparently.'

Cassie felt sick – and immediately wondered how Kelly was feeling.

'Then I should get ready,' she said, standing up from the bucket and heading for the bedroom, but Henry reached for her as she passed, his arms wrapping round her and gathering her into him.

'Not so fast,' he murmured, his cheek resting on her shoulder as he kissed her neck softly. 'I've missed you.' She sank back into him as his hand began to wander.

'I've missed you. I was beginning to think you were avoiding me.'

Henry's hand stopped and he shot her a guilty look from behind his eyelashes. 'Well, perhaps I was.'

She pulled back a little. So her instincts had been right, then? 'But why?'

'It's been a tough few weeks, all things considered, Cass: thinking I was going to lose Arch, actually losing the expedition, then running into your ex the very day I was working as a waiter . . . It's not been a great time for my ego.'

'Oh, Henry, you know I don't—'

'I know,' he smiled, squeezing her bottom affectionately. 'But as you well know, the male ego is an exceptionally fragile thing. I'm not used to feeling . . . redundant, I guess. In every sense of the word.'

'I would love you if you worked as a waiter, a circus clown or . . . I don't know, an optician.'

He laughed, a rich sound she realized she had heard far too seldom recently. 'Well, luckily for you, it's still going to be saying "Explorer" on my CV for a while yet.'

Something in his tone . . . She looked back at him, first in puzzlement, then excitement as she realized what he was saying. 'You've got the funding?' she whispered.

'Well, not for this year, sadly, but if I want it, I know a man who knows a man who's interested in associating his wealth with a good cause. He'll double the shortfall from this year, and if you factor in the club's grant too, we'll be able to go further next year, for longer.'

It was the benefactor they'd been waiting for! Cassie clapped her hands excitedly and did a little jog on the spot.

Henry grinned as he felt her body moving against his. 'And it gets better.'

'How? How can anything top that?' she squealed.

'The rent's now fully paid up till October. I just texted the landlord to let him know.'

'How did you do that?' she gasped.

'I've got a trip lined up – leaving in ten days.'

'*What?*' Cassie asked, a note of panic suffusing her excitement. This was good news, of course it was, but he was going *so* soon? 'Well, what is it? Where are you going?'

she asked, placing her hands flat against his chest.

Henry fell still and she felt the atmosphere between them change. 'It's a sailing trip.'

No. Her hands fell away, her gaze falling to the apple tree beyond the window as her jaw jutted.

Beau Cooper . . . She felt sick at the thought of that man taking another step into their lives. He radiated toxicity.

'Cass, someone dropped out. I had to take it,' Henry said urgently, finding her hands and placing them against his chest again. 'We needed the money – you know we did.'

'I know. But did it have to be with him?'

'This is the opportunity I've been waiting for. And, you know, I've been thinking – it was so weird running into Beau the other day and now this space has come up . . . it's like maybe this was meant to be.'

'Oh, so Archie's heart attack was all part of some divine plan to reunite you and your old partner in crime?'

His expression changed, but he didn't say anything further.

She instantly felt bad. 'And so . . . what? This is the trip with the boat made of bottles, is it? You're going to try to convince me that sailing the ocean on a boat made of taped-together plastic bottles, with less than two weeks' notice, is a good idea?'

'I know it sounds alarming, but nothing's going to happen to me.'

'Of course something's going to happen, Henry. There'll be a storm and it'll break apart in the swell; you'll be bumped by a whale and it'll break apart—'

His hand cupped her cheek. 'Hey, look, I know it sounds scary, but it's a lot more high-tech than it sounds. There's some serious corporate money behind it. Plus I've got more experience than any of the others combined; I'm co-skipper.'

'So it's all a done deal, is it? I don't get any say in the matter?'

He shook his head. 'The money was too good to turn down.'

She stared back at him, frustrated that he thought she'd accept that excuse. This was not just about the money and they both knew it. He wanted to do this; his ego needed it. Beau had tapped into his old friend's thirst for adventure, his hunger for the adrenalin rush.

'Listen, you know I wouldn't sign up for something without weighing the risks. Beau rang last night as I was on my way back from the hospital and we met up for a drink at his flat. He showed me the presentation they made to the sponsors on his iPad. It's boss. You wouldn't get big guns like Evian, Nike and the America's Cup involved with something like that unless they knew all the bases were covered. They can't afford to have six guys dying in the middle of an ocean on a boat with their logos on. This is an important ecological statement that has the weight of industry titans behind it. There's nothing tricksy or Hicksville about it. It's an absolute peach of an opportunity for me, Cass. You must see that it's got my name all over it?'

She sighed. 'Of course I do. But—'

He pressed a finger to her lips quickly. 'Just trust me. I'm doing this for us, Cass.' He trailed that finger down her neck, between her breasts . . . 'But if you're still not sure, I can tell you more about it while I treat you to a full-body massage.' He winked and she couldn't help but laugh, knowing full well just how persuasive those techniques could be.

Of course, Cassie knew she could make him stay if she let slip that Beau had her naked picture on his bedroom wall – she could bet her entire alimony that Beau wouldn't have allowed his old friend to catch a glimpse of that in the flat last night! – but that would only trample on his ego further. Nothing was going to change the fact that Luke had taken that picture and Beau had bought it, and besides, Henry needed to get back on track – he needed to get back on track more than she needed to avoid Beau Cooper's lascivious stares. He needed to get back to doing what he loved, doing what made him Henry and not just an optician or a waiter or a clown. As much as she didn't want Henry to go, it would be worse to keep him here in those circumstances, to position herself as a pawn between him and his new boss, his old friend.

'Just remember,' he grinned, his hands finding the hem of her T-shirt. 'If duffer, better drowned. If not duffer, won't drown.'

A reluctant smile escaped her as she rolled her eyes. *Swallows and Amazons* was his favourite book, and that was his favourite line.

He pulled her T-shirt off in one easy motion so that she stood naked before him in the beam of light – that mannered politeness of the last few days gone again. He was back to being himself. He would never convince her that sailing an ocean on a boat made of bottles was anything other than dangerous and reckless, but it was precisely those qualities that drew him to the job; this spirit of adventure was who he was – it was what made him the man she had fallen in love with.

His hands skimmed her curves with assured deftness and she felt herself respond to his touch. When it was just them, just this, everything felt so right and easy. She had no concerns about their now, their future. It was just the people in their pasts she was worried about.

Two hours later both of them were holding hands and smiling like fools on the McLintlocks' sofa, prompting lots of suspicious looks from Suzy as she intermittently tried to persuade Archie to 'give green tea a chance'. Velvet was playing in a small pop-up Barbie tent in the middle of the floor, and *The Jeremy Kyle Show* had been put on mute when Archie had actually looked, at one point, like he might burst into tears. Or have another coronary.

'So how many are there of you on this boat?' Archie puzzled.

'Six.'

'And it's made from water bottles?' He squinted over at Suzy. 'Or am I tripping on the drugs?'

'No, you heard it right,' Suzy muttered with a roll of her eyes.

'The craft's made up of twelve and a half thousand bottles, but it's a lot more sophisticated than that,' Henry said, while squeezing Cassie's hand reassuringly. She had seen the presentation before they had left the flat and she had to admit the boat did look significantly more secure than the *Castaway* raft she'd conjured in her mind. 'It looks like any other catamaran until you get up close to it.'

'And *that's* when you freak out?' Archie grinned, throwing a wink over to Cassie. His colour was, if not fully returned to its ruddy glory, at least an encouraging pink, but he had lost half a stone and it felt strange seeing him with sharper angles when everything about his personality was rounded and soft. 'I take it Cassie's not allowed within half a mile of it, then.'

'I'm not going to argue with him about it, Arch,' Cassie shrugged. 'He's going anyway. What's the point?'

'I'll be back in three months, which is the same as the Arctic trip, except I'm being paid almost double. What's not to like?'

'Just the sustained threat of imminent death for every moment of every day of those three months. Other than that, Mum's totally on board, so to speak,' Suzy quipped. It was Henry's turn to roll his eyes.

'So, any word on when you can go back to work?' Cassie asked Archie, pointedly changing the subject.

'Well, not for a month, at least. We're going down to Cornwall, where I can benefit from the "fresh air",' Archie said in a resigned tone.

'I don't know why you're saying it like that,' Suzy huffed. 'You're signed off work until September at the earliest, and London is no place to recover – all the noise and people and traffic and pigeons and—'

'Pigeons?' Henry laughed. 'How on earth are pigeons going to impede his recovery?'

'Everyone knows guano is a health risk, and Arch needs fresh air and open views, somewhere he can sleep with the windows open at night, a garden he can sit in.'

'We have a garden here,' Archie pointed out.

'Yes, with Easigrass and a Wendy house. You need somewhere with real grass and flowers.'

Archie rolled his eyes, making his views on the matter clear, but said nothing.

'Archibald Valentine McLintlock, don't give me that look,' Suzy said in her sternest voice, and making both

Cassie and Henry laugh as they always did when Suzy used his full name. 'After the fright you gave me last week, you jolly well owe me a quiet month in which you promise not to die.' She looked up at her brother. 'And that goes for you too.'

'Understood,' Henry said with a salute and a wink.

'So when are *you* going?' Cassie asked, feeling thoroughly despondent. First Henry was disappearing on her and now Suzy and Arch too?

'This weekend, we were thinking.'

'Oh brilliant!' Cassie said, throwing her hands up in the air. 'That's just what I need. All of you doing a disappearing act on me for the summer.'

'Come with us. There's masses of room. You've been to Butterbox Farm, right?' Suzy said.

Cassie shook her head. 'I feel like I have, though. You've told me about it enough times.'

'Seriously? You've never been down?' Suzy asked in astonishment, her brow furrowed in puzzlement. 'Oh yeah, I suppose you were always back in Hong Kong when we went. God, we had such amazing summers down there, didn't we, Henry?'

A light came on behind Henry's eyes. 'Sure did.'

'You've got to visit.'

'Sure, thanks,' Cassie nodded with a sigh. What else was she going to do with her weekends?

'Oh, has Gem got hold of you yet?' Henry asked his sister. He saw Suzy's quizzical expression. 'What? We speak on the phone.'

'And what's the latest with Lord?' Suzy's sarcasm was evident.

'Laird,' Henry reproved. 'And you can ask her yourself

when she rings – or at the party next week, whichever's soonest.'

'What party?' Archie asked, looking as alert as a spaniel on the peg.

'Nothing you need to know about,' Suzy said quickly.

'The team's send-off party. The sponsors are hosting it for us at the Blind Pig in Soho,' Henry said at the same time.

'*Really?*' Archie grinned, clapping and rubbing his hands together.

'Arch, no!' Suzy intervened. 'You are recuperating. Over my dead body are you—'

'Woman, my best man slash best mate slash blood brother is about to fly halfway round the world to set sail on the high seas on a pile of water bottles. If you think I'm going to miss out on buying him a farewell beer, think again!' he said loudly.

Suzy's mouth opened and then closed again, no sound coming out – Archie never raised his voice. Henry gave a small cheer and even Cassie was tempted to whoop, but Archie had eyes only for his wife, his hand reaching for hers. 'But *after* that, my darling,' he said in a softer voice, 'you can whisk me off to the ends of the country and sit me in a deckchair with a hanky on my head for as long as you like. I won't complain once, I promise, not even when you make me drink *that*.' His nose wrinkled in distaste at the now-tepid green tea, which looked like a witch's potion from a Walt Disney film.

'I'm going to make you drink a lot of that,' Suzy said crossly after a moment.

'I don't doubt it. And I'll be all the better for it, I'm sure.'

He tipped his head down, his eyes trying to make contact with hers and refusing to gloat in his rare victory.

There was another short pause. 'Well, you're not having a beer.'

'I don't want one, Duchess. I just want to buy one for this fellow here.'

Suzy sighed, casting her brother a hateful stare. 'You have a lot to answer for,' she grumbled, just as Archie grabbed her hand and tugged her over to him, pulling her down onto his lap and enveloping her in a bear hug that made even her smile.

Chapter Eleven

Cassie stood on the balcony, looking in at the party and watching as it pulsed without her. Flashes of the copper bar glinted back at her as the crowd constantly moved and shuffled, the leather chairs pushed towards the walls to make an impromptu dance floor. Henry was in there somewhere, laughing, charming, schmoozing, in his element, his formerly tattered ego now fully restored to beautiful, reckless invincibility. Usually, she could see his head above the crowd, but he was moving among fellow giants tonight – why were all sailors so tall? – and she hadn't caught sight of him for almost an hour now.

Her mood continued to fall and she turned away to face out into Poland Street instead. Unlike everyone else in the room, she found it hard to celebrate her fiancé disappearing round the world for three months, but she was seemingly alone in that opinion. Everyone seemed so delighted by the expedition – the crew, the backup teams, the sponsors especially so, it seemed, now that Henry was on board, but she just wished they were back at the flat, the two of them sharing a bath and eating supper on the bucket before rolling around in bed till the sun came up.

But there had been no getting out of this: tonight was as much a promotional event to drum up press as it was a send-off and Henry was contractually obliged to attend. Just as he'd been obliged to have countless meetings getting to know the team, charming the sponsors, running through the technical specs and navigation charts, getting the insurance set up . . . They'd scarcely had a moment alone together since he'd signed the contract.

The mood had been sedate to begin with, as Beau and Henry – both rakishly handsome in team navy blazers and chinos – worked the room as a unit, shaking hands, dishing out Hollywood-ready smiles and whipping up interest (much to Cassie's alarm) by bigging up the risks they faced. But no party that had Beau in it – or with a cocktail list that counted thermonuclear daiquiris in its number – was ever going to remain tame, and a hedonistic atmosphere had taken hold as the crew began to party hard, as if to make up for all the nights they wouldn't be on dry land. Newspaper photographers prowled the room, aiming their lenses at the prettiest girls and richest-looking men, and Cassie had seen for herself how valued Henry was in the team as the money men behind the trip vied to have their photo taken with the action heroes.

Cassie sighed, feeling out of the loop as she stood alone, waiting for Suzy to return with their fresh drinks. She well knew that more wine had simply been the excuse Suzy needed to move through the crowd and spy on Archie, who was clearly delighted to be back in the fray again.

'Hey, hey, hey! Here she is. I knew she had to be hiding around here somewhere.'

Cassie's stomach dropped as she heard Beau's distinctive cut-glass vowels aimed at her, and a moment later he was in her face. Quite literally.

'How are you, gorgeous?' he asked, swooping an arm

round her waist and kissing her hard on the cheek, his stubble rasping against her skin.

She pulled away with a look of undisguised contempt – his unpleasantness was only amplified with alcohol, it seemed – and matters weren't improved when she clocked Luke standing beside him, quietly watching on, a whisky in his hand.

What was *he* doing here? Were they joined at the hip?

'I had to come over and personally thank you for what you've done for me.'

'I haven't done anything for you, Beau,' she said stiffly.

'*Au contraire*,' he winked. 'I thought the whole shebang was going to go down the tubes when Freddy bailed on me last week. Two years we've been working on this project. I won't even *bore* you with the hassles we endured from the sponsors – wanting guaranteed media, carrying us over into their next year's marketing spends because some fuck-wit in accounts thinks they've overspent on paperclips. And then, just when we've got our ducks in a row, Freddy goes and almost ballses everything up 'cos he can't keep it in his pants and now his woman's about to drop a sprog.' He shook his head as if in despair, before a too-bright smile split his face. 'But then, don't you know, I remember my old mucker walking into the bar last week, looking just as bloody good as he did ten years ago, while the rest of us are withering into broken old men. I guess it's true what they say about a good woman.'

He winked at her again, but Cassie refused to respond in any way, shape or form. She intended to freeze him out of her personal space.

Not that it was working just yet.

'Henry may be the man of your dreams, Cassie, but he's

the man of mine too, trust me. Bloody experienced sailor, tried and tested in extreme conditions – South Pole expedition in 2008, wasn't it?'

She nodded, and glanced at Luke again.

'Strong as Popeye, doesn't drink all the booze on the first night and could charm the tail off a mermaid. Not that we'll be asking him to charm anything off anybody, you'll be relieved to hear.' He winked again.

She turned to go; she'd had enough already. 'Excuse me.'

But Beau caught her hand. 'Wait a minute, pretty lady. You don't have a drink. Let me get you a drink. What would you like?'

'Nothing from you.'

His eyes glittered and she knew they understood one another. 'You're sure about that?'

'She said no, Beau,' Luke interjected, firmly removing Beau's hand from her arm but with a matey smile. 'Look, Amy's over there looking for you. Why don't you . . . ?'

Beau looked back into the crowd. 'Shit, yeah . . .' he mumbled, staggering off with an exaggerated gait and leaving her alone with her supposed 'rescuer'. Only, he was just as bad. She already knew that. His gallantry was wasted on her.

'Sorry about that. He's drunk,' Luke murmured.

'You don't say,' Cassie said sarcastically, turning away from him.

'How about you? Having fun? I could get you that drink . . .'

She stared back at him – a thousand words, most of them rude, running over her face – before she turned away again. 'Just leave me alone, Luke.' Politeness in front of others had kept the smile on her face when they'd met at the polo two weeks ago, but she owed him no such courtesy now.

They were silent amid the noise.

'Look, Cass, I don't blame you for hating me,' he said after a minute, dropping the game and getting to the point. He tried to catch her attention with his gaze, but she simply turned away further still. 'I was an asshole, I know that.'

More silence. She wouldn't look at him. She wouldn't.

'But surely you know why I did it? You must have understood, even if you couldn't forgive?'

Understood? She whirled back to face him. '*What* justification could you have had for doing what you did? You betrayed me in the worst possible way. You took something that was private between us' – her hands had folded over her heart – 'and showed it to the world. *Him!*'

He stepped towards her. 'Yes, because I loved you, Cass. I was mad about you. I couldn't . . . accept that what we had was over. I was trying to hurt you back, to get your attention.'

'Well, you got that, all right. And my contempt besides.'

Her rocky words bounced off like pebbles on a giant. 'You walked away so easily, without even a backwards glance.

'No,' she refuted. 'Not without a backwards glance. I was miserable for a long time in Paris, but I had to go there. You knew that.'

'All I knew was that you chose to leave.'

'You could have chosen to wait. Did that ever occur to you? It would only have been for a few months, but it had to be "now or never" for you, didn't it? Your ego couldn't bear that I might even be *able* to leave you.'

He blinked at her, his hazel eyes steady, discerning. 'And

who says you would have come back? Look at you now, already engaged to another guy. When did that start, huh? Did you meet him just a few weeks later in Paris, or was it a few months later in London?' His eyes roamed her face, but she looked away, refusing to answer. She didn't need to explain her history with Henry to him. She didn't need to explain herself to him at all. 'Well, either way, it wasn't long, I know that much. You were *never* coming back to me. I knew it even if you didn't.'

She swallowed and they fell quiet again, the party thumping all around them like a giant heart. Was anyone watching them? Was Suzy? Henry? Arch?

'Listen . . .' he said, his hand reaching towards her, but she flinched and he took it away again. More silence and yet a running commentary in her head – all the things she'd wanted to say to him back then and hadn't. 'I don't want to fight. That isn't why I've come over. It was a long time ago now. We're different people. You've moved on; we both have, and believe it or not, I'm actually really happy that you've found what you were looking for. Henry seems like a good guy. Beau can't stop raving about him.'

Cassie wished she'd been looking at his face when he'd said that – had the words almost choked him? – but she continued looking out onto the street below.

'I'd really like to call bygones on this whole thing. Accept my apology, Cass. I'd like us to be friends again.'

She turned to face him, her hip leaning into the cold stone. 'But we were never friends, Luke.'

He stared back at her, both of them remembering exactly what it was they had been to each other. 'Maybe not, no. But . . . maybe we could learn to be.'

From the corner of her eye, Cassie saw Suzy approaching, her arms held high above her head as she moved through the crowd with the wine glasses. Beau was just behind her on the dance floor, making an obscene gesture behind her back, and Cassie remembered again his final lascivious words to her at the polo. Even now they made her skin crawl. He had seen her at her most intimate, a privilege he should never have enjoyed – and it was all because of the man standing before her now.

She looked back at him coldly. 'I don't think so. Anything that was between us you killed off a long time ago.' And she walked away, meeting Suzy just inside the French doors.

'Holy crap! Isn't that—' Suzy asked in surprise as she clocked Luke, just as Cassie grabbed her by the elbow and steered her away to another corner of the room. She had met Luke when she and Anouk had sprung a surprise visit on her in New York.

'He's still staring,' Suzy said without moving her lips, handing over her drink and clinking it with hers. 'What the hell's *he* doing here?'

'He's a friend of Beau's.'

'Ugh, that figures.'

Cassie arched an eyebrow. 'You know Beau?'

'He's a dim and unwelcome ghost from the past.' Suzy looked sheepish. 'And I may have snogged him once after one too many snakebites at a university ball.'

'Oh, Suze, you didn't!'

'I'm sorry. I was visiting Henry for the weekend and . . . well, it was a terrible lapse of taste *and* judgement.'

'At least tell me he's an atrocious kisser.'

'Mmm, yes, about that . . . Wish I could,' Suzy sighed

with a shake of her head. 'Still, he's an utter git. I can't believe Henry's hooked up with him again.'

'Well, hopefully three months in a tiny cabin with him will finally make the scales fall from Henry's eyes.' Cassie took a sip of her drink, surreptitiously checking Luke wasn't still watching, but he had disappeared from sight – hopefully the room and country too. 'Did you find Arch?'

'Oh yes. He's supervising the Drink While You Think.' Suzy rolled her eyes, pointing to the nucleus of fun in the room. Archie's red hair, even redder under the lights, flicked about like the Olympic flame as Cassie watched Henry cheering on someone out of sight from her position. She was sure he couldn't have seen Luke here. He wouldn't be smiling anywhere near as widely if he knew her ex was in the building.

'What are they trying to do?' Cassie asked, puzzled, just as the crowd parted momentarily and she glimpsed through the gap in the crowd a dazzling blonde-bobbed girl with a brilliant smile. 'And who is *that*?'

'Who?' Suzy craned to see. 'Oh, that's Amy, the co-skipper, Henry's opposite number.'

'Henry's got an opposite number?' Cassie murmured, watching as Amy gripped her hair with one hand, her eyes scrunched shut. She was clearly trying to think of something as everyone chanted a countdown to her. 'I thought Beau was the other co-skipper.'

'Nope. He's the expedition leader.' Suzy dressed the titles with faint scorn before noticing her friend's anxious expression. 'Hey, don't worry about her. She's one of the boys apparently. They all love her.'

'You don't say,' Cassie said with an edge.

'I don't mean they love her like that.'

'How do you know?'

'Arch told me.'

'Suze, just *look* at her!'

'Listen, what are you so worried about? Henry can see no one but you.'

'But she looks just like me, only better!'

Suzy soothingly placed a hand on her arm. 'Stop being so insecure. For one thing, she's got a boyfriend. And for another, there's no such thing as a better you.'

Cassie watched as Beau leaned in and said something in her ear, Amy throwing her head back in laughter in reply. Was he her boyfriend? Hadn't Luke just sent Beau over to her?

'Hey, guys!'

Both Suzy and Cassie turned in unison to find Gem bombing towards them like a pocket rocket. She was wearing a turquoise, brown and white crocheted dress with boy pants underneath and a black bra, her tanned skin winking through the vast openwork spaces. Her hair was still tightly bound in the cornrows, and attached to her hand was Laird.

Close up, he seemed less cartoonish than he had at the pub the other week. His eyes drooped slightly at the outer edges, giving him a vaguely melancholic air, and two weeks in England seemed to have taken the maroon tint off his tan. His hair was still improbably blond, but surrounded by the salty seadogs here tonight, it didn't seem quite so striking, and he just seemed fit, rather than buff, now that he was wearing a shirt and not a muscle vest.

'I'm dying for you both to meet Laird properly.' She looked back at him with bright eyes. 'These are the ones I was telling you about – Suzy, Henry's sister, and Cassie, Henry's fiancée.'

'Pleased to meet you,' Cassie smiled, holding out her hand as she caught sight of Suzy's expression and guessed at her displeasure at both of them being introduced only in terms of their relationships to Henry. Suzy wasn't Henry's anything. She was older – he was her little brother; or how about she was Archie's wife instead? Or just the elder cousin? Even just the one with the great boobs?

'Hi.' Laird shook her hand lightly. 'Sorry I didn't get a chance to meet you at the party.'

'It was a big party,' Cassie smiled, feeling guilty that she and Anouk and Bas had deliberately ducked into the crowd and disappeared – pretending to get separated – as Gem had led them over with Henry to make the introduction. 'I . . . uh, love your name. It's so unusual.'

'Thanks,' he said. 'My grandparents were Scottish. It's a Scottish name.'

'Ah yes, of course it is,' Cassie nodded. 'I used to live in Scotland.'

'Really? Whereabouts?'

'Halfway between the border and Edinburgh. The Lammermuir Hills?'

He shook his head apologetically.

'It's OK. No one outside of a ten-mile radius has ever heard of them.'

'Do you miss it?'

'Ha! You've got to be joking,' Suzy interrupted. 'Poor Cass was trapped in a terrible marriage the whole time she was up there. Her husband worked in Edinburgh and would only come back at weekends. It was just you and the cook and the gin cupboard, wasn't it, Cass?'

'Suze, you've just totally made me sound like an alcoholic!' Cassie protested with a laugh. She looked back at Laird. 'For the record, I do not have a drink problem.'

'Oh, I know,' he replied earnestly. 'Your skin's too good.'

'Oh, thanks,' she grinned.

Gem made eye contact with Cassie, flashing her a delighted smile that said, 'See?' as beside them Suzy cleared her throat.

'So, I just saw Archie,' Gem said, speaking up to her big cousin. 'He looks *so hot*.'

'He nearly died the week before last,' Suzy replied with an incredulous tone that suggested she was not of the same view. 'I hardly think he's looking his best.'

'*So?*' Gem cried. She placed a small hand on Suzy's arm. 'I never got what it was you saw in him till now. I always thought he looked like that *Fast Show* character – you know, the lord who's in love with his estate keeper?'

Suzy's mouth dropped open in mute horror.

'But now! The cheekbones, his eyes are so bright, and his teeth . . . He's got such good teeth. *Who knew?*'

Clearly not Suzy, who was now looking at her husband in the crowd with an expression approaching confusion. Were they talking about the same man?

'You're a lucky girl, cuz. We all are.' Gem looked back at Cassie again, sipping her drink like a child at her parents' dinner party. 'Have you and Henry set a date?'

Oh God, not again. The same old question. 'Not yet,' Cassie said with a tight smile. 'We're just enjoying life as it is now.'

Gem looked baffled by the answer.

'Cassie's still recovering from her disastrous marriage. She got married too young, you see,' Suzy butted in tactlessly. 'A decade wasted, her best years behind her and all because she rushed into it,' she tutted.

Cassie glared at her best friend – could she have been more unsubtle? – but Suzy's eyes were resting solely on Gem. Laird shifted his weight uneasily. He, at least, appeared to have got the point.

'Can I get anyone another drink?' he asked.

Cassie gladly accepted – mainly to help justify his escape – and she watched him slip into the safety of the crowd, her eyes coming to rest on Henry again, as he still stood horsing around in a tight-knit core with Beau, Arch and Amy.

'So I'm amazed Archie made it here tonight. He was saying he only got out of hospital, like, yesterday.'

'Yes, and if he tries to get off that stool, I'll personally drop-kick him back to the CCU myself,' Suzy said, eyes slitted as Archie enthusiastically began another count-down.

'When's he back to work?' Gem asked.

'Not for at least another month. His ECGs weren't great. He needs further monitoring before they'll sign him off. The doctors said he's got to fully relax and start gentle exercise.'

'I'll teach him yoga,' Gem offered excitedly, grasping Suzy's hand.

'Ha! You wish!' Suzy quipped. 'Trust me, there are farm-house tables with more flexibility in their legs than his.'

'You really don't need to be flexible to do yoga, you know,' Gem said, laughing. 'I know I could help him. I worked with some really knackered old blokes in Oz and it made *such* a difference to their well-being.'

Cassie had begun to get the giggles – for the first time

ever, Suzy's outspokenness was making no imprint on Gem's blunt-headedness – and she couldn't help but look over at Suzy's outraged expression.

'Well, you're very sweet, Gem,' Suzy said in her most patronizing tone, 'but we're not actually going to be around this summer. We're decamping to Cornwall.'

'To Butterbox?' Gem gasped, her eyes wide and her hand slapped over her chest.

'That's right. The fresh air and big views are just what he needs.'

'I couldn't agree more. It'll be so healing for him being by the sea. The soul needs that vista, you know. It's too easy to disconnect from nature when you live in these big cities; you don't even realize it's happening. There's just this silent erosion of something good and vital from our lives and then we wonder why we feel so out of balance.'

'Yes. Right. That's what I thought,' Suzy said warily.

'You know, this is how Laird and I connected in the first place. He'd be up for the surf and he'd go right past my dawn classes – just seven or eight of us on the beach. It was only a matter of time before we got talking and realized how connected we are.' Her eyes glazed with the memories. 'God, he'd love it down there. The surf's so sick at Polzeath and—' She stopped talking abruptly, her expression lighting up. 'Oh my God,' she breathed, her hand clamping suddenly on to Suzy's arm. 'We should totally come down with you.'

'What?' Suzy looked nauseous.

'Think about it! You and Arch need to heal – because you've had a terrible shock too, Suzy. Don't underestimate the pressure it's put on you – and Laird's just beginning to wilt, bless him, being so far from the sea. He loves me and he'd live with me in the Gobi Desert if I asked him to, but he needs that element in his life. And I can do my yoga anywhere. Plus, it'd be the perfect opportunity for us all to have some proper time together and really reconnect, you know? It's been so long, years really, since we all had proper time together.'

Cassie wondered how many more times Gem could bring the word 'connect' into the conversation.

'I don't think that's a good idea—' Suzy began, but Gem was on a roll.

'And of course, while we're there, all together, you can help me get my ideas for the wedding on track. Did Henry tell you?'

'Huh?'

'I mean, I'd pay you, obviously. I wouldn't expect any freebies, although mates' rates would be nice.' She laughed, joshing Suzy in the ribs with an elbow. 'But you've got to admit it makes sense: while Archie's getting the rest he needs, you can have a little project to tide you over to stop you going stir-crazy, and I can try to get my head around this crazy wedding lark. I mean, really, can *anyone* explain to me the point of favours?'

Suzy stared at Cassie – she did, in fact, usually hold very strong views on favours – just as Laird reappeared with the drinks.

'Babe, you'll never guess!' Gem gushed. 'We're going to spend the summer in Cornwall.'

'Cornwall?' If he'd drawn a blank with Lammermuir, Cornwall fared no better.

'It's the UK's surf central. Polzeath is totally, like, one of the top-ten surf beaches.'

'Oh yeah, yeah, I know Polzeath.'

'Well, we've got a family place down there. Aunt Hat's got one half, and I've got the other . . .'

Suzy's eyes slid over to Cassie's, Gem's point quite clear: Suzy had no jurisdiction over whether or not Gem chose to go. She co-owned the house.

'Suzy and Arch are going down there so he can recuperate. We can all bond, plan the wedding *and*' – she took a deep breath – 'you can surf every day again.'

Laird looked down at his diminutive fiancée, his expression as soft as warmed butter as he snaked his hand round her neck. 'Seriously?'

Suzy furiously mouthed, 'WTF?' as the happy couple kissed.

'Are you coming too?' Laird asked her, forcing Cassie to break Suzy's eye-lock.

'Sorry?'

'To Cornwall.'

'Yes! That would be so perfect! And there's loads of room,' Gem added.

Cassie shook her head 'Sadly not. I've got to work.'

'Ah, that's a shame,' Laird smiled with what seemed to be genuine regret, and she wondered whether he wanted her to act as some sort of buffer between him and Gem, and Suzy. She couldn't blame him. Suzy had been nothing short of terrifying so far tonight.

'It really is. Especially with Henry being gone so long.' Gem pulled an exaggerated sad face.

'I'm used to it,' she shrugged, trying to mask the white lie. She would never get used to being without him.

'Yes, are you sure you couldn't come down?' Suzy asked, rejoining the conversation. 'Now that you've got Ascot and the polo out of the way, aren't things calming down? I thought they were your big events.'

Cassie looked at her in surprise. 'Well, yes, but we've still got the smaller private events – birthdays, anniversaries, intimate weddings.'

'But I bet Zara could cover those. I mean, Jude's school is off for the summer holidays now, right? And she's always saying how bored she gets at home with Zara being at work the whole time.'

Cassie laughed. 'I'm not sure she'd thank you for signing her up to a summer of work, though.'

Suzy shrugged. 'It's worth an ask, though, surely? Let's face it, you're going to be thoroughly miz without Henry *and* me.'

'You're nothing if not modest,' Cassie chuckled, knowing full well that the only reason Suzy was now so desperate to get her down there was for the same reasons as Laird had asked – to act as a buffer between her and Gem. There was no doubt Suzy would be at risk of a heart attack herself if she had to spend the entire summer with her little cousin.

All eyes fell on Cassie – each with different agendas and needs. 'Look, it's not that I don't think it's a lovely idea, but—'

'Yeah, yeah, yeah, we get it,' Suzy said with a deep sigh, before holding up her drink and staring at it grimly. 'Cheers, then. Here's to the joys of an endless summer.'

Cassie felt instantly guilty, but what could she do? She couldn't take off for a month just because Suzy needed some backup with her family.

'Do either of you know where I could go to have a sneaky ciggie?' Gem asked, before quickly putting her hand on Laird's arm. 'I know, and I promise this is the last one. I'll start tomorrow, but my favourite cousin in the— I mean, my favourite *male* cousin in the world is disappearing round the world *just* as I've got back, which is such sucky luck. I need something to take the edge off.'

Laird rolled his eyes in disapproval and Cassie thought that was at least something he and Suzy had in common.

'Here, Laird, let me introduce you to Arch,' Suzy said with a burst of sudden friendliness that made Cassie's eyes narrow. 'He's a demon boogie-boarder. He can tell you all about the surf down there.'

Gem smiled as Suzy towed Laird away like a tug boat and Cassie realized as Suzy began making frantic hand gestures behind her cousin's back exactly what she was up to: this was supposedly Cassie's cue to halt the wedding in its tracks.

'Um, follow me, Gem,' Cassie said, leading her back to the spot by the windows where she'd been standing earlier with Luke. Was he still here? Her eyes scanned the crowd as they passed, but she could see no sign of him. Thank God.

They leaned on the balcony together, Gem lighting a roll-up she'd stashed in her bra, and both of them staring into the brightly lit madding street, their backs to the party.

'So I get the impression Suzy isn't very pleased about the wedding,' Gem said after a moment, watching as her own smoke ring wobbled into the big, wide world.

'What? Suzy?' Cassie asked in a new falsetto. 'No! She's delighted for you. Really, really happy. And of course, weddings are her business. She's actually got a not-so-vested interest in seeing you guys get hitched.'

Gem stared at her for a minute, clearly deliberating

whether or not to believe her. 'Well, Aunt Hats is distraught. She thinks I'm rushing into it.'

Cassie swallowed. 'That's only natural. From what I understand, you and Laird haven't known each other for very long.'

'But you like him.'

'Me? I think he's lovely. Really charming and sweet. And he's obviously mad about you.'

Gem smiled, her eyes on a shaven-headed security guard standing outside a nightclub across the road. 'Exactly.'

Cassie dithered, wondering how to strike the balance between supportive and annihilative. 'I do see why Hats is concerned, though. I don't see what the rush is for getting married so soon. What's so wrong with waiting a bit?'

'What's so right with waiting?' Gem countered.

'Well, it gives you time to be sure that you're doing the right thing. What Suzy said earlier was true: I got married at exactly your age and spent a decade of my life being miserable. If I could go back and advise my twenty-one-year-old self now, it would be to just let things hang for a bit. Marriage is supposed to be forever. Don't do what I did and rush in. Feelings change; passions cool. I don't doubt you and Laird are nuts about each other now, but are you sure he's still going to be what you want ten, twenty, forty years from now?'

'But who can ever be sure of that? You could put off your entire life according to that philosophy. We're all works in progress. If you'd told me three years ago, when I got expelled for having sex with one of the boys in sixth form, that I'd find peace in a sun salutation, I'd have laughed my head off. I was the angriest little bitch you ever saw, and yet now look at me: I'm Zen with a capital Z. Personal growth isn't linear, Cassie. None of us knows who we're going to become. I mean, did you ever think you'd be engaged again, so soon after your marriage broke up?'

The question momentarily floored Cassie and she watched as a fat pigeon ruffled its feathers on a telephone wire. 'Uh, well, honestly? No. In fact, to be perfectly honest, I never thought I'd get married again full stop.'

'Really?'

Cassie closed her eyes briefly as she remembered the last day of her marriage. 'Everything that happened with my ex and me, it made such a travesty of our vows. I'm not sure I could ever believe in them again.'

'But you obviously could, though, with Henry,' Gem said, looking up at her questioningly. 'Seeing as you're engaged to him.'

Cassie didn't reply. She was back in the library, overhearing Gil's voice as he let spill the awful secret that she'd never even suspected. She'd been that naive, that gullible. That trusting . . .

'Cassie?'

'What? Oh. Yes, I . . .' She hesitated. 'Of course.'

Gem laughed. 'Well, *that* didn't sound very convincing!'

'What? No, no, it is. I just . . .' She forced her mind to get back on message. 'I was just thinking about the vows, actually. You have to really think about them before you commit to them. They're not just hollow words; you're going to live your life *according* to them. I mean, "forsaking all others" . . . Is that really a decision you, as a twenty-year-old, can stand by for all of your life?' Luke's face swam into her mind, his words still a warm echo: *'Who says you would*

*have come back? . . . When did that start? . . . It wasn't long, I
know that much . . . You were* never *coming back to me . . .'*

She banished him from her mind. Gil. Luke. All the
ghosts from her past were revisiting her tonight, eddying
round her and setting her off-balance, off-kilter. 'I guess
what I'm trying to say is, just don't make the mistake I
made. Life is long. What makes you happy today may not
be what makes you happy a year from now. Keep your
options open.'

'Is that what you're doing?'

'I'm sorry?'

'Well, you said earlier you like living in the moment,
which is kind of the opposite to making plans to grow old
together, isn't it?'

'I . . .' Cassie wasn't sure how to respond. Exactly how
had this conversation become about her and not about
Gem?

'It sounds to me like you don't actually believe in marriage at all, anymore,' Gem said, flicking the stub of her
cigarette to the pavement below. 'Regardless of age.'

Cassie blinked at her, infuriated on the one hand, stunned
on the other; the girl was a champion debater, leading Cassie
along paths she'd had no intention of walking down. She
was more confused about what she thought and felt than
she'd ever realized. 'You know what?' she said defiantly.
'Maybe I don't. Maybe I bloody well don't. It's an outdated
institution that has no relevance to modern life and modern
relationships, it's just some hangover from a time when
women were like chattels; something to be traded. But
you're an independent, educated girl, Gem. Why do you
need a ring on your finger? It's just a form of ownership,
not really any different from being branded like cattle, '

Cassie said dismissively, straightening her back as she got into her stride. Oh Suzy was going to love this when she heard about it.

Gem looked at the ring winking on Cassie's own finger. 'Well, if that's how you really feel, why are you wearing that then?'

Cassie looked down at the ring, remembering the moment – the perfect moment – when Henry had given it to her. She'd been so swept up in the romance of it, so carried away by the glorious shock and drama of it all, that it would have been impossible, totally unthinkable, to give voice to these thoughts. And, of course, she just loved him so, so much. But these words – they shone with the shimmer of truth in them, they sprung from feelings that had, somewhere along the line, become instincts and she herself didn't understand how these supposedly contradictory feelings could co-exist within her. She crumpled like an autumn leaf. 'I'm not sure,' she said eventually.

'Don't you think you should tell— Oh hey, how long have you been standing there?' Gem asked, her voice brightening as she turned to face the party again. 'Henry?'

Cassie whipped round. How long *had* he been standing there? What had he heard? She was almost scared to see the expression on his face, but she needn't have worried – the crowd was already closing around him and all she could see was his halo of gold hair disappearing into the shadows.

Chapter Twelve

Even at such an ungodly hour, Heathrow was heaving. Cassie moved out of the way of a troop of Japanese tourists, all pushing their hard-ridged suitcases along on double wheels, going to wait instead by the trolley station. She resumed watching Henry, who was standing at the check-in desk and putting his passport back in his rucksack; even from this distance, she could see the tension in his bones.

He had left the party last night without her – something he had never done before – but he hadn't gone home either, and when he'd finally rolled up in a taxi at 4 a.m., Beau hollering something out of the window as it pulled away, she had pretended to be asleep. There had been no point trying to talk to him – to explain – when he was that drunk and angry.

But she hadn't fared any better this morning either. He'd had barely more than ninety minutes' sleep and the expression on his face kept the words stuck in her throat, unable to come out, as they got dressed. They had driven over together in silence, her at the wheel of his Mini, as he'd tried to get some more sleep, and now he was moments away from leaving. The rest of the crew would be here somewhere too and she desperately didn't want to say her goodbyes to him in front of them.

She watched as he lurched over – still drunk, no doubt – almost tripping over a sleeping student, but still looking distractingly good in his battered jeans, boat shoes and red and blue team sailing jacket. The very sight of him made her catch her breath, as it always did. He came and stood in front of her, gaze averted, his hands stuffed in his jeans pockets, like a reluctant schoolboy waiting for his mother's peck on the cheek at the gates.

Her hand reached for his arm. 'Henry, please don't leave like this. I can't bear for you to go when you can't even look at me. I've told you – I love you. I want to be with you. Only you. Why isn't that enough?'

He blinked, his eyes cold. 'Because it isn't. There's no commitment. No security. And I've spent long enough waiting for you, don't you think?'

'But you are the only man I want. I will never leave you.'

'And yet you won't commit to stay because it's like Gem said – you want to keep your options open.'

'That wasn't what I meant.'

'I heard you, Cass.'

'She just made me cross, that's all. She's infuriating to talk to.'

'Do you have *any* idea how it felt for me to overhear you talking to her – almost a complete stranger to you – about something that's so intrinsic to *us*?'

'I didn't know . . . I didn't know it was going to come out the way it did. I didn't realize it was how I really felt. They weren't feelings that I'd consciously admitted to myself.'

'So then you do admit it is how you really feel?' He closed his eyes, his face scrunched with pain and his fists balled, trying to contain himself as the emotions grew and the clock ticked. There was so much to say, too much . . .

Bloody Gem! Cassie swallowed hard, knowing time was already against her and she felt her own anger grow. Why was she always painted as the bad guy in this? 'Have you ever *tried* seeing it from my point of view? Some might say that if you really loved me, you wouldn't ask me to go back into something I've worked so hard to get over and away from; if you loved me, you'd just accept you've got me, without having to have some kind of ownership. You're trying to push me into something I just don't believe in anymore.'

She dipped her head low, trying to get him to meet her eyes, to forgive her, to see that love was enough, but the expression on his face floored her and she pulled back sharply. He withdrew his hand from his pocket and reached for her left hand, raising it to eye level, her Tiffany solitaire winking back at her like a cheeky child. 'Then why did you say, "Yes"?' he asked, the words spinning out slowly, his voice barely more than a whisper. It was exactly the same question Gem had asked last night – the one she didn't have an answer to, then or now.

'Because . . .' she faltered. 'I was just so happy to be with you I couldn't think beyond that moment. I wasn't even divorced when you proposed. I hadn't had time to take a breath.'

He blinked back slowly. 'Well, you've got it now.'

'What do you . . . ?' She couldn't finish. Her mouth felt dry, her heart pausing in its beats.

'While I'm gone, you need to make a decision.' His voice was deeper than usual, torn and ragged by sharp emotions. 'Do you want to be my wife or not? I don't have any doubts or fears about us, and I won't entertain "what ifs?". I don't want to live a half-life. I won't.'

Her mouth parted as she willed the words to come out, but she felt stoppered by the distinction he'd made. She wanted to be *his*, but she didn't know whether she wanted to be anyone's wife again. That was the honest truth of it.

His eyes, red-rimmed and bluer than usual, pinned hers, reading her mind, and he looked down again with a short, scornful laugh, his hands on his hips. She watched as he shook his head fractionally as though in disbelief.

'Henr—'

'Henry!'

Beau's toff shout filled the terminal, his voice and spirits seemingly unaffected by last night's excesses. Henry half turned, acknowledging Beau's signalling with an abrupt nod of his head.

He turned back to her, exhaling heavily as his eyes roamed her like a familiar land, seemingly consigning the sight of her to memory. She felt hollowed out by the sight of him so ravaged and her eyes filled with tears – grief that he was leaving, grief that he was leaving like this, rushing into the void. And then his hands were on her cheeks, his mouth on hers as he kissed her with all the passion and desperation of their first kiss, his tears mingling with hers so that she didn't know where his sorrow ended and hers began.

He pulled away just a little, his forehead pressed to hers, his eyes squeezed shut as though the sight of her was painful to him now, and she inhaled the scent of him – beery though he was – with rising desperation. He was going. He was really going, even as their relationship stood on the precipice.

With effort he stepped back, his hands dropped down, off and away from her for the final time, it felt like.

'Make your decision, Cass.'

And he turned and walked away, leaving both of them to head into the unknown.

'It's definitely just a rocky patch,' Kelly said calmly through the screen as Cassie took another deep gulp of her vodka and tonic – no lemon: Henry had forgotten to buy them before he left and Cassie had found it hard to find any enthusiasm to get off the sofa at all for the past three days – not even for the precious lemons that were 'de rig' for her perfect V&T. He had landed in Sydney two days ago now, and today was the launch date, the day he stepped onto that bottle-boat and wouldn't be safe and dry again for three months – and she had heard nothing. Not a text, not a tweet, not a peep.

'You said that last time.'

'And I was right then too. This is the same fight. Nothing's changed.'

'Everything's changed! Now he knows what I really think!' Cassie wailed, finishing with a signature hiccup.

'Well, it was going to have to come out one way or the other. Did you really think you could just go on putting it off?'

'Yes!' Cassie cried, closing one eye and staring into the bottom of her glass with the other – it made her thighs look *huge*! 'Oh God, why did he have to come over just *then*? A minute before, a minute after . . . It's all Suzy's fault, you know.'

Kelly arched an eyebrow as she sipped her water. 'How?'

'She bullied me into trying to talk her cousin out of getting married. She's only twenty and Suze thought it would be a great idea if I told her all about my own disastrous child-bride marriage!' Cassie threw her hands in the air. 'Oh yes, great idea!'

'Well, I can see her logic. You get to speak from experience.'

'No! No! Because she conveniently forgot to mention that her cousin has a PhD in arguing. She'd convert the Pope to Buddhism and have Vladimir Putin consulting his auras within twenty minutes of meeting them. She's impossible to talk to – she just twists your words and makes you say things you never knew you . . .' She trailed off. See? Gem had done it again and she wasn't even in the room!

Kelly's head tipped to the side, a sympathetic smile on her face.

Cassie double-blinked anxiously. 'What if this whole issue is too big for us to get past?'

'There's no such thing. It's just a matter of how hard you're prepared to work to find a solution. It's a long road that has no turns, Cass.'

Cassie was quiet. There was no future for her and Henry if she decided against marrying again. He didn't want to be happily unmarried.

'You think I should marry him, don't you?'

'It's up to y—'

'Yes or no? Gut response.'

'Fine, yes, I do. You're blissful together. It's nauseating to watch, but I'll be honest – I have sometimes wondered whether your year out after you left Gil wasn't a little too successful,' Kelly said. 'Being independent doesn't mean you have to be invincible.'

'Do I look invincible to you right now?' Cassie asked sardonically, indicating to her lank hair, pale complexion and the almost-empty glass in her hand.

'No,' Kelly conceded. 'But maybe you should let Henry see you like this. He probably has no idea that you'd fall apart without him.'

Cassie spluttered, suddenly, with laughter.

'What?'

'I just had an image of Anouk's expression if she'd overheard you say I should let him see me looking like this! "Are you mad? Looking like that? What is wrong with you?"' Cassie cried, mimicking their friend's accent perfectly. '"No man should ever see his woman looking like that. It is a wonder to me that you two are still together. Go wash your hair and match your lingerie. That is an order."'

Kelly laughed too. 'Ha! That'd be nothing! She'd die on the spot if she saw the shoulder-boulder bras I just had to buy . . .'

Cassie stopped grinning. She hadn't dared bring up the topic of the pregnancy yet. Kelly had determinedly kept charge of the conversation from the start, emitting non-verbal clues not even to raise the issue, but now . . .

'Really?' She kept her tone light.

Kelly nodded, looking down at her own bosom, which was impossible to gauge for size in a black silk shirt. 'They're ballooning, actually.'

'Oh right. Did that happen last time?' She was careful to keep any trace of hope from her voice. It had only been a week since their last lock-in, meaning Kelly was at eight weeks now, with only four to go till she was officially – and statistically – out of danger and Brett got to know he was going to be a father.

Kelly shook her head. 'But that doesn't mean anything, though,' she added quickly.

'No, no, I'm sure.'

'I'm still losing this baby next week.'

Cassie winced at the brutality of her friend's words. 'Kell, you don't know that for s—'

Kelly sniffed. 'Yes, I do. I know the pattern. It happens next week.' She stared back hard at Cassie – a warning for her not to push back.

Cassie looked away. She knew these hard-hitting words were Kelly's way of managing her own instincts, which were willing her to hope, daring her to dream that maybe this time, this time they'd get through . . . She shifted position, tucking her legs beneath her on the sofa.

'Well, then I guess I'd better get off my lazy arse and buy some lemons.'

There was a pause. 'Lemons?'

Cassie held up her glass. 'If we're going to make this a daily thing, I can't carry on drinking poorly made V&Ts. A girl's got to have standards, right?'

Kelly cracked a grateful smile, getting the unspoken point. 'Listen, I'm flying in to London the week after next. Are you—'

Cassie's eyes widened in horror. 'Kelly, you can't!'

There was a pause. 'Why not?'

'Because that will increase the risk of miscarrying. Even I know that!'

There was a heavy silence as Cassie realized she'd missed Kelly's cue, broken their cardinal rule.

'Cass, you promised,' Kelly said stonily. 'It doesn't help me to have you fighting me too.'

'I'm sorry. I'm sorry. I just—' She bit her lip, physically restraining herself from saying anything more, even though she practically vibrated from suppressed frustration. 'Sorry.'

Kelly inspected her nails. 'Besides, there's no actual evidence that flying increases the risk; it's nothing compared to what my own body can do to this baby.' For a second Kelly's face crumpled, every muscle contracting from the sheer force it took to hold back emotions stronger than hope. 'Obviously I wouldn't fly if it *didn't* happen,' she said in a voice so tiny it was only the fact that her lips were moving that convinced Cassie she'd heard it at all.

Kelly fussed with her drink, struggling for composure as Cassie hated herself from her spot on her sofa 3,500 miles away. How could she have been so tactless? She'd made a promise.

'So anyway, are you free on the Thursday?' Kelly tried again.

Cassie automatically went to nod 'yes', but pulled a face halfway through. 'Oh crap. Actually, I'm not sure. Possibly. I said I'd go to Cornwall with Suze and Arch for a bit, to help out with Velvet.'

Suzy had been wearing her down on the issue ever since Henry had left, although Cassie wasn't sure if it was in response to Cassie's utter dejection at the manner of Henry's departure – and his ultimatum – or Suzy's own growing panic at the thought of living cheek-by-jowl with Gem. Either way, Cassie had found herself somehow talked into a week's haitus, with the 'possibility'of staying longer.

'Suze doesn't know how taken up she's going to be with Archie yet and I'm worried she's going to murder her cousin.'

'Oh. Well, never mind.' Kelly shrugged, but her disappointment was evident.

'But look, let me see, OK? Nothing's firmed up yet. What are you coming over for, anyway?'

'Bebe's up for Best International Designer at the BFAs.'

'Oh God,' Cassie grimaced. 'So you really do need some backup.'

'God knows what she'll be like once she's raided her hotel minibar,' Kelly groaned. 'I'll be babysitting a monster.'

'Well . . .' Cassie thought hard. 'Do you know what, even if I am down there, I could probably get back for the night anyway. I think there are regular flights from Newquay, which is nearby. I'm driving down with Suze, but I could maybe fly back early.'

'OK, well let me know. It would be good to see you, and . . .' She hesitated. 'Well, I would imagine you're going to need to cry on my shoulder as much as I'm going to cry on yours. Sometimes even vodka isn't enough, am I right?'

Cassie frowned, puzzled. She sensed they had moved topic. 'Huh?'

Kelly gave a tense laugh. 'Wow, OK, so maybe not then. You really are over it.'

Cassie's frown deepened. 'Over what? What are you talking about?'

The smile disappeared from Kelly's face. 'Well, Gil and Wiz, of course.'

The distance between them contracted at the mention of her former husband and friend's names, all the air in the room sucked out in a vacuum so that Cassie felt her face was pressed to the screen as she waited for clarity. 'What about them?'

Kelly's amused expression changed as she took in Cassie's pallor. 'Oh Jeez, please tell me Suzy told you.'

Cassie didn't reply and Kelly groaned, dropping her face into her hands and shaking her head lightly. When she looked up, her eyes were wary. 'I'm going to kill her. She said she was going to tell you.'

'Tell me what?'

There was a long silence as Kelly struggled to find a way of softening the words she had to say. 'I knew you were taking it too well. I knew it,' she muttered to herself before taking a deep breath. 'Look, there's no easy way to tell you this. They're getting married in two weeks.'

Cassie felt the room rock. Her heart beat uncontrollably. 'How did Suze know, anyway?' Her mind went into overdrive. Why hadn't Gil told Cassie, his own ex-wife? He'd told Suzy but not her? It made no sense.

And then it did. Cassie groaned, closing her eyes. 'Oh God, it was in *The Times*,' she muttered.

'Cass, I'm so sorry,' Kelly said. It was her turn to sound tentative now as Cassie slumped back into the sofa.

Of course it had been in *The Times*. The union of Lady Louisa Arbuthnott and Gilpin Mathieson, two of the smartest families in Edinburgh, was never going to have passed unannounced.

'Cass, I'm sorry.' Kelly's voice was quiet. 'I thought . . .' Her voice faded to silence as she watched Cassie stare into nothingness, the past and the future becoming tangled in a messy knot.

Cassie came to, like she'd been slapped, and inhaled sharply. She looked back at the screen. 'Hey, what do I care? I don't! That ship sailed a long time ago.' Cassie's voice was flat, her free arm waving listlessly as vague punctuation to her words.

'OK.'

'They deserve each other.'

'Yeah.'

'I couldn't care less.'

Kelly paused. 'Right.'

They were both quiet. Cassie took a sip of her drink. Then another, swallowing loudly and smacking her lips together.

Kelly knew better than to offer platitudes.

'Well, it's certainly heartening to see that Gil's got none of my misapprehensions about marrying again,' Cassie said finally – and sarcastically – giving a massive shrug. 'I guess I really must be making this remarriage lark into a bigger deal than it needs to be.'

'No you're not.'

'Aren't I? Everyone else can walk straight back into marriage – why not me?'

'Because you're being wise, prudent. You had a bad experience and you've learned from it. Why *would* you just rush straight back in again? That's the very definition of idiocy. The guy's an idiot.'

Cassie shook her head with a stubborn expression. 'I'm over-thinking things.'

'Cass—'

She sat forward with sudden intensity. 'Do you know what? I reckon I should follow his example.' Cassie threw her arms up in the air. 'Yeah. Why the hell not? Sod it, I'm just going to go with my gut. I'm going to trust my instincts.'

Kelly brightened. She, too, was a fighter. 'Which are?'

There was a momentary silence as Cassie swallowed, deflating slowly, before falling back into the cushions like she'd been thrown into them. 'Damned if I know.'

Chapter Thirteen

Cassie sat in the back seat, watching *The Tale of Peter Rabbit* on Velvet's DVD monitor as Suzy swore at the slow drivers in front and Archie passed round the sandwiches. They had decided on the scenic route, hoping to point out Stonehenge to Velvet as they passed, but she was already asleep by then and Cassie was too engrossed in the film to look up.

By the time she did, they had passed through the small, winding valleys of Somerset, over the cow-dotted fields of Devon and were coming into the vast, domed moorlands of Cornwall, which sloped down to the sea in the distance. Everywhere she looked, ancient dry-stone walls ran ahead and around them like lines of mice, the now-familiar sight of white wind turbines revolving slowly in the breeze. Some tumbledown ruins were all that remained of the historic tin mines Cornwall had been so famed for in centuries past, and they drove through tiny villages where old-fashioned petrol pumps had long since been boarded up. In spite of the big sky above them, Cassie had a feeling of the walls of the world closing in.

'I can't believe you've never been down here before,' Suzy said, catching Cassie's eye in the rear-view mirror.

Cassie shrugged. 'I guess you don't know what you

don't know. I was always back in Hong Kong for the summer holidays.'

'Henry and I used to spend our entire summers down here. We'd be as wild as weasels by the time we had to go back to school. Mum never saw us from sunup to sundown.' She shook her head. 'I can't begin to imagine being that relaxed with Velvy now.'

'Different times,' Archie murmured, trying to retune the radio to anything other than static. 'God, are we by the coast or actually in the middle of the Atlantic?'

'Get used to it, babe. There's practically no mobile signal down here either, and I've left all the laptops and iPads at home. Cass has too, so don't think you can steal hers,' she said quickly as she saw Archie's look of absolute horror. 'The office won't be able to get hold of you even if they want to. Ha!' Suzy chuckled triumphantly. 'You. Shall. Not. Work.'

'Dear God, woman, what if they need to—'

'They won't! I've told your boss that if he even thinks about contacting you in the next month, I will have him tried for attempted manslaughter.'

Archie dropped his head in his hands.

They had turned off the A303 now and the roads were becoming significantly narrower, bosky hedgerows looming overhead at seven, even eight feet high, with multi-coloured and scented profusions of wild garlic, giant daisies, elderflower and honeysuckle.

They drove through Delabole – home to the world-famous black slate – a smile spreading on Cassie's lips as she saw a group of white-clad morris dancers sitting in the garden of a pub and enjoying a beer, their batons on the grass by their feet, the bells at their knees hanging silent for the moment.

'So when's Gem coming down?' Cassie asked, catching a glimpse of the sea as they passed the signs for Port Isaac.

'Germ? She's already there,' Suzy said in a sulky voice. 'They went the morning after the party, would you believe it? Lord's been pining for saltwater apparently, poor dolphin.'

'Gem. And Laird,' Archie said in mild rebuke. 'Behave.'

Suzy's eyes met Cassie's again in the mirror. 'Honestly, me and my big mouth,' she muttered. 'Why did I even mention we were coming down here? She never would have thought about it if I hadn't said. She hasn't been down here since I don't know when.'

'I don't understand why you're so stressed about it. Gem's not so bad, just a little wired,' Archie said calmly. 'And Laird's really very interesting.'

'I'm stressed because Mum's stressed,' Suzy replied hotly. 'She thinks Gem's making a huge mistake, and now I've got to help her organize a wedding for a marriage that none of us believes in, *as well as* look after you.'

'*I* am fine,' Archie said, leaning over to squeeze Suzy's knee. 'Just chill. Otherwise you'll be the one who needs looking after.'

Suzy harrumphed. 'Oh great. So I need looking after, and you do, Cass too. At this rate, Velvet's going to be in charge.'

Cassie looked across at the sleeping toddler, her rosebud mouth parted, her eyelids flickering lightly as she dreamed. She resisted the urge to stroke her cheek and risk waking her.

'Pah. Don't include me in your mass collapse. I am officially A-OK,' Cassie declared, giving a thumbs-up gesture in the mirror that fooled no one. If she'd been left reeling by the manner of Henry's departure, she had been flattened by Gil's news, and her puffy, deadened eyes and white skin told an entirely different story of sleepless nights and lack of appetite, which had seen Suzy commandeer the situation once and for all and ring Zara herself to clear Cassie's work diary for the next fortnight.

They turned off towards Rock, noticing a marked upturn in the smartness of the houses as they drew nearer. Even 1960s bungalows – the kiss of death anywhere else in the country – had been revamped with New England-style clapboarding in cool greens and Scandinavian greys, smart teak gates blocking off Chelsea tractors and only the wild flowers growing out of the old stone walls giving any indication of the bucolic wildness that surrounded them.

Cassie pressed her nose almost to the glass as they passed a small ribbon of shops – a butcher's, deli, fish shop, bakery and some boutiques. Slightly further on, there was the post office, newsagent, hairdresser's and an estate agent's, lots of signs for local galleries and a turn-off to a small cove.

They took a right turn at the top of a hill and swept out of the village again, driving beside fields banked high above them with long grasses that bent low as the wind danced on their heads. The lane was impossibly narrow here, single-vehicle access only, with just a few passing places, and they had to wait several minutes as a decorator's van coming in the opposite direction led a charge of cars and camper vans making their way back from the beach, surfboards strapped to the roofs.

'Come on, come on,' Suzy said impatiently under her

breath, her fingers tapping on the steering wheel, pulling out quickly before a Land Rover she could see at the back decided to tack on to the end. Which it did.

'Uh, Suze,' Cassie said as the two vehicles headed towards each other, the other driver – a blonde in designer shades – looking every bit as determined as Suzy that she wouldn't be the one reversing all the way back.

'*No problemo*,' Suzy said, just as they were practically within kissing distance of the other car's bumper. Suzy gave a triumphant smile – and the bird – to the blonde, swinging the car left into a sweeping driveway that led to the only two properties, seemingly, on the entire lane. 'Home sweet home.'

Cassie blinked as they passed two signs for 'Butterbox Farm' and 'Snapdragons'.

'Is this it?' she asked, peering at a modest whitewashed 1950s house, situated just inside the gates to the right. There was a large tarmacked driveway and two cars parked outside – a dented metallic-blue Renault Clio and a sleek black Jeep.

'Nope. That's Snapdragons. That's where Gem and Laird are staying.'

'Why are they in there and not Butterbox?' Archie frowned, before taking a look at Suzy's too-innocent expression as they continued up the drive. 'Oh God, what did you say to her?'

'Nothing! I simply pointed out that we have a very young child with us and . . . you know, if they value sleep . . .'

'Suzy! Velvet's been sleeping through the night since she was three months!'

'I know, but she's a child – there are never any guarantees, are there? And Gem and Laird are still practically teenagers themselves. I bet they sleep till noon and go to bed at dawn. It just wasn't practical to think that we could all sleep under the same roof for a summer.'

'You are a nightmare,' Archie sighed, as Cassie tried to suppress a smile.

'Plus I pointed out to her you could keel over at any moment. This isn't just a whimsical holiday by the sea for us, you know. We are here for the very serious business of convalescence. You need your rest.'

Archie twisted back in his seat to face Cassie. 'Are you going to deal with her or shall I?'

Cassie laughed as they drove through a second, grander set of gates with carved stone pineapples sitting atop the pillars. 'Oh, cool,' she breathed, taking stock of a much larger white house with more windows than she could count. It wasn't that old – maybe 1930s – or even that pretty, but it sat diagonally in its plot, the rear aspect facing west over fields where dairy herds grazed and down to the sea – Cassie guessed it would be a ten-minute walk, tops, to the beach. Nestled in a nook, between the fields and the beach, she could just make out the tip of a small church steeple.

'Oh, Suze, it's gorgeous,' Cassie said admiringly, undoing her seat belt and hopping out of the car to get a better look. The breeze lifted her hair off her neck immediately and she turned her face to the sky, instinctively wondering if Henry could feel it too – but no, she realized, in the next breath. He was in the southern hemisphere on the southern oceans. His sky was black right now.

'Leave the bags, Arch,' Suzy said, as he wandered round

to the boot. 'I'll get them. You take Velvet in and open up.'

'You'll be peeing standing up next,' he grumbled, taking the keys off her and hoisting their drowsy daughter into his arms.

Suzy watched him walk off, her face tense. 'He's going to be a terrible patient,' she said in an uncharacteristically small voice and seemingly to herself, before remembering Cassie standing beside her. 'And Henry buggering off to God knows where hasn't helped,' she said more loudly. 'Arch has been in a bad mood since he left. My brother's sense of timing is just classic. Classic.'

'Mmmm,' Cassie said, leaning into the boot and hauling out the heaviest bag as a distraction. There had still been no contact between them since he'd gone: no texts when he'd been in Sydney, and mobiles wouldn't work, of course, on the open seas. 'Well, we're four days down already. Only eighty-two to go,' Cassie said lightly.

'That's the spirit,' Suzy said, slapping her heartily on the back, so that Cassie almost fell head first into the car boot.

They trooped into the house together, Cassie's eyes wide as she took in the winding staircase, which covered three walls, the old stripped pine floors that needed to be re-oiled. The furniture was modest – armchairs and sofas with loose bleached linen covers in the sitting room, spoke-wheel wooden chairs and a refectory table in the kitchen – and the linings of the backs of the royal-blue velvet curtains in the sitting room were practically decayed from decades of enduring the blaze of the setting sun.

'How long has this house been in the family, did you say?' Cassie asked.

Suzy dropped the cool bags in the doorway and inhaled deeply, a smile on her face and her hands on her hips as she took in the familiar scene. 'Nana and Grumpy retired here in the 1960s. Me and Henry were baptized in the local church and spent every summer down here.' She closed her eyes for a moment, the tension in her shoulders slackening momentarily. 'Damn, it's good to be back. I always forget just how much I love it here until I step back in again and then – wham! Never want to leave.'

'Well, you have to. I need you in London. It wouldn't be the same without you,' Cassie said firmly, worried that her best friend might be getting ideas.

'Or we could all move down here together,' Suzy said, scooping up the bags again and walking through to the kitchen. Velvet was eating a spider web – hopefully minus the spider – as Arch went around opening all the doors and windows.

'Oh yes, I can just see it. You'd have me and Henry in Snapdragons as your gatekeepers while you and Arch played lord and lady of the manor.'

'Well, I just figured you'd have had enough of playing the chatelaine for one lifetime,' Suzy winked, hoisting the bags of Ocado groceries, which she'd had delivered at home an hour before they left, onto the worktop.

'That's true,' Cassie agreed, walking over to the glazed back doors and stepping out onto the terrace. She could almost taste the salt in the air; a herd of black-and-white cows munched at the grass not fifty feet away. 'So how far is it to the beach from here?' she called back into the house.

Suzy looked up from stocking the fridge. 'If you're running – which we always were, when we were little – six minutes. As a grown-up with all the bags, more like ten. That's Daymer Bay you can see from here.'

'Oh, I've heard of that,' Cassie murmured, stretching

lightly and turning back to the room. It was low-ceilinged but with enormous square footage, though it clearly hadn't been touched in thirty years. Old 1980s pine cabinets had been fitted against three of the walls in a U-shape, and a small island unit with cream melamine-topped work surfaces stood in the middle. A wipe-clean lino floor – good for sweeping up sand, no doubt – covered what presumably were the lovely boards she'd seen in the hall, and the fridge was white, unbelievably without an ice dispenser. How old school! What next? Cassie wondered – a TV that still stood on the floor? 'Suze, I just love it here.'

Suzy flashed her a beaming grin. 'Yeah? Me too. I know it needs loads doing. It's basically an interior designer's wet dream, but I don't need it to be spangly and perfect. Not like Kelly and Nooks would – can you just imagine?' she asked, one eyebrow arched and shaking her head. 'It's all about that, for me,' she said, pointing to the view.

'Agreed.'

'Come on, I'll show you the bedrooms.' Suzy, abandoning the vegetables, scooped Velvet into her arms and they sauntered up the long and winding staircase, Suzy pointing out the numerous bedrooms – all of them chintzy, with swags at the windows, sofas at the end of the beds and kidney-shaped dressing tables.

The place was so enormous there was no chance of Velvet ever having been able to disturb Gem and Laird, but the damage was done now, and she supposed they probably preferred having their own private space. She didn't imagine Gem was ever going to make a fortune from yoga, and Laird looked like he'd grown up in a coconut shy – or at least would have wanted to – so maybe even the little house was exciting to them.

Cassie's room was one of the best, situated at the back beside the master suite, with a long balcony that faced west. It was easier up here to see down to the beach and she stood for a long time looking out to the water, her mind constantly drifting back to her fiancé, who was, at this very minute, drifting too.

The tide was out and she could make out the dots of people still enjoying the last of the afternoon. A field on the far side had been given over to parking – the windscreens glistening in the sun – and several families were playing a game of rounders.

She helped Suzy draw a bath for Velvet in a bathroom so huge the bath sat in the middle of the room with at least seven feet of space around it on all sides, and Suzy didn't seem to care whether or not the geranium-pink deep-pile carpet got wet.

Archie called up that he was going to bike over to the store in the nearest village, Trebetherick, to buy some chicken and milk – which Suzy had deliberately left off her shopping list in case of traffic and high temperatures – scooting out before Suzy could remind him (as if he needed it) not to move up past third gear or come out of the saddle. 'Gentle exercise, the doctor said, Arch!' Suzy barked after him as he shot down the drive like he'd been catapulted.

The girls sat on the terrace, sneakily drinking a glass of rosé before he came back. Suzy was adamant that they should all abstain from drinking in front of him when he wasn't allowed alcohol, but that wasn't the same thing as abstaining entirely and Cassie wouldn't have been remotely surprised if Suzy had drawn up a list of things for Archie to do every evening at seven o'clock.

'I'd have thought Germ would have raced up the drive to see us the second she heard the car,' Suzy sniffed, slightly put out.

'She's probably at the beach, isn't she?'

'I suppose. Saying goodbye to the sun by plaiting her arms and legs.'

Cassie chuckled. 'You're just jealous because you have all the suppleness of that telegraph pole.'

'If only it was the girth,' Suzy smiled, patting her gently padded hips, which still carried traces of Velvet's baby weight.

'There's nothing wrong with your girth.'

'Oh no? Listen, if I went and stood next to that cow over there, you can bet your bottom dollar it would suddenly feel like it was having a thin day and want to put on its skinniest jeans.'

Cassie laughed, stretching out on the white plastic sunlounger and determinedly ignoring the slightly musty smell coming from the green striped cushions.

'So . . .'

Cassie looked over to find Suzy watching her closely. 'So, what?'

'You seem brighter today.'

'I feel great. Who wouldn't?' Cassie asked rhetorically, motioning to the setting and deliberately avoiding the subject.

'Have you heard from him yet?'

Cassie shook her head as she felt the pressure rush to her head again. It was the 'yet' that upset her, as though there was anything optional about it. He was out of contact, almost as uncontactable as if he were on the moon, or in Ikea. 'I told you, he's got no mobile coverage.' Her index finger tapped the lounger arm metronomically. 'All the radar equipment on the boat creates too much electro-magnetic interference. If he even wants to listen to his iPod, he's got to wrap tin foil round the headphones. This is it now till he gets back, or at least till they get to San Francisco, anyway.'

'Huh. I thought there was that telecommunications company keeping us in contact with them.'

'There is, in terms of informing us of their geographical positioning and any SOS messages, but they're hardly there to pass love letters between us.' Cassie knew she sounded defensive.

'Oh bummer.'

'Yeah.'

'Well, I still can't believe he went without saying good-bye. I mean, a text wouldn't have killed him.'

Cassie bit her lip and looked away, focusing on a particularly contented cow, its tail sluicing at flies as it grazed. She didn't reply, mainly because she couldn't believe it either.

'Having said that, I guess you can't blame him for being hacked off that you're suddenly having second thoughts about things,' Suzy carried on. 'You did pull the rug out from under him.'

Cassie shot her a look, wondering whose side Suzy was supposedly on. 'Excuse me! It's because of *you* that this has happened at all. If you hadn't got me entangled in your half-arsed schemes with your bloody cousin, everything would be fine.'

'Ha! Fat lot of good it did me. You've messed things up for you and Henry, *and* I've still got to single-handedly sabotage the wedding.' She frowned. 'And anyway, how exactly would it be fine? Henry asked you to marry him and you said yes. You've been engaged for the past year and a half. How can you come out now saying you don't believe in marriage? At some point, you were going to have to fess up.'

'I love him and want to be with him, and when he asked, I thought . . . I just assumed we could take our time with it all. I didn't count on there being so much pressure to *get on with it*. It's the institution I have a problem with, not him. I don't know why that's so hard to understand.'

Suzy sighed. 'Look, I get why you don't want to rush into marriage again, I do. But you have to bear in mind that he's never been married. He waited for you all that time, and what's seemingly dead for you is still alive with possibility for him. Are you really going to ask him to give up on his ideals because yours failed?'

'I'm not asking him to give up on anything. I want him. I want us to have a family. Plenty of people are happily unmarried.'

'You mean like Hugh Grant in *Four Weddings*?' Suzy asked.

'Exactly. Or Goldie Hawn and Kurt Russell – they're happily unmarried.'

'Madonna and her backing dancers,' Suzy suggested.

Cassie laughed. 'Richard Curtis and Emma Freud.'

'Kermit and Miss Piggy.'

Cassie laughed even harder. 'See? Lots of people have Happy Ever Afters without the ring.'

'Ha! As if you're going to give up that ring. Tiffany's finest! Poor Henry practically mortgaged Mum to buy it.'

'OK, not without the ring. Her fingers automatically

reached for it; it had become something of a soother for her and she would often fiddle with it when she was nervous or upset. 'But without the "I do".'

'You need to talk this through with him properly.'

'Well, he's made that a bit bloody hard now that he's done a disappearing act to the middle of the Pacific Ocean for three months.'

Suzy sighed. 'I know, but he's never been level-headed where you're concerned. I mean, when you married Gil . . . Most blokes would just go on a massive bender. He went to northern Norway and trained as an Arctic survival instructor! In fact, it's your bloody fault he's an explorer at all. He had a job all lined up in the City, but seemingly trekking the Arctic and biking across Siberia were the only ways for him to try to get over you.'

Cassie didn't say anything.

'He loves you, but he won't beg, Cass.' Suzy's tone had changed, the joking gone. 'And it would break my heart to see you two split up over a piece of paper.'

'We are not going to split up!' Cassie said, aghast. 'Look, this is all a storm in a teacup. It was bad timing that it came to a head just before he went' – and when she was excluded from the hospital ward, she didn't add – 'but he'll have forgotten all about it by the time he gets back.'

'Forgotten he wants to marry you?' Suzy guffawed, her eyebrows almost shooting to the other side of her head, but Cassie just took another sip of her drink and stared determinedly out to sea.

The front door slammed and they both looked back towards the kitchen, smiling as Archie sauntered through a moment later, two brown paper bags scrunched in his hands and an envelope.

'Bugger, drink up,' Suzy whispered, getting up from her lounger. 'I'll buy us some time.'

Cassie – who couldn't bolt a drink to save her life – took rapid sips of her wine as Suzy went into the kitchen to check on Archie's colour. There was only one sip left when Archie came out, looking very pleased with himself, a minute later.

'Ooh, what's that you've got there?' he asked.

'Huh?' Cassie asked, wide-eyed, as she hurriedly drained it out of sight before he could ask for some. 'Oh, you mean this? Ribena.'

'It didn't look like Ribena,' Archie frowned.

'I prefer it weak.'

'What's that you've got in your hands?' Suzy asked, quickly following him with a tray of glasses and a jug of sparkling elderflower.

'It's for Cassie, actually,' he replied, holding out the envelope.

'For me?' she asked in surprise.

'Yes,' he shrugged. 'It turns out they've got Wi-Fi at the cafe at the back of the store—' This time it was Archie's turn to look triumphant as Suzy gasped in horror, her great plan foiled. 'So I checked emails. Personal ones only,' he added, ever the pacifist. 'This was waiting for Cass in my inbox, so I printed it out.'

There was only one person who would know to write to her using Archie's email address. Suzy knew it too. 'Well, what did he do that for? I told him before we left that we wouldn't have reliable internet access down here,' Suzy said huffily.

'Don't worry. I've replied telling him we're here now. I'm

sure the *incessant mailing* will stop.' Archie rolled his eyes
as he handed the envelope to Cassie.

She forced herself not to tear it open in a rush, even
though the sight of the Inmarsat logo at the top of the
email – the expedition's satellite communications supplier
and the crew's only point of contact with land except for
the coastguard – made the words swim before her eyes.
He'd written. Even with ten pairs of eyes seeing this highly
personal letter between it leaving him and reaching her,
he'd written! She was forgiven . . .

But her mouth dropped open as she began to take in
what was written in the email. Not an apology, not a reconciliation . . . 'Oh!'

'Oh crap, what? What is it?' Suzy asked, hating being
out of the loop even for a moment. 'What's he gone and
done now?'

'It's a list.'

'Huh?'

Cassie looked up at her. 'He's written me a list for down
here.'

'Oh, you've got to be joking. Another one?' Suzy looked
at her husband for answers, though the expression on his
face told her he had none; he was as oblivious as the rest of
them.

Cassie clutched the paper tighter in her hands. It was
Henry's lists for her in Paris, New York and London –
devised to get her 'under the covers' of each city – that had
brought them together in the first place. In spite of her
friends' best efforts to spell out new identities for her, it
was Henry's lists that had been the tools that had really set
her on the path to self-awareness after she had lost such
confidence in herself following the breakdown of her

marriage that she couldn't put an outfit together, much less a new life. And now there was another list, just as she faced another crisis of confidence.

'He really can't help himself, can he? It's like some sort of compulsion. God forbid Cass should be allowed to just sit on the beach.' Suzy looked back at her. 'So what's he got you doing, then?'

Cassie smoothed a blonde tendril of hair back from her eyes. 'Well, I've got to catch a wave.' She bit her lip; she could barely balance on a yoga mat, much less a surfboard. 'Can we cheat and make it a Mexican one?'

'Actually, I think that's rather fun,' Archie said cheer-fully, while grimacing at the sugary taste of his drink and staring at it suspiciously. 'You can't come down here and not get in the sea. I'll join you. I've always wanted to learn how to surf.'

'Arch—' Suzy began.

'Gentle exercise, the docs said. What could be more gentle than standing on top of a board in the sea, darling?'

Suzy rolled her eyes, biting back the roll call of potential disaster scenarios – being swallowed by a basking shark, going into anaphylactic shock after a jellyfish sting, being carried out on a rip tide . . .

'What else?' Archie continued, before his wife could.

'Oh Lord, he says I've got to race a gig.' She pulled a face. 'What's a gig? It sounds like a long-legged bird. If so, I don't fancy my chances.'

Archie chuckled. 'It's a boat. A very big rowing boat. You'd better start eating lots of spinach and grow some muscles.'

'Ha, ha. And how exactly am I supposed to do this? Where would I even find a gig? Who would I race against?'

'Oooh, where there's a will . . .' Archie winked, looking over at Suzy. 'Gig racing's famous down here in the summer. I don't think it'll be too much of a problem to get you put in a crew.'

'"Give a Cornish gift."' Cassie looked up blankly. 'What the devil's that?'

'That's a local saying – it means if you've got something you don't want or need, then give it to someone else,' Suzy explained.

'You mean like my present-recycling drawer?'

'Yeah, sort of.'

'Were you in on this?' Cassie asked Suzy, eyes narrowed as she waved the list around. 'Be honest.'

'Categorically not. Henry doesn't tell me anything he doesn't have to.'

'Hmmm.' Cassie went back to reading again. '"Eat a pasty on the sand." Well, now that I can do . . .' She frowned. 'It says I've got to jump from the bridge into the Hidden Lagoon.'

Suzy's eyes brightened. 'Oh my God!' she gasped. 'The bridge.'

'Should I be worried? How big is this bridge? Are we talking suspension?' Cassie demanded nervously.

'I'd completely forgotten all about that place.'

'Where is it?' Archie asked, a little hurt. 'We've never gone there together. You've never even mentioned it.'

'Because I'd completely forgotten all about it, you daft nana! What did I just say? It's down on the Lizard, about an hour away. It's at the far end of a cove where you can only get to the beach at low tide. Bit of a tricky path down to it, as I recall, but so, so worth it. The water is turquoise. You'd never believe it was the Atlantic.'

'Well, that sounds good too,' Archie said, mollified, looking back at Cassie. 'This is a kind list. He's obviously going soft in his old age – there's nothing too scary on there at all so far. Is there anything else?'

'Just one,' Cassie mumbled.

Suzy's eyes narrowed as she looked at Cassie's expression and she stepped round to read over her shoulder.

'"Choose."'

He'd left the scariest for last.

Chapter Fourteen

They were all tucking in to muesli the next morning – Archie looking near tears as the bacon sat untouched and forbidden in the fridge – when Gem bounded in, using her own key.

'Morning!' she sang, stopping in her tracks at the desolate scene. 'Oh. Did someone die?'

'Beginning to wish I had,' Arch said mournfully, pushing his muesli – which did look like wet cement – around his bowl.

Gem laughed, hoisting herself up onto the island worktop. She was wearing a pair of rainbow-coloured tie-dyed leggings and a fuchsia-pink vest that had been seemingly shredded by something long-clawed, a light sheen of sweat glistening on her skin.

'You've been up for a while, then?' Suzy asked with a curl of sarcasm.

'Oh yes. I like to rise with the sun. I've already done an hour of yoga on the beach. I just love feeling the sand in my toes and that slight instability – it's so good for tightening the smaller support muscles and really engaging your core, you know?'

'Not really,' Suzy grumbled. 'The last core I found was in a tub of Ben & Jerry's ice cream.'

Gem laughed, as though Suzy was joking. 'How about you? Did you all get a lie-in?'

Arch went to reply, but before he could get a word out, Suzy got in first. 'No. Velvet had a bad night. We've been up for hours too.'

Cassie tried not to choke on her food as she heard the lie tripping so easily from Suzy's tongue. Suzy's arm extended across the table towards hers, rubbing it sympathetically. 'Sorry, Cass. It's so unfair on you to have to put up with it. We're used to it, but you must be shattered.'

'No, no, it's OK,' Cassie mumbled, glaring at Suzy for including her in the deception. Again.

'You do all look pretty rough,' Gem said sympathetically.

Now Suzy almost choked on her breakfast.

'Is everything all OK in Snapdragons?' Cassie asked brightly.

'Loving it. It's so *cute*. It's got the same flowery wallpaper I remember from when we were little. Nothing's changed at all. And I think some of the chutneys and dried herbs are original too,' she laughed, giving an all-over body shiver.

'So what are you up to today?' Cassie asked, wondering if it was bad form to put sugar on the muesli.

Gem shrugged happily. 'I dunno. We thought we'd see what you guys wanted to do first.'

Suzy's eyebrow lifted up like it was being pulled on a string. 'Oh, well, don't let us hold you back. I bet Laird wants to do loads of sightseeing, and we're probably going to be really old and boring and just stay here and chill for a bit. Arch needs to convalesce. Velvet needs her naps. You know . . . boring.'

'Oh.' Gem's face fell and it was like the sun going behind a cloud.

There was a small silence and Cassie felt bad at how Suzy kept pushing her cousin away.

Then Archie gave a slight cough. 'Actually, Cass and I were going to have a surf lesson this morning. Care to join us?'

Cassie looked at him in surprise. 'Wait, I know the list said to catch a wave, but I don't think he meant *twelve hours later.*'

'No time like the present, though, eh, Cass? If my heart attack taught me anything, it's that,' he winked. 'Carpe diem.'

'Oh.' It was hard to argue with someone who now had the benefit of near-death wisdom.

'But are you up to it, Archie?' Gem asked, jumping off the island and coming over to the table, concern on her face.

'The doctors are actively encouraging me to do exercise.'

'Gentle exercise,' Suzy said sharply.

'Exactly,' Archie beamed, not looking at his wife. 'Join us.'

'Join you? I can do one better than that!' Gem squealed delightedly. 'Laird can teach you. He'd be totally stoked if you'd let him. He's just itching for an excuse to spend the day in the water.'

'Brilliant!' Archie declared, as if he'd known she was going to say that all along. 'What are the tides in Polzy? You guys got a tides book yet?'

'It's low tide at 11.04 a.m.,' Gem said, glancing up at the wall clock. It was just gone ten now.

'Even more brilliant,' Archie exclaimed again, pushing

away his muesli. He couldn't have looked more pleased with himself. 'As long as someone turns the mirrors to the wall so I don't have to see myself in my budgie-smugglers, we—'

'Budgie-smugglers? Arch, wear that bloody wetsuit we bought for boogie-boarding or you'll die before you get your knees wet. You're bad enough when the shower runs cold when I run the taps downstairs.'

Archie chuckled, reaching over to kiss his wife on the cheek. 'Quite right, darling. Well, then, I think we should be ready to go in . . . what? Half an hour? That'll give us time to get down there and find Cass a suit and board.' He clapped his hands together. 'Perfect, no?'

'No!' Cassie and Suzy replied in unison.

Gem laughed, jogging happily back down the hall. 'Brilliant. We'll meet you down there. I'll go tell the others.'

The door slammed behind her as Suzy and Cassie looked at each other in despair.

'Hang on a minute,' Suzy frowned. 'What others?'

It wasn't quite *Baywatch*. For one thing, the surf guards sat in their red-and-yellow Jeeps rather than prowling around in red skimpies in beach towers, but the black-and-white chequered flags flapped noisily in the breeze, and there were enough people in the water who knew how to ride to imbue the rest of the beach with some serious surf cool.

Everyone parked their cars on the hard-packed sand at the back of the beach, and Cassie spent a rather ignominious twenty minutes in the rear of a high-sided truck trying to zip herself into a long-limbed wetsuit as a guy with a hot-pink goatee threw various colour options in her size at her. She took the first one that fitted. Getting into these things was like jamming balloons into drainpipes.

She came down the steps self-consciously, hoping no one would pay any attention to her, but before her foot even touched the sand, Archie had taken a photo of her on his phone. 'As proof,' he smiled before she could protest.

Archie threw the phone back into their car and held out the board she had been fitted for before getting changed. It was at least half her height again, and bright, shiny yellow with a red rim and purple hibiscus print on the underside. His wetsuit was still rolled down to his waist to stop him overheating – Suzy was keeping a very close watch on his colour as she played with Velvet in the rock pools – and even with his recent weight loss, he looked well padded.

'Laird's meeting us down by the water,' he said, tucking his board under his arm and heading off with a jaunty stride. Cassie trotted by his side, wishing she hadn't zipped her wetsuit all the way up now. She was so hot, and the waterline was a good quarter of a mile away. As they walked, she watched the smattering of serious surfers kicking turns over the waves, the more amateur boogie-boarders thrashing in the surf further up the beach between the red-and-yellow flags.

'Arch, I'm actually quite nervous about this,' she said, as they drew closer and the waves seemed to increase in height.

'Really?' Archie asked, but she was sure his voice had gone up an octave too as they watched a surfer get dumped by a roller.

'When I fall off, you will check that I resurface, won't you? I mean, I don't know Laird that well and—'

'There's absolutely nothing to be worried about, Cass,' he laughed, striding onwards.

'Yeah, but . . . you will, right?'

'Of course!'

Laird was already in the water. He was easy to spot, skimming the surface of the water with a relaxed agility that even Cassie could see showed he was used to bigger and badder seas than this. She watched in awe as he manipulated the board with the merest ankle flex, carving 180-degree turns with a shift of his hips and trailing a languid hand through the underbelly of the wave before allowing the board to slow and sink below the surface as the wave crashed and the power and speed dissipated.

'That'll be us by the end of the week,' Archie quipped as Laird spotted them both, throwing his arm up in greeting before hoisting himself, face down, on the board and paddling in quickly to them. He ran through the shallows looking every inch Patrick Swayze in *Point Break*, water droplets cascading off his hair and a smile that could light Wembley Stadium on his face. His shyness from the party the other night had completely gone. He was, quite literally, in his element.

'Hey,' he panted, drawing level and nodding happily at the sight of them both in full kit. 'Looks like they know what they're doing at the rental place all right.' He inspected the boards quickly. 'You ready for this?'

'Mm-hmm,' Cassie said, not quite trusting her voice to convey a sense of excitement right now. She was a good swimmer, but she was also the girl who had to hold her nose every time she jumped in the pool. How exactly was she supposed to cope with being tossed about like a cork out there?

'Now listen, mate,' Archie began. 'I don't want to be a bore or anything, but as you probably know, I very nearly popped my clogs a couple of weeks ago, and if I was to overdo it and die out here, my wife would absolutely kill me all over again. And probably you too.'

Laird laughed.

'So, by all means, strut your stuff, but I'll have to make some judgement calls along the way as to what my old ticker can put up with. *I*, obviously, want to go all cylinders firing, but Suzy's very . . . overprotective, as you've probably gathered by now, so if you see me hanging back a little, it's simply to pacify her. Don't worry at all.'

Laird smiled, nodding with what seemed to be perfect understanding as Cassie gawped in open-mouthed disbelief. Arch was even more terrified than she was!

Laird looked at Cassie. 'And how's your heart?'

'Hers is a little bit dodgy too, at the mo,' Archie said, throwing an arm round her shoulders and giving them a little squeeze.

Cassie smiled. 'Shit-scared, to be honest.'

Laird laughed. 'Well, listen, that's totally normal, and actually, we're barely even going to go in the water today.'

'We're not?' Archie asked with evident relief.

'Nope. We've got to master the basics on dry land before we get wet. First things first, we need to learn the pop, establish how to paddle and practise the standing position on the board.'

'The pop,' Archie echoed dubitably.

'That's the explosive movement when you go from lying down to standing. It's got to be quick and neat. You only get a few seconds at most to plant your feet in exactly the right position. Here, I'll demonstrate.'

He threw his board down on the wet sand and lay on it on his stomach, his arms held out and bent as he pretended to paddle. 'Now, at the right moment, you've got to plant your hands here, like this, and push – like a mini push-up – as you tuck your legs in tight under your hips and plant your feet wide, front foot facing forward, back foot angled to the side. Like this.'

And in a nanosecond he quite literally popped up from his prone position to a standing one.

'Well, that looks easy enough,' Archie said, his voice brighter.

'Really engage your stomach muscles when you're doing it,' Laird said encouragingly, tightening his hand into a fist. 'It keeps the back tight and allows you to move much more dynamically.'

Archie looked down at his pale, spongy stomach. 'Dynamically. OK.'

'And you, Cass. Let's give it a go,' Laird said.

Cassie let her board drop to the sand with a thud and gingerly lowered herself down onto her stomach.

'OK, so arms out like this,' Laird said, taking her arms at the elbows and pulling them out like wings. 'And when you're ready, tuck yourself in tight and – pop!'

She gave it a whirl, sucking her tummy in along with her breath and trying to move as dynamically as she could from her favoured sleeping position, but it wasn't so much a popping motion as a flopping one. First she lifted her bottom up before she planted her hands so that she almost went chin first down on the board. Then she lifted her hand too late so that her knee didn't know which way to go round her arm and her feet ended up too far back, which

– had she been on the water – would have sent her flying backwards, overboard . . .

Archie didn't fare any better. He had a tendency to use his stomach as a launch pad, rolling on it like a Weeble to get up.

Laird, to his credit, didn't laugh and they tried again. And again.

After half an hour of popping – or rather, flopping – they moved on to paddle technique and balance exercises so that by the end Cassie felt like she'd endured an SAS training drill. There was a knack to it that was as much about belief as strength, and by the time Laird took them into the water – to cool down, rather than surf, Cassie suspected – neither of them was capable of anything more than lying on their boards in the shallows and letting the waves break over them.

'Well, that looked exhilarating,' Suzy trilled as they dragged themselves back up the beach after an hour and fell, exhausted, onto the towels.

'Oh, darling, the thrill of the open seas, that horizon, being part of nature . . .' Archie panted as Velvet staggered over and sat on his stomach, prompting him to groan loudly. 'It's quite something.'

Cassie laughed as she unzipped her wetsuit, rolling it down to her waist and exposing her bikini top. 'We're alive, at least. And look – I didn't even get my hair wet. Bonus.'

'Well, yes. Surfing on sand has that advantage,' Suzy quipped as she handed round bottles of cold water.

'I reckon tomorrow we'll get onto the water, don't you, Cass?' Arch asked. 'We were definitely getting the hang of it by the end.'

'Oh, absolutely,' Cassie agreed, taking a sip of her drink and hugging her knees up as she watched Laird paddling out to deeper water with misleading ease. 'I thought Gem was going to join us, though.'

'Oh no, she's terrified of the water. Won't go near it,' Suzy replied.

'You mean because of you guys scaring her with the sea-weed?' Cassie rummaged in her rucksack for her oversized sunglasses. Henry had told her that story the night of the party.

'Well, she says it's that, just to make light of things, but she nearly drowned when she was little once.'

'God, no. Really?'

'Mmm. Caught a current when she was on a lilo in Spain with her parents and couldn't get back. She was lucky someone on a pedalo realized and scooped her up.'

'The poor thing.'

'Yeah. She says she hasn't been in the water since. We'd better hope it's not the case that the couple that surfs together stays together.' Suzy frowned, puzzled. 'Or actually, maybe we should hope that.'

'Leave them alone,' Archie mumbled, already very nearly asleep.

Suzy cast a sly glance at Cassie and winked.

'So, where is she now?'

'She watched you guys here for a bit, but she wanted to pop over to Padstow to get some fish. They want to do us a barbie tonight.'

'And since when has a barbie ever included *fish*?' Archie asked with a note of panic, suddenly wide awake again. 'If ever a man is entitled to some burnt meat, that's the time:

burgers, snags and ribs. I can see I'd better be in charge of the charring tonight.'

'You're supposed to be reducing your cholesterol and that means less red meat, *much* less. Besides, I think prawns and mackerel sound very healthy. I'm intrigued to see how they taste barbecued. And Gem was saying bananas are a barbecue revelation.'

'Bananas?' Archie spluttered, redder in the face than he had been during the entire surf lesson. 'I'm not having barbecued bananas!'

'Oh, do shut up, Arch,' Suzy sighed. 'Have you got any sunscreen on?'

Chapter Fifteen

They were all as pink as shrimps by the time they got back to Butterbox. Suzy, Archie and Laird had gone ahead in the car with Velvet to prepare her tea, but Cassie was grateful for some solitude and preferred to take the longer, slower clifftop walk home. Their day together had been quietly eventful, relaxed but full on, as it always is with children: Archie had spent hours building Velvet a speedboat in the sand, which she immediately proceeded to fill with buckets of water, and when he and Suzy had fallen asleep, Cassie had taken her off for a play on the grassy banks just above the rocks where they were sitting, the two of them watching in quiet raptures as the wild golden-haired rabbits nibbled on the clover and sea thrifts. They had had pasties for lunch – another thing they could tick off the list (which was proving to be disarmingly placid so far) – vegetarian for Archie, eating them in the brown paper bags they came in and trying not to get sand in them, and it was only when the incoming tide started nudging the bottom of their multicoloured striped windbreak that they were finally forced to move.

The journey back was uncomplicated and straight out of a Daphne du Maurier novel. As Archie had directed, she had to head up the steep hill and take the right footpath onto the cliffs, following the coast round, past the golden crescent of Daymer Bay until she saw the church whose steeple she had spied from the house. If she headed left there, she could follow the hedge line along the fields and would come to the stile that entered their garden.

It had taken her almost an hour from Polzeath, not because the distance was great but because the beauty of the landscape was so distracting and she had stopped frequently to absorb the shape of a land that felt so remote and foreign from the rest of England that she half expected to find the border had been sundered altogether and this county that felt more like a country was bobbing in the sea beside it.

By the time she threw her leg over the stile, Laird was already firing up the charcoals and Archie was on a desperate hunt for something stronger to drink than Purdey's.

'Hey!' she called as she strode up the lawn in the denim shorts and pink vest she'd left in. 'I hope I haven't missed anything?'

'Not a thing. We've only just finished feeding Velvet,' Laird smiled as he looked up. 'Suzy's gone up to have her shower.'

'Oh good,' she smiled back, taking off her sunglasses and peering at the platter of fish that Laird had arranged on crushed ice, with samphire and mussels on the side.

Laird's expression changed. She didn't have time to ask why because suddenly she heard Archie bellow from inside the house, 'Lairdy, m'lad!', appearing at the doorway a moment later with a bottle of Merlot and a delighted smile. 'Look what I just f— Oh! Good God!' he exclaimed in astonishment as Cassie sauntered up to him with a tut.

'I'll take that, thank you,' she said in a sing-song voice.

'It's more than your life's worth, or mine, to let you have that, as well you know.'

'But—'

'No buts, Arch!' she called behind her as she strode through the kitchen and into the hall beyond. 'We'll keep you alive if it kills us all.'

She skipped into her bedroom with a happy smile, tossing the bottle onto the bed and wandering into her bathroom to get the shower running. Only when she caught sight of herself in the mirror did she realize the real cause for Laird and Archie's reactions: her face was as rosy as an apple, but round her eyes, two giant white moons beamed back at her. Panda eyes writ large.

By the time she emerged downstairs, forty minutes later, she had used half a tube of her Clarins green concealer, which was supposed to minimize redness in complexions and which she sometimes used on her cheeks to offset her tendency to blush. She had left her hair down to act as a curtain and hopefully mitigate the full extent of Suzy's scrutiny.

To no avail.

'Holy crap!' Suzy burst out laughing as she took one look at her in the kitchen. 'Did the goblins get you?'

'Oh, don't!' Cassie wailed, her hands flying to her green-tinted face. 'The green's better than the red.'

'It really isn't.' Suzy walked over to her bag and pulled out some baby wipes. 'And as your best friend in the world, I am staging an intervention.'

'But my eyes! They're bright white.'

'Yes, and you'll put everyone off their food sitting there like you're radioactive.'

Cassie laughed in spite of herself, obediently wiping her

face clean and grimacing at the green wipes as she threw them in the bin.

'Just keep your sunglasses on,' Suzy instructed her. 'It's light till nine anyway, and then we'll just blow out the candles and sit in the dark.' She pointed to a chilli-flecked green bean salad on the counter. 'Carry that out, will you?'

Cassie pulled her sunglasses down from the top of her head and followed her out with the dish, setting it on the large oval table. Laird and Archie had done a fine job of finding all the cushion covers for the chairs in the summer-house and lighting the stash of taper candles that were reserved for power cuts, ingeniously planting them in a terracotta pot full of sand. Cassie counted seven place settings.

'Shouldn't this be five, Suze?' she asked.

Suzy counted on her fingers. 'No. Us three, Gem, Laird and the couple who are staying with them.'

'Oh. I didn't realize that they had guests too.'

'No, me neither,' she said in a lowered voice and checking Laird wasn't listening. 'Gem conveniently forgot to mention it. Guess I really am excused now for keeping them in the lodge house, huh?'

Cassie shrugged. 'What are they like?' She remembered all the trendy types at the Cross Keys and her hands went to her sunglasses, pushing them further up her nose. Great – strangers; these would definitely have to stay on all night now. That or excuse herself from dinner by nine.

'No idea. Gem's been showing them the sights all afternoon,' Suzy said under her breath. 'But I reckon it's no bad thing: they can distract her from us and provide some much-needed breathing space between her and me.' She rolled her eyes and leaned in closer. 'Honestly, while you lot were busy *not* surfing, she was driving me potty. By the time she asked me where she should take them this afternoon, it was all I could do to stop myself from suggesting Carlisle.'

Archie came over, breaking up their secretive conversation and handing Cassie a drink of Purdey's with a disapproving look – although whether that was because she had hijacked his Merlot heist or was wearing sunglasses in the gloaming she couldn't be sure.

'Thanks, Arch,' she smiled apologetically. 'Have you started to stiffen up yet?'

'Who, me?' he asked, stretching his neck. 'I have a residual fitness level that I just never lose, Cass. I guess it comes from being so sporty in my youth.'

'Yes, really fit. Hence the near-fatal heart attack,' Suzy scoffed, but softening her scorn by affectionately flicking the tea towel at his retreating bottom.

'Ugh, I've got to start running more regularly again,' Cassie sighed, rubbing her thighs lightly through the thin cotton of her baby-blue dress. 'I may need a piggyback up the stairs tonight. I'm not sure I'll be capable of popping even a champagne cork by tomorrow.'

There was the sound of squeaking from the near corner and they all turned as a side gate swung back on its hinges.

'Hey! Here you all are. What a lovely sight,' Gem cried happily, crossing the lawn. She ambled up to Laird and kissed him lingeringly on the lips. 'Miss me?'

'Of course,' Laird grinned. 'Where've you been? I was expecting you back ages ago.'

'Where haven't we been?' she asked back, accepting her Purdey's from Archie with a grateful smile. 'We went to

Padstow, then on into Wadebridge to get some *proper drinks*.' She winked at Archie. Suzy looked like she was going to have a stroke. 'Then we went for a drive to Port Isaac. It is just so *cute* there. Honey, I wish you'd come with us. I know you wanted to ride the waves, but you'd have loved it. We'll go again tomorrow, shall we? It's this heavenly little fishing village, just teeny tiny, and we found the best fudge shop.'

'Sounds great. Where are the others?'

'Just coming. Amber's trying to find a cover-up. She feels the cold so easily.'

'Did they enjoy the sights?'

'Loved it. *Loved* it! Luke says he never wants to leave.'

Cassie almost dropped the glass from her hand. What had Gem said?

'And you'll never guess who I saw today—' Gem continued, just as the side gate squeaked open again and they all turned to see a tall, lean couple making their way over the grass. 'Oh, look, they're here. Come over, guys!'

Cassie felt the ground shift beneath her feet as she took in a silhouette that she knew all too well. No, he couldn't possibly be here . . . Not again.

But he could and Suzy realized it, too, in the next moment, giving a small gasp and turning to Cassie in horror. They watched in silence as the couple approached, their hands intertwined, long, lean legs striding in unison.

'Amber, Luke, I want you to meet Suzy, my biggest and best cousin, her hubby, Archie, and Cassie, who's engaged to my other cousin, Henry, who isn't here – he's sailing across the Pacific as we speak,' she said proudly.

Even the mention of Henry couldn't pierce the smog of

shock that had descended over Cassie at the sight of her ex-boyfriend crossing the grass.

'Happy to meet you, Luke,' Archie said, oblivious to the tangled web that interconnected some of their group and thrusting out his hand. 'And, Amber, what a pleasure.'

Suzy, for once, didn't say a word, instead shaking their hands like a dutiful wife and waiting for Cassie to take the lead on whether or not to reveal that they were already . . . acquainted.

For a long moment Cassie just blinked at them all from behind her giant sunglasses, grateful now for their protection in the fast-fading light. Amber she'd have known by name even without an introduction. She was one of the models of the moment, with ad campaigns for Dolce & Gabbana, Jimmy Choo and Burberry this season. And Luke was her boyfriend. She was whom he'd meant when he'd said at the party that he'd moved on too. He hadn't been lying, then.

'Hello,' she said finally, shaking Amber's delicate hand, scared she might lift her off the ground. She looked over at Luke; his expression was hidden from her by his own mirrored aviators, but the tension in his body was plainly apparent – he was standing too still for one thing, like a samurai alert to any movement at all.

They weren't going to be able to deny knowing each other.

'Hello, Luke. Nice to see you again,' she said stiffly, not sure whether he'd even respond with civility. They'd hardly parted on friendly terms last week, when she'd thrown his attempts at diplomacy back in his face.

Gem looked astonished. 'You guys know each other?'

'Vaguely,' Luke said quickly, before she could reply. 'We

met in New York a few times. We've got some friends in common, right? Bas, Kelly Hartford . . .'

'Uh, yes, she's Kelly Cole now,' Cassie said cautiously, trying to guess his game. 'She got married a few years back.'

'Oh yeah, that's right. I'd forgotten. Who can keep track, right?' He cracked a slight smile. 'Do you still see her?'

Cassie just nodded. She wished she could see his eyes. They'd had this very conversation at the polo. This was a game, role play.

'Kelly's an absolutely top pal of Suzy's too,' Archie said, oblivious to the undercurrent. 'The girls were all at school together. They go back yonks.'

'Funny, isn't it?' Luke asked, stuffing his hand in his pocket and looking across at Archie with interest. 'It's just such a small world.'

'Never fails to astound me,' Archie continued. 'I remember one time . . .'

Cassie tuned out, watching Luke deliver a seamless performance that betrayed no hint of the intensity that had once existed between them, of the fierce passion that had led to them not leaving his apartment for four days one time and her losing three pounds just from sex. Her eyes travelled over to Amber, yet another in the long line of models who had both preceded and succeeded her. A photographer dating his models was just an occupational hazard, he'd once told her. Actors dated other actors; nurses dated doctors . . . How else was he supposed to meet girls when he was trapped in an airless, windowless studio for fifteen hours in every day? And frankly, though he'd never said this outright to her, why wouldn't he?

Every man on the planet would want to trade places with him.

Cassie tilted her face to make out that she was listening to the men's conversation, but her eyes were taking in Amber's silver 'H' Hermès sandals and denim cut-off shorts, which were so tiny the pocket linings peeked out of the bottoms. Her long, rich brown hair – while not blow-dried – had still clearly been styled into rough 'beachy' waves, and she had some sort of dry oil on her skin, for it glistened as she moved, minute flecks of gold reflecting in the sunset. A hair-thin gold bracelet with a single diamond dangled round one dainty wrist, and it was apparent she had been named Amber on account of her lion's-yellow eyes.

'Well, it's an amazing place you've got here,' Luke said, still to Archie, and Cassie knew he was deliberately avoiding engaging Suzy in conversation directly. She *did* know the truth about their relationship and he couldn't be sure yet how her loyalty to Cassie would manifest itself – although fiercely would be a good guess. 'I can hardly believe the view. I always think mine is pretty special in Manhattan – I live on the forty-eighth floor and can see all the way to Brooklyn – but this is really something else.'

Cassie tried not to remember his apartment – the industrial chic with exposed-brick walls and steel girders he'd pioneered long before the crowds, the massive custom-made bed, the state-of-the-art coffee machine, the light box where he'd first seduced her . . .

Why was he here? Had he known she was here? He had to have known! Surely he didn't expect her to believe it was just a coincidence to find themselves in the same shabby house on a remote lane in the furthest corner of England?

'So how do you guys know each other?' Cassie asked Gem, accidentally, in her haste, talking over the punchline of Archie's joke about the Frenchman and the toast.

'Oh, Ambs and I connected in Sydney last year. Lululemon was doing this mass live yoga session for the launch of their flagship and Amby was one of the models.'

'Why did they have *models* for a yoga session?' Suzy asked disingenuously.

'Oh, 'cos it all goes hand in hand in that market. I mean, everyone's always asking you about your figure and how you exercise and what you wear, right?'

Amber groaned and rolled her eyes. 'Jeez, if I had a buck for every time I've been asked about my fitness regimen or my diet, I wouldn't have to freaking work!' she laughed.

Gem, Luke, Archie and Laird laughed too. Suzy didn't – Cassie could see her friend was watching her husband's blood pressure rise by the second to be in the presence of a bona fide model.

'Anyway, so Amber was one of the girls doing the demo and I was leading the yoga workshop; we just got chatting and really connected.' Gem put her hand on Amber's arm. 'Hey, remember the silent retreat in Goa?'

'Oh, man, we got the giggles so bad,' Amber laughed, leaning in to Luke so that he draped his arm round her shoulders, planting an easy kiss on the top of her head. 'I mean, three days without speaking? Come *on*!'

'It wouldn't be Suzy's forte either,' Archie said. 'She talks so much sometimes I think she's being paid for words per minute.'

'Oh, ha, *ha*!' Suzy said indignantly, walloping him on the arm.

'Wow, so then you're here because *you two* are such good friends,' Cassie murmured, scarcely able to believe her bad luck. It had been bad enough seeing Luke at the polo and the party with Beau's crowd; that at least made sense – he and Beau were friends – but now there was another connection linking their worlds?

'Yeah, but it's not like we're able to see each other much,' Gem shrugged. 'In fact, we haven't seen each other for months. Amber's always travelling for work—'

'Always,' Amber sighed wearily.

'And I was in Oz for all that time. We'd slightly lost touch, to be honest.' Gem looked sadly at Amber, who was nodding solemnly back at her. 'But then we bumped into each other again at Henry's leaving party last week because Luke's a mate of Beau's. Can you believe it?'

'Sadly yes,' Cassie muttered into her drink.

'So when Amber told me she was with Luke and Luke knew Beau and Beau knew Henry and, of course, *you're* with Henry and he's *my* cuz and *your* bro' – she looked over at Suzy – 'I thought . . . wouldn't it be just so much fun?' Gem held her arms out in delight.

'Amazing,' Suzy said, shaking her head and looking over at Cassie. 'Isn't that just amazing?'

'Amazing,' Cassie echoed limply.

'It was just the perfect opportunity for us all to be together. I mean, there's so much to do and talk about.' She squeezed Amber's arm as she looked over at Suzy. 'Amber's agreed to be my bridesmaid, you see. How could I pass up the chance to have her and you – the very best wedding planner in London – together, all to myself? I just couldn't resist holing us all up here. You don't hate me, do you?' she teased.

This time, neither Suzy nor Cassie said a word. Neither one of them had the strength to lie.

Chapter Sixteen

The sky fell down in the middle of the night, Cassie awaking to find thick layers of cloud rolling in off the sea as she lay in bed looking out past the open doors onto the balcony. She had wanted to go to sleep to the sound of the cows moving quietly in the field, but instead had fallen into a fitful state of unconsciousness where memories of a former life flickered behind her eyelids like backlit stills on a silent-film projector.

It was not yet seven and the house was silent, Velvet sleeping more soundly than Suzy could ever afford to let Gem know. Cassie rarely saw this time of day; she was famous for her ability to sleep anywhere, through anything – but not this morning. Her legs kept kicking out, her toes and fingers scrunching tight, as though her bloodstream was infected with something feverish.

She got out of bed and dressed quickly, pulling on yesterday's shorts and a sloppy grey V-necked T-shirt that had 'Super Loved' written across the front in faded script. Henry had bought it for her when he'd seen it in the window of a boutique he'd been passing, even though it had taken him a week to recover from paying over £100 for a T-shirt.

She pulled on her plimsolls and let herself out through

the side door by the pantry, walking with swinging arms as she headed over the lawn and towards the stile. The humidity was intense, even at this early hour, and her bare arms and legs felt clammy and cold within minutes. The hedgerows were heavy with brambles and newly budding blackberries, which were still green, and she had to hold her arms above her head in places to keep from being scratched as she followed the footpath between the two fields, which had been worn bare.

The cows were all lying down in the fields, their legs bent awkwardly beneath the heft of their bodies, noses nudging the ground as flies buzzed around their ears. She walked past with silent speed, crossing into the links golf course – which already had a few people pulling their bag carts over the greens – feeling a desperate urge to outpace something, her hair swinging wildly over her shoulders and her breath coming heavily, even though she was marching downhill.

She reached the small church in minutes. A thick hedge walled the graveyard in a protective square, and the church itself was sunken into the grassy banks that surrounded it, like a pin in a cushion, its pointed grey stone steeple looking more like an upturned ice-cream cone up close, weathered but resilient in the onshore breeze.

She walked through the stone lychgate and up the stepped lawns, falling into an agitated heap at the top. The beach was mere yards away from here, the tide still on its run out, but some dog walkers were already visible by the waterline, throwing balls with long-handled plastic sticks, and she didn't want to see anyone. Not yet.

She dropped her head in her hands, feeling buffeted by the storm of emotions raging inside her: frustration and fear anytime she thought about Henry; frustration and anger anytime she thought about Gil; fear and anger anytime she thought about Luke.

She had been hoping, as Suzy had, that she'd find some kind of escape here, a few days off from normal life to try to get her head around the obstacles that sprang up in her anytime she thought of the words 'I do.' Instead, here she was, confronted with a man from her past who was one of the very reasons why she now said, 'I don't.'

It was clear she would have to leave. They had got through last night somehow, without Gem, Laird or Amber picking up on the full, ugly truth about her and Luke (although she was quite sure Suzy would have given Archie the lowdown the second they'd closed their bedroom door), but something would trip them up, something would give them away that would throw a neon light on the lies they'd already told; and besides, how would it look to Henry when he found out she had effectively holidayed with her ex while their relationship hung in the balance? No, there was no choice. They couldn't both stay here.

She watched a few boats tracking up and down the now-narrow passage of the estuary, their Cornish-red sails (which were actually brown) filling with wind and bellying out as they tacked and jibbed in neat, rhythmic zigzags. The heavy-bowed clinker boats were a world away from the ocean-going, state-of-the-art craft Henry was in at this very moment, his sky falling dark as hers brightened, another day done for him as she woke to another to endure.

She thought of the list she wouldn't get to complete, and she wondered what he had been hoping to achieve from it this time. How was eating a pasty on the sand or racing a boat going to have pushed her past the almost visceral fear that stopped her from wanting to commit again? How was jumping into a lagoon going to have saved them? Because he had made it clear that unless she jumped into marriage again, they had no future.

The wind blew her hair in front of her face and she rested her elbows on her knees, her hands like barrettes, keeping her hair pinned back. Even just the thought of splitting up seemed wholly unreal and impossible to her. Yes, they were floundering on the same rock, over and over, but they were crazy about each other, made for each other; there was simply no way she could conceive that they could ever be without each other. If she still continued to say, 'No,' would he *really* go through with it?

Up till now she had thought time was the answer – delaying, fudging, filling their diaries with trips and holidays and work dos and events so that there was simply no space to pencil in a wedding. Everything was so much fun, so perfect. But time was running out, or so everyone kept telling her anyway. She was thirty now; it was time to start thinking not just about 'settling down' but about the *next* phase, the *next* chapter. Those were the questions that were beginning to come thick and fast now – from her mother in Hong Kong every time they spoke on the phone, from Hattie, their friends. Had they talked about starting a family? How many did Henry want? A boy first, or a girl? Couldn't she just imagine a mini-Henry? What a tearaway he'd be – and so handsome too!

No one realized these questions elicited the same panic in her as 'Have you set a date?' They didn't seem to understand that Gil's greatest betrayal hadn't been his infidelity with Wiz; it had been his love for Rory, their secret child, her godson. Cassie had loved him herself, treasuring him and delighting in him as if he had been her own, and to find out that he so *nearly* was had been the killer blow . . . nearly wasn't enough. Just like that day in the hospital, she was locked out. She had so badly wanted a family of her own – it had been Gil's promise that they would begin trying for a baby after the anniversary – but there was no room for her in that one. Blood trumps law. Son trumps wife. It was the little boy who had truly broken her heart, far more than Gil had managed. Was it any wonder that the idea of family felt so tainted to her now?

But she was falling behind life's curve, the proverbial hare: the girl who'd been first off the starting blocks and married at twenty-one, had fallen asleep by the road, while everyone else was already passing over the finishing line. They had gone on without her: Suzy, Kelly . . . Would Henry too?

She watched as the gulls followed a fishing boat down the estuary, wheeling in the sky before diving for mackerel in the wake, screaming noisily and drowning out the black choughs cawing in the treetops. This, then, was the sound-track to the place Henry had told her about so often.

He knew and loved this place well; he'd grown up to the summers here. This view had been his as a child, his long, bare brown legs running down the bald footpath as Hattie and Ed, his late father, struggled after with towels and bags, his love of the sea nurtured, no doubt, on this very stretch of water.

She sat there until the chill began to set in, watching the wind running over the long grasses like a child playing Duck, Duck, Goose, fat clouds scudding towards the horizon like skimming stones. She rose, knowing she ought to get back. She hadn't left a note explaining where she was and there was every chance Velvet would decide to be her alarm clock, making a bolt for freedom when Suzy took her out of her cot and bursting through the doors to see Auntie Kiss-Kiss and negotiate a story in bed together. If they found she wasn't there . . .

She walked through the churchyard with slow steps. Some white and purple flowers from a recent wedding still clung to the church door, scraps of confetti marbling the damp blades of grass. It was a wildly beautiful spot to be married, the deep hedge providing an effective windbreak from the sea winds, and her hand trailed lightly over the moss-fringed headstones, their engravings in-filled with yellow and white lichen. She stopped as her eyes fell to a pair that were visibly newer than the rest: '*Here lie Phillip and Emily Warrender, beloved parents of Gemma, taken too soon. October 2006.*'

A fire, Suzy had said. She hadn't said that they'd been buried here. Was it so surprising that Gem would want to spend more time here then? Cassie bit her lip, feeling a rush of sympathy for the child left behind, even now – nine years later – looking for love, roots and stability. Looking for home.

She stepped through the deep lychgate, onto the path, and was immediately sent flying as something jabbed her hard in the side. She fell onto the grassy bank with a cry.

'Oh shit!'

She looked up in confusion as much as pain, to find Luke staring down at her in horror, the sharp nose of a surfboard pointed in her direction under his arm.

'Cass, I didn't see you until . . . Are you OK?'

She rubbed her ribs – the board had scored a direct hit – but she couldn't check for a bruise without lifting her

T-shirt and clearly *that* wasn't going to happen. 'I'm fine.'

He offered her his hand and helped her back to standing, although she made a point of snatching her hand away. He flinched at the gesture, a pause opening up. 'What are you doing out here at this time, anyway? It's not exactly your favourite time of day.'

Her eyes flickered irritably to his. Even just a throwaway line like that was privileged information, a personal detail he had no business using anymore – precisely the kind of thing that would trip them up in front of the others.

'You're not jet-lagged too, are you?' he smiled, even though he must have known it was highly unlikely *she* would have left the country since seeing him at the party last week. Unlike him. He'd probably flown to Haiti and Tokyo since then.

'Just enjoying the view,' she said in a surly voice, refusing to smile back.

Gently, he set his board down on the path. She looked back at him, taking in properly the sight of a wetsuit rolled down to his hips, his sand-coloured T-shirt wet at the hem. 'Since when did you learn to surf? You're a New Yorker,' she said with as much scorn as she could muster.

'Pirelli calendar,' he said, almost apologetically. 'There's so much damned waiting around on these tiny tropical islands.'

'Huh, bummer,' she muttered, with a sarcasm that he didn't miss.

His head tipped to the side as he scrutinized her, his eyes tracing her ridiculous tan lines, which were now on glaring display – she had left her sunglasses in the bedroom – and which had only faded overnight by a few degrees to Schiaparelli pink. 'Look, Cass, about last night—'

'Oh yes, congratulations, by the way.'

'What?'

'You and Amber. She's beautiful.'

He looked stumped by the comment, baffled by her wide-eyed insincerity. 'Thanks.'

'How long have you been together?' She was guessing two weeks.

'Since November.'

Eight months? She couldn't keep the surprise from her face. 'Oh.' That was far longer than any of his other relationships. Longer than they'd lasted, anyway. 'She must be special.'

'Yeah, she is.' He looked down at the ground, clearing his throat lightly. 'Look, Cass—'

'Well, you'd better watch out. One week – no, one day with Gem as Bridezilla and she'll—'

'Cass!' His tone stopped her in her tracks. 'I'm *really* sorry.'

She paused, too weary to keep up her exhausting patter of sardonic comments that fooled neither of them.

'I'm sorry for what I did in Paris – it was a shitty thing to do, exhibiting the pictures in the show like that—'

'Selling them was even worse! You *profited* from my humiliation.'

'Actually, I gave the money to charity . . . It didn't feel right.' He had the grace to look sheepish. 'I'm sorry for turning up here. I had no idea you'd be here.'

'Oh, come on!' she scoffed. 'You don't expect me to believe that?'

'Look, I admit I barely know Gem and Laird. I'd never even met them before last week, but I got on well enough with him at the party, and Amber . . . well, she doesn't have many friends, not proper ones anyway – you know what the fashion world's like – so when she said she wanted to come . . .' He sighed. 'She needs to put down roots. We both do. We're trying to build a new life for ourselves.'

Cassie blinked at him. This wasn't the Luke she knew. Repeated apologies? Donating money to charity? Long-term relationship? Putting down roots? Surfing before breakfast?

He nodded, as if reading her mind. 'I've changed, Cass. I'm not the man I used to be.'

She continued staring. He certainly looked the same – better, if anything, his year-round tan particularly burnished at the moment so that his hazel eyes seemed to glow brighter in contrast, his dark brown hair a little longer and wilder than it used to be, and he'd put on more muscle since her time with him. 'A nation rejoices,' she said defiantly.

He looked stung by the words – yet another slap-down – and she saw the expression change in his eyes from earnest, placid and benign to something darker and more familiar to her – a flicker of anger, of patience being worn thin, passions lurking just below the surface; but she wasn't going to let him off the hook that easily. She still stood by what she'd said to him at the party – his betrayal had been unforgivable. It wasn't good enough to turn up two years later with a surfboard and a hippy haircut and tell her he'd changed. What remained unchanged was the fact that his actions meant bastards like Beau Cooper could buy her naked image and hang it on a wall; call it art and throw cocktail parties where everyone could see it; hang it in the bedroom and stare into her eyes while he banged his

241

girlfriends; meet her in the flesh and strip her bare with a knowledge and possession and intimacy that told her he owned her.

'What does Amber say about it all? Does she know what you did?'

He hesitated before replying. 'Actually, she doesn't know about us.'

Cassie blinked in surprise. She'd been so certain he would have had to come clean behind closed doors. 'Well if you being here is all so innocent, why would you lie to her about it?'

'I'm not *lying* about it, but where's the good in telling her about you? It would only make her feel insecure, and she's beginning to have a really good time down here. She thinks you're great, and she says Suzy and Archie are like some kind of double act. Obviously if I'd known we were going to be seeing you, I'd have warned her.' He stopped. 'Actually, no, that's not true. We just wouldn't have come.'

The admission was unexpectedly painful for her to hear.

'But as it was, I thought we both handled the situation well last night.' He gave a light shrug. 'No one would ever have guessed we made such a mess of things—'

'*We* made a mess of things?' But the momentary flicker of irritation she'd seen before had gone. The eyes looking back at her were as open and clear as a child's.

'What difference would it make anyhow? It's water under the bridge, right? You're engaged. We're happy.' He shrugged again.

Cassie stared back at him, her instincts and suspicions tempered by this continued chivalry, this persistent politeness that betrayed a new apathy about her. A little over two years ago he had offered her everything he had in

New York, and when she had rejected him, his subsequent revenge in Paris had been as blinding as his passion. But now, here . . . even with the two of them alone, when there was no more need for play-acting in front of strangers, he was behaving as neutrally towards her as a stranger giving directions. The heat between them, the fire that had once made her so convinced they could never see each other again, it had gone out.

He raked a hand through his hair, his eyes watching the uncertainty in her features as she absorbed this new, passive dynamic. 'Cassie, please, let's not hate each other.'

She continued staring at him, searching for the trick, the sleight of hand that would reveal his ruse, but there was nothing that she could see or read in him that alarmed her.

Slowly, she turned, stepping back onto the path and making a point of waiting for him as he picked up his surfboard again. It was if not a peace treaty, at least a cease in hostilities.

They walked a short way in silence.

'So, how did you and Amber meet?' she asked quietly, glancing over. 'Or do I even need to ask?'

No. She didn't need to ask. He raised an eyebrow, giving her the answer without words. 'She's different, though. She's the one who's got me back on the straight and narrow . . .' He stopped himself and she wondered what he had been going to say. Back on the straight and narrow from what? Her? Or was she inflating her ego to think that her departure had been quite that devastating? 'But she's sweet and kind, which is really saying something for NYC. And we make each other laugh. I can talk to her. It's the simple stuff.'

'Oh.' Cassie couldn't imagine him embracing the simpler

life. When she'd been with him, everything had been very designed and stylized, international and top tier.

'I guessed from Gem that Henry is Suzy's brother, yes?' She nodded.

He inhaled deeply, his ribs opening out like bellows. 'Well, that certainly explains a few things. You guys go way back. That's how he knew with the list in New York . . .' He was talking more to himself than her, it seemed, his eyes on the horizon ahead. 'Have you heard from him?'

She looked across at him, puzzled at how he talked about Henry so easily, as though he was a mutual friend of theirs. 'No, not much,' she mumbled. She knew it would infuriate Henry to know Cassie ever discussed him with her ex. 'I've had one message, but it's hard obviously, when everything's being filtered through twenty other people first.'

'Yes, of course. I can see how that could be . . . limiting.'

They paused as they got to the golf course again, both looking left and right to check for incoming balls before crossing the fairway.

'I guess you're used to him being away for long stretches, though, huh? Beau was saying about all the incredible expeditions he's done. It's such a boon for them to have him on the team.'

She couldn't help looking back at him, searching for sarcasm or scorn, but he met her eyes with a guileless smile. 'He's very experienced,' she agreed.

'Beau said he was recently made a professor at the Explorers Club.'

'A fellow, yes.'

'That's a big fucking deal. You know that, right?'

'Of course.'

'Did you go?'

'Excuse me?'

'Did you go to New York for the ceremony?'

'Yes.' She remembered the ludicrously extravagant Valentino dress, how it had felt walking across the hotel lobby, Henry's hand in hers, the snowy polar bear standing guard above them all as everyone drank and laughed and talked and revelled in her fiancé's daring. She missed him so much suddenly it hurt, and her hand instinctively covered her stomach.

He abruptly stopped walking. 'So when was that?'

Cassie looked surprised. What did he care? 'Around Easter, I think. Why?'

He gave a small laugh, jabbing his finger. 'I *knew* it was you. I saw you getting a cab.' She remembered the taxi sluicing past, his face a pale flash in the window. He looked back at her. 'You were wearing red, right?'

She nodded, surprised he'd remembered that small detail.

He nodded too. 'That's always been your colour,' he said after a moment. 'It would have made a great image. Really . . .' He remembered to walk and she quickly fell in step too. 'Really striking with all the other colours, you know? That was what caught my eye. I wished I'd been quick enough to take a shot. It was like a Tiffany's ad in motion – yellow cabs, tail lights, the red dress, your bright hair.' He stared at her intently. 'You were wearing red lipstick too, right?'

'That's right.' How had he noticed that from a passing cab?

'You never usually wear lipstick.' He was reading her mind again. 'Hell of a surprise seeing you like that, though.

I wasn't sure if you'd seen me too.' His eyes were intent upon her, scanning her like a laser.

She shook her head. 'No.'

'No?'

'No.' She wasn't quite sure why she'd lied about it. What did it matter one way or the other whether or not she'd seen him?

'Huh.'

They walked in silence past the hedgerows where the brambles were trying to rule supreme, Luke letting her go first on the narrow path before catching her up as they passed where the cows were grazing, the house just ahead of them now.

'Well, I'm this way,' he said as they got to the stile, indicating towards the side gate and the garden beyond for Snapdragons. He raked his hand through his hair again as another awkward silence began to stretch like a lazy cat. 'So I guess I'll see you later, then.'

'I guess so.'

He gave one of his new, unfamiliar benign smiles and she watched as he walked off without a backwards glance.

She didn't see Suzy standing on the terrace in her dressing gown, her hair blowing about her face and a large mug of tea in her hands. And as Cassie crossed the lawn, perturbed and unsettled, Suzy slipped back into the house, as silent as a shadow.

Chapter Seventeen

They made an unlikely four – Cassie, Suzy, Gem and Amber – all in Suzy's car as she hooned around the tiny wet lanes the next afternoon, with the recklessness that only ever comes from the suicidal or the local. Suzy considered herself the latter, nipping down farmers' tracks and green lanes in her Volvo estate as Amber tried not to whimper – the boot had already flown open once – and Gem laughed her head off. With the rain having set in for the day, they were on their way to a bridal boutique in Wadebridge, or as Suzy had said under her breath with a mutinous look in her eye, 'Phase One'.

The town was large and sprawling, with supermarkets and ring roads and plenty of buses. They had passed several large bridal boutiques – Gem jabbing the windowpanes with her finger and pointing them out to her cousin – but Suzy kept repeating she'd found something 'more bijou' and navigated her way away from the centre, towards a residential pocket at the back, where old stone terraced houses replaced the shops and the streets were narrow with free parking.

'Here we are,' Suzy said, pulling on the handbrake so hard it squeaked. Archie, Laird and Luke were in charge of Velvet this afternoon, a motley crew of men who looked utterly flummoxed by the proposition of entertaining the toddler for the afternoon, and the last she'd heard, they'd been doing a toss-up between bowling and crazy golf.

They filed out of the car, Amber standing in the middle of the road and looking at the boutique's window display with ill-concealed horror.

'Are you sure this is right?' she asked. Kelly – in reply to some scurrilous overnight texts from Suzy – had told them that Amber had walked for Miuccia Prada, Karl Lagerfeld and Christopher Bailey, so Cassie reasoned she had probably never seen polyester lace before.

But if Amber was dubious, Gem was oblivious.

'Oh. My. God,' Gem said dramatically, pausing at the door. 'This is, like, a seminal moment in every girl's life, isn't it?'

'What? Coming to Wadebridge? You need to get out more, Gem,' Suzy joked.

'I mean trying on a wedding dress for the first time!' Gem laughed, with an emotional tremble in her voice. 'I'm warning you now I might cry. In fact, I probably will.'

Amber – seemingly forgetting her horror at the dresses and getting into the bridesmaid-slash-cheerleader spirit – gave an excited squeal, clapping her hands together and skipping lightly on the spot as a minicab hooted for her to move out of the road.

'Fine. I consider myself warned,' Suzy said with a tight smile, leaning heavily on the door and falling in. They all filed in after her, silence falling on them like the stiffened veils that had been thrown like poachers' nets on the mannequins.

Suzy caught Cassie's eye as their small group congregated in the middle of the room – she, at least, was clearly very pleased with what she saw. The small boutique – merely the width of one of the neighbouring terrace's sitting rooms but extending right the way back to where the kitchen would ordinarily be found – was the pokiest, most budget-looking salon she had been able to find on her frantic Google searches and she was confident Gem wouldn't be getting her much-hoped-for Cinderella moment in here.

A black nylon carpet flecked with silver bristled beneath their feet, the pale lilac walls adorned with crystal-studded tiaras hanging from plastic hooks.

A woman with a perm – 'A perm!' Suzy mouthed in delight – jumped up from a silver rococo desk in the far corner, where she'd been reading *Hello!* magazine. She smiled at the disparate band of women, trying to ascertain which one of them was the bride.

'Welcome,' the woman smiled.

'Hi,' Suzy said, grabbing Gem by the shoulders and positioning her in front of their group. 'My cousin Gem, here – she's getting married.'

'Oh! Many, many congratulations!' the woman cried, as though the revelation was a completely unexpected surprise to her, her enthusiasm managing to override even Gem's.

'Ah, thanks so much. That's really nice of you,' Gem said, shaking her hand enthusiastically.

The woman looked up at Gem from under her lashes. 'Might I possibly ask to see the ring?'

Cassie knew this wasn't so much a bonding exercise as a chance to get proof there was actually a wedding in the offing. Suzy had told her lots of boutiques used it to stop hordes of girls just coming in and trying on the dresses. No ring? Not getting in.

'You might,' Gem laughed, proffering her hand and showing off a ring with a brightly striated caramel stone.

'What is *that*?' Suzy asked, peering at it with an incredulous look.

'Tiger's eye. It represents the grounding energy of the earth – that's Laird – and the elevating energy of the sun – that's me,' Gem said, her eyes fixed dreamily on the stone.

Cassie felt bad that she and Suzy hadn't asked to see her ring till now – to have done so could have been misinterpreted as approval or encouragement, but still, standing here in a bridal boutique about to try on dresses, it felt a little mean.

Suzy tutted sympathetically. 'He spent a month's salary on that, did he? Hmm, well, I suppose surfing's never going to bring in a reliable income.'

Gem appeared not to hear her. 'It's what it represents that I love, you know?' she said to the woman.

'Which is why you can't go wrong with diamonds,' Suzy said firmly. 'They're popular for a reason. They represent eternity and you'll have them forever. They're indestructible. Not like these . . . fashion stones,' Suzy frowned. 'Still, maybe he can upgrade in a few years, when he's had more of a chance to establish his career.'

Suzy cast Cassie a wink as she turned away.

'I think it's dead original,' the woman said, nodding as though the ring had unlocked the secret of Gem's soul, her eyes running up and down Gem's tiny but perfect figure in her cobalt-blue harem pants, aqua vest and flip-flops. 'And I'm guessing you'll want something equally unique for your dress too.'

'Of *course*,' Gem grinned with wide eyes.

'Well, before we go any further, let me just start by telling you that *I* am Paula.' The woman raised a hand to her heart, lest anyone should be in any doubt as to whom she was referring. 'And this afternoon I want you to think of me as your fairy godmother. Your wish is my command.'

Gem clapped her hands together excitedly and Amber trotted her feet on the spot again like a frisky filly. Cassie looked from one to the other, wondering if it was some sort of synchronized routine they'd devised, like footballers celebrating a goal.

Paula raised a finger in the air. 'And I have a feeling your first wish is for some champagne. Am I right?'

'Oh my God, yes!' Amber cried, drilling her heels as fast into the floor as a woodpecker's beak into a tree. 'We had Purdey's last night. I am *desperate* for some Krug.'

Paula looked at her quizzically for a moment and Cassie could see her trying to place Amber's face – there was no doubt this tall, willowy creature with smoky eyes and tight knees inhabited another world – but in the next instant Paula had tossed her head and the query out of her mind and disappeared to a back room, returning moments later with a bottle of Tesco's prosecco and five glasses.

Cassie looked around the room anxiously, feeling increasingly claustrophobic and wishing she'd been more forceful with Suzy as she'd cajoled her into coming along and 'helping' her with Gem. For one thing, she had brought down a book from London that she had had lying on her bedside table for months – Henry hadn't once given her a moment to get to it – and she wouldn't have minded a few hours just to herself. For another, it was hardly tactful of Suzy to make her spend an afternoon here, given that the thorny issue of marriage was the source of all her woes.

Her eyes flitted lightly, warily, over the gazar ruffles and plissé silk details that edged out of the racks, and she stopped as she caught sight of a sleeve threaded with seed pearls. She walked over and brushed it through her fingers, remembering the excitement she'd felt trying on her wedding dress for the first time – it had been in the Harrods bridal suite, her mother sitting opposite on a huge silk chaise and waiting for the moment she stepped out of the vast changing room, looking like a princess in ivory duchesse satin with a smooth bodice and globe pearls sewn along the scooped neckline and bracelet sleeves. Her mother had cried as the salesgirl had carefully draped the veil over her face, placing a bouquet of silk roses in her hands for effect – Cassie had too.

But they'd also both cried as she rang her mother from a hotel room at Heathrow, ten years later, to tell her that the marriage was over – and why.

She thought of Wiz, no doubt patronizing the smartest boutique in Edinburgh, her dress bespoke and triumphal, more suited to a coronation than a wedding. It was happening this Saturday – eleven o'clock in the chapel on the estate. Cassie still hadn't talked to Suzy about it, and she had made Kelly promise not to tell Suzy she knew: as far as Suzy was aware, Cassie had no idea Gil was getting remarried. Cassie wasn't sure why she didn't want her to know she knew – possibly because she'd make her talk about it, dragging up the past again when all she wanted was to let the earth beneath her feet settle, and to let new shoots grow. And what really was there to say? Their love had died a long time ago now and she had moved on with Henry, she really had. Gil's upcoming wedding was just the turning of the lock on that door to her old life; that was all. Her hand dropped down and she moved away from the racks towards the centre of the room again, where Paula was handing out the drinks.

'So,' Paula said, 'have you seen anything specific, or are we just going to work our way through the stock?'

'Work our way through the stock!' Amber cried, punching the air and making Gem laugh. Cassie was almost a hundred per cent sure that Amber had, at school, been a cheerleader.

'Come on, then, ladies,' Paula said, leading the charge and taking them over to the first closet of dresses. 'Now, these are what I call my Bo Peeps – full hoops, puffy sleeves, lots of gathers, very traditional, so they'll never date and they flatter *every* body type. No one has a fat day in one of these.'

'Was she looking at me?' Suzy mouthed to Cassie in indignation as they moved on to the next alcove.

'And in here we have what I call the Goddess range – long, sculptural columns, usually strapless, but there's one or two with asymmetric detailing if that takes your fancy. They're generally much plainer, for the more contemporary bride.' She pronounced 'contemporary' slowly and in a half-whisper, as though it was an unusual and foreign concept that had to be tolerated occasionally.

They took in every 'theme' in the shop, Paula cherry-picking what she thought would most 'favour' Gem's 'diminutive frame' and 'idiosyncratic style'.

'And what were you planning to do with your hair? Any thoughts on up or down or . . . in,' she asked Gem, pointing to her cornrows as they walked towards the dressing room, a bundle of dresses piled atop her arms. 'It might be hard to get a tiara on with them – that's all I'm thinking.'

'I'm not really a tiara type of person, Paula, if I'm honest, although I wouldn't be averse to a floral wreath. Something living and pure. My fiancé's really into nature and animals and stuff. He's a surfer. I keep telling him he should go pro . . .'

They disappeared round the curtain and Cassie and Suzy slumped on the hot-pink velveteen Victorian three-way love seat that resembled a clover leaf, so that their backs were angled towards each other.

'Cheers,' Suzy murmured, pouring them each another glass of prosecco.

Amber hovered by the Goddess alcove, clearly unsure where to stand now that her friend and ally had disappeared.

'Another drink, Amber?' Suzy asked after a moment.

Amber came over with a grateful smile, perching awkwardly on the third seat so that she wouldn't be sitting back to back with Cassie.

'Cheers,' Cassie said with a determined smile, and they all took a sip of their drinks. 'Did you see anything you liked?'

'Loads of things,' Amber sighed. 'I mean, I wasn't sure when we first got here. This place is hardly . . . Well, it's not Milan, let's be honest. But actually . . .' She nodded approvingly, lowering her voice. 'Paula may have no taste in interiors, but she knows her wedding dresses. There are some beauties hiding away in there.'

'Ha! You would say that. You could make anything look good,' Suzy said, peering into her glass.

'Oh, you're so sweet,' Amber smiled. 'I guess it's more that I just love fashion. I kind of understand the energy the designers want to express in their clothes, you know? I love it all – high, low and everything in between.' She drained her glass. 'I'm going to be the *worst* when the time comes to choosing for me.'

'Really?' Suzy levered up an eyebrow. 'D'you think Luke's going to propose, then?'

'Oh, well, I wouldn't—' Amber demurred coyly.

'He's *so* going to propose!' Gem gasped, overhearing their conversation and popping her head round the curtain.

'Gem!' Amber squealed, laughing as she playfully swatted the air between her and Gem.

'You've got to tell them.'

'They won't get it!'

'They will. They were young once too, you know. Just tell them, Ambs!'

Amber gave an exaggerated sigh as Cassie and Suzy swapped horrified stares. Had . . . had Gem said they were *old*? 'Well, it's not . . . I mean, it's not a *conventional* . . .' Amber ran out of words, as if fretting about how to explain it. She leaned in closer. 'I guess the thing you have to understand is, our world isn't like everyone else's – fashion is, like, a whole other planet. So if Luke was going to propose, he wouldn't choose something standard like a solitaire.'

'I'm not with you,' Suzy said, a baffled expression on her face.

'What she's trying – and failing – to say,' Gem laughed, across the room, 'is that she found a Love bracelet in his bag when she was looking for something the other day.'

'What's a Love bracelet?' Cassie asked, her voice weirdly scratchy and her question confirming Gem and Amber's opinion of the two of them as out of touch, past it, over.

'Cartier. Solid gold and it comes with a special little tool, like a screwdriver, to get it on or off. It's like a chastity belt but for the wrist, basically. A signal of surrendering your-self completely to the other person. What better way to show your commitment to someone? It's modern and dead sexy, I reckon.' Gem winked. 'Luke's got amazing style. *He'd* never do a diamond either.' And she disappeared into the changing room again, leaving Suzy staring back at her, agape.

'I bet you looked amazing in your wedding dress, didn't you?' Amber asked, sipping her drink and angling her knees towards Suzy. 'You and Archie make such a good couple. I want Luke and me to be like you when we're older.'

Suzy took a moment to respond. So many inadvertent insults, so little time. 'I had to go with pretty much the first dress that fitted . . . Wide back,' she muttered.

'I bet you're just saying that,' Amber said generously as Cassie peered at her over the rim of her glass and resolved to get up early to cycle to Trebetherick and Google 'Cartier Love bracelets' on her iPhone first thing tomorrow.

Suzy realized everyone's glasses were empty. 'Any more?' she asked the others, holding out the bottle.

They all accepted, Suzy filling the glasses almost to the brim just as the curtain whooshed open and Gem stepped out in a snow-white silk dress with spaghetti straps and a low scooped back. It had been cut on the cross with a small kick hem, and tiny covered buttons ran down the back seam, along her spine and over her bottom. The simplicity of it highlighted her figure to perfection, and even with the cornrows in, there was no doubt that this was *it*. This was 'the Dress'.

Amber jumped up with a small shriek as Gem did a neat

turn, her hands up to her mouth in mute exhilaration, her eyes shining as brightly as fire embers.

'I do not bloody believe it,' Suzy whispered under her breath, without moving her lips. 'The first freaking dress? Are you kidding me?'

Cassie realized Suzy's glass was tipping prosecco over her lap and righted it for her.

'So what do you think, ladies?' Paula asked, with righteous pride, fawning around Gem, smoothing seams and flattening straps as she went.

'Paula, you *are* her fairy godmother!' Amber cried, taking her by the shoulders and bending down to hug her excitedly. 'I never would have guessed you had it in you!'

A look of puzzlement crossed Paula's face as she too wondered whether this was a compliment or not.

'What do you think, ladies?' she asked, looking at Suzy and Cassie on the couch.

'Well, I'm . . .' Suzy began, rising and making a stately procession around Gem, before blowing out dramatically through her cheeks. 'I'll be honest . . . I'm not sure.' She held her hands up. 'I mean, don't get me wrong. It's a beautiful dress and Gem looks stunning in it. But then Gem would look stunning in a bin bag, and is it really . . . ? Well, is it really *you*?' She addressed the question directly to Gem.

Gem's face fell and she turned to look at herself in the mirror again, making tiny twists one way and then the other as she tried to grasp Suzy's point.

'I mean, that's just my opinion. Maybe I'm wrong. What do you think, Cass?' Suzy asked, beckoning for Cassie to back her up. 'Cruel to be kind,' she whispered. 'Cruel to be kind.'

'Um . . .' Cassie dithered. Gem did look utterly spectacular in the dress. What could she possibly say? 'I think I probably agree with you, Suze? Gem looks glorious, but . . . maybe not very . . . relaxed?' Everyone's eyes swivelled from Cassie back to Gem in consideration. 'I guess it's just not a look I associate with Gem. It's all a bit buttony and sleek.'

'Buttony,' Paula echoed.

Cassie desperately threw out her hands like she was framing plumes of steam. She felt so mean saying these things when in truth Gem was a vision of bridal perfection in the dress. 'She's much freer, in my mind.'

'Freer,' Paula echoed again with a contradictory nod and a look of puzzlement.

'Suzy's a really big wedding planner in London,' Gem said to her as Paula fiddled with the straps again, as though their placement an inch to the left would change everything. 'She dresses brides all the time. All these socialites.'

'Oh,' Paula said, her face falling as she bit her lip, giving one last tug on the back seam. 'Well, hey! It is only the first dress you've tried on. There's plenty more to go, right? We can always come back to this if you want to, Gem.'

'Brilliant. Thanks, Paula.'

Both gave brave smiles.

'But first . . .' Paula said, running off to the back room again and reappearing with another bottle of budget bubbles. 'We can't have anyone getting thirsty, now can we?'

'Hey, you know Amber's getting married soon too?' Suzy said suddenly.

Paula screeched to a halt, almost leaving tyre marks on the carpet. 'You're not!' she breathed.

'Oh, but—' Amber protested.

'Oh my goodness, yes! You should totally try on some dresses!' Gem squealed. 'We can do it together.'

Cassie looked between them all in utter bewilderment. Hadn't Amber just said that he *hadn't* proposed yet? And that was even if he was planning on proposing. After all, who proposed with a bracelet? There was modern and then there was downright ridiculous!

'See what I did there?' Suzy said under her breath as she turned away to face Cassie. 'We'll put all the spotlight on Amber and take it off Gem. We can't afford to have her finding another dress – finding the dress is always the biggest obstacle. I was banking on at least a month of delays on that alone, but she's going to look good in everything. Trust me.'

'Oh, I do,' Cassie murmured, trying not to move her lips.

'I do this for a living. I know these things.'

'I know, I know,' Cassie breathed, smiling as Gem looked over.

'Oh my God! And Cassie as well!' Gem said, pointing to her.

'What?' Cassie's voice dropped an octave as Amber and Paula looked at her too. Paula looked like she might spontaneously combust. Three brides in one group?

'Cassie's engaged to my cousin.'

'No, wait!' Cassie said, her hands straight up in protest. 'I don't even have a date set yet.'

'Nor do we!' Amber trilled, hopping on the spot again.

'Well, actually, gals . . .' Gem said, in a coy voice that prompted them all to turn back and find her chewing, cartoon-style, on her knuckles.

'Oh, good God, no,' Suzy said loudly, already a step ahead.

'I kept trying to tell you the other night – I ran into Father Williams the other day at St Enodoc's. I stopped in there because obviously I know him from when he . . .' Her expression changed. 'When he buried Mum and Dad.'

Cassie remembered the clean-looking gravestones, the simple words that couldn't contain the loss behind them that continued to seep and bleed even now. Amber walked over and grabbed Gem by the hand. Gem smiled gratefully.

'I wanted to give him my news, you know?' she said, looking up at Amber. 'I thought it would be nice to tell him something good and show him that my life's happy now.'

Cassie shot Suzy a dark look, but she didn't need to. Even she looked stricken with guilt.

'He must have been so overjoyed to see that you got your happy ending after all,' Amber said.

'I think he was, I really do, because then he made a few calls and said that if we wanted to, he could marry us at St Enodoc's next Saturday at four.'

'No!' Amber and Suzy both shrieked together, albeit with very different tones.

Gem picked up on Suzy's, looking over at her quizzically.

'I just mean . . . there's so much to do, that's all,' Suzy said hastily. 'I mean, weddings, they take weeks – months, really – to prepare. And it's got to be perfect, right? This is the biggest day of your lives. It's the very least you deserve.'

'I don't need it to be perfect. I just need to be Laird's wife. Besides, we may have already found the dress, so that's one thing to tick off the list.'

'But . . .' Suzy stammered, looking to Cassie for help.

'But what about Henry?' Cassie asked, coming to the rescue for once. 'You asked him to walk you down the aisle and he's *so* excited about that.' She slapped her hand over her heart. 'Oh my goodness, he didn't stop talking about how honoured he was that you'd asked and what a big day it would be for you all.'

Gem smiled sadly. 'In the perfect world, Henry would be here to walk me down the aisle too, but he's not back for three months. I wasn't looking to make it happen just now and yet somehow it's worked out that way; it feels like karma, you know? And what, really, is there to do, if we've got the church and the vicar? We can have a party at the house, flowers from the hedgerows, a dress from here . . .' She smiled at Paula. Everything was falling into place so easily.

'It's not physically possible. The banns need to be read out for at least three weeks in advance. We're looking at the end of July at the very earliest,' Suzy said with seeming reluctance to be the bearer of bad news.

'Ordinarily, yes. But the vic says I can apply for a common licence because I have a special connection with this church, you know, because of my parents.'

'Well, food, then. You'd need to sort out the food,' Suzy said with a note of desperation.

'But aren't you in catering, Cass?' Gem asked with exquisite simplicity, so that Cassie could only look back at Suzy apologetically. 'I think hampers on the lawn sound fab. Right up our street.'

'Invitations! They take ages to sort and do the proofs and get sent out. And then people need six weeks' notice, minimum. It's the height of the wedding season now. No one will be able to come.'

'As long as you guys are there and Auntie Hats . . .' she shrugged.

'But . . . Laird's parents? They'd have to come from Australia.' Suzy's voice was already in another octave.

'He's an orphan too, like me. It's what first connected us. He's got a brother, though. Laird wants him as his best man, so he said he'd look into flights. We told him last night.'

'I don't believe this,' Suzy muttered, draining her glass and striding back towards the bottle of fizz.

'I don't suppose . . .' Paula said in a voice that barely contained a rising excitement, 'that you've considered a three-way wedding?'

A *Daily Mail*-style photograph of a mass wedding in North Korea filled Cassie's mind; Suzy started coughing as her prosecco went down the wrong way; Amber looked as horrified as she had standing out on the street.

'No? No? It was just a thought,' Paula said quickly. 'Right, well, shall we try some more dresses on, then?' she asked, scooping Amber and Cassie into her fold and herding them towards the dressing room.

Cassie stared at the bride in the mirror, telling herself it was the drink. Gem and Amber's mutual excitement had led to her and Suzy drinking far more than was wise and things had gone too far as usual. In trying to protect Suzy's 'cover' that they were all in it together planning this wedding, she had been brought face to face with her worst fears, and now she was in a dressing room, in a wedding dress, admiring herself, while Suze called Archie to tell him to pick them up. Emotions and memories were clamouring at her – the unfamiliar weight of a wedding dress remembered again, the fancy rustle of the silk underskirts, the squeeze of corsetry . . . She looked self-assured and elegant, like a woman who knew herself. It wasn't the type of dress she'd chosen to wear to marry Gil – in fact, it was almost its opposite – but what if she had? Would it have changed things? She remembered Gil's face as he stood expectantly at the end of the aisle waiting for his demure, insecure bride; she remembered Gil's face in the study that last night as the secret was exposed. Between those two moments, he had changed her for ever, and her new taste in dresses was but the tip of the iceberg. She blinked at her confident, elegant reflection. Was this how Wiz was going to look a few days from now?

'Hurry up, Cass!' Suzy called from across the room. 'What are you doing in there? Digging your way to freedom?'

Cassie shook her head and stepped out from behind the curtain quickly.

'Go for it, Suze,' she ordered, her eyes to the floor and praying she'd be brutal. Suzy, drunker than all of them, had been having a whale of a time passing judgement from the love seat as they each paraded a whirl of ill-advised dresses. After the disaster of Gem finding the perfect dress, she had put on her professional hat and declared she would 'edit' the selection for everyone – leaving Paula merely to zip and button them in and fetch more prosecco – and she'd had a glorious afternoon laughing at Gem in ruffles, Amber in sateen and Cassie in gothic lace.

Only, this dress had slipped through the net. It wasn't shocking or cartoonish, dated or cheap. It was ivory silk tulle with a straight front, thin straps and old-rosebuds gathering the fabric in finger-pinches at the hips. It high-lighted her slender shoulders and elegant back, her flat stomach and good height. It was narrow but not tight, modest but not frigidly so, modern but romantic. It was a dress worth getting married *for*. Not that she'd ever be so daft as to do that, but she wished she'd never put it on and she needed Suzy to do her worst.

But Suzy wasn't speaking. Her hands were up at her mouth, tears in her eyes as she twirled her finger in a circle, indicating for Cassie to do the same.

'Oh, Cass . . .' she murmured as Cassie slowly revolved on the spot, both Amber and Gem stepping out of their changing rooms and cooing as they picked up on the peculiar silence.

The sound of the door opening made Cassie look over her shoulder, freezing on the spot as Luke walked in backwards leading in Laird, who had his eyes closed.

'Well, it's the right place,' Luke said to him, turning into the room. 'Don't open your—'

Amber and Gem gave little screams and disappeared into the changing rooms. 'You can't see us in our dresses!' they shrieked, their eyes peering round the curtains. 'It's bad luck!'

'Well, that's why I closed my eyes!' Laird laughed.

'I didn't realize that . . . you were,' Luke stammered to Amber, but with his eyes on Cassie as she stood there frozen in the middle of the room. Why wouldn't her feet move?

'Gem made us,' Amber trilled nervously from behind her curtain. 'I never would have otherwise. We're just playing at it! You know what us girls are like when we get together.'

'We've had *way* too much to drink,' Gem piped up, just as she seemingly lost her balance and they all heard a loud thump behind the curtain.

'Babe! You OK?' Laird asked, advancing towards the changing room.

'Fine! Fine! Don't come in!' Gem laughed. 'It's bad luck.'

'We make our own luck, baby,' he said, his cheek to the curtain and his voice low. A second later Gem peered round the curtain – at his knee height.

'Awwww,' she cooed. He bent down for a kiss.

Cassie, watching, glanced back at Luke. His eyes were still on her.

She darted back behind her curtain, cheeks flaming that she'd been caught dressing up, playing at being a bride when she wanted to be anything but! She took the dress off roughly, feeling humiliated and exposed and raw, not wanting to see herself in it for another minute, as Suzy offered the boys a drink.

'I rang for *Arch* to come and get us,' she said, in a slurred voice.

'Yes, but he had to give Velvet her bottle – we're not qualified,' Laird said with a smile. 'So, it looks like you girls have been having a fine old time of it here.' Cassie could hear the sound of the champagne bottle being replaced on the table, beside the four empty ones.

'Like you wouldn't believe,' Suzy hiccuped. 'I'm tempted to redo my vows with Arch after this.'

Cassie stepped out of the changing room, back in her clothes and handing the dress to Paula with averted eyes.

'No?' Paula asked, dismay on her face. It had been as much of a sure thing, to her mind, as Gem's first dress.

'It's not me,' Cassie murmured as Gem and Amber followed too, with heaps of dresses in their arms.

'Ladies? Any decisions?' she asked hopefully as they piled them high.

'Paula, we're going to come back next week and do another fitting when we're sober,' Gem smiled, swaying slightly as she held on to Paula's arm.

'Oh.' Paula's face fell. She had turned the 'open' sign to 'closed' once the others had started trying on dresses too – and it had all been for naught.

'But I promish you this – I will buy my dress from you, come what may. We did *not* just clear you out of all your champagne for nothing.' Gem, whose head was hanging down like it was too heavy for her neck, gripped Paula's arm reassuringly – and for support.

'OK, well, you just let me know . . .' Paula said to their backs, nodding bravely as they trooped out, Amber holding on to Luke as she wobbled on her tiny ankles, Laird grasping Gem by the hand and Suzy and Cassie linking arms.

Suzy sat in the front on the way back – on the pretext of showing them the route back home – as Laird drove, and Cassie squeezed in the middle between Gem and Luke, who had Amber on his lap. No one said very much on the journey home. Suzy was asleep, and Gem was trying to meditate to stop the world from spinning quite so quickly. Amber chatted excitedly about the 'girlie fun' they'd had, but neither Cassie nor Luke, thighs touching in the darkness, said a word.

Chapter Eighteen

There was no surf. The sea was as calm and flat as a cup of tea as she sat astride the board, legs dangling in the water while she watched Laird demonstrating to Archie, again, the explosive power needed to get from lying down to standing in under two seconds.

'Cass,' Laird said, looking across at her, 'do you want to give it a go?'

She nodded reluctantly and lay tummy down, moving into a slow crawl with her arms before suddenly planting them on the board and pushing up as she tucked in her feet, but unlike on the sand, and even without any waves, the board wobbled on the water's surface; although she got her feet down, she couldn't find her balance enough to straighten her legs and in the next instant she was in. Again.

She surfaced with a gasp. The water was shockingly cold, even with a wetsuit, and she was sure a jellyfish had missed her face by inches. That would have been all she needed – red welts to decorate her sunburn. She felt her sense of humour – and her sense of adventure – desert her.

'Good effort there, Cass. You nearly had it,' Laird said encouragingly.

'You think?' she asked drily, heaving herself back onto

the board with a groan. Who were they kidding? She and Archie had spent four days having lessons now, trying just to stand on the boards, and this was the first time they'd made it into the water. Conditions couldn't have been better for novices like them yet they seemed doomed to spend their time lying on their tummies. 'I'm beginning to think I'll make an excellent boogie-boarder.'

Laird, hearing the tone of her voice, paddled over, pushing himself up to sitting easily. 'Don't give up, Cassie. I know it's depressing, this stage. You think you'll never master it, but believe me, all this groundwork you're doing, it's creating muscle memory that's going to come together. And when it does' – he flashed her a winning smile – 'nirvana. There's nothing like it in the world, trust me.'

She shrugged, feeling useless, feeling angry, feeling depressed. Everything in her world was just wrong right now, like it had tipped off kilter by one degree, leaving her unbalanced and lurching slightly.

'Shall we give it another try?'

'If you want.'

'That's the spirit.' He turned back to Archie, who looked like he was trying to nap on his board. 'Arch, shall we try again?'

'OK, boss.'

They lay tummy down and went into crawl again. Twenty seconds later there was a double splash.

'How was that?' Suzy asked brightly, chopping tomatoes for a salad as they walked with a squelch into the kitchen. 'Oh.'

'I'm going to have a long, hot shower and then a lie-down,' Archie said morosely, opening the fridge for a beer and finding only elderflower. He closed it again and walked off in an even bigger grump.

'Don't wake Velvet – she's having her lunchtime sleep,' Suzy called after him, but he didn't reply. She looked over to Cassie for an explanation, but she was just as unforthcoming.

'Still not standing, then?'

'I've decided I'm going to go back tonight. There's a train at half seven,' Cassie said, ignoring the question and walking over to the fridge too. 'This just isn't working for me. It's lovely down here, Suze, but thrashing about in the ocean, swallowing seawater on an hourly basis and getting sunburnt is not what I need right now.' She opened the fridge door and looked in.

There was a short silence as Suzy stopped chopping and put down the knife. 'Oh right. Uh-huh. I see.'

'What?'

'That's the reason, is it?'

Cassie glanced back at her. 'Yes, why wouldn't it be?'

Suzy watched her. 'It's got nothing at all to do with your ex next door.'

She turned sharply, her hand on the handle. 'Of course it hasn't! We haven't even seen them for three days.'

'Exactly. That's what I mean.'

Cassie blinked at her. 'Suzy! I told you, there's nothing there. He's apologized, I've accepted his apology, and we've both moved on. He's a different person now.'

'Oh yes, I totally agree he's changed. He and Amber seem very settled. I have to admit it's not played out the way I feared it might with him. I was dead worried when I saw him coming over the lawn that first night – I thought he'd followed you down here to win you back, but . . .' She shrugged. 'Well, he's clearly moved on too. In fact, I almost quite like the fella. I saw him and Amber in town earlier, walking hand in hand eating an ice cream – they actually looked kind of cute.'

Cute? Luke? That man was all about sex in the shower, not teddy bears and love hearts.

'And Arch thinks he's great, although if he actually knew the truth about you and Luke . . .' She pulled a face.

Cassie frowned. 'Do you mean to say you haven't told him who Luke is yet?' She had simply assumed Archie was fully accepting of the fact that they had both moved on. After all, Luke was here with Amber, and she was a model.

'Who Luke *was*, you mean? No.' Suzy shrugged. 'Why bother? It'd only make him feel like he had to hate him on Henry's behalf, and really, he so doesn't need that kind of stress right now.'

Cassie exhaled impatiently. 'So then what is your point? Why would I be leaving because of Luke if everything's cool between us?'

'Because I think it's rattled your cage that he's over you.' She held her hands up defensively as Cassie gasped in indignation. 'Hey! Don't think I don't understand it – I do! Every girl should be able to get an ego-boost from her ex. He should remain bitterly in love with you forever. It's all very well *in theory* you both moving on and behaving like grown-ups, but it's quite another thing to have his new-found bliss flaunted in your face – especially when things are so dire with you and Henry right now. I get it, really I do.'

'No, dire is not the word. It's just a rocky patch – Kelly said so.' Cassie stuck her head back in the fridge and scanned the cheeses on the top shelf. She rather liked the look of one of Velvet's Babybels. Instead, she pulled out a pack of prosciutto. 'And I couldn't give a stuff about Luke and his bliss. Ugh, starved,' she said, closing her eyes and chewing belligerently.

Suzy sighed, scraping a chair out from under the kitchen table and sinking heavily into it. 'Well, then I don't understand why you want to go.'

'I just do.'

There was a pause. 'I really don't get what's going on with you at the moment. You're all over the place.'

'No I'm not.'

'Cass, you and Henry are seemingly at breaking point over something we all thought you'd agreed to a year and a half ago! If that's not "all over the place" I don't know what is.'

'We've been over this, like, a million times,' Cassie groaned. 'You know why I feel how I feel.'

'I reckon it's a timing thing. You're out of sync with one another: you want career and fun; he wants to settle down. You want more time to live the life you missed out on, but, Cass, time is passing – you're getting older, hon.'

'So you're saying I'm embarrassing myself?'

'No,' Suzy demurred, before adding under her breath, 'Not yet.' She watched as Cassie replaced the prosciutto and started on the pack of mini Peperamis. 'Well, if you and Henry are just in a rocky patch and you're cool with Luke, why the big rush to escape? You know I need you right now.'

'You really don't,' Cassie said with a mouth full of food. 'Archie is almost fully back to normal as far as I can see, and I've already proved my utter uselessness with Gem – not only, as you pointed out, did I sabotage my own wedding instead of hers, but now I'm providing the bloody catering for hers too! I'm doing way more harm than good.'

'Exactly. You're doing the catering. You can't disappear now,' Suzy said, pivoting the conversation around again. 'Gem needs you. I am not discussing soufflés with her. She'll want them wheat-free, gluten-free and sprinkled with flipping unicorn's tears or something. I don't have the patience, I really don't.'

Cassie rolled her eyes. 'I'll come back in time for the wedding next weekend. I need to get all the kit from home anyway.'

'You really don't. Because that wedding is *not* happening,' Suzy said firmly, slapping her palm against the table and completely contradicting herself. 'This isn't a game, Cass. I've only just put the phone down again to Mum stressing about it. She's not sleeping – she's on the phone to your mum almost every night because she's up at Hong Kong hours. Can you imagine her reaction when I had to tell her Gem's gone and set the date for less than a fortnight's time? Go on, just try. No, don't bother. I'll tell you – she nearly had a stroke, that's what, and you know Mum – she's as stoic as a battleship.'

'They seem happy, Suze,' Cassie sighed, shutting the fridge and slumping down at the table too. 'Laird's a good bloke.'

'I'm not saying he isn't.' She leaned in and dropped her voice to a whisper. 'But I'd be a good bloke too if my fiancée was about to inherit her parents' estate on her next birthday at the end of summer.'

Suzy waited for Cassie's eyes to meet hers. 'That's right. Half of this place and two mill in the bank. She's going to be minted, Cass. Don't you think it's just a little bit suspicious that her boyfriend's so keen to get married? I mean, what male did you ever know who wanted to settle down in his early twenties?'

'I wouldn't judge anyone by your taste in boyfriends before Arch,' Cassie said pithily, although she couldn't deny the revelation about Gem's inheritance did throw a new complexion on things.

Suzy threw herself back in her chair, disappointed by Cassie's lack of suspicion. She drummed her fingers on the table. 'I won't let you go back to London. How are you going to get to the station? Hmm?'

'Arch can drive me.'

'He's not allowed to drive.'

'I'll call a cab, then.'

'With the mobile reception here? Ha! Good luck.'

'Fine, so I'll hitchhike.'

'Cass, you can't leave me here!'

'You're being overdramatic, Suze. I have to get back for work anyway. You know this.'

'Not for another week you don't! You know I've got it all sorted with Zara. You'll only mess up our plans if you go back now.'

'Talking of which, have you nicked my diary?'

'No. Why?'

'I can't find it anywhere.'

Suzy shrugged, but Cassie wasn't convinced. She wouldn't be in the least bit surprised if Suzy had pinched it to stop her from going back to work and to force her to stay down here.

The phone rang and Suzy slipped lower in her chair,

dropping her head into her hands. 'Oh God, if it's my mother *again* . . .' she groaned.

'I'll get it,' Cassie said, standing up and crossing the kitchen. 'Hello?'

'Is that Cass?' a female voice asked.

'Yes,' Cassie said warily. The woman sounded familiar. Certainly her tone of voice suggested they knew each other.

'It's Betsy. We got that place you was after.'

Cassie straightened up, straining to hear. There was a lot of background noise coming through from the other end of the line. 'I'm sorry, who? What place?'

'In the gig. Sarah can't make it. She needs to do a double shift, and Emma's still got her arm in plaster, so she's no good. It's as well you called when you did or we'd have been up the ruddy creek. See you eight o'clock, yeah?'

'But I didn't c—'

'Oh, and ignore the forecast. We's always baking by the time we get to Newlands, so keep it light and easy to strip. Catch ya later!'

Cassie stared at the handset in shock as the caller rang off.

'What just happened?' Suzy asked, watching her.

'I don't know.'

'Well, who was it?'

Cassie pulled a face, trying to remember. 'Betty? Betsy?'

'Oh, Bets!' Suzy replied cheerfully. 'Good news?'

'No! I think she was telling me there's a space in the gig tonight.'

'Amazing!' Suzy laughed, smacking her hands down on the table. 'Talk about saved by the bell! That's a stroke of luck. Now you've got to stay.'

'No I don't. I'm going, Suze. I've had enough.'

'Of course you have. Henry's thrown a wobbly, and you can't even get your ex to flirt with you. It's shitty, but it's time to move on now,' she said, patting Cassie on the shoulder and going back to her chopping.

'Yes, straight back to London, thanks, away from *you*.'

Suzy shrugged, an infuriating smile on her face. 'Not tonight, babe. There's a gig out there with your name on it.'

'But I've never even seen a gig before,' Cassie protested, getting crosser and crosser.

'Google it. And eat pasta for supper. And wear your bikini.'

'You seem to know an awful lot about this,' Cassie said, her eyes slitted. 'Who made the call to Betsy in the first place?' As if she needed to ask . . .

'Henry and I belonged to the Gig Club when we were teenagers. Betsy and I go way back.'

'Oh really? Uh-huh. I see,' she said defiantly, planting her hands on her hips. 'Well, you can jolly well row with her tonight, then.'

'No can do,' Suzy said, sauntering from the room as they heard Velvet begin to yell upstairs. 'I'd love to help you out, really I would, but it's not my list.'

Chapter Nineteen

Rock was rammed. Bunting had been strung up all the way from the Sailing Club to the railings of the car park – which was the furthest point in the village – and people were milling everywhere. The tide was in, slapping noisily against the harbour walls, and more boats than she could count were bobbing about in the estuary. The winds had picked up since this morning's dead calm, and a gauze-thin mist was beginning to roll in, dampening skin and making hair frizz.

'Oh, Suzy, come *on*,' Cassie said in a nervous voice as Suzy scanned the crowds on her behalf for Betsy. 'This isn't reasonable. I thought it was just a little thing, but there are hundreds of people here. I can't possibly be expected to—'

'Oh, I see her!' Suzy cried, waving her arm in the air and taking off at a sprint towards a group of women on the slipway.

'Arch, talk to her,' Cassie pleaded, turning round to Archie, who was holding Velvet in his arms and looking longingly as people walked past with pints in plastic beer glasses.

'You know what Henry's like with his lists,' he shrugged sympathetically, giving her a quick squeeze.

'Yes, and it's thanks to you he got the list to me in the first place,' she tutted. 'You're his lackey. I don't know why I thought you'd do anything to help.'

'Listen, it won't be all that bad. There's five others in the boat with you; I reckon so long as you just keep rhythm with them, no one will notice whether you've got a clue about technique or not.' He winked at her. 'Come on. It's just one race. Suzy's going to give herself a hernia if she keeps waving at us like that.'

They trotted down the quay, beside the lifeboat station, to where Suzy was standing with a heavy-set girl with beautiful bright orange hair that from a distance looked like a mass of flames. She was wearing it pulled up in a messy top-knot, with a hot-pink vest and black sports shorts on, seemingly oblivious to the cold and gusty wind.

Cassie's eyes fell again to the white horses rippling down the estuary, the water a dark air-force blue, and she heard the flap and rattle of the ratchets on the Sailing Club's toppers and picos, all safely stowed on the quay for the night. Out on the water, sails were being lowered on the clinkers and skiffs as people tried to neutralize their positions and not drift with the winds. It was hard to believe they had been enjoying millpond conditions for their surfing lesson just this morning, and she could only guess at the size of the waves that must now be thundering into the wide beach at Polzeath. Laird would be in seventh heaven, no doubt. Luke too, maybe.

'Cass!' Bets greeted her, holding out an oar in place of a hand. 'It's good to meet you. And oh boy, do we need you! You couldn't have volunteered at a better time. I'll tell you, I'm going to kill that Emma when I see her next. She did it slipping on a spilt beer in the Mariner's, you know.'

But Cassie didn't reply. She was too busy looking at the enormous oar. It was at least 2.5 metres high, and so thick her fingers didn't close round it. How was she supposed to row with this thing? It could prop up a house.

'How much gigging have you done, did you say?' Betsy asked.

'I didn't,' Cassie replied, just as Suzy's arm shot forward and pushed her out of the way of a crew who were jogging down the slipway, holding their yellow gig between them.

'Polperro,' Betsy said, her eyes narrowed as she watched them stop by the water's edge and lower the boat down. She turned slightly to Suzy. 'Remember their cox in '95?'

'As if I could forget,' Suzy replied in a dark voice, her arms folded menacingly across her bosom.

Archie and Cassie swapped arched eyebrows but said nothing. People had begun to move forwards towards the waterline now, and someone called Betsy's name.

'Come on, Bets!'

Betsy turned with a wave, and Cassie saw a group of women in the same hot-pink vests as her, manoeuvring a blue boat – '*Speedwell*' written in large white letters along the side – towards the water.

'Time to go,' Betsy grinned, tossing Cassie one of the pink tops. 'Our crew colour. Put it on. Dress like a team, row like a team, we say.'

Betsy grinned and jogged down to the others. Cassie – realizing she was out of time to try to argue her way out of this – hurriedly pulled off her grey marl hoody and mint Sweaty Betty T-shirt and put it on. She went to put the hoody back on, but Suzy stopped her.

'Trust me. You won't need it.'

'I will. It'll be a lot colder on the water.'

'Not with the amount of work you're going to be doing. It'll be a miracle if you keep your bikini top on.'

Cassie frowned, but reluctantly let Suzy keep hold of the hoody.

'Go get 'em, tiger,' Arch smiled, giving a small punch in the air to rally her fighting spirit. It didn't work.

'I bloody well hate both of you,' she muttered. 'But I love you, darling,' she whispered to Velvet, giving her a quick kiss before jogging dejectedly down the slipway to where the others were now sitting in the boat. A tiny woman in a yellow sailing jacket and navy baseball cap was holding the prow to keep it steady against the quay.

Betsy, who was doing some energetic shoulder rolls, stopped and turned in her seat at the front. 'Everyone, this is Cass. Cass, this is Lorna, Stevie, Sall and Jacqs. And Debs here' – the woman in the yellow jacket nodded – 'is our cox.'

'Hi,' Cassie smiled, raising a feeble hand and seeing a space in the fifth seat back. Hers, she presumed. The seats were positioned left and right alternately down the boat. Cassie saw her seat was on the left, meaning her oar would go into the water from the right.

'Hop in,' Betsy said, resuming her shoulder rolls. 'You're at five. We need to get into position. The other crews are at the start already.'

'You jump in – I'll pass the oar over to you when you're sitting,' Suzy said brightly.

'Where's the start?' Cassie asked her in a quiet voice, stepping down tentatively into the boat and trying not to shriek as it rocked.

'See the blue tug out there?' Suzy said.

Cassie, sitting with relief – although not comfort – in a

blue plastic bucket seat fixed to a bench, turned to see the small boat Suzy had pointed to. It was at least 500 metres away, in choppy waters, and as the girl who tended to have second thoughts about getting into Jacuzzis, she didn't fancy her chances of going anywhere in these conditions. A wind wrestled with her briefly and she shivered, her eyes meeting Suzy's apprehensively as she reached for the oar.

Sympathy was what she was hoping for. Surely even Suzy could see this wasn't simply unreasonable, it was downright unsafe? But Suzy just winked, helping her slot the oar into the bracket and holding the boat secure as Debs hopped in and everyone gripped their oars. Cassie took a deep breath and looked at how the other girls were holding theirs. They seemed to hold their outer hand – the one that was on the tip of the oar – facing them around the oar, the inner hand cupped over the top.

'Ready?' Suzy asked, and at everyone's nod (except Cassie's), she let go of the boat, pushing it away from the harbour wall. Away from safety.

Cassie scrunched her eyes shut and automatically launched into the Lord's Prayer – the first time she'd recited it since school.

'Right, girls, let's keep this tight,' Betsy said calmly as the boat floated freely on the water, lurching from side to side so that the dark water splashed threateningly over into their laps. Cassie winced at the shock of the cold and gripped the oar tighter, willing herself not to scream, before realizing the crew was already moving in a unified rhythm that righted their direction; within five strokes they had faced the boat into the waves, rather than side-on to them, so that the chop cut around them and the boat bobbed gently on the surface as they rowed.

Cassie forced herself to calm down. They weren't sinking; they weren't sinking . . .

She watched the team's steady rise-and-fall rhythm, knowing she couldn't just sit there like a lemon while they did all the work. She counted as they leaned back in unison, pulling the oars into them, before sitting up on the forwards push on the count of three.

'Cassie, pick it up!' Debs said through her little tannoy, her eyes hidden beneath her cap but clearly seeing how Cassie struggled to fall into line. The principle of it was fine – down two, up two – but the weight of the water on the oars meant she found it hard to push them through and get back up in time, so that she was perpetually leaning behind as the others sat back up again.

Another gig – red – glided past, the crew a symphony in motion, backs straight, arms strong. Cassie could see Debs watching her and knew she must be able to tell that Cassie had never set foot on a gig before. 'Oh God, oh God,' she muttered.

'Twist your wrist on the forward push,' Jacqs murmured, from behind her.

What? Cassie stiffened in surprise – she hadn't been aware she'd expressed her panic out loud, but she did as instructed and the oar sliced cleanly through the water, like a blade through butter.

Oh!

'Thank you,' she whispered back as she did it again and again, beginning to catch up with Sally's rhythm and maintain it. Their speed seemed to increase a little – or was that just her imagination? – and she felt a bolt of relief as she integrated into the team's coherent motion. This wasn't so bad after all, she thought, as she rose and fell with the others. She hadn't fallen in. She hadn't dropped her oar or hit anyone else's – although there was still time.

She clenched with tension again, concentrating so hard on not messing up that she was surprised when Debs gave the cue for them to stop rowing and drift.

She turned and saw the blue tug just ahead. Really? Already?

Jacqs reached over and patted her on the back. 'Good going,' she said encouragingly.

Cassie beamed as relief and pride surged through her. Phase One was complete – she'd made it to the start line at least, now just the finish line to go – and as she stretched out her back and arms, she allowed herself the luxury of looking around at last.

She was amazed by what she saw: yellow water taxis chugging away at a distance, filled to capacity with spectators yelling out the names of their favoured teams – 'Swift!', 'Shearwater!', 'Bonnet!', 'Hope!' – as those on the smaller crafts did the same. There were so many boats on the stretches either side of them that from the shore it had looked more like a Normandy landing, but here, sitting amid them, it felt like a festival on the water.

It took a while for them to get the boat into position. No sooner were they in line with the tug's prow than they drifted forwards again as they waited for the last gigs to line up. Cassie sat on the boat, her hands gripping the oar tightly, nerves beginning to kick in again as she looked left and right. Padstow sat to their right (the place of pilgrimage for seafood lovers the world over) and Rock to the left (the postcode with some of the highest retail values in the country), but the sea mist had stripped them of clarity and all that she could really see was the vast channel that surrounded her on all sides and had seemed so menacing from the shore. Beneath them, she could just make out the pale shimmer of the drifting sandbank, called the Doom Bar and historically the undoing of so many vessels.

But not this one – this gig was buoyant and beautifully hand-crafted in the ancient tradition, these girls strong, and as they bobbed about, just like plastic water bottles on the sea, waiting for the off, Cassie suddenly understood exactly why Henry had put this on her list. Being on the water was what this place was all about – not buying olives from the deli or eating at Rick Stein's, or even paddling in the tame shallows of Daymer Bay or wave-jumping at Polzeath, but rowing out to the deepest, darkest depths when the wind was up, the sun was setting, the air was like cobwebs and the sea had a snarl to it . . . This place had a wild, savage beauty that either touched you or frightened you, and it was here that Henry's love of adventure had been moulded and nurtured. This – right here in the middle of the sea – was where he had become the man she loved.

'Nervous?' Jacqs asked, tapping lightly on her shoulder.

'You could say that,' Cassie confessed with a shy smile, twisting in her seat slightly. 'Is this an important race?'

'North coast friendly,' Jacqs said with a dance in her hazel-green eyes. 'Of course, we say friendly. What we mean is, a fight to the death.'

'Oh yikes,' Cassie managed to grin.

A bell rang somewhere and everything suddenly fell quiet, like the sky emptying of birds in the moments before a storm. The yells from the spectators stopped and Jacqs gave her a fist-bump. Cassie took a deep breath, her hands tingling from the adrenalin. This was it, then . . . The crews in the eight gigs all assumed identical positions, heads tipped down slightly, arms poised to pull.

The tug gave a long blast of its horn and suddenly the girls were rising and falling again in perfect synchronicity, Cassie a half-beat behind, as the gig began to move through the water to the cheers and toots of the supporters. At first the boat felt heavy, as though tethered to the seabed beneath them, but repetition rapidly brought momentum and within a minute the boat felt if not quite powered under its own steam, at least like it was rising out of the water and skimming across the surface.

Cassie kept up the pace, concentrating on the twist of her wrist as she realized she still had no idea exactly where they were rowing *to*. There was a huge rock at the mouth of the estuary, but they wouldn't be going all the way there and back. Would they?

It was probably better she didn't know, she decided, having to put all her concentration into just keeping up.

Debs was shouting instructions at them – 'Heave', 'Aft' – but before they'd even reached the distinctive hump of Brea Hill, at the near end of Daymer Bay, her arms were already beginning to burn. Usually, the most exercise her arms ever got was lugging heavy picnic hampers up and down her stairs, but this was a different kind of pain, the muscles burning but not seizing as they contracted and released over and over again.

She had no idea where they were in the race, only that she could see two other gigs from her back-facing position. That had to mean they weren't last, right?

'*Speedwell!*'

'Go, Cassie!'

Cassie turned her head only fractionally as she pulled

back, but it was enough to see Suzy and Archie waving dementedly from a yellow water taxi as the gig cut past, Cassie beaming back with . . . exhilaration, she realized.

She had forgotten all about the cold wind as she took huge, deep breaths, trying to power her body on, and she knew her face must already be pinker than their crew tops. She stared grimly at Sall's back, barely aware of the way her right wrist instinctively twisted on the push forwards now or of how she clenched her core on the roll backs.

The first she knew of their route was when the rock island came into her peripheral view on the left-hand side of the boat – her worst fears confirmed.

'We're at Newlands! Starboard double up! You can do this!' Debs hollered, the rock staying to their left as they coursed round it. The waves grew bigger in this expanse of open water and a shot of alarm jangled Cassie's nerves as the rough sea slammed into the sides of the gig and sprayed high into the air, drenching them all, but there was barely time to process it. They just kept on rowing, the rock staying to their left and then beginning to pull forwards in her vision until eventually she was staring straight at it, its bulk receding as they made their way back into the protected waters of the estuary and towards the finish.

Her muscles were screaming now, the fibres tearing minutely with every stroke, and her heart felt like a jackhammer. Every stroke hurt; she couldn't think, could barely see beyond the pain, but she knew they were getting close, as the number of taxis and boats around them increased again, short horn-blows bursting over the wind in encouragement alongside the cacophony of shouts and yells and cheers.

Cassie wasn't sure she had enough left for the finish. She

had moved past exhaustion long ago, and yet somehow she kept moving in time, her body overriding her conscious controls like a computer outsmarting the technician; she groaned with every stroke, desperate to keep the pace, not to let down the team.

Behind her, she heard the long toot of a horn, followed by several shorter ones and a crescendo of cheers. The first boat had to be over the line. Was it much further? Could she keep going long en—

The blue tug shot past them, Cassie staring at it with a removed sense of recognition, her stomach taut and arms syncopated. It was a moment before she realized everyone else had stopped rising and falling and was slumped forward and back in their seats like felled skittles, that Debs had stopped shouting and was punching her arms in the air.

She wanted to ask if it was over, but there was no breath left in her to do it and she dropped her head onto her lap, her cheek by her knees and her eyes closed as she luxuriated in the exquisite feeling of not moving anymore. She felt her heart in her chest in a way she never had before. It pounded wildly like a boxer's fist, as if trying to show her not just that she was alive but *so* alive.

Henry's message was clear; she got it now: if she wanted to drift through her life – half asleep, uncommitted – she was with the wrong man.

Chapter Twenty

Date: 09/7/15
From: Haycock, Neil
To: Fraser, Cassie
Subject: Message In a Bottle

Hi Cassie,
Thanks for your message for Henry, which we forwarded on 08/7/15. He has responded that he is very well and enjoying the views.

Conditions are set fair and they are proceeding at 34 knots. If you would like to track their progress on radar, they are 9°26′S; 159°59′E.

Kind regards,
Neil
Communications specialist,
Message In a Bottle Project,
Inmarsat

Cassie turned the page over, her elbows red and sore from lying on them so long, but she had to finish this chapter while she could. Suzy's incessant talking about Gem and Laird every time she sat down meant she hadn't got past Chapter Four and she was determined to finish a book on this holiday. This was a precious window of opportunity – last night's exertions had bought her a grace period from the list, as there were no surf lessons for her today (although Archie had disappeared off with Laird), but Gem had stopped by at breakfast, wondering if they could 'chat' later about food for the wedding, and Suzy and Velvet would be back from the shops any minute.

She bit her lip, engrossed and swinging her leg idly in the air behind her, only vaguely aware of the feeling of the breeze on her bare skin. She certainly wasn't aware of the sound of footsteps over the stile at the bottom of the garden, or the soft crush of grass as someone approached.

It took a small cough to achieve that.

She looked up in surprise to find Luke standing with his board watching her.

'You always did that,' he smiled, setting the board down on its end.

'Did what?'

'Swung your leg about when you were reading. I used to have to clear a swat zone when you were reading the papers.'

She laughed lightly, wishing he'd put a T-shirt on with his rolled-down wetsuit, but it was too hot for clothes today. In fact, she was in her full bikini today, for the first time, no wetsuit to protect her modesty (or hide her wobbly bits) because she'd assumed she had the place to herself.

'Are the others still down there?' she asked, politely turning down a corner of her page and closing the book.

He nodded. 'Arch managed to stand.'

'No way!' she gasped jealously. 'You're kidding me?'

'No,' Luke laughed. 'Although, you'd probably feel better if you'd seen it for yourself. I use the word "stand" in the loosest possible sense.' He indicated to sit down. 'May I?'

'Sure,' she shrugged. 'Where's Amber?'

He pulled a face briefly. 'Promise you won't laugh?'

She shrugged her acquiescence as he leaned back on straight arms, his torso long and perfect. He looked like he hadn't shaved for five days, his stubble denser than usual. It suited him. A beard would suit him, she thought idly.

'She and Gem are having their cards read. Some woman in Tintagel apparently.'

Cassie laughed.

'You said you wouldn't!'

'I'm laughing at how you pronounced "Tintagel". It's "Tin-taj-el",' Cassie corrected.

'Right, that's what I said,' he protested. 'Hey, look, I'm American. What'd you expect? Besides, you're a fine one to talk. You can't say "Chance".'

'Oh, don't start that up again,' she groaned, still convinced that they'd only seen so much of his friend Chance in New York because it made them all crack up to hear her pronunciation of his name: they used the flat 'a' of 'apple', whereas she used the 'ah' of 'aria'. 'At least I—' She stopped herself abruptly. What was she thinking, falling back into their past jokes?

'So where's Suzy?' he asked, after a moment that felt considerably longer.

'Wadebridge. We were out of nappies and muesli.' She rolled her eyes. 'Poor Arch. I think he'd sell Velvet for a bacon butty right now.'

He smiled and she wondered where he'd been for the past few days. She hadn't seen him since he and Laird had surprised the girls at the bridal boutique, and she couldn't help but wonder whether his absence had been deliberate. She remembered the shock on his face at seeing her in the dress. Had it bothered him, seeing her dressed as another man's bride? Or was she, as Suzy had said, reading too much into it, unable to accept that he had moved on, once and for all?

She shook the thought away. No, Suzy was wrong. Cassie had Henry. She didn't need her ex to bolster her ego.

'He looks good on it, though. Arch, I mean,' he said after another pause. 'He's caught some sun and shifted some timber, to use his words.'

'Yes. He's looking much healthier.' She sighed lightly, wishing she could get up off her elbows and move to a sitting position – her arms and shoulders were tender after last night's brutal exercise – but her bikini suddenly felt too much like a bra and knickers in his company and she kept herself shielded instead, with only her back and calves on display.

She knew it was stupid to be so coy. What would he care to see her in her bikini? He did swimwear and lingerie shoots in his sleep. And besides, nothing he had done in all the times they had seen each other here had betrayed anything other than genuine contrition and what seemed to be a certain nostalgic fondness. But even knowing all that, she couldn't pretend that he hadn't seen her naked or forget that he knew what she liked in bed, and she felt that knowledge run like a current between them at all times.

'So . . . I heard you had a fun night,' he said, yet again trying to ignite the conversation, and she nodded brightly, knowing she had to at least try to help them move on. 'You came fourth, was it?'

'Yes, unbelievably – given that they were effectively a man down . . . or girl.'

'Archie said you were brilliant. Determined, I think was the word he used.'

'Well, I'd never hear the end of it if I failed at something on the list.'

Luke's mouth parted in surprise. 'Oh, I see. This is another of Henry's famous lists, is it?'

She smiled and gave an awkward shrug, knowing they both recalled how the list for New York had brought such tension into their relationship – the Christmas present on it, particularly, had almost led to a fight between them.

'Good to hear he's still going strong with that.'

Cassie looked at him but couldn't read his tone and she started studying a blade of grass instead, wondering how to change the subject. 'Anyway, it was great fun. I may even try it again.'

'Really?'

'Yes, they have training sessions on Wednesday nights and Sunday mornings, so if I do stay here . . .'

'You mean you might be going?' he asked, shocked.

'I . . . don't know. Maybe.' She shrugged. 'Work. You know . . .'

The truth was, she wasn't sure now about whether or not to stay. Last night had changed things. Working that hard had felt cathartic somehow, like she'd sweated some of her restlessness out of her system. Did it matter if she was in Cornwall or London? Gil was still going to remarry on Saturday; Henry was still going to be in the Pacific on a bottle-boat.

'Well, that would be a shame,' he said quietly, looking out to sea.

Would it be? she wondered. She stared at his profile, so handsome, and wished he'd never stepped back into her life. Could she really stay down here, with the possibility of seeing him round every corner? She never knew when, or where, she was going to see him next, or whether his intentions were benign or not, and she felt unsettled and jumpy.

Cassie looked away and picked at the grass. It was no good. As they sat there alone, just the two of them, the tension between them crackled. They didn't even need to look at each other to feel it. It didn't matter that they had moved on to new relationships, they were never going to be able to do the 'just good friends' gig. They could be polite, civil, but they had never been friends in the first place; the chemistry between them didn't allow it. They had a past that meant they could have no future, no matter what shape it took.

'Oh my God!'

The voice at the gate made them both turn.

'You are not going to believe what we've just seen!' Gem said, shooting through the gate like she was jet-propelled. 'Oh no, Luke, you can't hear this. You're a boy.'

'Where's Amber?' Luke asked, sitting straighter.

'She's gone to have a shower. It's so hot!' Gem puffed, pulling her T-shirt away from her neck and blowing air on her own face.

'I'll go join her,' Luke said, before freezing momentarily as he realized how that had sounded.

'I bet you will!' Gem gave a dirty laugh, smacking him on the bum as he got up and passed by, his eyes meeting Cassie's in the briefest of glances as he nodded his good-bye.

'So,' Gem said, falling into a lotus position. 'Can you guess?'

Cassie shook her head, her mood soured by the conversation that had just passed, and she wasn't sure she had the patience to indulge Suzy's hyperactive, self-obsessed little cousin right now. 'Nope.'

She watched as Gem reached into the back pocket of her linen shorts and pulled out a flyer: 'Rock Oyster Festival, Diningfold Hall, 11–12 July.'

'What is it? A festival?'

'Duh! That's what it says, doesn't it?' Gem laughed. 'Look, it's music, food, circus acts . . .' She clasped Cassie's hands. 'Have you ever been to Glasto?' she asked Cassie with the earnestness of a discussion about organ donation.

Cassie shook her head again, now violently wishing Suzy would come back.

Gem looked at her with sudden pity. 'Oh, you really must! You haven't lived. It's a rite of passage, Cass, and I mean that.'

'Well, I—'

'Which is why this is *so* great.' She stretched out 'so' like it was a limo. 'It'll be Glasto but smaller. Way smaller. More intimate. Which I prefer.'

Cassie also violently wished Gem wouldn't speak in bullet points. 'I take it you and Amber are going, then?'

'Me and . . . ?' Gem gasped, eyes burning. 'Cass, you don't get it! Of course me and Amber are going. We *all* are. This isn't just going to be any old festival, you know.'

'What's it going to be, then?' Cassie asked carelessly, picking up the book again and looking for her page.

Gem leaped up and did a perfect cartwheel, finishing

with an extravagant showgirl flourish of her arms. 'My hen night!'

Cassie walked out of the village store, confused. She could have sworn Archie had said he'd picked up his emails from the Wi-Fi cafe at the back of the shop, but the two tables and chairs that passed for the cafe had only laminated menus to their name – sadly there was no Wi-Fi here, like the rest of the village – and she had had to buy a cobbler loaf, just to mask her confusion.

She threw the bread into the basket and her leg over the bike frame, staring unseeing down the lane towards Polzeath. The tide was way out, the exposed beach glimmering in the sunlight, the die-hard surfers but coloured dots. If Archie hadn't picked up his emails from here, then how had he received Henry's list? Henry hadn't known she was coming down when he'd left for Australia, so he couldn't have written it in advance. It begged the question . . . No, two questions. Where had he got it from? Suzy had banned all gadgets from the house and Cassie wouldn't put it past her to have done spot checks. And if Henry was getting emails out from the boat, why wasn't he sending any to *her*?

Her phone buzzed in her shorts pocket and she took it out, amazed to see that she had four bars of mobile signal – the advantages of stopping on a hill – and a new text message. From Brett. Instantly, her heart dropped to her feet.

'Hi, Cass. Have u heard from Kelly? She went to the Hamptons while I was out of town but was supposed to get back today and is not answering her cell. Prob nothing but unlike her 2 b uncontactable like this. Am trying every-one. Call me if u know anything? Thanks, Brett.'

Call him if she knew anything? Of course she knew something. She knew everything; way more than he did! Was this it then? Had it happened? She felt her pulse quicken, the first shoots of panic beginning to spur through her. She tried to think rationally. She couldn't call him first. No way. Not yet. Kelly's disappearance may not be down to the miscarriage – it could be something far more inno-cent, completely innocuous – and Kelly would never forgive her if she spilled this secret on a false alarm. No. She had to get hold of her first. Kelly – if she'd tried to get hold of Cassie – would have probably called her on her BlackBerry. Kelly was always in 'work' mode and assumed everyone else was too. Plus it got better signal.

When had Brett sent this? she wondered desperately as she began pedalling away from Trebetherick's green-trimmed village store, rising out of the seat to get past the small hill before the lane swooped away, downhill almost all the way back to Butterbox. Her mind was on speed as her hair flew out behind her. It was almost eleven o'clock here, meaning it was only 6 a.m. there – possibly he'd been up all night trying to find his wife, in which case it didn't look good for her 'innocent' theory; their very worst fears were being realized and the worst was happening. But she couldn't be sure. She had no signal at all in the house; if he'd sent this last night, it was highly conceivable the mes-sage only got through now that she was in range of a phone mast. Kelly could be back home already.

Oh God, but what if the worst *was* happening? Her mind wouldn't let it go. Today was 10 July; that meant Kelly was officially nine weeks gone now. Cassie bit her lip, feeling ashamed. She had been here for nearly a week and hadn't called Kelly once. Yes, Suzy's ban on gadgets and zero broadband at the house had meant Skype was an impossibility, but she couldn't blame it all on that. The truth was that the distraction of dealing with Luke again meant her promise to buy lemons and connect daily had gone out of her mind. She was a terrible person, an awful friend, a rubbish girlfriend . . .

She was back at the house in minutes, tearing up the long drive past Snapdragons – both cars were in the drive – and throwing the bike on the ground as she fumbled for her keys in her pocket and struggled with the door.

'That you, Cass?' Suzy called through from the kitchen, *The Archers* playing on the radio.

'Won't be a minute!' Cassie called back, sprinting up the stairs two at a time and grabbing her BlackBerry, which she had left charging by the bed.

No messages from Kelly there either. Dammit.

She clicked on FaceTime on her phone and found Kelly in her contacts. 'U there?' she wrote into the blue bubble, but the signal was typically weak and she ran to the windows with it. No luck. She opened the doors onto the balcony and stepped out, leaning over the railings, her arm held aloft.

Two bars. Damn. Should she go back to the store?

She held it there for longer.

She checked the screen again. No reply.

'Talk to me, Kelly,' she typed in a new bubble. 'Has it happened?? Let me help.'

She held the phone up once more, her heart clattering like a tin soldier in her ribs.

'What *are* you doing?' a bemused voice below asked. 'Have you made contact with life forms in deep space?'

Cassie looked down to find Suzy standing on the terrace, a jug in one hand and a glass in the other.

'Just trying to get a signal,' Cassie said weakly. When Kelly had told her not to tell anyone, she hadn't really meant Suzy too, had she? Cassie had never kept a secret from Suzy in her life. Not successfully, anyway.

'Nup. Never gonna happen.' Suzy's blonde hair swung sympathetically, gleaming as it caught the sun. 'Fancy some home-made lemonade?'

Cassie shook her head. 'Maybe later.'

Suzy pursed her lips, looking up at Cassie quizzically, before she headed back inside.

Cassie turned a circle on the spot, one hand clutching her hair. What could she do? What could she do from here? What could she do from here with no laptop and practically no Wi-Fi?

She stared out into the distance, for once not seeing the view. She did, however, see the figure walking up through the fields, surfboard under one arm and wetsuit rolled down, the man who spent half his life on tropical islands with supermodels and still always got a signal.

She caught up with him by the side gate.

'Hey!' she panted, jumping out from behind one of the hedgerows and alarming Luke so much he almost dropped the board on his toes.

'Jeez, Cass! You scared the shit out of me.'

'Sorry, sorry,' she said, holding her hands up apologetically.

He took one look at her flushed cheeks and wild eyes. 'What's wrong?'

'Can you get a Wi-Fi signal down here?'

'Yes.'

'Have you got a laptop?'

'Of course. What's going on?'

'I need to borrow it, your laptop.'

He tipped his head down, trying to get her to slow down. 'Cass, slow down. What's wrong?'

'I don't have time to explain. I'll tell you everything after, but can you please just help?'

He looked at her for a moment, then nodded. 'Come on, then.'

They jogged through Snapdragons's garden – so much smaller than Butterbox's, but more densely stocked with foxgloves and delphiniums – Luke propping the surfboard against the wall by the back door and letting them both in to the house.

It was quiet in there, and dark. The primrose cotton curtains had been left drawn in the sitting room – 'to keep the room cool' – and Luke ran silently and swiftly upstairs to get his laptop from the bedroom.

'Amber's still sleeping,' he said quietly, one finger raised to his lips, as he came back down again moments later. He handed it over to her with a questioning look.

Amber was still sleeping? It was almost eleven o'clock, but Cassie didn't have time to care. She took the computer from him and opened it hurriedly on the pine kitchen table, clicking cluelessly on various icons on the desktop. It went to email.

'Uh, Cass, if you could just tell me what it is you need, I can get it for you,' Luke said quickly, angling the laptop away from her. 'Is it about Henry? Has something happened?'

'*Henry?*' Cassie echoed sharply, before catching herself and giving an apologetic sigh. 'No. It's Kelly. And it's an emergency,' she added. 'I need to Skype her.'

He cleared his throat, quickly typing on the keyboard before turning the laptop back towards her again. 'Be my guest. But it'll drive you nuts – I'm warning you now. There's not enough bandwidth for video.'

'But you said you had Wi-Fi!'

'And I do. But you need more for video. Certainly more than you can get here.'

Cassie slapped a hand to her forehead. It wasn't enough just to talk to Kelly. She had to see her, scrutinize her. She couldn't necessarily rely on her friend to tell the full truth at a moment like this. Kelly was a master of disguising her emotions. 'I'm fine', coming from her, covered everything from bored to breaking point. 'I need to see her. It's really important, Luke.'

His eyes examined her with his expert appraisal, taking in her rising panic. 'Then you need to go to Rock. That's where I've been chatting with my agent most days. They've got a good connection in the cafe in the deli. Decent coffee too. You know it?'

She shook her head. Suzy had been doing all the deli trips, enjoying being able to push Velvet along the pavements in her pushchair. 'But I'm sure I can find it,' she said quickly, straightening up. Rock wasn't a big place. How long would it take to cycle there? Some of it was uphill. Ten minutes? Maybe slightly more?

Dammit. Why was everything so slow down here? It had been twenty minutes, already, since she'd got the text and Kelly had potentially been missing all night.

'Luke? Baby, is that you?' Amber's voice – croaky with sleep – drifted down the stairs.

Luke's eyes met Cassie's, the room seeming to become smaller somehow.

'Come on, I'll drive you,' he whispered after a moment, lifting the laptop off the table and grabbing the keys to the Jeep. And together, as silent as thieves and feeling just as guilty, they crept from the house.

The screen stayed white until the fourth ring.

'Oh, hey, Cass,' Kelly said, a note of drowsy surprise in her sleep-addled voice as she tossed her hair off her shoulder. 'How's it going?' She frowned. 'What time is it?'

'How's it going?' Cassie echoed in a shrieking whisper. 'Kell! I just picked up a text from Brett telling me you'd gone missing! How do you think I'm going?'

'Oh.' There was a long pause as Kelly disappeared from the screen suddenly, and as the walls in the background changed from charcoal to Prussian blue, Cassie could tell that Kelly was getting up and walking out of the bedroom. 'I'm sorry. He totally shot the bolt on that.' Kelly rolled her eyes as she set the laptop down on the kitchen counter and gave a big yawn. She looked pale, even though the Hamptons summer season was already in full swing.

Cassie blinked at her, her heart rate climbing even higher at this anticlimactic explanation than it had after reading the text. *He shot the bolt?* That was it?

'Kell, I just about had a heart attack! Where were you?' she demanded, hands splayed.

Luke, who had been advancing with two coffees, caught sight of her body language and did a quick about-turn back towards the speciality pasta section.

'The Jitney was delayed and my cell was dead. Honestly, talk about overreact. I'm so mad with him. He called, like, everyone.' She leaned in closer to the screen. 'You see now what I mean, though?' she whispered. '*Way* too protective of me.'

'But everything's still OK? The baby's . . . ?'

Kelly glanced behind her quickly, to check they were still alone. 'Everything's *fine*, Cass.'

There it was – the word: the one Cassie had known she'd get, the one Cassie had known she'd have to see Kelly's expression to understand. She stared hard at her friend's beautiful, pale, fine-boned face. 'But you're at nine weeks now.'

'I know.'

'I thought—'

'I know,' Kelly nodded, her mouth drawing into a thin line. 'It'll be any day now.'

Cassie sighed, the finality of the fact like a punch in the face, and slumped slightly in the seat now that her adrenalin was allowed to ebb away. 'I just wish I could do more to help. I feel so useless being so far away from you.'

'We have these sessions.' Kelly gave a tiny shrug and tired smile, but Cassie pulled a face – what help could they really offer?

She saw Luke glance across and, seeing her less frantic, begin to make his way over. 'I'm so sorry I haven't called before now. There is *no* Wi-Fi. Like, none. And Suzy's banned everything electronic from the house. She's terrified Arch will start working on the sly and his stress levels will go up again.' That reminded her – she'd have to ask Arch where he'd downloaded the list.

'That's fair enough. So where are you calling from now, then?'

'The cafe in the deli. Lu—' Cassie stopped short. She had been *that* close to saying Luke's name, and Kelly had been closer than anyone to Luke and Cassie's relationship in New York. She wouldn't believe in their born-again friendship any more than Suzy had initially, and Cassie didn't have the energy to explain. 'I just got lucky with a superspecced laptop.'

Kelly seemed to accept the explanation at face value. She was too sleepy to be suspicious.

'So Archie's doing well?'

'Better than that. We're learning to surf and he's already standing up!'

'Jeez, is that safe?'

'Doctor's orders – sort of.' She shrugged. 'Let's face it, Suzy wouldn't let him anywhere near it if it wasn't safe.'

'True. But whose idea was it to try surfing? The temperatures in the Atlantic our side are enough to give you a heart attack.'

'Henry's, actually.'

Kelly looked astonished. 'Is Henry there?'

'Ha! I wish. In spirit only. He's written me a list.'

'Oh, of course he has!' Kelly laughed lightly, scratching her head with red manicured fingers. 'So what have you got to do this time?'

'Well, the night before last he had me rowing the Camel estuary in, like, *a storm*, with a bunch of strangers.' Well, it had been windy . . .

Kelly shook her head. 'You're crazy. I don't know why you go along with it.'

'You try saying no to him.'

'Well, we all know *you* can't!' Kelly quipped, with a dirty laugh.

Luke had reached the table and was standing on the other side, out of sight of the laptop. Cassie hoped he hadn't overheard.

'Here,' he murmured, putting down her coffee.

'Thanks,' she said quietly, her eyes flicking up to his briefly.

'Who's that?' Kelly asked.

'No one,' she said quickly.

'Well, it had to be someone.'

'I mean, it was just the . . . you know, the guy behind the counter.'

'Oh.' Kelly yawned again. 'Listen, it's still dawn here and I'm wiped. I better get back to bed before Brett realizes I'm not there and sends out another search party.' She gave an ironic wink.

'Sure. Listen, I'll try calling you tomorrow, OK? And call me if there's anything in the meantime. *Anything* at all. Now that I know about this place, I can get over here in a few minutes and we can talk face to face.'

'Sure thing. And remember to let me know about meeting up next week,' Kelly smiled, blowing her a kiss and quickly disconnecting before Cassie even had a chance to push back that there was a chance Kelly could still be pregnant next week and therefore wouldn't fly.

'The guy behind the counter?' Luke asked with a wry smile as he sat down at the table too, forcing her to slide along the bench.

'Well, what else was I going to say? I couldn't very well tell her it was you.'

'Why not? Aren't we allowed to speak to each other anymore?'

She tutted. 'You know what I mean.'

He was quiet for a moment. 'Yeah.'

They sipped their coffees for a while, watching as a young mother walked in with her mini-me twin eight-year-old girls in tow, all three of them wearing navy-and-red Breton-striped dresses.

'So, everything all OK now?' he asked.

'Yes, emergency diverted.' She gave him a grateful smile. 'Thanks for your help.'

'No problem. Although you gotta tell me what the emergency was. You did promise.'

She sighed. It was true, she had. 'Brett texted me last night saying Kelly hadn't come home. He was worried about her.'

Luke stared at her. 'And . . . ?' he prompted.

'And the Jitney was late,' she shrugged.

Luke exhaled incredulously. 'You're telling me that you and him both had a massive freak-out because the bus was late getting back from the Hamptons?'

'It's not that simple. I thought something had happened to her. I had good reason to believe that—' She stopped mid-flow, realizing she had said too much.

'Go on.'

She blinked back at him. She'd promised not to tell. 'It's nothing.'

'Cass, you wouldn't have come looking for *my* help if you could have possibly helped it—'

She blushed wildly, mortified that he'd read her awkwardness around him so accurately. His eyes – hazel brown and as steady as an eagle's – held hers and for a moment it was like time warped. They were no longer sitting in a cafe on the north coast of Cornwall – alternately polite and scratchy with each other, unable to establish a safety zone – but in a bar in Manhattan, his hand on her thigh and his lips by her ear as he whispered all the things he was going to do to her that night.

'What did you think had happened to her? Who am I gonna tell, huh?'

'She's pregnant.' The words came from her like they'd been pulled on strings.

Luke blinked, breaking the spell. 'Well, that's great.'

'No, not great. It's her fourth pregnancy in a year. She can't carry past nine weeks. And this is nine weeks.'

'Oh shit.'

'Yes, exactly.'

'But she's OK?'

'For now.' She took another sip of her coffee, looking away and making a mental note to avoid further eye contact.

'No wonder Brett was freaking.'

She looked back at him again. 'No, he doesn't know. I'm the only one. She's not telling him till she gets the all-clear at twelve weeks. She says it isn't fair to make him go through it all again.'

'But it's OK for her to go through it?' Luke asked, incredulously.

'I know! That's just what I said!' Cassie exclaimed, feeling vindicated. 'Her view is, there's no choice for her, but there is for Brett. She thinks she's being kind. Crazy, right?'

'Totally,' Luke agreed, his eyes holding hers again and spinning them both back to another time, another place.

'Well, that really does explain why you were so demented to get hold of her,' he said finally, looking away first.

'I wasn't *demented*,' she retorted with mock indignation. 'I was a concerned friend.'

His eyes glittered with amusement. 'Demented.'

'Concerned.'

'Demented.'

An exasperated smile tugged free from her and she joshed him in the ribs with her elbow, making him laugh. 'Concerned.'

Chapter Twenty-One

'And how, pray tell, are you paying for this?' Suzy asked, rooted to the spot in the entrance to the yurt, Cassie and Amber clustered by her shoulders as Gem walked around the 'living space' – a hexagonal area with a kilim rug and wood-burning stove – her arms outstretched and face turned to the sky. The four futon beds were arranged in a fan-shape around the edges of the rug, coloured Moroccan pendants with tea lights inside hanging down low from the ceiling trusses.

'I've put it on my credit card,' Gem shrugged lightly. 'No biggie.'

'Hang on. You told me you put your flights back from Oz on your cards too. And the cost of your homecoming party. How much credit do you have, exactly? And more to the point, how are you going to pay it back?' Suzy asked bossily, finally walking into the room and throwing her rucksack down on the middle left bed. 'You do understand about interest rates, don't you?'

Gem laughed. 'Suze, you're such a riot!'

Suzy shot Cassie an alarmed look. What kind of answer was that?

'Relax. It's all covered. You know I'm twenty-one in a

couple of months, right? Repayments aren't going to be an issue.'

Suzy gave a depressed sigh – it wasn't always easy being right – throwing herself back on the bed and staring up at the turquoise and hot-pink swags that dressed the ceiling.

Cassie bagged the bed beside her to the right, Gem taking the bed to Suzy's left and Amber taking the one furthest to the left.

'Do you think Arch will remember to put Velvet's cream on behind her knees?' Suzy asked, her hands behind her head.

'Probably not.' Cassie threw herself down on her bed too and immediately regretted it: there wasn't much bounce.

'It always gets worse in the heat, her eczema,' Suzy fretted.

'We're back tomorrow night. She's with her father. It'll be fine,' Cassie said soothingly, reaching for her rucksack and wondering whether what she had packed was funky enough for a festival. Wasn't there supposed to be a whole 'look' for these things now?

'Where are the boys staying again?' Suzy asked Gem and Amber, twisting back to face them.

'In the normal camping bit. Laird said glamping was for wimps, but then he grew up in the bush. He thinks a camp-site with running water and showers is cheating,' Gem smiled proudly.

'Poor Luke. I think he'd have much preferred a nice hotel to go back to tonight,' Amber smiled, pulling out a tiny rainbow-stripe seersucker cotton playsuit that looked like it would fit a ten-year-old and holding it up with a considered pout.

Cassie felt a flash of panic at the sight of it, really not

sure now about the navy-and-red Breton-striped dress she'd seen in the window of the boutique opposite the deli yesterday. It was the same dress she'd seen the yummy mummy wearing, although Luke had said she looked much better in it, when she'd tried it on.

'Well, just as long as we don't see either one of them,' Gem said, hauling her bag onto the bed too and pulling out clothes like they were ribbons from a magician's hat. 'It's not cool for them to have the stag night where we're having the hen party. *I* had the idea first.'

'Well, given that you're putting this wedding on with only twenty minutes' notice, it was either this or a pub crawl in Newquay, and you *really* don't want them doing that,' Suzy said with a shiver.

'Is Arch OK about being left behind?' Amber asked, this time holding up a pair of denim cut-offs. Cassie bristled at how casually she used his pet name, as though she considered herself part of their group.

'He's delighted,' Suzy sniffed with an indignation that suggested she fully expected him to take advantage of a near-empty house and hunt down her hidden stash of Sauv Blanc.

'It must be so hard for him, though, to see us all going out together, having a great time—'

'Yeah, well, nearly dying comes with paybacks. He can't do without proper rest and a proper diet right now. This place would effectively be a death trap for him.'

'Oh.' Amber looked chastened.

'And obviously someone had to look after Velvet too,' Suzy added after a moment in a softer tone. 'It was me or him, and frankly, after the aggro he's given me over muesli and elderflower these past two weeks, he jolly well owes me a break.'

'Yeah. Payback,' Cassie echoed loyally, pushing the striped dress to the bottom of her bag.

'Well, I, for one, am really glad you're here,' Gem said, rooting in the depths of hers. 'It's Girls On Tour this weekend and it just wouldn't have been the same without my Big-Sister Cousin.' Her eyes lit up as her hands found what they were looking for and she pulled a magnum of champagne out of the rucksack.

'Er, it's two o'clock,' Cassie said, apprehensively.

'Exactly. Ladies, it's time to get this party started.'

They trooped out of the tent, arm in arm and dressed like it was Woodstock 1969. Cassie's wardrobe apprehensions had been unfounded – not because she had packed well but because Amber had gone into full fashion-diva mode and styled them all with a seemingly limitless supply of props and accessories from her and Gem's bags, making pronouncements with an authority that even Suzy didn't argue with. Gem, as the hen, was put in a frothy white tutu with neon-pink leg and wrist warmers, and a denim jacket. Suzy, who had almost keeled over at the sight of the tutu, was in a short turquoise kaftan that made the most of her good legs, peacock-feather drop earrings, reflective Ray-Bans and a panama. Cassie was a 1970s throwback in washed-out chambray hot pants with a grass-green ribbed tank, rainbow-striped knee socks and her hair in a plait with a silk daisy chain resting lightly over the crown of her head. (She couldn't even begin to imagine Kelly and Nooks's faces if they could see this.) Amber was in the playsuit with wedges, neon rubber bracelets stacked up her arms and a Stetson.

It turned out there had been two bottles in the bag, and by the time they'd finished dressing up, both had been drunk and the yurt looked like it had been raided by Cossacks.

'So, where first?' Amber asked as they took in the sight before them. In the next field, where the action was based, the grassy swathes that had still been visible when they'd arrived were now lost from view as thousands of people milled between the tents and stages. It wasn't exactly how Cassie had imagined a festival would be. In fact, at first glance, it all seemed rather 'Middle England' and well behaved, not very Glasto at all. A farmers' market was doing a roaring trade as people shopped for artisanal breads and prize-winning tomatoes; teams from Jamie Oliver's Fifteen restaurant in Watergate Bay and Michelin-starred Nathan Outlaw in Rock were holding demonstrations and workshops, and at every turn people could sample Porthilly oysters, Roskilly's ice creams, Cornish-orchard scrumpy and ciders, and Cornish curries that were being cooked on huge paella-style woks.

'Well, we're not going to go hungry,' Suzy said in a satisfied tone as they began to walk past the huge three-metre-high towers of shredded ribbons flapping in the breeze, which acted as a visual location guide for visitors in far-off lanes.

Cassie smiled as Suzy readjusted the angle of her hat. She had never seen Suzy look so trendy before, and she had to admit Amber had done a great job of getting them all into the festival spirit, even if they were probably a little overdressed. Her striped dress would have been perfect, after all. There were lots of families here, with loads of kids running around in named hoodies, and many people had cagoules tied round their waists, in case the showers that had been forecast materialized.

'I think we should go over to the sound stages,' Gem said, pulling up one of her leg warmers. 'The warm-up acts are going to be on stage soon and I'm dying to find out who's the mystery band.'

'There's a mystery band?' Cassie asked, looking over at the distinctive humped shape of the music stage, with huge lighting rigs and video backdrops. A three-towered circus tent had been pitched on the opposite side of the field, along with a tall red-and-yellow helter-skelter.

'Really? I'd quite like to check out those cheeses,' Suzy said, squinting at a nearby stall and heading towards it.

'Suze! Stop being so middle-aged. You're at a festival, not Waitrose!' Gem complained, pulling her away.

'Cheese is not middle-aged. Look at Alex James. He actually makes cheese now.'

Gem looked puzzled. 'Who?'

Suzy groaned. 'Ugh!'

'Actually, Gem, it might be an idea to go check out the food stalls. It could give us some ideas, and we really need to sit down and talk about the food for the wedding,' Cassie said.

'No, that's admin stuff and this is my hen night!' Gem said with a whine, reaching into her bra and pulling out a cigarette.

'Aren't you supposed to have given up?' Suzy scowled.

'I nearly have,' Gem smiled, lighting it with a wink. 'Anyway, Cass, I reckon we could eat berries off the bushes and drink dew from the grass and feel like we'd feasted.

Our wedding day is going to be so full of emotion. All that trad stuff like flowers and food . . .' She made a dismissive gesture with her hands and pulled a face. 'I mean, don't get me wrong, I know it's important, but—'

'You're damn right it's important,' Suzy butted in, before whispering into Cassie's ear, 'Especially when our digestion will probably last longer than the marriage.'

'Tomorrow, I promise,' Gem said, squeezing Cassie's arm. 'We'll go over the menus then. We just want it all really simple anyway.'

Cassie inwardly groaned. A ham sandwich was simple, but she didn't think they'd be wanting that. She could already see this was going to be more work than she'd bargained for.

They wandered en masse past the rows of shopping stalls, garnering both admiring and amused glances, stopping to coo over silhouette-printed linen scarves and shells set into sterling-silver jewellery. Cassie stopped outside a surf-school stall and watched as a couple of children balanced – rather expertly – on what appeared to be a short oval board rolling over a plastic cylinder. She watched as they swung the board back and forth hypnotically, arms outstretched and making it look easy. 'What are those things?' she laughed.

'They're called Indo Boards. Fancy a go?'

She turned to find a guy with dark shaggy hair and a strip of zinc oxide on his nose smiling at her. He was wearing a purple rash vest and lime-green baggies, which, while cool on the beach, looked a little daft in the middle of a field.

'Oh, thanks, but I've already had a bit too much champagne for that,' she demurred, taking a step back.

'Oh, go on, Cass!' Suzy said, stepping between them and looking like she'd been teleported in from a Vegas pool party. 'You've been trying to stand up on the damned surfboard for days. Maybe this'll help.'

'You're learning to surf?' the guy asked.

'Trying to, but failing badly.' She rolled her eyes.

'Who's teaching you?'

'A friend. He's really good. An Aussie,' she added, as though nationality alone confirmed his skills. 'It's not his fault; it's mine.'

'That's true,' Suzy sighed, patting Cassie on the shoulder. 'Cassie's such a control freak. Anything outside her comfort zone and she just freezes.'

Cassie shot her an annoyed look as Suzy pushed her glasses back up her nose with a pleased smile.

'Come on, let's give you a whirl,' the guy said, grabbing a spare board and setting it by her feet. 'If it is tension that's holding you back, the champagne will probably help.'

'Oh, but—'

He placed his hand on her elbow and she stepped onto the board gingerly.

'Put your hands on my shoulders,' he said. 'That's it. Now plant both feet shoulder-width apart . . . Turn your right leg out slightly so that it's facing forward . . .'

Cassie took a sudden breath as she felt the cylinder roll beneath her and she gripped her hands harder into his shoulders to keep from falling. She gave an apologetic smile, embarrassed to realize people were watching.

'Uh . . . How did the kids make this look so simple?' she laughed nervously.

'Easy. They're a lot smaller, so their centre of gravity is lower.'

'Oh.'

'Now, just begin to slide side to side. Arms out and try to keep your shoulders level. All the movement should be in your hips . . . That's it. Now when you feel ready, let go of my shoulders . . .'

Cassie bit her lip as she carefully lifted her hands away, still keeping them close enough to him, however, to grab at a moment's notice.

'You see?' he grinned as she began to rock – barely – from side to side. 'I told you the champagne would help.'

'Go, Cass!' Gem trilled as she began to 'surf' a little faster.

'You're doing it, Cass!' Suzy cheered, filming her on her phone. 'You can show Henry when he gets back.'

Cassie laughed, sticking out her tongue, as she began to find the rhythm, her confidence growing fast. It was really quite easy once you got the hang of it.

'There she goes!' the guy laughed, clapping as Cassie gave an extra hip wiggle. Across the field, a band had come onto the stage and launched into a cover of 'Sweet Child o' Mine'.

'Oooh, I know this one!' Cassie laughed, waving her arms above her head and beginning to dance a little as she continued to 'surf'.

'I want a go!' Suzy cried, clapping her hands and beginning to rock out too.

'Me too!' Gem echoed, followed by Amber, and the guy and his colleague ran around placing the Indos at their feet and helping them get set up.

Amber's board was placed just in front of Cassie's, the two women facing each other once the surf guy had been released from her grip. Amber got it almost immediately, yelling out a 'Yeehaw!' and pretending to throw a lasso above her head. The way she moved was so slinky and knowing it was like she was strutting down a catwalk or doing her best Jessica Alba impression in leather chaps – as nervy as she was one to one or in a small group, she seemed to grow in stature and confidence with the eyes of the crowd on her. Cassie's own eyes narrowed. She didn't trust that kind of actorly 'look at me' insecurity.

'Who thinks they can take it to the next level?' the guy asked, holding out some hula hoops.

'Me!' Cassie, Amber and Gem all shouted out together.

Suzy, who didn't seem to be faring quite so well – an air-guitar riff had thrown her off her stride – kept quiet.

The guy walked around them all, handing out the hoops. 'It's a lot harder, OK? It's a bit like rubbing your tummy and patting your head at the same time. Remember to keep your shoulders still.'

Cassie got going with it first, as Amber struggled to get it over her Stetson, before deciding to dispense with the hat altogether and tossing it to the ground like a stripper's bra.

A small cheer went up around them and Cassie realized their small crowd had grown, with many more groups of lads with pints watching than before. She heard Amber's name ripple through the crowd like leaves rustling on a tree and realized her star had been spotted.

Amber got going again, not so much hula-hooping as doing the Dance of the Seven Veils, with exaggerated hip swings that would have hypnotized a cobra. The crowd was really getting behind them now, people beginning to clap.

Cassie swung her hips a little harder. Gem wasn't really in the mix. The layers of her tutu kept catching the spin of the hoop and within moments she hopped off to have a cigarette instead, so that it was just her and Amber, surfing and hooping in time with the music.

Amber had begun to sing, letting her pretty head loll against her shoulder as her body worked its magic and the crowd fell under her considerable spell. Even Cassie, who was trying to concentrate on her own moves, caught the allure. Was it any wonder Luke had decided to stop with her? She was an ultra-woman: beautiful, dainty, delicate, entrancing. She didn't look like anyone else here in this crowd of thousands. Even if Cassie hadn't walked away from him, even if she hadn't chosen Paris over him, even if she hadn't chosen Henry, they would have ended anyway. She wouldn't have been able to hold on to a man like him. She was the girl next door. Amber was from another planet.

Amber was beginning to dip now, drop lower through the knees and show off the tautness of her slim thighs. Cassie wondered whether she had a secret background in pole dancing and gave it a go too, but the shift in the distribution of her weight – coupled with the hooping and the side-to-side sliding of the surfing – was a progression too far and she went flying backwards suddenly, the cylinder shooting out from under the board like a missile.

'Whoa!' the surf guy laughed, catching her and holding her up under the arms as she sagged like a bedraggled scarecrow.

'Oh my God, I'm so sorry,' she spluttered, mortified. 'Did I break the board? Did I break *you*?'

'I'm fine. But I think maybe you just cleared out my stock,' he laughed, setting her upright again and pointing to a line of customers holding Indo Boards as his colleague tried to get the card machine to work.

'Oh.'

Amber – who had clearly 'won' – hopped off the board like a gazelle. Another cheer went up and she gave a cute curtsy, blowing kisses into the crowd. She gasped. 'Baby!' she cried, throwing her arms in the air and running into the sea of people, which parted for her, to reveal Laird and Luke, both standing holding their pints, bemused grins on their faces. 'Did you see me?'

Gem immediately stamped her cigarette out on the ground, hoping that Laird hadn't seen *her*.

'As if I could miss you,' Luke replied, his chin on her shoulder as she wrapped her arms around him, pushing her body into his and instantly making Luke the most hated – and envied – man there. His eyes drifted up, meeting Cassie's almost apologetically, but she looked away quickly. What was he apologizing for?

'Tell you what,' the surf guy continued, drawing Cassie's attention back to him. 'Let me give you the hula hoop. As a thank-you.'

'What? Oh no, really, I couldn't,' Cassie protested as he held out the lilac-and-silver hoop.

'Take it, Cass!' Suzy laughed. 'It's a bleeding hula hoop, not a diamond necklace. Velvet can have it!'

'Well . . . thank you,' Cassie said quietly, taking it from him and throwing it over her head and onto her opposite shoulder, like an across-the-body bag.

'No. Thank *you*,' the guy winked. 'I'm going to have to redouble my stock orders before you go viral.'

'Excuse me?'

'Some people were filming you and that model on their phones. I'd pay good money to bet you'll be a YouTube sensation by the end of the day.'

Oh great, Cassie thought miserably to herself.

She and Suzy made their way over to the others. Gem – in spite of having been upset about Laird having his stag night at the festival too – looked delighted that they were reunited after four long hours apart and had jumped onto him, her lips locked on his and her legs wrapped round his waist. Laird, in turn, looked delighted by the sight of his diminutive fiancée in a tutu.

'All right, all right, just break it up,' Suzy said, wading in and separating the two happy couples. 'This is supposed to be a hen night. If you're going to snog anyone tonight, it definitely shouldn't be your fiancé.'

Laird chuckled, putting Gem down.

Cassie hung back, pretending to look around at the site but really just trying not to catch either Amber or Luke's eyes. She gripped the hula hoop on her shoulder.

The loss stung.

'You girls all look very . . . colourful,' Laird said, taking in their get-ups.

'Amber dressed us,' Gem said, striking a pose. 'You like?'

'Obviously,' Laird winked, smacking her pert bottom. 'I don't think I'd have recognized you, Suzy.'

Suzy preened happily. It had been a while since she'd really given fashion a second thought and most of the time, these days, she dressed for comfort and practicality with Velvet.

'Well, these girls hadn't done any festivals before and I just thought . . . let's do it right,' said Amber proudly. 'I mean, Gem's been going to Glasto since she was fifteen, and we love Coachella, don't we?' Amber rolled herself into Luke's body again, her back against his chest and holding his arm over her torso. 'And I've been talking for a while about making the move into styling, haven't I?'

Luke nodded.

'Because you know, in my industry, life is short. It's no different to being an athlete. This body can't stay at this level indefinitely,' she said with a dismissive gesture at her flawless physique. 'I've only got another couple of years at the top and then I'll *have* to diversify.'

'Oh, I know just what you mean, Amber,' said Suzy. 'I was a model too before I went into wedding planning.'

There was a horrified silence before Amber realized she was joking. 'You always get me!' she laughed, jabbing a finger towards Suzy.

Cassie could tell from Suzy's expression that Suzy didn't like the way Amber had laughed *so* hard.

'Anyway, where next?' Laird asked.

'I really want to get to the front by the stage. There's no point being right at the back. You may as well watch it on TV,' Gem said with a pout, which Laird immediately kissed.

Cassie rolled her eyes. The persistent coupledom was beginning to get to her.

'Have you seen the size of the crowd already? That mosh pit is sixty-deep!' Luke said. 'We won't see anything anyway.'

'A mosh pit? Uh-uh. I am way too posh to mosh!' Suzy said in an alarmed voice. 'No way can I risk being trampled to death at a concert, especially for some unidentified band.'

'The rumour is it's Coldplay.' Luke took his arm away

from Amber so that he could swap hands for his pint. His eyes flickered towards Cassie, who had fallen quiet.

'Coldplay? You're kidding?' Gem shrieked. Could her night get any better?

He shrugged. 'That's what people are saying, but what do they know, right?'

'Oh my God, I can totally risk it,' Suzy said, turning to Cassie, her eyes even wider than her little cousin's. 'Me and Chris Martin, it's meant to be. Haven't I always said it?'

Cassie smiled her assent.

'And Arch knows that, does he?' Laird asked, bemused.

'Oh, totally!' Suzy said, rearranging her kaftan and checking her legs. 'He's my freebie.'

'Your what?' Amber asked, looking for Luke's arm again.

'You know – if ever our paths were to cross and the opportunity came up, then I would totally be allowed to bonk him. Special pass. One-time-only deal.'

Everyone laughed, except Cassie, who had heard this before and knew Suzy was deadly serious.

'Arch has got Heather Graham as his freebie,' Suzy added, pinching the crease of her panama.

'Oh. Who's yours?' Gem asked, looking behind her to ask Laird.

'I'm allowed one?'

Gem shrugged. 'Why not? Maybe that's their secret to a happy marriage.'

'Then I guess Ana Ivanovic?'

Gem frowned. 'You said that way too quick! You didn't even have to think about it!'

Laird's face fell as he realized he'd 'failed' the test. 'Well, what about you?'

'Jared Leto,' Gem said as fast as she could.

'Amber?' Laird asked.

'My man,' she said silkily, burrowing back into Luke again.

'No! That's cheating,' Suzy said crossly, taking it all very seriously. 'It cannot be him. You cannot cheat with your own husband slash boyfriend.'

'Well, then I guess it would have to be . . .' She strung the last word out in deep contemplation. 'Bradley Cooper.' The look on Amber's face as she said his name suggested she expected Luke to now challenge the man to a duel.

Cassie stepped in. 'I'm just going to put this hoop back in the tent. It's really annoying,' she said quickly, turning and darting off before anyone could remotely try to stop her. She didn't want to listen to this. She didn't want to hear Luke's answer or have to give her own.

She wove through the crowds, feeling ridiculous in her clothes as she slipped past the rustle of anoraks. What grown woman thought knee socks with shorts was a good look anyway? She looked like a skater girl at a ramblers' convention.

She was back at the yurt in minutes, throwing herself down on the bed with a groan of despair and almost winding herself as she landed on one of the empty champagne bottles that had been hidden beneath a pile of clothes. She reached for it and set it carefully on the floor, before dropping her head on the pillow again.

This was the worst hen night ever. Not only was the stag present, but she wasn't even drunk – the best she had managed was a mild buzz before they'd left the tent, and now the combination of fresh air and losing to Amber had left her feeling flat and tetchy. She checked the bottle for remnants, but it had been emptied to the dregs.

'Knock, knock.'

She twisted round in surprise to find Luke standing in the doorway.

'Hey,' he said with a bashful look, like a boy who knew he wasn't allowed in the girls' dorm. 'Can I come in?'

She scrambled up to a sitting position, instantly on alert. 'Luke, what are you doing here? Where's everyone else?'

'Apparently Amber's met the band a couple of times. They're going to try their luck with getting VIP backstage passes.'

'So then what are you doing *here*? Why didn't you go with them?' she asked in bafflement. Who turned down the opportunity to go VIP with Coldplay?

'You know why.'

The air sucked out of the room. What did he mean? He couldn't—

'Well, how else would you know where they all were?' he shrugged. 'I said I'd take you round to them.'

'Oh.' She nodded. Of course.

She got up from the bed and, embarrassed by the mess, feebly picked up some of the clothes and folded them in a pile.

Luke walked over and lifted them out of her hands. He stared down at her. 'It'll keep.'

They walked outside together. The food stalls were beginning to shut up shop, the lights of the domed main stage beginning to overpower the pale sky now that the sun was making its slow approach back to earth. There were fewer children running around, and several groups of lads in drag told her theirs weren't the only hen and stag dos there.

'You don't have a drink.'

Cassie looked down at her empty hands. 'No.'

He stopped walking. 'You can't be at a concert and not have a drink, Cass. There are rules about these things.'

'Really?' But before she could so much as arch an eyebrow, he had grabbed her hand.

'Follow me.'

His touch was like fire and every instinct told her to break the contact, but his hand had firmly gripped hers as he pulled her through the crowds, which were growing denser as the other activities closed down, herding everyone by default to the stage area. She heard 'Coldplay' in the crowd more than once before they ducked into a beer tent.

Half the festival seemed to have had the same idea and Luke practically had to scrummage his way through to the bar. When he finally got there, he ordered several drinks for each of them.

'What?' he asked, as she stared in astonishment at the sight of the eight beer bottles wedged between his fingers. 'I'm not queuing again. Are you?'

She took three with an arch look. 'Come on, then, let's find the others,' she said, beginning to turn and head out of the tent.

'Can't. You've got to drink up first. No glasses allowed anywhere but here.'

She looked back at him in disbelief. He expected her to drink four beers with him? They would be here for hours!

'This is farmland, you know,' he said earnestly before swigging his drink. 'We have a duty to behave responsibly for the animals. I've become very partial to cows in the past week.'

'You're all heart,' she said drily, clinking her bottle against his. 'Cheers, then.'

She wished she could drink quickly, but she was famously slow – something he'd clearly forgotten, and as they swigged their beers, looking to the people around them like a regular couple, she wondered what else had slipped his mind about her. Maybe he really didn't remember half of her peccadilloes or quirks; just because she recollected his preferred sleeping position and that breathing in his ear rendered him powerless didn't mean he ever thought about the one time he had made her knees buckle or how she took her coffee.

'You look great, by the way.' His eyes flickered over her retro-chic outfit.

She shrugged. 'Nothing to do with me. It's all Amber's handiwork.'

'No it's not. I was there when you sculpted those thighs, remember? When Kelly had you tower-running and doing early morning runs around the park?' he laughed softly. 'I had to massage you better, I do believe.'

Cassie couldn't find her voice. She couldn't believe he'd said that out loud, referenced something intimate between them that they could never – either of them – afford to refer to. She drank faster, confused by his behaviour. His touch just minutes earlier had felt electric, yet he treated her like a 'mate'; he had followed her to the tent, but only to bring her back to the others. Was she imagining things, misreading signals tonight? Putting subtext into actions that wasn't there? Reading innuendo in meanings that were perfectly clear? She turned away. It had to be the alcohol.

'I hope it is Coldplay that's on.'

He missed a beat and she knew he was staring. 'It probably isn't. Why would they do a little gig like this?'

'Well, they are from Devon. That's the next county to here, and people from the West Country stick together.'

'Then it probably is them, then.'

She glanced at him, his tone too acquiescent, his mind clearly on something other than the line of conversation. 'Yeah.'

He hesitated. 'Do you remember when they played Madison Square Garden? We tried for hours to book online.'

'Sold out in an hour,' she murmured. 'Yes, I remember.'

'So then maybe tonight is . . . karma. Restoring what should have been ours all along.'

Oh, come on! She wasn't imagining this! She looked at him, her heart pounding way too hard and fast again. What the hell kind of game was he playing here?

'Hey! The universe owes us a Coldplay concert. Am I right?'

There it went again, the conversation taking a slippery bypass away from where she'd thought it was heading. Jeez. She laughed, a frown on her face as he slipped away from her suspicions again. She must be drunker than she thought; she was all over the place tonight.

'Come on, drink up. These'll go warm,' Luke said, tapping the other beers. 'Race you.'

'Oh! Wait . . . !'

Chapter Twenty-Two

The sky rose above them like a phoenix, raging red, its fiery wings spread from one end of the world to the next, but even that couldn't compare to the lightshow on the stage before them. Strobes pulsed like galactic sabres, the ground trembling beneath their feet as the bass began to boom and the crowd's shouts rose to a towering crescendo. 'Coldplay' was on everyone's lips now – God help the band coming out if it wasn't them, Cassie thought, as Luke led her through the crowd again, the shock of his hand on hers dulled now by four beers and a couple of chasers.

Something in the way he held himself made people stand aside for him. Was it the white smile that contrasted so cleanly with his rough stubble? His expensive jacket? The self-assurance that came from success? Could they tell he came not just from another country but another world? Her other life?

She followed him, hoping they would at least get close enough to see the band on stage, even if they did have to watch the video screens to tell who was who. There were more people here than she could fathom, white lights of phone screens already held aloft, set to 'pause', as they waited for the band to come on. The warm-up acts had done their work with aplomb – the mood was electric – and with the sun almost set, what else was there to wait for?

Nothing.

In the next moment the lights went down and the crowd went wild. An explosion of white lights more like fireworks set the stage alight and suddenly a man with an elephant mask was singing at a mic, his head filling the hundred-foot screen.

The crowd erupted as Chris Martin's distinctive voice carried over the field and down to the creek behind. Cassie threw her arms in the air with a scream, jumping up and down dementedly and whooping as loudly as she could.

She couldn't believe it. They actually were here! Here she was, in a festival in Cornwall, listening to Coldplay – part of a *scene*. She felt the energy lift her up like a wave. Why had she never done this before? It was yet another thing she had missed out on in those lost years of her life. She looked across at Luke and was surprised to see he was already watching her, a quiet smile on his face as she over-reacted for them both.

He leaned in. 'Can you see them?' he called across to her.

'Sort of,' she shouted back.

He dropped down to his knees. 'Come on.'

She looked at him in horror. 'Luke, what the hell are you doing?'

'Get on my shoulders.'

'No!' she laughed.

He looked back at her. 'Yes. You've always wanted to see them live. Do it.'

'Luke—'

'Cass! Do it before I get trampled to death!'

The crowd was tightly knit and moving by degrees. She threw one leg round his right shoulder, having to hold on to his head as she put her left leg over too. It seemed for a moment as though he couldn't stand up with the weight of her on his shoulders, but then his hands found hers and moved them away from his eyes.

'That's better.'

'Oh!' she said nervously, as he started to get up and she felt like he might pitch forwards, throwing her into the backs of the people in front; but he smoothly rose to standing, sending her rocketing up to ten feet in the air.

Cassie gripped his head harder, convinced she was going to fall, but his arms folded round her socked calves, holding her tightly in place just as Chris Martin pulled off the elephant head and ran from one side of the stage to the other. Without even thinking about it, Cassie let go, her hands in the air as she whooped at the top of her voice, laughing as she made eye contact with the other girls enjoying this privileged vantage point.

The first organ chords of 'Fix You' rang out, a white laser beam sweeping over the crowd like a prison-yard spotlight. Cassie swayed to the beat, her head thrown back as she sang loud and proud, 'When you try your best, but you don't succeed; when you get what you want, but not what you need . . .' She knew she was part of a collective moment that would stay forever with every person here. She felt transcendent, transported – so much so that when an image was beamed onto the huge screens, a hundred feet high, of a beautiful woman with bright blue eyes and pinked cheeks, her mouth spread wide in an excited laugh and her sexy boyfriend between her thighs, it was a moment before she realized it was her.

Chapter Twenty-Three

It was quiet in the tent. Everyone was still sleeping, even though the new day was peeking belligerently through the gaps and demanding their attention. Cassie lay on her side, her back to them all, staring into the mirrored turquoise shawl that was draped down one wall. The hangover was fierce – champagne followed by beers followed by shots had been a *really* bad idea – and she felt so rotten she wasn't sure she could move from this position, much less this bed.

But that wasn't why she was awake. Beyond the throbbing pain of the hangover, her nervous system still seemed to be jangling from last night's euphoria – a slightly elevated pulse, rapid eye movement, her senses seemingly set on a higher alert . . . Her body was inert, but her mind was racing, her stomach tight and fizzing. She had the impression of standing on a clifftop, her toes wiggling over the edge as a giddying wind whirled around her, lifting her hair, tickling her skin and making her laugh, making her careless . . .

'You awake?' Suzy's voice was feather-light in the gloaming.

Cassie froze.

'I know you're awake. I can tell by your breathing.'

'I'm just *breathing*,' Cassie muttered after a moment, irritated that she couldn't even doze in peace without Suzy knowing best.

But Suzy didn't reply and a moment later Cassie rolled over reluctantly, keeping her eyes closed and resting her hands beneath her left cheek. 'I'm dying,' she said quietly, which was code for 'Leave me alone.'

'I'm not surprised. You were out of your tree by the time we caught up with you.'

'That wasn't my fault,' Cassie protested, remembering Luke's overzealous ordering in the beer tent.

'It never is.'

Cassie refused to be provoked. 'Did you get to go backstage?' Specific memories of last night were murky – so much for the moment staying with her forever!

'Yeah, for all the good it did us.'

Cassie opened her eyes. 'What do you mean?'

'Well, it's not all that great being *back*stage when the band's *on* stage. We ended up mainly watching them on a monitor.'

'But what about afterwards, when they'd finished? Surely Chris Martin has seen the error of his ways?'

'Huh, as if! I never even got to see him. Amber had gone off in a strop by then, and without a famous model by our side as confirmation that we're not a bunch of crazed stalkers, we had to leave.'

'Why had she—'

But Suzy didn't get to finish. The door to the tent flapped open and Gem wandered in, cradling something in her arms and cooing softly. Both women sat up in astonishment – Cassie because she hadn't even realized Gem had been up and out; she could just make out tufts of black-and-white hair in Gem's arms.

'What the hell . . . ?' Suzy demanded, her face darkening.

Gem looked up at them both with soft eyes. 'I am *so* in love.'

'That is a puppy,' Suzy said sternly.

Gem gave a gentle laugh. 'Top marks.'

'What the hell are you doing with a puppy?'

Gem rested her cheek on the top of the dog's head. 'He's my wedding present to Laird.'

'*What?*'

Even Cassie jumped at Suzy's tone.

'Don't you think he's just adorable? Before Laird's parents died, his family ran an animal sanctuary. He just loves animals; he's amazing with them. He says he'd love to go back and reopen the business again, finish what his folks started.'

'Where did you get him from?' Cassie asked, unable to resist reaching out a hand and stroking its velvety head.

'The couple in the pink camper van, three up from here.'

Suzy scowled. 'You're seriously telling me they're selling puppies at a festival? There's laws against that, you know!'

'Chill, Suze. They're not puppy farmers. I got chatting to them last night when they asked about my tutu. I began moaning that I didn't know what to get Laird for a wedding present and they suggested one of their pups. Their bitch had her litter a week early, so it's thrown out all their plans; they had to bring the pups with them to this, which, let's face it, no one in their right mind would ever do! Apparently it's been, like, a complete nightmare!'

'No shit, Sherlock.'

'Can you imagine four puppies running riot in a camper van? Bess said they've eaten through the lino already.'

Suzy appeared to be speechless.

'What's his name?' Cassie asked.

Gem shot a shy look over to Suzy. 'I'd like to call him Rollo,' she said, sinking to her bed and opening her arms so that the puppy rolled gently onto the mattress, ears cocked and his tail wagging as he registered the heady scents of flat champagne, stale tortillas and hairspray in the yurt. 'He's so like Rover, don't you think? Even down to the white flash on the top of his head.'

'Don't.' The word was a warning, hard and flinty, and Cassie looked between the two women. She well remembered how much Suzy and Henry had loved the old dog. Suzy had cried every night for weeks after he'd died; she'd called him her 'first love' and had refused even to consider having another dog ever since. Cassie, herself, had loved him almost as much, and their shared exeats and holidays at West Meadows, Hattie's house in Gloucestershire, had revolved around trying to get him to roll over and walk on hind legs.

Everyone watched as Rollo scampered off the bed and onto the floor, nose sniffing madly before promptly dropping his hindquarters and peeing on one of the rugs.

Suzy gave a bitter laugh. 'You paid a damage deposit on this place, right?'

Cassie noticed, as she looked over for the first time, that Amber wasn't in bed; in fact, her bed appeared not to have been slept in.

'Hey, where's Amber?'

The others looked over at her with mild surprise.

'Don't you remember?' Gem asked.

'Remember what?'

There was a brief pause. 'She and Luke left last night.'

'What? You mean *left* left?'

'No! They went back to Snapdragons.'

'Oh, I thought you meant—'

'As if Amber can leave before the wedding! She's my bridesmaid, remember?'

'Oh yes,' Cassie faltered, her brain trying to shift into another gear. 'Why?'

'Well, she *said* she had a headache,' Gem explained, but there was a tartness to her tone now that the cuddly puppy was out of her arms.

'But . . . ?'

Gem looked over to Suzy, as if for help, but Suzy couldn't take her eyes off the puppy. He was pressing down on his forepaws, bottom in the air, his entire face stuck in a shoe as he shook it from side to side.

'Huh?' Suzy asked, realizing she was supposed to say something. 'Oh. She freaked when she saw you on Luke's shoulders.' Her eyes slid back to the dog again.

Cassie felt herself go pale at the thought of Amber 'freaking'. What did that mean? Had she thrown things, called her names? Was she going to grab her by the hair and bitch-slap her the second she walked back in the door at Butterbox? And what of Luke? If Amber had ordered him home as a result of her freak-out, was he going to come clean about their past and tell her the truth about them after all?

'Well, leaving the festival seems an overreaction, doesn't it?' Cassie asked with a forced laugh. 'He was just trying to help me see the stage.'

'Mmm, yeah, I know *technically* it was all above board, but . . .' Gem's eyes were steady upon her. 'It just didn't look good.'

There was a heavy silence, Gem's stare protracted and weighty with accusation.

Cassie was taken aback. 'Wow. So you're saying Luke and I aren't allowed to be friends?'

'No, I'm not saying that, but to be honest, I can see where Amber was coming from. There are grey areas, aren't there? Sometimes you can feel something's a bit dangerous, even if it seems perfectly innocent . . .'

Cassie stared back at her, wondering exactly how much Gem knew about her and Luke's past. Had someone told her – Suzy? Arch? Henry? – or had she guessed? Was she guessing now?

'Put it this way, I wouldn't have been pleased if I saw Laird like that with another girl, and I reckon Henry would've reacted exactly the same if he'd seen you.'

Cassie felt her hackles rise at the mention of Henry's name, at the assumption Gem knew Henry best, at the implied threat in her words. 'Well, that's because you don't know Henry the way I do,' she replied coolly.

Gem straightened her spine a little and Cassie was reminded of a snake getting ready to strike. 'I've known him all my life. He's more like a brother to me than a cousin. He tells me everything.'

'He tells you nothing,' Cassie said sharply. She had had her fill of Gem's incipient possessiveness of Henry. 'Even if he *was* your brother, which he's not, a brother's nothing to a lover. I know him intimately – his every thought, desire, dream . . . He shares them with me, not you. You're eight years younger, a hurt little girl he simply still feels protective of. He's incredibly fond of you, but you're as amusing to him as that puppy. That's it. So *I'll* tell *you* how he reacts, not the other way round, OK? Because you talk about grey areas, Gem, but you're in one yourself, right now, and I can "feel"' – she sarcastically made speech marks in the air with her fingers – 'that you're not as innocent as you're making out to be either.'

Gem looked back at her, her face impassive but her eyes stony cold and Cassie could tell she wasn't used to losing. 'Amber said—'

'Amber can say what she likes. I'm not interested. Henry would never be so petty as to be threatened by something like that, but if Amber wants to "freak" at Luke about it, well, that's her business.'

And without another word, Cassie reached down and grabbed her purple trainer from the puppy's mouth. 'And you'd better get your dog under control too.'

Cassie was lying on the sofa, one leg dangling idly over the arm, utterly determined this time to get to the end of Chapter Four, when Suzy walked in.

'Oh. Hey.' Suzy flopped heavily into one of the wing chairs that would be so *au courant* if it was covered in a jazzy tartan, but instead looked tired and dated in a mossy velveteen fabric.

'Hey. I thought everyone had gone out.'

'Me too.'

Cassie's eyes fell to the glass of wine in Suzy's hand. 'Gosh, it's a bit early, isn't it, Suze? It's not even lunchtime yet. I'm surprised you can even look at alcohol after last night.'

'I *need* this.' Suzy stared at the wine glass like it was an elixir.

Cassie recognized the tone in her voice. 'Oh God, what's she done now?' she asked with a sympathetic groan.

Suzy shot her a hateful stare, which, had it actually been intended for Cassie, would have made her turn to ash. 'She's bloody snuck in with that dog and *left* him here, with a water bowl and a cardboard box.'

'You are kidding!'

'I wish I was.' Suzy took a deep glug of the wine. 'He's in the boot room.'

'Well, take him back again.'

'Just tried that. She says it's only till Saturday, so that it's a surprise for the wedding. I mean, what's she gonna do? Have him jump out of the cake?'

Cassie tried not to laugh at the image this conjured in her mind. 'Unbelievable.'

'*Un*believable,' Suzy concurred, nodding as she stared into the wine glass again, a positively frightening look on her face.

'Where's Velvet?'

Suzy blinked herself back into the present. 'Huh? Oh, Arch has taken her for a walk along Greenaways.'

There was a pause. 'Oh. Right.'

Suzy scowled again, her mood blacker than Cassie had appreciated. 'What do you mean, "Oh. Right"?'

'Well, is it OK for him to be walking alone with Velvet? What if he . . . if something happened again?'

'I took his blood pressure this morning and it was fine. His colour's good, appetite healthy. He just wants to be treated normally again. Is that too much to ask?' Suzy snapped.

Cassie shook her head, even though she felt hurt by her friend's sharp tone. Suzy had so much on her plate – a toddler, a convalescing husband, a stressed mother, a wedding to sabotage and now a puppy to look after. Little wonder her patience and temper were stretched thin.

She stepped back onto safer ground. 'God, Gem's got such a nerve dropping Rollo on your doorstep like that,' she tutted sympathetically. 'You'd have thought she'd learned her lesson about not pushing too far this morning.'

Cassie recalled the short, tense journey back from the festival – the three of them hung-over and irritable, their bruised egos bristling against each other in Suzy's car. The glossy black Jeep hadn't been in the drive when they'd rolled past Snapdragons and Cassie had wondered whether Amber had insisted she and Luke leave immediately, after all.

Not that she asked anyone outright. She had gone straight back to bed – angry, frustrated, depressed all over again, as though the highs of the past few days had never happened – and when she awoke, it was in a marginally brighter mood, the spat with Gem merely a faint sour note in the background.

Suzy was staring at her.

'What?' Cassie asked, bringing back her thoughts.

'Nothing.'

'No, you said something. What was it?'

'I just said I thought she had a point.'

Cassie's mouth dropped open – had she misheard? – and she shuffled herself into a more upright position on her elbows. 'Sorry?'

'Gem. She had a point.'

Cassie was gobsmacked. 'Are you seriously telling me you're on her side? *You?*'

'Give me a break,' Suzy snorted.

'So then what are you getting at?'

'Just that I think you were wrong when you said Henry wouldn't have minded about you . . . wiggling about on Luke's shoulders. I think he'd have flipped, actually.'

'I wasn't wiggling! I was dancing! It was a concert! He was helping me see the stage!' Cassie protested, scarcely able to believe they were having this conversation.

'And he's your ex. Your very attractive, sexy ex whom you nearly got back together with in Paris.'

'Yes. And the pertinent point here is . . . he's my *ex*. Added to which, as you've already, so kindly pointed out, he's completely over me.'

There was a fractional pause. 'Yes, well, I've changed my mind about that.' Suzy blinked at her. 'I don't think things have finished between you after all.'

'*Seriously?* You're honestly telling me you think he and I are rekindling our lost lust because we got drunk and danced with fifty thousand other people at a concert? Jeez, give me a break!'

'There's still unfinished business there.' Suzy presented the statement as irrefutable fact. 'It isn't over.'

'Right. Yeah. I get it. Totally,' Cassie said with impressive sarcasm. 'Because I sat on his shoulders to get a better view, that means we can't keep our hands off each other. Meanwhile all the other times we've been together *without incident* don't count. And I suppose him skipping hand in hand through Rock with Amber is all a front too, is it?'

'All I know is every time I look over at him, he's looking over at you,' Suzy replied with irritating calm that only served to wind up Cassie further. 'And he looked like he'd been shot when he came in and saw you standing in that wedding dress.'

She'd seen it too, then.

'It was Amber he was looking at, actually. They're not even engaged yet, remember? What bloke wants to see his girlfriend playing the bride when he hasn't even proposed?'

'Well, I'd bet our house that until *you've* got a wedding ring on *your* finger, Amber won't be getting one on *hers*.' An anger came into Suzy's rich, dark eyes that Cassie had seen many times before – but never directed at her. 'Henry's my brother, Cass. Do you really think I'm just going to let this happen right in front of me while he's away?'

The sudden playful wind that blew over the precipice – where Cassie had felt herself balancing all day – felt chilling now, and black.

'I'm not even going to dignify that with a comment,' Cassie said angrily, picking up her book and pointedly looking at the page, 'Chapter Four' swimming before her eyes. Her heart was pumping at double time, and her hands were tingling. 'I have done *nothing* wrong.'

Silence crept like a stain between them. The air seemed solid – thick and unbreachable – changing their views of each other into something hazier and less defined. They never fought; their last fight must have been at school, it was so long ago, but there was a far more threatening undercurrent to this than whether or not Cassie had pinched Suzy's shoes or eaten the last of the bread.

Suzy got up from the chair finally. 'What kind of sister would I be—'

'What kind of friend are you *being*?' Cassie spat back.

'One who calls it as she sees it. And Gem wasn't wrong in what she said this morning.'

Cassie looked back at her, tears stinging her eyes. 'I can't believe you're on her side, after everything I've done for you.'

'This isn't about sides! It's about Henry! He deserves better than this.'

'Better than this? Or better than me?'

'That isn't what I said and you know it.'

'Do I? All I know is that I'm being punished for being precisely the person you all wanted me to be. You wanted me to be strong and independent and living life on my terms at last, but now all you and your mother and Henry go on about is setting a date and starting a family, as though the divorce and the betrayal and the lies never happened,' Cassie cried. 'Well, newsflash! They happened to me! And the hurt and shock doesn't just go away because your brother gave me a ring. It doesn't work like that. You can't use a new engagement to get over an old marriage.'

'Of course you can't, but neither can you stay in this limbo you've created for yourself. You're caught between lives, Cassie – you want to party like you're twenty-one, but frankly it's not a good look anymore. It's getting old. At some point, your life has to start moving forwards again.'

'Oh, like Gil's is doing, you mean? Five days from now and it'll be the first day of the rest of his life.' She inhaled deeply. 'Thanks for telling me, by the way.'

Suzy blinked, looking shocked. 'I . . . I was going to tell you.'

'When? When he was on honeymoon? Were you worried

I might secretly try and reignite my relationship with him too?'

'Don't be flippant, Cass.'

'Why not? Isn't it a *good look*?' Every word was dripping with a sarcasm she barely recognized herself capable of.

'I was trying to protect you . . . Who told you, anyway?'

'Kelly. Because she *is* a good friend.'

'When?'

'A couple of weeks ago.'

'So, about the same time you started freaking out on Henry, then?'

'No. Because *I'm* not the one freaking out. He is. You are.'

'You find out your ex-husband's getting remarried in the same month your fiancé pushes for commitment and your ex-lover suddenly appears out of the blue, and you're seriously trying to tell me you're not freaking out? Cass, your world's spinning so fast right now it's a wonder to me you can walk straight.'

'Ha! Pot. Kettle. Black.'

'What's that supposed to mean?'

'That you're out-of-your-tree stressed and projecting all of it onto me. That wedding's going ahead on Saturday and nothing you have done has stopped it. She's got the dress, the vicar, the church,' Cassie said, counting on her fingers.

'Yes! And you're doing the bloody catering. Between you and Henry and Arch and my mother and that bloody Germ, is it any wonder my life's a mess right now?' Suzy shouted, her voice splintering from the weight of the words. 'There. I've said it. My life's a bloody mess. *Are you satisfied?*'

Cassie swallowed, instantly stricken with remorse as she saw two swollen tears slide silently and defiantly down Suzy's reddened cheeks. Suzy never cried. She was Boudicca, her warrior friend.

Suzy brushed the tears away angrily with the backs of her hands – as though she had let herself down – turning as she got to the door. 'Well, I'll tell you this for nothing, Cassie. Maybe everything in my life is wrong at the moment, but I know as sure as an egg's an egg that I'm not wrong about you and him.' And she stormed out of the room, sucking the air out with her.

Chapter Twenty-Four

The lagoon lay slick and still, like an unblinking turquoise eye, as the sea frothed against the other side of the rocks that encircled it like a wall, the cold Atlantic Ocean several feet lower than the pool now, as the tide continued its race out towards the horizon. Their soft and pale bodies looked vulnerable against the scarred black rocks, which rose in a circle from the water, all of them leaning into the serpentine stone and trying not to scratch themselves against the thick encrustations of mussels and limpets.

Cassie and Archie were wearing their new wetsuits, but Laird and Luke were in long board shorts, and Gem and Amber were in just their string bikinis. Suzy was still on the beach with Velvet – the rocks being too perilous for the little girl to navigate – and all their bags.

Cassie wished she had stayed with her, even though they hadn't spoken now for three whole days, Suzy pointedly leaving the room every time Cassie entered it. But as much as Suzy's silence was terrifying, Cassie would still rather brave that than this. The sight of the azure water – from twenty feet up – was beautiful; the cold crush of wet sand beneath her feet would be so much more soothing than the scaly damp stone, and rips of terror leaped through her every time her toes lost purchase on the sheer rocks.

But she couldn't leave. It had taken her twenty minutes to get up here and the only way back down was through the air. This was the bridge Henry had specified on the list – the bridge (it turned out) being a narrow strip of rock that formed the upper arc of a vast, hollowed-out cliff on one side of the lagoon – and she had to jump from it, or, as Laird had said, 'tombstone'. Obviously that did not sound good, and although he said it with his signature laid-back smile, Cassie couldn't help but wonder whether Gem had relayed to him her 'strong' words on Sunday.

Even if she hadn't, he surely couldn't have failed to register the tension simmering between all the women: in addition to ignoring Cassie, Suzy – for reasons unknown – was barely able to adopt a civil tone with Gem; Gem kept shooting Cassie death-stares, and Amber had yet to look at Cassie at all. When Cassie had asked whether she'd like a coffee at the cafe earlier, as they'd sat on the grass and waited for the tide to fully recede and expose the beach in the cove below, Amber had studied her nails and muttered that she'd 'rather die'. Luke had overheard – she could tell by the way his head had angled back slightly, towards them – but he had neither said a word nor looked at her – in fact, this was the first time she had even caught sight of them since the ill-fated weekend – and she wondered how many different ways Amber was making him pay for his so-called treachery.

'How are you feeling?' Archie called up and across to her. Bless him, he appeared to be as oblivious as ever to the bitter politics that were on the verge of erupting in the uneasy group. It had been at his insistence – after examining the best combinations of tide times, wave height and weather forecasts – that they had all travelled down to the

Lizard peninsula today to watch Cassie enact the last remaining order on the list before they entered the count-down to the wedding and – to quote Arch – 'things would get stressy'.

'How do you think I'm feeling?' she shouted back. 'I'm going to bloody kill him!'

Archie laughed. 'Don't blame you! I wouldn't want to be where you're standing! I think I can feel another heart attack coming on just looking at you.'

'Me too!'

'You must be at least forty feet up!' he hollered.

'Stop talking now, Arch!'

'Are you going to jump?'

'No! But I will start throwing rocks at you if you don't shut up!'

She looked down into the water. Laird had estimated the depth at around eighteen feet, and it was so clear that even from this height, she could make out bright orange spider crabs, the size of dinner plates, scuttling across the sandy floor.

Everyone had agreed she had to go into the pool first, not only because it was her list and her challenge, but also it was more important to keep the water clear given the height she was jumping from. There was only one sub-merged rock in the water, to the right of where she stood, but as long as she jumped outwards, she would clear it easily. Nonetheless, Laird had solemnly agreed with Archie that the sand shouldn't be eddied about, with the net result that the five increasingly hot and bored faces, twenty feet below her – and they were still twenty feet above the water themselves – were turned towards her, waiting for her to find the courage to jump.

Behind them all, from her superior vantage point, Cassie could see Suzy and Velvet running in and out of the shallows, hand in hand. Unlike the way the sea slammed onto the abrupt rocks of the lagoon, the water was lapping gently onto the beach, and she watched as Suzy lifted Velvet, swinging her into the air – the toddler's legs flying out behind her, her face tilted to the sun – before gathering her close and nuzzling her neck, the little girl wriggling with laughter. Her best friend and her god-daughter, two of the people she loved most in the world and who would become family, if she could just find the courage to make that leap too. But the question of what would happen to them all if she didn't – couldn't – hung over her like a threat. Already they were fracturing under the strain. She and Suzy were estranged because the words 'I do' sank like concrete blocks in the pit of her stomach.

It was a moment before Cassie realized a tear was slinking down her cheek, unseen, unbidden, and she felt a sudden rush of white-hot fury at herself course through her veins. Why couldn't she do it? Gil could. In three days' time, he was drawing a line under their life and history together that even the divorce hadn't been able to achieve. It was one thing to end a marriage, quite another to embark on an entirely new one. Why couldn't she just put her foot forward and take that next step too? It wasn't that she wanted Gil back – he was nothing compared to Henry –and it wasn't that she didn't love Henry enough. She just didn't want to feel . . . trapped or owned again. She didn't want to relinquish her freedom.

'You can do it, Cass!' Luke called up, breaking her trance. 'Don't over-think it. Trust your instincts.'

Amber's glossy head jerked up – at the easy (and revealing) way he'd called her Cass? – and Cassie saw Gem gently place a sympathetic hand on her arm. Her gaze fluttered back to Suzy and Velvet momentarily – had she ever been more isolated? – and it hit her for the first time that maybe the freedom she craved wouldn't take the sexy, selfish, indulgent shape she expected were she to hold on to it. She would lose Suzy, Arch and Velvet for sure if she lost Henry – they came as a package; they were already family. First dibs. She would be free, but she would also be alone.

Adrenalin spiked in her bloodstream, a tingling rush flaring through her limbs as she looked down to the cool, still pool. Henry had tricked her – there was no other way down from this ledge – and she knew exactly what he was trying to teach her: she had to jump. She had to face her fear and ball it up and step into the unknown anyway.

She put her hands on the rock behind her and pushed her bottom away so that only her feet and hands kept contact with the cliff face. She just had to trust in herself, her own ability. She could do this. She looked to the horizon and inhaled, ready—

'Fuck it!'

The girl's voice and then a sudden splash made Cassie look down; a vortex of white water had opened up in the middle, the crabs lost from sight, the sand, the rock . . . But she couldn't see what or who was in the water. There was no time. The abrupt movement was all it had taken to unbalance her from the shallow lip and she slipped, the rough surface grazing her skin like a cheese grater on silk as she began to fall through space, her arms and legs flailing wildly as she screamed.

Time warped, splitting and stretching, as the blueness rushed at her and, beneath it, the rock.

'No! Cass!'

The first touch was like stone, her skin burning up as the tense water held, just for a fraction of a moment, before it splintered beneath her weight, unyielding and unforgiving as she hit it side-on and went in. Almost immediately she heard two explosions above her, but she couldn't see past the bubbles; there was no colour down here, no light, just the breathtaking shock of the cold, the fire of her skin, pressure screaming in her ears as water filled her nose and mouth – there had been no time to catch her breath or to take one, no time to push away or jump out, and her airless body plummeted down through the water, straight towards the rock . . .

Her arm . . . Something had her arm, jerking her away in a violent whiplash motion, away from the rock and back into blue space. She felt skin on her skin, hands on her arms, and in the next instant she broke through the surface, coughing and spluttering, gasping for breath, barely aware that she was being held up, powerful legs that weren't hers propelling her through the water back to the rocks.

The water peeled from her face as her body was slipped through its silky embrace – smooth and acquiescent now – droplets in her eyes fracturing the vista into split screens as the rock wall drew closer. She could see everyone screaming, but she couldn't hear them. Laird and Luke were in the water beside her, manoeuvring her onto a shallow shelf; Amber, she saw, was clinging to a half-exposed rock on the other side of the pool, her hair wet, dark and slicked back like a kelpie, terror in her eyes as she watched the drama.

'Are you OK? Are you all right?' Luke was asking her. 'Cassie!'

'She's in shock, mate. We need to get her out of—'

'No. I'm OK,' she protested as the wracking coughs subsided, her eyes falling to Archie. He was pale, halfway down already from his previous perch, leaning as far as he dared from the rocks to see her, desperate to just jump in – like the others must have done, she realized – but his older, weakened body warning otherwise.

'Cass, did you hit the rock?' Luke was asking, urgency in his eyes, his eyes roaming her face, looking for signs of injury.

She frowned. It was so hard to know what exactly had happened, to break it down from sensory experience to factual recollection. She had slipped and fallen . . . Her eyes travelled back up to the bridge. She had fallen all that way? She shook her head. 'Something knocked me out of the way, I think.'

Luke grabbed Laird by the shoulder and squeezed him hard.

Laird shrugged. 'Surfers and rocks – you learn to act fast, mate. It was lucky this pool's still. It would have been almost impossible to grab her in the surf.'

Luke looked back at her. 'So then you're not hurt?'

'Well, I didn't say that,' she groaned. 'My skin hurts like *hell*. I feel like I've been whipped and then pickled.'

Laird grimaced. 'Yeah. You may bruise – you went in badly, although thank God you've got your wetsuit on. That'll have saved you some bruises for sure.'

'But you've not got any numbness, any—'

'Luke, I'm OK.'

'Really?'

She managed a faint smile. 'You're worse than my mother.'

'Listen, *you* didn't just have to see that. I don't think I'll ever sleep again.'

'I'll second that. It was way worse for us,' Archie said, reaching them all finally and grabbing her hand to kiss it fiercely. 'I thought I was going to have to tell Henry you were now an omelette.'

Cassie laughed, a growing sense of euphoria beginning to rush through her as her nerves caught up with her body and realized the danger had passed. She was actually OK. She had fallen forty feet onto water that had felt like concrete and she had survived. She wasn't going to do it again anytime soon, of course – like, in this lifetime – but she had done it. One more thing to tick off the list. OK, so strictly speaking she hadn't jumped off the bridge – she hadn't *made that leap* that Henry had wanted her to make; she had slipped and fallen in . . . But it would still count, right?

'Well, now this is more like it,' Archie murmured as he lay on his stomach, his hands resting below his cheeks and his eyes firmly closed.

'Mmm, I think we're belly-boarders at heart, Arch,' Cassie replied in the tone of voice more usually reserved for one of Bas's iconic Indian head massages, as the heavy swell of the ocean intermittently rolled beneath their boards, leaving the two of them drowsy with inertia. 'I'm exhausted. I want to go to sleep.'

'You always want to go to sleep,' he mumbled, just as sleepily.

Somewhere behind them – in the thick of the action – Laird was catching the waves that they were supposed to be netting, but after half an hour of failed pops, Archie had dubiously and ominously pleaded 'a strange feeling' in his chest, and no one was pushing Cassie into anything after her fall earlier.

They were back at Polzeath for a 'sunset surf', as Laird had put it. In all honesty, Cassie had had more than enough of the beach for one day but she desperately didn't want to go back to the house. Suzy still hadn't really spoken to her, even after she'd heard the horror of Cassie's 'tombstone' attempt becoming all too literal – the most basic, mumbled platitudes without any eye contact didn't count – and Amber's apology for jumping the starter's gun had been as truculent and insincere as a grounded teenager's.

Cassie allowed her eyes to close. She was beginning to ache all over from the fall and it had been a long afternoon. The adrenalin buzz that had buoyed her in the moments afterwards had ebbed away to leave an antsy and fragile shock. They had travelled for almost two hours to get to the cove and she hadn't wanted everyone to have to get straight back into the cars on her account, so she had sat quietly on the sand, applying a wet towel as a cold compress to her red and bruised skin as everyone began playing hide-and-seek in the labyrinthine tunnels that meandered through the double-sided headland to both beaches. They weren't anywhere deep enough to have been useful to smugglers in times past – the fact that they were completely submerged during high tide also rendered them useless – but what started as a game for Velvet had soon morphed into an adults' version, as Gem and Amber – quickly forgiven, it seemed; certainly more quickly than Cassie had been for-given for her 'lapse in judgement' – dodged in and out, wild-eyed and as frisky as ponies, with Laird and Luke in hot pursuit, the girls' squeals and giggles of delight as they were invariably caught echoing back to the beach.

Cassie had pretended she hadn't noticed that she was the odd one out – the gooseberry – choosing instead to go off for a solitary walk on the outer headland, a large, grassy outcrop that became an island at high tide. And when she came across Amber and Luke kissing in a remote nook, she silently turned and pretended she hadn't noticed that either.

Her life seemed to have become a hologram of itself, she thought, as she and Arch bobbed in easy silence; it felt flat and spectral, everything in it that she'd always felt so certain of – her foreverness with Henry, her sisterly tie to Suzy, her contempt for Luke – now suddenly unpinned and unanchored, ready to drift away from her.

'You'll have to be careful how you tell Henry you fell from the bridge. He's going to be wracked with guilt,' Archie mumbled, sounding half asleep. Cassie had visions of both of them drifting out to sea like toddlers on lilos and having to be rescued by the RNLI.

'Why?' Cassie asked, lazily opening one eye like a dozing cat. 'It's not like he pushed me.'

'No, but he'll hold himself responsible for making you do it.'

It wasn't guilt Cassie knew he was going to feel; it was disappointment. 'He didn't march me up there at gunpoint either.'

'True.' There was a small pause. 'Maybe I should march Suze up there with a gun and make her tell me what's going on with you two.'

Now both eyes were open. 'What do you mean?'

'Oh, not you too,' he groaned. 'Don't deny it – spare me that. It's so obvious you've had a fight – even *I* can tell it, and we all know I've got the emotional intelligence of a jellyfish. Not to mention the muscle tone.'

Cassie laughed at the unexpected joke and he winked.

'Come on, spill. I heard her crying in the bathroom earlier and she tried pretending it was the Epsom salts. And you and I both know my wife only ever cries when we're out of cava.'

'Is this why you dragged me out here?' she moaned, as a particularly large swell rose beneath them like a sea monster rising from the depths. 'You want to be our mediator.'

'More of a hostage negotiator. I'm not letting you back on dry land till you meet my demands.'

She chuckled. 'I see.' Cassie was quiet for a long moment. How did she tell Archie – not just Suzy's husband but Henry's best friend – about Amber and Gem and Suzy's baseless suspicions? He hadn't been at the festival – he hadn't seen how innocent it all was, but maybe he'd think there was no smoke without fire?

She decided to go for the catch-all explanation. 'It's just everything getting on top of her, that's all – she's really worried about Hats—'

Archie shot her a stern look.

'Fine,' Cassie sighed. 'Gem and I had a little contretemps in the yurt yesterday morning and Suzy decided that, for the first time in her life, she was on her cousin's side. Her cousin whom she cannot bear and also is not now talking to, in case you hadn't noticed.'

'Her side? What are we, eight?' he asked wryly.

'If we have to be,' she riposted, knowing she sounded childish. 'Aren't you going to ask me why she's not talking to Gem?'

'OK. Why isn't she talking to Gem?'

'I don't know. I was hoping you could tell me that.'

Archie groaned. 'Well, I know she's livid about having to hide the puppy from Laird until Saturday. It's given her loads more work to do, as if she wasn't already busy enough with me, Velvet and her mother. Of course! Throw a puppy into the mix! Did you hear it crying last night?'

Cassie shook her head.

'No. Me neither. But she did. Was up three times in the night, and then of course Velvet woke up early for once.' He groaned. 'Oh Christ, I don't know. This is all way above my pay scale. No wonder men talk sport.'

They were quiet for a moment.

'Tell me what you think of Laird,' she said. 'You've spent more time with him than me or Suze.'

'I think he's a decent bloke – obviously batty about Gem, down to earth, sporty, good with his hands. And Luke too. I'm really enjoying his company, I have to say. We've been spending a lot of time together. His job's so fascinating. Absolutely fascinating.'

Cassie felt sick at the words. When he found out who Luke really was – or rather, had been – and surely he inevitably would, he'd feel utterly traitorous for having befriended Henry's nemesis. She knew she ought to tell him, that now was the time, but the words wouldn't come. She still didn't want to consider the possibility of Henry knowing Luke had been here and the suspicions that would arouse.

'So you don't think it's dodgy that he wants to settle down so young? Hats and Suze are convinced he's after Gem's money.'

Arch shrugged. 'He's an orphan too. I reckon things are

different when it's just you against the world. You'd want to start building your tribe sooner rather than later.'

'Do you know what happened to his folks?'

He shrugged again. 'I didn't like to ask. But it explains a lot, don't you think?'

'Yeah, maybe.' She pulled her hands out of the water, shaking them dry and resting them under her cheek like Archie.

'My darling wife and her mother are making their lives far more stressful than they need to, by fretting about this wedding; it's not like we don't have enough going on at the moment, what with me trying not to die.'

'Oi. Enough of that talk, mister.'

Archie winked at her again. 'Gem's nearly twenty-one: she can make her own decisions. Frankly she *should* make her own decisions. What's the worst that can happen? They divorce.' He gave a lackadaisical shrug.

'Arch, you say that like it's no big deal, but I've got the T-shirt, remember? It's pretty bloody bad. I feel like I've had to grow a new skin, a new heart, getting over it.'

Arch reached over and patted her hand.

She tried to go back to the point. This was about Gem, not her. 'Plus, when they divorce, he takes half her fortune – *that's* the problem Hats and Suze are worried about. Gem's robust – she'll bounce back; but that inheritance is her parents' legacy.'

'Laird's not materially minded. Look at him back there. He's all about the spirit, catching the perfect wave.'

'Even more reason, then, why he'd be up for a quarter-share in Butterbox and Snapdragons. This is one of the top ten surfing beaches in the world.'

Archie pulled a shocked face. 'So sceptical, Miss Fraser! I never knew you had it in you.'

'That's the thing about divorce, Arch,' she muttered, closing her eyes again. 'By the time you come out the other end, you automatically see the worst in everybody and don't trust anybody.'

'Not even yourself?'

'Myself least of all. No one ever said survival was pretty.'

There was a small pause. 'Henry's not Gil. He would never—'

'I know.' Dammit. They were back to her, again.

'But . . . ?' Archie asked, opening both eyes to look at her.

She looked back at him. 'But every time I think of becoming a Mrs again – a *wife* – I feel trapped and power-less, like I'm putting my entire life in his hands. I know Henry would never abuse my trust, but then I never thought Gil would either. It's not as simple as just putting another ring on my finger. I have to give up my name, change my passport, my driving licence, my bank details . . . Everything that says I'm *me*. Nothing changes for you. You lot don't even have to wear a ring if you don't want to. It's the girls who do all the giving up, renouncing their own identity, not the men.'

Archie's face fell. 'Christ, when you put it like that . . . I feel bloody awful now to have asked Suzy to be my wife.'

Cassie laughed, splashing him with water. 'Stop it. You know what I'm saying. When you get married for the first time, you place hope over experience. It's different second time around. And none of these feelings are about doubt-ing Henry – it's not personal or about him. They're just the scars of divorce.'

'Once bitten, twice shy, huh?'

It wasn't the first time she'd been told that. She stared at him. 'Surely you can talk to him for me, when he gets back? Try and get my point across? Whenever I try, he takes it as a rejection of him, and it's not. And then we fight.'

'Hang on a minute, I'm supposed to be negotiating between you and Suze, not you and Henry.'

'I'll pay you a commission.' She pulled a face. 'I seem to be at war with everyone at the moment. Can't do right for doing wrong.'

'It'll all make sense with hindsight. That's what I always tell myself when I'm on a balls-up bender of my own.'

'Yo!' They both lifted their heads to find Laird paddling towards them, a grin on his face. 'Look who's come to join us for a few rides before sundown.'

They glanced behind to see a dark head, powerful shoulders and arms, paddling fast in their direction, wetsuit still rolled down.

Cassie felt her heart drop. Oh great, what was *he* doing out here? One of the reasons she'd come out in the first place was to avoid having to see him, along with the others, at the house.

'Luke, old boy,' Archie said happily, struggling to sit up, wincing as the cold seawater slapped around him from the movement.

'Hey,' she nodded quietly, sitting up too as he approached. She watched as he pushed up into a sitting position, legs astride the board, his eyes dancing with the same delight as Laird's.

'It was too good an evening to pass up,' Luke grinned, bumping boards with Archie in greeting and noticing his bone-dry hair. 'Caught any good waves so far?'

'Well, *I've* been ripping it up, but these two have been holding a mothers' meeting,' Laird laughed. 'I thought they were going to whip out a flask and start serving up coffees at one point.'

'I'll have you know we've been putting the world to rights over here. Poor Cass has got a lot on her plate at the moment. Falling off the bridge this morning was the least of her worries.' Archie gave her a comradely wink.

'Oh yeah?' Luke said, jamming his arms into the sleeves of his wetsuit and rolling it over his shoulders. 'Like what, Cass? I thought your life was pretty perfect.'

Cassie stared at him. Like he didn't know! It was his fault that she'd fallen out with Amber, Gem *and* Suzy! She'd told him she didn't want all those beers; she'd told him she didn't want to get on his shoulders, and look at the result! He hadn't even been allowed to talk to her since the concert. How could he pretend nothing was wrong, for either one of them?

'Arch is telling porkies. We were actually discussing whether he should go ahead with the operation for his ingrowing toenails.'

'Eww!' Laird laughed as Archie gasped in indignation.

'Suzy would never stand for my toenails getting that long.'

'Your wife clips your toenails, mate?' Laird asked, slapping his board with hilarity. 'Oh, dude, that's even worse!'

Cassie chuckled – glad she'd moved the conversation on – but she was aware of Luke's stillness amid their silliness, his eyes upon her, just like Suzy had said.

'Well, whatever you've got going on, it's time to ride,' Luke said after a moment, reaching his arms up behind his head and tugging the tape on the back zip. 'These waves are perfect for you. I learned on surf like this.'

Archie wrinkled his nose. Apart from his legs dangling in the water, he had dried off. 'To be honest, I think I'll just—'

'Uh-uh-uh. There's only one way back in, mate,' Laird said, slapping one hand onto Archie's shoulder. 'And that's standing up. Come on, you've done it once before. I'll lead you in.'

'Cassie? Want me to guide you?' Luke asked her, running his finger inside the neckline of his wetsuit, adjusting it fractionally.

'It's all right,' she demurred. 'I can't stand up. I'll just belly-board in.'

He looked at her in surprise. 'That's it? You're just going to give up? I never thought of you as a quitter.'

'Listen, I've spent over a week trying to get up on this thing. No one can say I haven't tried.' Frustration tinted her voice.

'Then we'll do it together. Surfing's all about knowing when to make your move. You can't go for just any wave. We'll line up just after the break there and when I say go, you pop, OK?'

She shrugged with a teenager's carelessness, wondering what the fallout would be when it got back to the girls that the two of them had been surfing together too. Archie might have to become her character witness. 'Fine, but Laird said exactly the same thing and I know it's not as easy as you make it sound.'

'We'll see you back on shore, chaps,' Archie said as Laird began paddling away.

Luke nodded, watching them go before turning back to her. 'You OK?' he asked in a different tone of voice – concerned, intimate.

'Why wouldn't I be?'

'I mean everything that's been going on with Amber and the girls. It seems like you're having a tough time.'

Cassie immediately looked away, taken aback by his kindness, a wall of blocked emotion rearing up inside her and taking her completely unawares. Why was she upset? She didn't understand . . .

'Amber feels so bad about earlier. I mean, really, really bad. She was in a bit of a state when we got back to the house, to be honest.'

Cassie shrugged. Amber hadn't looked in much of a 'state' in that hidden nook at the far end of the beach when she'd stumbled across them kissing earlier, but she wasn't prepared to go over it with him.

She looked down, noticing that her hands were beginning to tremble. She'd been in the water for too long. That, probably, and the shock . . .

'We should go,' she said.

He reached out to stop her board. 'Wait. Look . . . I just wanted to explain why I've, you know . . . disappeared. It's not your fault, but if I so much as look at you, she freaks out.'

Her *and* Suzy, it seemed. 'Whatever. I don't care.' She raked one hand hard through her hair, refusing to look at him. He appeared to have gone very still. 'I take it she knows now? About us?'

He hesitated, before nodding. 'I had to tell her.'

'I don't know why it had to be a secret in the first place.

I sincerely doubt I'm the first of your exes she's come across.'

'No. But you were the only one who mattered.'

She looked across at him, taken aback by the tone in his voice, the look in his eyes. She could feel the nearness of his leg in the water beside hers – the displaced water pushing against her skin as their boards bumped and nudged each other in the swell. 'We need to go,' she said, quickly lowering herself onto the board.

'Cass—'

'The others will be waiting.' She began paddling inshore.

Luke caught her in two strokes, but he didn't try to stop her; instead, they cut through the water, side by side, in silence, positioning themselves six feet short of the break, alongside the line of other surfers, all sitting on their boards, waiting.

They bobbed on the surface, the moment that had just eluded them darting around them like a shadow in the depths, but keeping a safer distance.

'OK. Two back,' Luke murmured after a while. 'See it?'

'Yes.' Nerves fluttered inside her.

'When I say, start to paddle. And you pop on my command, OK? No hesitation.'

She gave a small, dry laugh. 'Pop on my command . . .' It sounded funny, but he wasn't laughing; he wasn't even smiling. His eyes were on the wave that was heading straight for them – unbroken, its power still hidden below the surface, its twin threat and promise still just a suggestion from here.

She stared at his profile, outlined against the deep pink sky – so handsome, so unsettling, so familiar. She had traced it a long time ago with her fingers, her tongue . . .

Her stomach twisted. They didn't have to ride this wave that was heading straight for them. They could let it just slip past, flow beneath them, ignored, and their heads would stay above water. They could drift over it as if it had never been there at all. But—

'Paddle.'

Her arms began to move, slicing the water in powerful arcs, and he was alongside her, the wave only feet away now. She could hear it gather and build below her like a storm, the rolling concentration of energy still pent up and leashed.

'Now!'

It seemed too early to her, but there wasn't time to think or argue. Instinct took over. She could feel the sheer force of the wave immediately lift her up, her board only just ahead of the froth as it began to crest and break, and her feet made contact with the waxed surface. Every muscle in her core was tensed, her body hard and concentrated on this one moment as she felt the momentum begin to carry her and take over, doing the work for her. Her arms spread wide, her legs bent but steady as the wave toppled in on itself, her board nosing just ahead, riding its energy effortlessly.

'Woohooooo!'

The jubilant scream wasn't hers – she couldn't see whose; her focus was resolutely on the water just ahead of her – but she claimed it as her own anyway, the same rush of exhilaration gathering in her as she somehow stayed up, her body instinctively finding balance in small twists left and right – not dramatic, nothing as impressive as the swooping turns of the pros, but enough to keep her upright, to keep her going.

A delighted laugh escaped her. She was doing it! She was actually surfing!

'Oh my God!' she screamed, her eyes wide with amazement and joy as she suddenly 'got' it. This was the rush everyone talked about it, the almost-spiritual transcendence that came from harnessing nature and riding its rhythm. How could she have come this far in her life and never experienced it? How could she have deprived herself of knowing this? It was the ultimate freedom . . .

Wait, no . . . Too soon, the wave began to die, sinking down into itself like a collapsed soufflé, and the board began gently submerging as the energy it needed ran out, until she was neck deep in water again and her feet touched the sand.

No! She wanted more! Longer, faster, higher . . . She wanted to do it all over again. One hit and already she was hooked.

Luke sliced to a dramatic stop beside her, a giant rainbow of droplets showering outwards like fireworks in the sky. His overwhelmed expression matched hers as he gathered her in a tight hug.

'I did it!' she laughed incredulously, as she pulled back, her mouth open as wide as her eyes. 'I actually did it!'

'You did it, Cass,' he laughed, his eyes dancing with happiness.

'Well, strictly speaking, *we* did it,' she laughed, aware of the role he'd played in her success, aware suddenly she was still in his arms. 'I needed your prompt to get it right.'

His expression changed. 'We did it, then,' he echoed, his voice so low she could feel the bass rumble from his chest against hers, his eyes on her lips, droplets falling from his face onto her cheeks.

He looked back at her and her smile faded as she realized she was trembling – but not because of the cold. She saw the truth in his eyes, heard the echo of Suzy's words – *'It isn't over . . .'* – and she knew the wave had broken over them at last.

Chapter Twenty-Five

'Come and get it!' Archie called, almost entirely enveloped in smoke as the wind changed direction yet again and the smell of burnt sausages drifted over to the cows.

Cassie, who was lying upstairs in the bath, winced at the prospect of having to go out there. Yet again, she'd been hiding away, escaping to her room the moment she'd got back and pleading chills from the sea. But she couldn't stay in here forever, appealing though it was.

The others were already on the terrace by the time she appeared fifteen minutes later, her hair towel-dried and wearing her favourite tracksuit bottoms.

It was almost ten o'clock and the temperature had dropped sharply, although a large fire pit was saving them from the worst of the night coolness for now and throwing a flattering, flickering light over everyone's beach-tight skin. Cassie automatically stood in front of it, holding her hands up to be warmed.

'Not still cold, are you? Here, I had to save you one,' Archie said, handing her a hot dog with a wink. 'Bunch of gannets, the lot of them. Even I can't eat that quickly.'

'Hey, some of us have earned this meal. We worked up an appetite,' Laird protested, taking a huge bite of his own hot dog, a bottle of beer in his other hand. 'Isn't that right, Luke?'

Luke, who was standing on the other side of the vast fire pit, staring outright at her as flames leaped between them, nodded. 'Yeah.'

She looked away quickly. She had heard his voice outside her window as he chatted to the guys – coming over early to help – for well over an hour and she knew he'd been waiting for her to show. She knew that, now, with absolute certainty.

'Where's Suzy?' she asked, taking a bite of the hot dog, ketchup splattering over her white T-shirt. 'Oh great, first bite,' she muttered, as Archie laughingly ran over with a tea towel and began dabbing at her chest, something Cassie had seen him do endless times with Velvet.

Archie suddenly realized the inappropriateness of what he was doing and straightened up. 'You'd better do it,' he said, holding out the towel.

She laughed and took over the job; Archie wouldn't make a move on her if his life depended upon it.

'Suzy's setting up the monitor,' Luke offered, watching the skit with reserved cool.

'Oh right. What's the film? Did we decide?' She directed the question to her chest, keeping her eyes well away from his. The moment in the sea earlier – fleeting though it was – had been like a scald and she knew she had to keep her distance now. They couldn't be friends. It was a lie, a charade. She had been so naive to suppose it could ever have been different between them. Something – a spark, an ember – was still alight between them and they couldn't give it oxygen.

'Well, *we* had to decide without you, given that you were

in the bath for two hours – using up all the hot water,' Archie admonished.

'You said not to hurry, that dinner was going to be late tonight!' she protested. 'If it's not dark till ten, there's no point in me hanging around and getting in the way from eight o'clock, is there?'

'Yeah, but leaving it to ten to ten?' Archie raised his eyebrows and she knew he knew perfectly well that she was avoiding Suzy. 'Anyway, we're watching *It's a Wonderful Life.'*

'Oh, *what?'* Cassie's shoulders sagged. 'Arch, you've made me watch that film every year for, like, fifteen years! I know it backwards.'

'Well, we may end up watching it backwards if Suzy can't remember which way to put on the reels,' Archie guffawed.

'I've never seen the film, actually,' Luke said, swigging from his beer. 'It's one of those classics I've never got round to watching.'

'Oh, you'll never forget this experience, let me tell you,' Archie said proudly. 'Our garden film nights really are something else.'

'I'll bet.'

Cassie, feeling a tap on her elbow, turned.

'Hi.' Gem was standing behind her, an apologetic smile on her face.

'Hi.' Cassie's eyes flitted over to Amber, who was on one of the sunloungers and studying the most recent issue of *Brides* magazine by firelight with a studious fervour better suited to *The Odyssey.*

A pause.

'So, I just wanted to clear the air about yesterday,' Gem

started. 'I was being overprotective; you were hung-over . . .'

Cassie frowned. If this was supposed to be passing for an apology . . .

Gem gave her a sudden dazzling smile, arms out-stretched. 'Friends again? Henry would hate it if he knew his two favourite girls were fighting, and I don't want any-thing to blot my happiness right now. It's just three days till the wedding and it means so much to me to have you at the very centre of it.'

Cassie didn't think providing the food really counted as being at the centre of it, but there was no time to debate the issue – Gem had already thrown her arms around her, pin-ning Cassie's arms to her sides so that her right arm was bent at an awkward angle as she tried to keep her hot dog away from Gem's pretty grey cotton jumpsuit. Gem pulled away again as Cassie straightened up with a tight smile. The word 'sorry' hadn't actually made an entrance, but that was being picky, right? The girl was getting married in three days. She was allowed to be unreasonable, unlike-able. Hysterical, even.

She realized Gem was holding something out to her. 'What's that?'

'The menus for Saturday. They're just ideas, you know. Obviously you know best, so if something doesn't work or . . . I don't know, isn't in season . . .'

Cassie felt a nibble of panic in her stomach. She had assumed (and rather hoped) that their falling-out yesterday had meant she was 'off the job', particularly when that argu-ment had been almost immediately superseded by her and Suzy's more serious fight, and she hadn't given Gem – or her food – any more thought.

She supposed it wasn't like they were talking big numbers, just the seven of them here, plus Hats and her plus-one (which Gem had taken as a sign that she was 'coming round' to the idea), and potentially Laird's brother and his wife, who were, according to Archie earlier, going to try for a standby flight from Melbourne.

'Anyway, have a look through and give me your thoughts. We don't want anything fancy. You know what we're about – the day is just a modest celebration of our love, shared with the people we love most.' She squeezed Cassie's arm for a moment, holding her gaze with a disingenuous smile, before turning and walking back to Amber, who immediately muttered something under her breath that Cassie couldn't hear.

Cassie – holding the entire hot dog in her mouth for a moment as she freed up a hand to unfurl the sheet of paper – looked down: bitter melon; barberries, wakame, kohlrabi . . . Cassie's jaw dropped open. *Modest?* It made Yotam Ottolenghi look like a fussy eater. Half this stuff was so rare she'd only be able to source it in London, and the other half was either out of season or so time-intensive she'd need a team of chefs to have started prepping for her three days ago. She glanced at Gem, wondering whether this was, in fact, a form of revenge. At best, she had to be joking.

Archie's name was barked from a short distance away and he stepped back, peering over to the far side of the house. Cassie noticed for the first time that the three saggy sitting-room sofas had been carried out onto the lawn and arranged in a vague U-shape facing the large gable end.

'I think we're probably good to go,' Archie said, pleased. 'Come on, chaps, grab a pew.'

Gem and Amber jumped up from the sunloungers,

bridal magazines scattered on the ground around them and an empty bottle of prosecco lying on its side, as they raced each other to 'bags' the best seats.

'Don't you want to put a cardy on, Amber?' Archie called with a worried tone as she ran past in a slip of lilac silk. 'You'll catch your death in that skimpy top . . . dress thingy.'

'It's a kaftan, Arch,' Amber purred, stopping dead in her tracks as she got to Luke and threading her arm round his hips, deciding Gem could win. 'And anyway, it's all sorted. Plus, I've got my man to keep me warm.'

Cassie kept her eyes dead ahead, still eating her hot dog, as they all walked over to the sofas. Gem had already bagged the large, central four-seater sofa for her and Laird (nabbing the best view, no doubt), Amber took the three-person one on the far side for her and Luke, leaving the nearest one for Cassie, Suzy and Arch, the biggest-bottomed bunch of the group.

Archie stared down at the two-seater dubiously.

'Here, Cass, you sit beside Su—'

'No, I'll grab a blanket and sit on the ground. You shouldn't be on the damp grass, Arch.'

'No.'

'Uh-uh! I mean it,' she said firmly as he automatically protested. 'You two are really noisy snoggers anyway. I wouldn't hear a thing sitting beside you both.'

Laird and Archie laughed loudly and Cassie grabbed one of the itchy tartan blankets that hung across the back of the sofas, wrapping it loosely round her shoulders so that its length fell to just below her hips. Suzy, who had been in the house, came back with a faded beanbag from the playroom that was leaking tiny Styrofoam balls all over the grass.

'I got thi— Oh.' She stopped short as she saw Cassie sitting cross-legged on the blanket. 'I was going to sit there. I've got to work the reel anyway.'

'I told Cass I'd sit there,' Archie said, 'but she was having none of it. She thinks the damp grass will try to kill me.' He considered for a moment. 'God, it would be embarrassing, though, if it did.'

'Well, if you want this . . .' Suzy muttered, dropping the beanbag beside her on the rug, without making eye contact once again.

'Thanks,' Cassie mumbled back, shifting herself onto the beanbag. The grass was already dewy, and the film was long.

'Yes, but now I can't see,' Archie complained. 'Your head is blocking my view.'

'Urgh! The screen is a thirty-foot-wall Arch!' Cassie grumbled, getting up and dragging the beanbag over to the far side of the sofa. 'There.'

'Thanks,' he winked, as Suzy draped a blanket over his lap. 'Tch, I'm not eighty,' he protested to her under his breath.

'Shut up,' Suzy hissed back, draping one over his shoulders too, before bending down to a piece of 1930s equipment by her feet. 'Everybody ready? All got a drink and been to the loo?'

'Would you listen to yourself?' Archie asked her, as Gem giggled, looking like a loved-up teenager, her legs on Laird's lap, one of the tatty blankets draped over the two of them too.

'God, I'm f-freezing,' Gem said, inching closer to Laird.

'Why didn't you come and stand by the fire pit, you daft girl? You'd have been warm as—' He stopped. 'Oh.'

Tenderly, he kissed the top of her bumpily cornrowed head.

Cassie wondered what he'd meant but was distracted by the sight – and sound – of Amber ceremonially tucking a voluminous orange blanket with giant 'H' motifs around them both. Not for her an itchy wool car rug, and she made a point of purring as she snuggled down into what was no doubt an acre of cashmere.

Suzy sighed and pressed down on one of the push buttons that was more like a piano key. Instantly, a whirring sound started up, a dazzling bright light igniting on the large expanse of wall and then, suddenly, shapes formed as the opening credits came up.

Gem aaahed happily, dropping her head on the cushions. She looked almost harmless, Cassie thought, watching her from her position on the outer flanks as she blankly chewed on the sausage that was so chargrilled it was like eating coal. Did she have any idea of the chaos that trailed in her wake? Did she know the stress she was causing everyone around her?

She tried to get comfortable in the saggy beanbag, finding the best position was to sit upright, her elbows perched on her bent knees as she watched Jimmy Stewart bowling through town, a charmed fellow who made friends at every turn.

Behind them all, the cows mooed intermittently, disturbed no doubt by the unusual sounds and light glare refracting off the building. It was a dark night – which helped – great banks of cumuli towering into stacks in the sky and bringing the threat of winds and rain tomorrow.

She was dreading it already. Gem wanted them all to go back to Paula's to get Amber's bridesmaid dress sorted, and Cassie was going to have to draw up a new, truly more modest menu and shopping list. They were in Wadebridge, not Westbourne Grove. Cobnuts didn't come as standard here.

She sighed, giving up on the carbonized hot dog, forcing her gaze back to the film showing on the side of the house. It was one of her favourite scenes – the one where Donna Reed jumped into the flower bushes – but her concentration kept wavering.

He was looking over at her again; she just knew it. The weight of his stare was a physical thing upon her, pressing down on her chest so that her breath felt shallow, her head light. She turned her face further away so that she was almost in profile to him, her right hand cupping her right cheek and trying to block his view. But he was sitting across the lawn in darkness, just watching and waiting, she knew, for her to acknowledge the moment that had passed between them in the surf.

Five minutes passed.

Ten.

Twenty.

Her eyes slid over – bitter and resentful that he was doing this to her, refusing to let it drop. What did he think was going to happen? What did he want? Their gazes joined like magnetic fields, instantly locking on to one another in the flickering darkness, and she widened her eyes angrily in a silent 'What?' expression.

His response was an impassive stare that she recognized only too well from those nights in New York when they'd stayed out late with his friends and all he really wanted to do was get her back to the apartment . . . She looked away again, agitated and restless.

A sudden small shriek from Amber made everyone turn, and Cassie looked over just in time to see her tuck her legs up onto the sofa, her eyes trained on something small but advancing at speed towards her. 'What is *that*?' she cried.

Cassie turned a full 180 degrees back again, just as Rollo launched himself into the air and grabbed the last remaining piece of her hot dog from her hand. 'Oh my God!' she shrieked in turn, falling backwards into the beanbag.

Gem immediately jumped up from the sofa, Suzy too, but the dark little dog was too fast for them to catch and didn't seem particularly taken with his given name, as he didn't respond to it being called at all.

'Oh my God! Suzy! How the hell did he get out?' Gem wailed, reaching for and missing the puppy as he ran laps round her.

'How should I know?' Suzy demanded, joining in the chase. Everyone was on their feet now – everyone except Archie who, having tried to get up, had been shot down by his wife with a stern look and a single pointed finger instructing him to stay where he was.

'Well, you were the one looking after him!' Gem said accusingly.

Suzy whirled round to face her. '*I* never signed up to that! He's your puppy! You just left him here without so much as a "please" or "than—"'

'Stop it! Stop . . .' Gem pleaded, keeping her back to Laird and trying to stop Suzy from incriminating her further.

'I take it you're going to replace my new French Soles, which he's completely destroyed?' Suzy demanded, immediately exploiting the situation.

'Of course,' Gem agreed hastily.

'Hang on a minute,' Laird said as the two women resumed lunging and swiping for the puppy. 'Since when did you get a puppy?'

Gem deflated; the secret was out anyway. Of course it was. 'It was my wedding present to you,' she said plaintively, her mouth pushing into a small pout. 'I know how much you love dogs and I just fell in love with him. I wanted it to be a surprise.'

'Well, it's certainly that!' Laird laughed, getting up and clasping her head in his hands. 'And you got Suzy to babysit it?'

'It was more than just babysit!' Suzy huffed crossly, her fingers only just brushing the feathers of the dog's tail. 'He's got such bad separation anxiety I ended up sleeping in the bloody kitchen with him the past two nights.'

Rollo jumped onto the empty sofa, where Gem and Laird weren't sitting.

Gem went limp in Laird's arms as she stared into his eyes. 'I thought it would be the start of our family unit, you know?' she said in a little-girl voice as Laird kissed her and Suzy made an impressive lunge across the sofa behind them – still missing the dog. Rollo jumped back onto the grass and then disappeared into the shadows. 'And it would have been such a perfect surprise if Suzy hadn't ballsed it up.'

'*Me?*' Suzy exploded, gathering herself from the cushions with a pop that would have made Laird proud and straightening up to her full impressive height. 'You're lucky I even tried to help! You're lucky I went along with this charade for as long as I did, especially as you know and I know that you've got no right even owning a dog.'

'What?' Gem's voice was a croak.

'How dare you pretend that you care about any living creature after what you did?' Suzy's eyes blazed as she locked Gem in her sights.

'No.' Gem shook her head. 'Please, Suzy. Don't.'

'Oh no. I bet you don't want Laird hearing about that.'

Everything went still.

'Baby, what's she talking about?' Laird asked, looking down at Gem with an apprehensive expression.

'Nothing. It's really nothing. She's lying.'

Laird looked over at Suzy, who was physically shaking, her eyes bulging with long-suppressed rage. 'Suzy? What's going on?'

Arch stood up, looking concerned at his wife's fury. She wasn't just on the edge; she'd gone over the other side, pushed too far. 'Darling—'

'She killed my dog. Your precious fiancée, who would like you to believe that she couldn't pull the petals off a daisy, killed my dog,' Suzy cried, real tears sliding down her cheeks.

'No,' Laird revoked, looking back at Gem in shock.

'It was an accident!' Gem pleaded. 'I didn't see—'

'He was standing right in the middle of the drive. You couldn't miss him. I saw the whole thing happen from my window.' Suzy's voice cracked at the memory and Cassie wanted to run over and throw her arms around her. But she couldn't, because in Suzy's eyes, she was the enemy too, now.

'But I . . . I wasn't thinking straight. I wasn't looking. I had dropped my phone.'

'Was that the same phone Mum had just tried to confiscate from you because you'd been caught sneaking out at night again?' Suzy asked sarcastically. 'The one you ran out of the house with, and that's why you were speeding down the drive?'

'I'm sorry!' Gem quavered. 'You know I am! I came straight back into the house to ring the vet.'

'How very good of you,' Suzy said with withering scorn.

Gem stared back at her bigger – in every sense – cousin, their dark history glistening between them in the shadowy garden. When she finally spoke, her voice was hollow, as though its substance had been thinned out. 'It was an accident.'

'Brought about entirely by your temper,' Suzy countered, merciless now.

'I haven't driven a car since. I can't—' She squeezed her eyes shut, her body braced as though for the impact again. 'Aunt Hats and Henry forgave me.' She looked back at Suzy, desperation in her eyes. 'Why can't you?'

'Because you act as though you've got the copyright on grief. You behaved as badly as you wanted, but that was OK because you were an orphan. But we'd lost Dad barely a year before the fire.' Suzy's voice was thick and unfamiliar to Cassie's ear, as the sarcasm she used as armour finally gave way to a hurt and grief that had been put on hold for too long. 'Do you remember that, or is it only your grief that counts? Our family was already in pieces before yours was, but we had to put all that to one side to deal with you. Mum was a box-fresh widow when she lost her brother too, but you never gave her a moment to grieve. No sooner had she got the news about the fire than her every thought was about what was best for you. And in return, you behaved like a little bitch. "Oh, you killed the dog? Never mind." If the fire had been Mum's fault, you couldn't have been more cruel. No one else's pain mattered. No one else mattered.'

'They were my *parents*,' Gem screamed suddenly, drowning out even Suzy. 'And they left me. They left me, don't you see that? I was alone.'

There was a long silence, the two cousins standing as rigid as chess pieces in the light beam, while *It's a Wonderful Life* flickered over them.

When Suzy spoke next, her voice was quiet. Restored again. The anger – having broken through – had seeped away like a hill mist. 'They never left you, Gem; they were taken. There's a difference. And you've never been alone – you had Mum and Henry and me. There hasn't been one day since the fire when you've been on your own, and that's the problem. It's why I don't believe this marriage will ever work. I know you and Laird love each other, I can see that, but you are damaged, Gem. You've never recovered because the whole rest of your life has been spent denying the horror of what happened.'

'I don't deny anything. I live my life in an open way; I'm open to love, open to new experiences—'

'Gem, you haven't driven a car since you hit Rover; you won't go in the water since you drifted off on that lilo; you won't get near a fire pit because of the flames. You're running, and everything you do – your search for Zen, this off-the-cuff, hippy-go-lucky wedding – it's just a desperate attempt to distract us all from the fact that inside, you are burning up with *rage*.'

Suzy's voice was so quiet Cassie almost had to strain to hear, but her words had clearly hit their mark. Gem was crying, her head shaking from side to side, refuting the truth, but she was shaking as violently as if she was febrile.

'I think . . .' Laird looked across at Archie, who nodded

back in wordless agreement. Laird led Gem away in silence.

Archie wrapped his arms around his wife. 'We're going inside now too,' he said gently but firmly, walking her back towards the house. For once, Suzy didn't protest. She was all out of words.

Cassie stared across at Luke and Amber, both of whom were mute with shock at the scene they'd just witnessed.

'Holy crap,' Amber breathed as they watched Archie and Suzy disappear inside the house, forgetting, temporarily, her enmity with Cassie. 'Who *knew*? I mean, I knew Gem had some serious shit going on, but . . .' She gave a low whistle.

Luke, who was only half listening, raised an eyebrow as he twisted first one way, then the other. 'Uh . . . anyone see where the dog went?'

'What?' Cassie gasped, suddenly looking down onto the blackened ground. In all the commotion between Suzy and Gem, they had completely forgotten about the puppy.

She turned and looked behind her towards the fields. There were cows in the immediate field but sheep in the ones beyond, and if he worried them, the farmer would shoot him on sight. 'Oh bugger, we've got to find him.'

'What's his name?' Luke asked, walking towards her, his eyes locked on Cassie again as he moved in front of Amber's line of sight. The dark passion in his eyes rooted her to the spot and for a moment, just one, she thought he was going to do what he would have done in the sea earlier, had she not leaped like a salmon out of his arms. But he bent down and switched off the projector as Amber gathered the Hermès blanket tighter round her shoulders.

'Rollo.'

'Rollo?' Luke repeated, his voice benign but his eyes burning as he stalled for time.

Amber was still behind him, out of eyeshot of them both, and Cassie felt her breath hitch. She had to get away from him. 'We'd better split up. You go that way; I'll look over here,'she said quickly.

'What about me? I'm barefoot. I can't go traipsing over fields in the dark with no shoes on,' Amber whined.

'Then go and put some shoes on,' Luke said, before seeing her reluctant expression. He sighed. 'Or don't. Make some coffee.'

He headed off into the darkness, using the light on his phone as a torch and calling Rollo's name. Cassie followed suit, moving in the opposite direction as she headed for the stile.

The fields and hedgerows took on a different aspect by night. She had walked along this path dozens of times in the past ten days, but the thorns on the brambles seemed exaggerated in the shadows cast by the moonbeams, and the sheer bulk of the dozing cows was altogether more menacing in the dark.

'Rollo!' she called. 'Here, boy!'

But there was no response: no bark to indicate he'd heard, no whine to tell her he was hurt or stuck some-where; no sound of padded paws thundering over the grassy, baked earth.

She shone her phone light into the nooks and crevices in the dry-stone walls and hedgerows, but her head was full of the news Suzy had just spilled. It made sense, at least, of their uneasy relationship – how Henry had been able to laugh and joke, when Suzy couldn't; how he'd been able to forgive what he knew, when she couldn't forget what she'd seen.

'Rollo!'

Cassie remembered the unsettling look she'd seen in Gem's eyes when she'd 'won' their showdown, the mania that accompanied her every move. Suzy had been right – Gem was damaged. But was that really so surprising, given the circumstances in which she'd lost her parents? It was certainly no wonder Hattie – whose feathers were famously never ruffled – was fretful and sleepless about this marriage.

The world darkened suddenly, spun too fast, as she felt her hand caught, the scent of vetiver and sandalwood cloud around her, an aftershave she herself had bought.

'Don't—' she managed in the moment before his lips crushed hers, his hands spread across her back, pushing her in and keeping her close, as though she was the one who'd been lost and not the worn-out puppy she could feel sniffing the ground by her feet.

Luke pulled back, his eyes glittering darkly. 'Let's just stop this now. You know we can't carry on pretending, Cass. It's too hard . . .' He kissed her again, the feel of his mouth on hers so familiar, all the same desires she had long ago tucked away flickering into being like one of those reigniting birthday candles – no matter how hard she tried, the flame wouldn't blow out.

She hated that he could still do this to her, that after everything they'd done to each other – the rejections, humiliations, punishments – the chemistry wouldn't let it just go, fade, die.

She put her hands to his chest, pushing back, trying to breathe, to think. 'Luke—'

'It wasn't over then, and it isn't over now. I knew it when I saw you again in New York – and you knew it too, Cass.'

She swallowed, knowing he was calling her on the lie, the pointless one she had tried to hide behind that day in the garden last week. He knew she had seen him, he had seen for himself the effect he had had on her, frozen still in the freezing night.

His eyes burned into hers, seeing it all. 'It isn't over.'

She stared back at him, her breath coming hard and fast, her heart like a boxer's fist on her ribs as she remembered the effect of him on her, seeing him in the cab in New York, seeing him at the polo. 'I know.'

His eyes came alive. 'So then *be* with me. If it was a hundred per cent right with him, you wouldn't have hesitated, you'd be his wife already.'

She didn't reply. Emotions were swirling and crashing around inside her, her heart saying one thing, her body yet another.

'He doesn't understand what you went through, the person you've become. That year changed you, Cassie. I've only ever known you like this – free, independent, strong – but he wants you like a caged bird, the person you once were.' He saw the resistance in her eyes. 'I know you love him. I know you do. Just like I love Amber. But it's a matter of degrees, isn't it? "Almost" just isn't enough in the end. We want it all, you and me – we want the rush, the right now, the energy. No one could ever touch us when it came to sexual chemistry. We weren't just on fire; we *were* the fire. There'll never be anyone else like that for us – you must see that.'

She tore her eyes away. He made it so hard for her to

think, putting words in her mouth, thoughts in her head. She just needed to—

'You were looking for something the first time round, and you didn't think I was it. You couldn't let yourself *believe* that you could have found what you were looking for so quickly, so easily. So you called me the rebound guy, right?'

She swallowed. It was exactly what she'd called him, how she'd 'managed' the memories when he had popped into her head, anytime she saw one of his images in a magazine, at a bus stop . . .

'But what if I wasn't? What if I was the real deal all along and you just weren't ready to face it?' He stepped forward – Rollo coming with him, Luke's belt looped through his collar to form a makeshift lead – his finger hooking up under her chin, making her look at him again, that touch alone making her want him. 'Just let go, Cass. You're fighting something that's right. We both know it. I never gave up on us. Look.'

He pulled something from his pocket – a bangle? It was solid and gold, tiny screw-heads dotted round it. 'It's a symbol of love. Once you put it on, you don't take it off. Like a ring, I guess.' He studied her face as she looked at it more closely. Recognition dawning . . . 'It represents never letting go. And I never did.'

She didn't need to see the little red box to know it was the Cartier bracelet; she remembered Amber and Gem's excitement over it – a very modern proposal, they'd fancied. 'No. You bought this for Amber,' she said firmly, pushing back. Did he think he could just switch girls for the gift?

'No. Look.' He shone his phone light on the inner radius. She squinted.

'December 31st 2012.'

A hand flew to her mouth as she took in the date of the party he'd thrown for her in New York to convince her to stay – all her new friends lined up as proof that she had a life there, it could work . . . 'It was meant to mark the first day of the rest of our lives, but . . .' He blinked, his eyes fierce with emotion. 'You left before I could give it to you. I've had it with me ever since: it was in my pocket at the gallery in Paris that night of the private view; I had it in London at the party . . .'

'But why?' she whispered.

'In case the opportunity ever came up to . . . convince you we were real.' He blinked at her. 'I've tried letting you go. And I've tried just being your friend. I actually did.' A small laugh escaped him as though the very idea was ridiculous. 'As if *that* was ever going to work.' His hand found hers, squeezing it hard. 'You're under my skin, Cass. Nothing I can do about it.'

A moment passed. 'I don't know what you want me to say,' she said quietly, almost flattened by his words, scared by the truth in them and what would happen if she responded, what would happen if she didn't . . .

'Just say no.'

She looked at him in surprise. '*No?*'

'Say you won't marry me. Let's live happily ever after.'

Chapter Twenty-Six

London blared. The sounds seemed louder, the colours bolder than when Cassie had left, not two weeks earlier, and she wove through the Pimlico Farmers' Market with an energy that hadn't been hers when leaving nearly a fortnight ago.

'Hey, Cassie, you're back!'

She looked up to find Martin, her man for mushrooms, smiling at her. He got up at 4 a.m. to travel from Dorset for this farmers' market, but he'd still had more sleep than her. She'd been awake all night, her mind racing, Luke's words – his unproposal, so modern after all – ringing in her ears, offering her another way, another life.

'I thought Zara said you weren't around for another week. How was Cornwall? You've caught the sun.'

'Have I?' Her hand moved to her cheek. She felt flushed – high, again – even in spite of no sleep.

'Catch any waves?'

The phrase made her think of Henry – his signature list and some greater meaning attached to it; it made her think of Luke and their euphoria as they rode the wave together.

'Just one.'

'Only the one?' Martin laughed. 'Get back down there and try harder, missy.'

'I'm going back tomorrow, actually.' She held up the list and rolled her eyes. 'Got a wedding to cater for on Saturday.'

'Blimey, Saturday? What you doing back up here, then?'

She adjusted her hat – a wide-brimmed, floppy fedora that kept the sun from her eyes. 'It's transpired that the bride's got rather niche tastes. There wasn't time to get everything delivered down; it was just easier to pop back here and do it myself.' After the revelations last night, Cassie had resolved to do the best job she could for Gem; they may never be bosom buddies, but the poor girl had bigger things to worry about than menus.

It had also given her the perfect opportunity to escape, partly from Suzy – there was no guessing the mood she'd be in this morning – partly from Luke. Especially from him. She'd deliberately switched off her phone. She didn't want to have his voice – low and beguiling, that delicious accent – next to her ear, like he was on the pillow beside her. She didn't want to see his eyes – vivid, intense, rapacious – undressing her, caressing her, talking her into things she knew were bad and dangerous, yet felt so good. She thought he could probably talk her into anything and that was why she had left; there was no perspective when he was near and she needed time to think. The cliff winds were swirling round her again but this time they were warm and caressing, enticing her to cast off her fears and finally make the leap of faith that had seemed so impossible before.

She knew she was at a crossroads, perhaps the biggest of her life. This was it. Where her life ended up would be traced back to this moment, this decision. So much of what had happened to her up till now had been out of her control: the consequences of Gil's affair had made divorce inevitable, not because of her anger or refusal to forgive –

she believed she could have done that – but because there was a child involved who needed a father and she had refused to be the person standing in the way of that happening. She had had to go.

Equally, falling for Henry had been easy, thoughtless, as instinctive as breathing, and up till now she hadn't questioned it; she hadn't needed to. Why dwell on the one piece of grit in their relationship when everything else sparkled? But the tectonic plates of what he wanted and she didn't had been pushing against each other for two years, betraying their presence only in the warning tremors that occasionally made the ground shake beneath their feet; and the pressure was constant now, fracture of some kind inevitable. To move forwards, one of them would have to break.

And it didn't have to be her. She could have exactly what she wanted with Luke; she didn't need to splinter off a piece of herself to be with him. He wasn't pushing her into something in which she had lost faith. They were on the same page and everything that had been between them before was still there, just waiting . . . She remembered his kiss last night and the self-control it had taken to push him away before they'd lost themselves to something more.

'I'll take the oysters, thanks, Martin,' she said brightly, holding out the money, her eyes falling to the golden glint on her wrist. Gem had been right. It really was modern. Vervy. Cool. She imagined their life in New York: dinner eaten out of steaming takeout bags; the two of them walking through the Village for coffees, her head on his shoulder; idle walks in Central Park; the look that would come into his eyes when they were alone, properly alone, again – it had always made her catch her breath, that look. Their chemistry was undeniable, unstoppable. Maybe Luke had been right – he'd been more than a rebound. After all this time, even after finding intense happiness with other people, the universe had somehow boomeranged them back to each other. They fitted; they wanted the same things, crucially, at the same time; they belonged together.

Martin handed over the paper bag and her change. 'Enjoy Saturday.'

'Oh, I won't,' she laughed.

'I'm gonna wanna hear about this wedding. All the gory details,' he called after her as she slipped into the crowds again. 'I love it when them brides is mad.'

She stopped at all her usual stalls – the cheese, the chutneys, the purple carrots – knowing the traders by name and chatting with extra gaiety as they all commented on how 'well' she was looking. She was having a ball, shopping in the sunshine and mingling with the crowds; she felt lighter and freer than she had in months. She hadn't realized what a burden it had been constantly trying to fend off a life she didn't want. She felt giddy with relief.

In under an hour the list was almost ticked off and her neon-orange string shopping bags were bulging. The flat was only a three-minute walk from here and already her palms were striated from the weight of the groceries, but she couldn't make herself walk faster. After twelve hours of living in her head, reality was beginning to bite. Luke's proposal had seemed so easy, so *obvious* when they were standing in the moonlit field, a puppy snuffling at their feet, but she didn't know how to walk into her and Henry's home and be presented with their own life interrupted; how to stand with a stranger's eyes in her own hall and face everything that they shared. She wasn't sure she could meet Henry's gaze in the numerous photos she had proudly dotted on every surface when they'd moved in, their togetherness as tangible as a Saharan wind. She didn't think she could look at what she was supposed to walk away from.

She stopped walking, feeling fluey, her body aching and suddenly so, so tired she thought she could curl up on the pavement and go to sleep.

She didn't want to go home, but neither did she want to go back to Cornwall. Not yet. She still had to think. To be *really* sure . . . The bags in her hands sagged another inch closer to the ground. Luke's face last night shimmered in her mind, the pretending over. She was further than ever from knowing what she wanted. Suzy had said she was caught between lives and she'd been right. She'd been right about all of it. But just because Suzy had been right, it didn't meant that what Cassie felt was wrong.

No – coffee, that was what she needed. She was just tired. After a sleepless night and long, early morning journey, coming straight to the market had taken it out of her. She needed some fuel to get her through this next bit; it wouldn't help her to go home when she was already depleted. She was tired and emotional as it was.

She looked over at the cafe on the other side of the road. The tables had been set up outside with red-striped parasols, and almost all of them were taken.

Cassie walked over, heading for the nearest free table; it was in the sun and she'd need to somehow move the giant umbrella if she wanted any shade but she was already focused on the double espresso (the way Anouk took her coffee) that was going to restore her energy – and courage.

She was just about to release her bags from her poor, reddened hands when she noticed the women at the next table

– a halo of bright blonde hair flashing in the sunlight.

Cassie stiffened as she immediately recognized the dazzling smile that accompanied it, the same dazzling smile that had aroused such insecurity in her the first time she'd seen it. What . . . what was *she* doing here?

Cassie's feet took her to the table. 'Hi.' She had interrupted the girl's conversation without thinking about it, without noticing the quizzical expression of the girl's lunch companion, who was looking her up and down, her eyes sticking at the bulging shopping bags in Cassie's hands; the blonde girl shielded her eyes to get a better look at the dazed stranger standing over her and staring.

'You're Amy.'

Amy frowned. 'That's right.'

'Why aren't you on the boat?'

Amy gave a curious but unamused laugh. 'Sorry, *who* are you?'

'I'm Cassie, Henry's—'

Amy's face brightened. 'Oh yeah. Henry's fiancée! I know all about *you*. How are you?' she asked, like they were old friends.

'Why aren't you on the boat?' Cassie repeated. She suddenly didn't feel right at all. It didn't make sense. There was no reason that she could think of as to why Amy would be sitting here and not sailing the Pacific.

She shrugged. 'They didn't need me once Henry came on board.'

'But you're the co-skipper.'

'There was only ever supposed to be one. The cabin was too small for six.'

Cassie was confused. 'Do you mean you were taken off the team because of Henry?'

'Mm-hmm.' Amy seemed blasé about it.

'But why? Why did they need him if they already had you?'

'Beau was doing a favour for a friend.' Amy shrugged. 'Hey, listen, it wasn't like I cared either way. Three months in a tiny cabin with five blokes is so not my idea of a good time.'

'Yeah, right, like you'd have lasted three months,' Amy's lunch companion laughed. 'You told me you and Beau were going to get off at the first water stop and holiday in the Solomon Islands for a few weeks.'

Amy laughed too, putting a finger to her lips. 'Sssh! I told you not to repeat that.'

'I don't understand,' Cassie said, looking between them both.

'No, you wouldn't,' the friend said in an unfriendly tone, fiddling with the straw in her water and clearly willing Cassie to leave.

Cassie stared down at them both, confused and uncertain, but Amy's amused smile had gone now and her bright face had folded into a harder, more inscrutable expression that discouraged further questioning.

Cassie stepped back, sensing that she'd stumbled into something but not sure what, and she didn't notice the weight of the bags pulling on her hands anymore as she staggered home, lost in theories and ideas that slipped from view like figures in the mist whenever she tried to calculate more than two steps ahead.

She put the key into the lock of the building's front door and slowly trudged up the stairs. She was going to get into the flat and go straight to bed. She wasn't well, she didn't feel right. She felt as wiped out now as she had felt wired an hour earlier.

'And honestly, she said it was like having every bone in her body snapped.'

'She said that – and yet still did it?'

'I know, right?'

Cassie's feet stopped moving as the accents – familiarly wry and sophisticated – drifted down to her ear. Surely . . . ?

She turned the corner to find Kelly and Anouk sitting on her doorstep. The bags dropped from her grasp.

'Finally!' Anouk exclaimed, getting up and wrapping her arms around her shoulders. But Cassie couldn't take her eyes off Kelly and she stared at her in mute despair over Anouk's shoulder, taking in her friend's pale complexion and unchanged figure. If she was here, then . . .

How could she explain to her friend that she hadn't been able to get the laptop again to call? That to get it, she'd have had to go to Luke and she couldn't possibly have done that after the festival; they'd spent all this week playing cat and mouse, avoiding and hiding from each other, before breaking into the chase again.

Anouk released her and Kelly stepped in for her embrace. 'Not a word,' she murmured into Cassie's hair.

Cassie blinked her agreement in silent reply. No one knew and now no one ever would, not even Brett. Especially not him.

They stepped apart. 'Bebe here?' Cassie asked, with deliberate levity.

Kelly rolled her eyes, playing the game too. 'Holed up at Claridge's waiting for her finest hour. She's having lunch with Philip Treacy and the Porter team.'

'Ah. At least that'll keep her off your back for a while.' Cassie was aware that her voice sounded odd.

'Are *you* OK? You look pale. Doesn't she look pale?' Kelly asked Anouk, who immediately squinted and nodded.

'Really? Everyone else has been telling me how well I look. I've got a tan, you know,' Cassie said breezily, putting her keys into the lock and trying to shake off her unsettling conversation with Amy. So she'd been ousted from the team? So what? If she wasn't bothered, why should Cassie be? Beau had done his old friend a favour and given Henry a job; that was the most important thing. She wasn't remotely surprised to learn that Beau had been planning to skive off for most of it.

'How did you know I was here?' Cassie asked, stepping into the hallway but keeping her eyes on the floor as she fussed over the bags. She wasn't sure whether it was a help or a hindrance to have the girls with her here in the flat. They could distract her, but could she keep up the act in front of them?

'Suze,' Kelly said, helping with a bag. 'She said you were back for an overnighter before the wedding.'

Cassie stiffened. Had she told the others about their fight and what it was about?

'Actually, that reminds me,' Kelly continued. 'You should probably call her back. Is your mobile off? She just called again a few minutes ago, asking if you were here yet. I told her I thought we'd missed you.'

'Right. Yes, thanks, I will,' Cassie murmured, with no such intention of returning the call. It was going to be hard enough talking face-to-face.

'I take it this means you two didn't manage to stop the wedding, then?' Anouk asked, going straight into the kitchen and switching on the coffee machine. 'You were supposed to talk to her, weren't you?'

'Yeah, and that went so well,' Cassie said with a groan, dropping the bags onto the kitchen floor. 'So well, in fact, that far from talking Gem out of it, I somehow talked myself into doing the bloody catering! Hence . . .' Cassie gave a small sweep of the groceries with her hands. 'I am the Mr Bean of sabotage.'

Anouk chuckled, shaking her head. '*Désastre.*'

'Whose wedding are we talking about, and why on earth were you trying to stop it from going ahead?' Kelly asked, a scolding tone in her voice.

'Gem, Suzy's cousin. Hattie's her legal guardian and both Suze and Hats are dead against it. They think she's too young and that her bloke is after her money. I definitely mentioned it to you . . .'

'And is he?' Anouk asked, her eyes sliding discreetly over to Kelly, clearly remembering that, years earlier, Kelly had been scammed by a man for exactly that.

'Well, *I* don't think so,' Cassie said with a quick shrug. 'He's very nice, actually. He's been teaching me to surf.'

'Oh yeah!' Kelly laughed. 'And how's that working out for you?'

'Brilliantly, actually,' Cassie giggled, flicking her with a tea towel. 'I'll have you know, I caught my first wave yesterday.'

'Oooh. Was it a spiritual moment?'

Cassie remembered the rush of that moment, again, the feeling of Luke's arms around her as they revelled in her success, the realization that they could fight the feelings between them but not deny them. She felt almost drunk on it. She looked at her two oldest, dearest friends – her family really – and realized how far she had strayed from the path of her own life. They thought they knew everything about her – the name of the first boy she kissed and the humiliation of their braces clashing, her favourite song, the secret ingredient in her famous lasagne – but they didn't know that Luke was back in her life, back in Cornwall waiting for her, much less that last night she had been back in his arms. How could she even begin to articulate to them the predicament she was in? To anyone?

She was close to her mother, in spite of the distance and time difference with Hong Kong, and they spoke regularly on the phone, but she had kept quiet about her recent and growing troubles with Henry, worried her mother would think she was 'failing' again, feeling ashamed by her inability to do what everyone wanted her to do, to just 'move on', unhurt, unwounded, fully restored to unblemished emotional health. That alone was bad enough; there was no question of confiding in her about her confusion with Luke too.

'You're out of caffeinated,' Anouk said, holding up the Nespresso coffee tray accusingly.

Cassie pulled an apologetic face. 'Oh . . . yeah, about that. Henry's been trying to get me to cut down on my caffeine intake recently. We're drinking decaff these days.'

Anouk muttered something furiously and rapidly in French under her breath. Coffee without caffeine in it clearly wasn't coffee.

'So, what? You're going back again?' Kelly asked, decanting food into the fridge.

'Yes, tomorrow afternoon,' Cassie sighed, already dreading the long journey. 'I'm taking the car down. I have to – there's too much kit to carry for the train.' She struggled with the lock on the back door, tugging it open with effort and basking for a moment as a rush of warm air burst in, refreshing the stifled little flat, which had simply been locked up and left.

'Will your car make it?' Anouk asked drolly with an arched eyebrow as she placed down the three coffees.

'Oh, ye of little faith. I'll have you know it's fresh back from the garage.' The herbs in her window box were looking thirsty, she noticed, reaching into the cupboard under the sink for the small enamel watering can. 'That still doesn't mean it'll make it,' Kelly drawled.

Cassie flipped her the bird and both women laughed. 'So what were you two talking about as I was coming up the stairs just now? Something about snapping bones? It sounded grim,' she said, stepping out onto the fire escape and watering the parched soil, watching as the water splashed onto the dry, dusty leaves. Her ears picked up on the busy chatter coming from the apple tree and she was surprised how much she had missed it. Without ever realizing it before, those little birds' songs had become the soundtrack to her life here with Henry. She felt her heart contract sharply, like a stitch.

'Beni Omar. You heard of her?' Kelly asked.

Cassie shook her head.

'Well, she's this hot new model – walking for *everyone*, got the Vuitton campaign. Bebe's desperate to book her for the next campaign, but, like, ha! – as if! Anyway, she was telling me about body resculpt. It's a Japanese massage that manipulates the bones closer to make you look more petite.'

'Ugh, sounds disgusting,' Cassie grimaced.

'Yeah, but if you have it done enough, it can make your waist so tiny it looks like you've had a rib removed.'

'Really?' Anouk breathed, perching elegantly against the worktop.

'Even *more* disgusting,' Cassie gurned as her friends edged closer together.

'Apparently all the top girls are getting it done. Bebe was telling me on the flight who's had it. It's the new thing.'

Cassie watched as Anouk encircled her waist with her hands. There wasn't much space between them. 'Oh, Nooks, you wouldn't! Come on! How can that be good for you?'

Anouk shrugged, looking back at Kelly. 'How bad was the pain? Did she say?'

'You ever crack your knuckles when you were little? I did, all the time.' Kelly's point was clear. She reckoned she could take it on.

'Well, it would have to be someone who really knew what they were doing,' Anouk said, both cautioning and encouraging her in the same breath.

Cassie groaned as she watched the two of them talking each other into it. She would always be the gauche girl in their company – the girl who wore Pond's Cold Cream instead of Terry, converses instead of heels, a T-shirt to bed instead of No. 5. 'I can't believe you're seriously considering this. Either one of you.' She shot a look at Kelly.

Kelly shrugged and Cassie turned away to put the watering can back under the sink, but not before she caught Kelly throw a wink to Anouk that clearly meant 'Book it.'

Was this a flash of defiance? Cassie wondered as some of the water splashed onto her bare legs. Was Kelly telling herself this was one of the perks of *not* being pregnant?

'Oh, hey, here – before I forget, I got you something,'

Anouk said, reaching down to her bag. 'I was going to drop it through your door while I was here.'

'What is it?' Cassie asked, straightening up and reaching for her coffee.

Anouk handed her a small envelope and Cassie peered inside, gasping in genuine shock as she saw the contents. 'Oh my *God*!' she exclaimed, pulling out a small, silver Tiffany heart-shaped locket.

'The authorities in Paris are clearing the bridges. It's out of control with the whole love locks things. There's tens of thousands of them now and they're so heavy the bridges in some cases will collapse. They want people to do selfies and #lovewithoutlocks instead, but . . .' She pulled a face. 'Anyway, I thought I should rescue it for you before it disappeared forever. It's not like all the other bike locks and padlocks. It's valuable. It's Tiffany, *non*?!'

'But how did you even know where to find it?'

'Easy. When you guys went to Venice that time, Henry left me a note with the coordinates: Pont des Arts, Left Bank side, second section, nine links in, twelve links up, just beneath the pink heart lock—'

Kelly chuckled. 'Typical Henry.'

'Even with that, though, it took me so long to find it. It was completely buried. Can you imagine the looks I got? People thought I was a thief!'

'Or a bitter ex,' Kelly grinned.

Cassie handled the tiny cold pendant. It had been Henry's first move – given to her at Christmas, a box within a box within a box, sitting at the bottom of the tree in the Fifth Avenue store. She'd worn it the rest of her time in New York, until she'd moved to Paris, where he'd 'accidentally' locked it on to the bridge with the other love lockets – an obscure, underground trend at the time that had since gone viral.

She had often thought of it, 'their' heart sitting above the Seine in the city of lovers, frozen in the snow, tinder-hot in the sunlight. Constant. Always there. She hadn't ever expected it to come off. She'd thought their locket would still be locked to that bridge in Paris for generations to come.

But now the bridges were being cleaned up, all that love swept aside. Was . . . was this a sign?

She stared at it, so small and simple in her palm. When had everything become so complicated?

'I did . . . do the right thing, didn't I?' Anouk asked, placing a hand on her arm and looking across at her with concern.

Cassie looked up. 'Y-yes, yes, of course. I just . . . It's a surprise, that's all. I wasn't expecting . . . Hang on, *how* did you get it off? You don't have the key.'

'*Non*. But I have some jeweller's tools that meant I could . . . how you say? . . . jimmy the lock?'

'Oh,' Cassie exhaled. 'Right.'

Anouk and Kelly swapped glances as Cassie reached over and gently placed the locket on the windowsill. It glinted in the sunlight like a Cupid's heart.

'What's that?' Anouk asked.

'What's what?'

'That.' Anouk pointed to the small arc of gold that could be glimpsed beneath her cuff.

'Oh, that's nothing. It's—'

'*Cartier?*' Kelly breathed as Anouk grabbed her hand, holding her arm still, an expression of wicked delight on her face. 'Henry got you a Love bracelet?'

'Um—'

'I thought you guys were broke! Do you have any idea how much those cost?' Kelly almost screeched.

Cassie shook her head.

'We're talking Birkin money, Fendi fur . . .' Kelly looked impressed, taking Cassie's arm off Anouk and getting a closer look herself. 'But it's not even that. I'll be honest, I didn't know Henry was so clued up. These babies are fashion's inside track. I wouldn't have thought these were his bag.'

'Tell me you have got the little screwdriver that goes with it. Don't lose that,' Anouk said sternly. 'You think a Tiffany locket is hard without a key? Pfft.'

'Oh, uh . . . yeah. Right.'

'Ha! Who needs a wedding ring? I guess that's one way round the remarriage problem!' Kelly guffawed, holding Cassie's wrist in her hand as she examined the bangle.

'What do you mean?'

'Well, he's got you well and truly shackled with that, hasn't he? This baby's like a handcuff . . . Hey, what's that?' she asked, peering at it more closely.

It was a moment before Cassie caught up and realized what Kelly had seen.

'It's nothing!' she said sharply, snatching her hand away, tugging roughly at the cuff again.

But it was too late. The expression on Kelly's face told her she'd seen the inscribed date – a date that she remembered well herself: she'd been there. It was a date that led to only one conclusion. Her hand dropped down, a look of stunned astonishment on her face as Cassie turned out of the kitchen and stepped onto the fire escape, her heart pounding, her mind racing. But there was no alternative explanation for this, nothing she could say to mitigate the shock of what she was already embroiled in.

Kelly's voice was quiet behind her. 'Care to explain?'

Chapter Twenty-Seven

'How does Brett put up with you?' Anouk tutted, trying to pull back the pintucked eiderdown from Kelly. 'You are such a hogger.'

Kelly, who was sitting beside her on the other side of the bed, shrugged. 'I know, but at least I'm not a kicker. Cassie's the worst kicker, don't you remember?'

'I am not!' Cassie protested from her position at the foot of the bed. They were sleeping like sardines tonight, but Cassie was sure she'd been put in the tails end so that Anouk and Kelly could both face her like an inquisition – or firing squad.

'We're going to wake up with concussions tomorrow,' Kelly chuckled, prompting a kick from Cassie, whose earlier tears had left her veering wildly between outright defiance and forlorn exhaustion, and she was still fragile, even now after several hours of improvised spa treatments in her bedroom, which were supposed to try and relax her (although Kelly had had to go into the room and turn over all the pictures of Cassie and Henry first).

Scented candles flickered delicately from every surface, trying to overpower the synthetic scent of nail polish – Chanel's Mirabella decorated their toes, still peeking out from the bedcovers – and they were lying on the bed with their hands held up, smothered in an expensive anti-ageing cream Anouk kept in her bag, while Kelly tried to rub open the latex gloves that Henry kept in the cupboard under the sink for plumbing emergencies; supposedly they were going to wake up tomorrow with the lily-soft hands of five-year-old princesses. Every so often, Cassie got another, slightly hysterical fit of the giggles as she took in the sight of Kelly and Anouk with Bircher muesli on their faces, which only a sharp reflexology dig in the solar plexus region of her right foot could stop.

'So, you seem a little calmer,' Anouk said, holding her hands still for Kelly to roll on the gloves. It reminded Cassie of surgeons being gloved in a medical drama.

Cassie just blinked. 'I feel paralysed. I don't know which way's up anymore. I certainly don't know which way's forward.'

'I just can't imagine you without Henry,' Kelly murmured quietly, ineffable sadness in her voice.

Cassie looked away, assailed by another violent rush of emotions. She couldn't imagine it either.

It was odd. She *could* imagine being with Luke – all the feelings she'd once had for him were still there; she had simply boxed them away and now she'd let them out, acknowledged them, they were coexisting alongside her feelings for Henry. But the one thing she couldn't do was imagine *not* being with Henry. Her mind wouldn't go there; her heart wouldn't let her. The very thought was impossible.

'You still love him, right?' Kelly asked.

'Of course I do! I will always love him! He's the love of my life,' Cassie said with too-bright eyes. She slumped further into the pillows, her voice flattening. 'But I just don't think that's going to be enough anymore. It's clear we want very different things. He's forcing this issue and I can't pretend that I didn't go through what I went through. You don't just walk out of a ten-year marriage without there being some kind of payback, and he just doesn't *get* that. I don't know how I can explain myself any more clearly. Why would I go back to something that makes a prisoner of me, locks me in regardless of how other people behave? I don't ever want to leave him, but I have to be free to leave; that possibility has to be there for me now. I've got to keep a door open.'

Kelly looked sad at her words. Anouk didn't.

'Well, I quite agree,' Anouk sighed. 'People place so much weight on ownership, like they've got to possess you. Why? Surely it is more comforting to know that the person you are with has *chosen* to stay. They could go, but they choose not to.' She arched an eyebrow. 'It is much more seductive, no?'

'I couldn't disagree more,' Kelly said, rubbing even more furiously on the latex glove, which merely flapped in her hands like a dying fish. 'When you make the choice to dedicate your life to that one person, and one person only, you build an intimacy that your so-called freedoms could never touch. It's way sexier.'

'In the beginning maybe,' Anouk shrugged. 'But twenty years from now you'll be obsessing over that hair that's sprouted at the end of his nose and wondering why the hell he can't see it and get rid of it. Everything you love now will be driving you crazy by then.'

'So what's your answer? Keep turning them over? Be with younger guys as you get older? Where's the peace in that? You'd be paranoid about your looks, your allure.

How long will they stay? Are they seeing anyone else? Should you leave them before they can leave you?'

'Actually—'

'OK, girls. Time out?' Cassie said tiredly, making a T-sign with her hands, the bangle sliding down her wrist. It was smeared with muesli, but she couldn't get it off – Luke had the screwdriver and nothing in Henry's toolbox was small enough to fit it. 'I appreciate the debate, but there's nothing hypothetical about my situation. If I don't marry him, he says we're f-finished,' she stuttered. 'I've got to give a "yes" or "no" answer. It's that simple. And that impossible.'

'Sorry,' they both murmured.

Cassie's face fell, twisting with pain as another surge of anxiety reared up inside her and she grabbed her hair by the temples, oblivious to the fact that she hadn't yet got her gloves on. 'Oh God, I am fucking up.'

'No, you're not. Not yet, anyway. Only if you make the wrong call,' Kelly said quickly. 'And nothing has been done yet that can't be undone . . . Right?'

It was a moment before Cassie realized what she was getting at. 'No. We just kissed.' But even that was a betrayal, just on a sliding scale of degrees, something that would have been unfathomable – abhorrent – to the version of herself sitting here two weeks ago. She had kissed another man. She was planning on leaving Henry, leaving here, this life, this path, and stepping onto a new one. How had she got here? *How?*

'How are you feeling now you're away from them both?' Anouk asked, twiddling a biro between her fingers and Cassie could tell she was gearing up for a cigarette.

She shrugged weakly. 'It all seems so distant now. I mean, Henry's somewhere in the middle of the Pacific;

Luke's in Cornwall. It's hard to believe either one of them is waiting for *me*.'

'And yet they both are,' said Kelly. She gave a heavy sigh. 'Tell me this. Would you still be walking away from Henry if you didn't have Luke to go to?'

'If I do go – *if!* – I'm not leaving Henry *for* Luke. But there's unfinished business there. I can't pretend there isn't.'

'This would all be a helluva lot more simple if he'd just stayed on his side of the Atlantic,' Kelly said crossly. 'I mean, I cannot believe he's staying in the exact same place as you.'

'I know. It is weird,' Cassie sighed. 'His girlfriend knows Gem.'

'Or maybe it is fate, uh?' Anouk asked.

Kelly shot her a look that suggested Anouk was being unhelpful. 'I just don't understand why you stayed on once you realized he was there too. Surely you knew what might happen if you and Luke were together again?'

'Honestly? No! I hated him so much after Paris.'

'Too much, in retrospect, uh?' Anouk asked.

Cassie shrugged again. 'Yes, maybe.'

There was a pause.

'Look, it's a sex thing with you and Luke,' Kelly said, changing tack. 'The chemistry was always incredible between you. God knows, it was in *my* face long enough. Man, I will never forget the time I found the two of you in the bath—'

'Thanks!' Cassie shrieked, preferring not to go into specifics, even though the exact same memory had played through her mind several times in the past twenty-four hours.

'The point I'm trying to make is that you two didn't get to let things take their natural course. You upped and left for Paris after New Year because that was the date we'd arbitrarily agreed on at the outset, but you and he weren't done. You hadn't played yourselves out. The relationship didn't get a chance to die; it just ended, *like that*.' She clicked her fingers. 'So it's maybe not that surprising that this has happened.'

Cassie sensed there was more to come. 'But you think that we would have ended if we'd had more time?' she prompted.

'Oh yeah. Absolutely,' Kelly said resolutely.

'You have no way of knowing that,' Anouk argued. 'You're making assumptions because you see her with Henry and want that to be the answer – but what if it isn't? They've got problems. Cassie and Luke don't.'

'If Henry could hear you—' Kelly started.

'Hey! I love him as much as you, but this is about what's right for Cassie. This is the rest of her life we're talking about. There are no second chances with this. Whatever direction she chooses – whichever man – she can't go back.'

Cassie slumped further down the pillow, feeling her anxiety and confusion begin to marble again. Both Kelly and Anouk fell silent, feeling guilty. As much as they shared a style DNA, they had always disagreed about what was best for Cassie. Kelly had rendered her a Park Avenue blonde during her New York stint, Anouk a bobbed brunette. Kelly had had her running Central Park and eating sushi; Anouk had introduced her to the joys of the hammam and a full-bodied Merlot. They weren't likely to make it a first and agree, now, on this.

'And Suzy has no idea?' Kelly asked after a moment.

Oh God, Suzy. Cassie dropped her head into her muesli-coated hands again. 'She had her suspicions. We had a big fight about it. She was right and I was . . . I was putting my head in the sand. I didn't see it clearly like she did. I believed Luke when he told me he'd moved on. I mean, he's dating Amber Taylor, for heaven's sake! Hello! Why would I think he was pining over me? It's laughable.' She swallowed as they remained silent. There was nothing funny about it. 'She doesn't know about last night.' Her face crumpled, the muscles falling slack with despair. 'How can I tell her? If I go back to Luke, I'm betraying her as much as I am Henry. She'll never forgive me. She won't. I'll lose her too.'

Kelly and Anouk glanced at each other. Confirmation. There were no platitudes to offer here.

'Did you tell Luke you were leaving?' Kelly asked quietly.

She nodded.

'So then he's waiting for you.'

'Yes.' Cassie met their eyes. 'Oh Christ, what do you think I should do? Someone please just tell me what to do.'

It was a moment before either woman spoke.

'Well, I know there's one thing you can't do,' Anouk said slowly.

Cassie blinked. 'What's that?'

'You can't go back there alone.'

'Jeez, it would've been quicker coming by mail,' Kelly grumbled from the seat in the back, a hamper on her knee as they passed a sign for Bodmin.

'This is nothing – you should see Henry's car,' Anouk drawled. 'We almost had to cut the roof off to get Bas out.'

Cassie laughed, winking at Kelly in the rear-view mirror.

OK, so it had taken seven hours instead of five, but she was really rather pleased (not to mention relieved) that her Morris Minor had made the motorway journey without incident – no black smoke belching from the exhaust (as it had done on the road to Bath once), no burst tyres (en route to Norfolk) or the clutch going (a wedding in Warwickshire). The poor little car was so full its back bumper was practically kissing the tarmac, as Cassie had expertly wedged baskets, rugs, glasses, cutlery, ice buckets, food trays and best friends inside.

'Right. Bas says he can get the first train down in the morning,' Kelly said, reading from her texts.

'Did you tell him where the spare key is?' Cassie called back. 'It's under the—'

'Yeah, yeah. He says he's in. Reckons he'll be with us by eleven tomorrow.'

'I can't believe we missed him. It must have been by minutes,' Cassie said sadly, shaking her head. 'Such crummy luck.'

'Well, maybe next time he will think to text beforehand to check you're there,' Anouk said. 'It is rude to turn up unannounced, *non*?'

But Cassie already had a feeling as to why he may have turned up at her flat without notice. The couture shows were starting in Paris next week, but if he'd turned up a few days early to see Luis and things hadn't quite panned out in the way he'd hoped . . .

She bit her lip, hoping it wasn't that. Let one of them be lucky in love, at least.

She swung along the back roads via Delabole as the sky reddened into black, her grip tightening on the steering wheel as the miles to Rock were counted down on every road sign. They were too late for dinner now, in spite of their best plans, and she had texted Archie from the Tiverton services to appraise them of their new ETA. 'If you're tired, don't wait up. Big day tomorrow!' she'd signed off, in the vain hope – she now realized – that Archie would spread the word and scatter their guests back to their rooms. If she could just *not* see Luke for one more night . . . If she could just have another twelve hours to herself while she reached for clarity, achieved perspective, settled on the answer that her heart told her was right.

Her hands tightened at the wheel again.

'You OK?' Anouk asked, her eyes on Cassie's blanched knuckles.

'Me? Yeah. Just tired.' She had barely slept again, her nervous system scarcely touched by the holistic, relaxing treatments her friends had prepared last night, and she had been working in the kitchen for several hours before Anouk and Kelly had woken up, their rubber gloves still on and bits of porridge oats stuck in their eyebrows.

'I'm not surprised. You worked like a fever today.'

Cassie shrugged. 'It was good to get ahead with the prepping. I reckon it's going to be fairly stressy in the house tomorrow, no matter what Gem says about it being low-key. At least all I've got to do now is roast the lamb and stack the macaroons.' A sixth sense told her that tomorrow was going to be difficult in lots of ways – not only with Luke wanting an answer, but also being faced with Suzy's stonewalling again. Her eyes flickered towards Anouk in the passenger seat beside her. 'I couldn't have done it without your help, you know. You guys were amazing, pitching in like that.'

Kelly and Anouk had stood in the kitchen doorway, their eyes on the bowls already filled with washed, chopped and colour-coded ingredients, and had immediately put aprons on over their pyjamas, recognizing work as catharsis when they saw it. They had stayed like that all day – no one, not even Anouk, taking a shower or getting dressed till they'd been ready to start packing the car, Kelly and Anouk obediently following Cassie's instructions with an understanding that sometimes, just sometimes, it was better to do than to talk. They had made great sous-chefs. (Notwithstanding the moment Anouk accidentally sliced off a nail and made such a fuss that for several moments Cassie had thought it had been a finger.)

'I've got to say, I never realized how intense your job is,' Kelly piped up from the back. 'It seems to me you've got to have ten arms, plus eyes in the back of your head.'

Cassie chuckled. 'It certainly feels like that sometimes.' It had been revelatory for her to be the 'expert' among her friends for once. Her tutelage under her late friend and mentor Claude Sautans in Paris had been a first-class education and she rarely got a chance to indulge, to show what she was really capable of doing; her job usually meant working to very tight budgets and briefs, but Gem's ideas had been so obscure and unrealistic – not to mention last-minute, having maintained all the way through that she didn't want to be 'hung up' on the superfluous details of the day – that Cassie had felt vindicated to take carte blanche and produce a menu to her vision.

Hence she'd planned individual hampers, starting with terrines of jellied ham, parsley and quail's eggs, then moving on to a salad of pea tops with edible pansies, and rare lamb and butternut squash roasted with hazelnuts. For pudding, she'd whipped up some deliciously tart gooseberry fool and elderflower jelly, and in lieu of a formal wedding cake – which would have needed to have been started six weeks ago – she had baked several trays of rose petal-infused macaroons, ready to stack into a croquembouche (her and Claude's signature dish) in the morning.

'I can't believe the scale of things down here,' Kelly murmured as ten-foot-high, pink-tufted hedgerows whistled past the car with only inches to spare either side, the scent of wild garlic a pinch of sweetness in the night air. 'It's like Lilliput, everything's so tiny. They must operate a one-way system like New York, right?'

'Nope.'

'You're kidding? They get two-way traffic down these roads?'

'I know. It's crazy. And most of it's tractors too.'

The lanes were quiet as they slipped through the hilltop village, the snake of traffic down to the sailing club mercifully dispersed for the night and the drunken babble from the Mariner's pub too distant to discern from here. A fox skipped across the lane a short distance in front of them, its casual cock of the head telling them it had no fear, took no heed of the rounded car from another era bumbling towards it.

'Well, this is it,' Cassie said a few minutes later, turning into the long drive and past the cream pebble-dashed pillars. 'That's Snapdragons on the right.'

'Oh.' Anouk's voice betrayed disappointment as they passed the 1950s house, the Renault Clio and the Jeep parked outside at jaunty angles, a light shining through the downstairs window.

'I know. It's not a beautiful house, but wait till tomorrow when you see the setting and the views. It's sensational.'

She slowed as they approached Butterbox. Every light

was blazing so that from a distance the house appeared almost aflame and there were various cars in the drive – Suzy's Volvo, of course, and an old orange Beetle that she recognized as Hattie's, but there was another, glossier one too, with a rental sticker on the back bumper. Had Laird's brother caught a standby flight after all, then? Archie's bike was propped up against the hydrangea bush, the day's issue of *The Times* still rolled up and now damp with dew in the basket.

They disembarked with care. Cassie was the only one who hadn't had a hamper on her lap and they each had to stretch out, after hours of sitting hunched. They piled the hampers in a tower in the porch by the front door – some of them had been filled with the wine glasses and cutlery, others the jellies and pansies – ready to bring in shortly with a little help from the others.

'Well, here goes,' Cassie said quietly, her key in the lock and taking a deep breath as Anouk and Kelly both squeezed her shoulders. 'Remember, say nothing yet to Suzy, OK? You're just here to . . .' She faltered, not having thought through an alibi.

'Here to see her,' Anouk said. 'She's been trying to get me down here for years.'

'And I'm so desperate to get away from Bebe I'll even spend seven hours in your tinpot car,' Kelly quipped, taking the sleeve of Cassie's light jumper and maternally tugging it down, over the bangle.

'OK, yes. Good. Great,' Cassie nodded uncertainly. She had a sense of standing on the precipice again, not sure if she was going to jump or be pushed.

They stepped into the hallway, dropping their bags onto

the sagging blue damask wing chair opposite the stairs. The house's distinctive musty, salty tang had sweet and fresh top notes, thanks to an armful of long-stemmed pale pink roses lying out on the hall console.

'Beautiful,' Anouk whispered, rushing over.

'Well, Hats must have come round to the idea of the marriage, then,' Kelly murmured, lifting one and smelling it with her eyes closed. 'I carried these at my wedding, do you remember?'

As if she could ever forget. 'Maiden's Blush,' Cassie nodded. It was the perfect wedding flower, albeit a rare, old-fashioned variety these days, which Hattie grew in her noteworthy dedicated rose garden at West Meadows. They had been the catalyst that had brought her and Henry together at last, and the sight and smell of them were almost painful to her now.

The sound of voices in the sitting room carried down the hall – earnest conversation, some talking over each other, the tone harried and humourless. The women all looked at each other. Perhaps Hattie hadn't come round after all? Were she and Suzy launching a joint last-minute offensive on Gem?

'Hey. I'm back,' Cassie called through casually, her eyes on Archie standing by the fireplace, the safest person she could cling to as she walked into the room. His arm dropped from the mantelpiece as he saw her. 'Guess who I found wandering the streets of Pimlico.' She stepped to the side to let Kelly and Anouk into the room too.

Suzy clapped her hands over her mouth at the sight of them, tears springing to her eyes as she rushed over, clutching them both in a giant bear hug, her speciality. 'I can't tell you how good it is to see you,' she sobbed.

Kelly and Anouk met Cassie's eyes in silent concern. Cassie looked at the floor, uncomfortable at Suzy's emotional reaction. Was she trying to garner sympathy, bring them on side? In a moment of clarity, Cassie knew her friend would never forgive her for the decision she was going to make; she would never support her as her friend; she would stand against her as Henry's sister. Cassie was going to lose them both. Fact.

Out of the corner of her eye, she could see Laird and Gem on one sofa, but instead of Gem's legs stretched over Laird's lap, she was curled up beside him like a baby animal seeking warmth; Luke and Amber were on the other sofa, Luke's arm slung lackadaisically across the back seat cushions, but she saw how he stiffened at the sight of her, and a frisson of electricity surged through her to be so close to him again. Even in her peripheral vision she could see how good he looked in his grey T-shirt and jeans; she could isolate his scent in a room full of others. Everything about him put her senses on high alert. Her heart was pounding, her nerves scorched and fried. She wanted to both run to and away from him at the same time; she wanted to kiss and slap him in the same moment; she wanted everything and nothing to do with him. She wished she had never met him; she couldn't imagine not having met him. She didn't regret a moment they'd shared of their past anymore, but was that the same as regretting not sharing a future? Cassie tugged on her sleeve, taking care to hide the dratted bangle from the others – it could give them away in a moment; hadn't he thought of that? – as she stole a glance at him. She couldn't help herself – and as his hazel eyes, apprehensive for once, locked with hers, she was taken aback by the force of the instincts that suffused every fibre of her mind, body and soul. Suddenly she knew. She knew exactly what she was going to do. She could feel it – the answer had come to her finally and it felt so right, so real, she thought she could bite down on it.

'Where have you *been*?'

She turned back to find Archie staring at her, a look of ashen desperation on his usually florid face.

'You know where. I went back to London to get the food sorted. I said I'd be back tonight.'

'Yes, but your phone . . . it's been switched off!'

She swallowed, not daring to look at Luke again. 'That's right. It, er . . . ran out of juice and I didn't have a charger.'

Archie ran a hand through his hair. 'Cass, we've been trying to get hold of you.'

She felt bad that she hadn't told them in person. Maybe a note had been too abrupt? She could only imagine the grief Suzy had been giving him as Cassie disappeared forty-eight hours before the wedding. With the way things were between them at the moment, Suzy probably doubted Cassie's promise that she'd be back in time, and the caterer going off radar with two days to go was every wedding planner's nightmare, much less *this* wedding planner's with *this* wedding.

'Well, there's really nothing to worry about. Everything's sorted. I shopped yesterday and prepped today, thanks to my sous-chefs.' She shot a relaxed smile across to the happy couple. 'We're good to go. I think you're going to be very pleased.'

'Great,' Gem nodded, her smile weak.

Cassie looked back to the others, baffled by the strangely muted mood in the room. Was this wedding on or not?

Gem and Laird must have reconciled after the fallout from her fight with Suzy the other day, else they wouldn't be sitting together, on the sofa, but there appeared to have been a seismic shift in dynamics.

She became aware of glances sliding across the room like skaters on ice.

'Look, there's something—' Arch began.

'God, sorry! I'm being so rude not introducing you guys,' Cassie said at the same time, remembering her manners. 'Gem and Laird, Luke and Amber, meet Kelly and Anouk, our oldest friends.'

'And dearest,' Suzy said – proprietorially? – dabbing her eyes again.

Everyone obeyed protocol and robotically shook hands, Luke greeting both Kelly, whom he knew well, and Anouk, whom he'd met once, with cautious reserve.

'Drinks?' Suzy asked, seemingly highly strung and fidgety tonight. Cassie wondered whether she was even aware of the way she kept balling her hands into fists.

'Please,' Anouk replied gratefully. 'Anything red.'

'I don't suppose you've got any coconut water?' Kelly asked hopefully. Cassie glanced across at the super-healthy option and she felt a kernel of anxiety that they hadn't had a moment alone yet. She had to get some time on her own with her. How was Kelly able to keep up this pretence that all was well? How was she able to keep something so devastating a secret when Cassie couldn't keep it under wraps that she'd kissed her ex?

'*Coconut* water?' Suzy pulled a face, looking more like her normal self for a moment. 'Listen, you're not in Manhattan now, honey. If you want even sparkling water, I'll have to give you a straw and you can blow the bubbles yourself.'

'Fine,' Kelly laughed. 'Then I'll keep Arch company and have whatever he's having. I'm trying to get healthy too.'

'Says the woman who planks before bed just for kicks,' Suzy muttered, wandering over to the drinks table. 'Honestly, there are Olympians who'd be intimidated by you.'

'Look, Cass—' Archie began again.

'Lemon, Kell?' Suzy asked.

'Thanks. Or if you've got any lime. Apparently it's really good for the liver because of the—'

'Would you all please just shut up and listen to me?' Archie suddenly yelled.

They all looked at him in amazement. Archie never raised his voice.

'There's something you need to know.' His eyes were on Cassie and she felt herself go cold. 'We've been frantically trying to get hold of you, but your phone was off.'

'Oh, she's here! She's here! Thank God!' Cassie turned to find Hattie calling back up the stairs, before advancing down the hall towards her with her arms outstretched. 'Oh, my poor lamb.' She hugged Cassie close.

Cassie – who was now rigid with anxiety – stood as stiff as a board, waiting to be let go, to be told what was going on. Hattie stared back at her, hollow-eyed and hollow-cheeked. 'Now, darling, it's all going to be OK. I can feel it. In my bones, I can. I'm his mother and I *know* it's all going to be OK.'

Cassie's mouth opened but no sound rose from her throat; her eyes blinked, but they couldn't see – instead Suzy's tears, Gem's quiet, Archie's agitation, Luke's fear balled together in her mind. Her phone had been switched off. It had been switched off!

The sound of feet – small, light, hurried – coming down

the hallway made her glance over. They sounded echoey and she thought she was hallucinating at the sight of the slight, tidy woman running towards her. How could she be here? Why was she here?

There could be only one reason.

Gravity loosened its grip on her and she felt herself begin to float. She thought this must be what shock was, a total suspension of conscious control: she couldn't take a step if she wanted to, couldn't swat a fly or duck a punch. All she could do was wait – wait for the words that would spin her out of this self-protective cocoon and into freefall, because she already knew what they were going to say.

But they were too slow – or rather she was too fast – and as she fell to the floor, the words remained unsaid. Unreal. Untrue.

They were untrue.

Chapter Twenty-Eight

She came to on the sofa, her mother sitting beside her, rubbing her hand in her own, as she always had done when she'd been a little girl. No one else was around, although she could hear voices in the hallway, the sounds of doors banging.

'What happened?' Cassie croaked, disorientated. 'Where is everyone?'

Edie, her mother, leaned forwards and kissed her forehead. She looked older than she did on the Skype screens, worry etched into the corners of her eyes, threads of grey at her blonded temples, her round blue eyes, which Cassie had inherited, watery from tears. 'You just fainted, darling. I told them all to give you some air. It was terribly stuffy in here.'

They blinked at each other, both knowing that wasn't why she'd passed out. Cassie realized she was holding her breath again. 'Tell me the truth, Mum.'

There was a tiny pause. 'They've lost contact with the boat, darling. There was a typhoon.'

'Typhoon?' Cassie had grown up in Hong Kong. She was well accustomed to storms of this kind and she knew their power – how they whipped up tsunamis in the oceans and snapped communications towers like kindling twigs when they hit land. She remembered how her father used to lash the garden furniture to the balcony railings, religiously clearing out the gutters to make sure the water could run faster than it fell.

Her mother squeezed her hand tightly. 'But the good news – and what we really have to hold on to at this point – is that it was forecast. They knew the typhoon was coming and they had time to head towards the nearest land mass – some islands, we think.'

'But if they've lost contact . . .' Cassie prompted. She didn't want to know, but she had to. Imagination would be so much worse than reality. There was no bliss in ignorance.

'Then they must have been caught up in it, yes. Of course, it could be that some of the communications equipment was just damaged but the boat is fine. They may well be sailing along, absolutely tickety-boo, just without radio contact.'

'When was the last contact?'

'Tuesday night.'

'*Tuesday?*' Cassie echoed. It was now Friday night, but her phone had been switched off from yesterday. 'But . . . but I was here till yesterday morning. Why didn't we hear about it before then? I never would have g—'

'No one here knew till Archie saw it in the papers yesterday, after you'd left. He got in touch with the communications people and . . . that's when they told him. They thought we already knew. An email had been sent out apparently.' She shrugged. 'I don't know. They're looking into it internally but . . . well, that's a fight for another day. Right now, the only thing that matters is making sure that everyone on the boat is OK.' She squeezed Cassie's hand again. 'Everyone's been calling you constantly since they found out.'

Cassie remembered the call she hadn't returned to Suzy.

'Archie even wanted to fly up and go to your flat to tell you, but Suzy's not letting him out of her sight. He's terribly stressed about it all and she's worried sick about him. This kind of strain's not good for him, so soon after his attack.'

Cassie blinked, her head swimming again. While she'd been shopping and chopping, everyone here had been desperately ringing her, and all that time Henry had been – what of him? Was he desperately clinging to an upturned raft? Were the bottles scattering in the ocean, one by one, littering the seas and doing the very thing they were protesting against?

She frowned. 'How did you get here so quickly?' Hong Kong was a twelve-hour flight away.

'I was coming anyway, darling. I wanted to surprise you.' Edie smiled. 'I've been trying to support Hats through this wedding malarkey. Honestly, that poor family is going through the wringer at the moment – first Archie, then Gem, now Henry.' She sighed. 'Between you and me, I'm not sure how much more she can take.'

'But you're so terrified of flying.'

Her mother shook her head. 'I'm *more* terrified of letting down my best friend. She needs me right now. How could I put my irrational fear before her very real trauma? Frankly, a Valium and a couple of gin and tonics was the very least I could do to support her.'

Cassie smiled wanly – she knew the cost to her mother's nerves would have been significantly graver than she was letting on – but her concern was elsewhere. She stared into space, trying to make the words real. She felt numb and disconnected, the words bouncing off her like rubber bullets: the boat was missing. The boat made with bottles in a typhoon-whipped ocean had lost contact with land, with the people who could read the satellites and keep them safe and bring them all back to the people who loved them.

It was hideous but true: Henry was missing.

'So w-what next?' Her voice shook like a leaf about to fall.

Edie sat straighter, pushing back her shoulders. 'We wait, darling. That's all we can do. Obviously, the satellite and communications people are in constant contact with the authorities. The boat will show up on a radar somewhere – military or commercial or what-have-you. We'll hear something soon. Any minute. *Any* minute.'

The tears came then, small, tight budded ones as she tried to imagine the number of people searching for the man she loved, lost in the vastness of the Pacific Ocean. Reassurance was hollow when weighed against the bald facts, the overbearing odds as to what had happened.

'Oh, darling, please don't cry,' Edie soothed, her voice cracking too. 'He'll come back. Everything will be fine, you'll see.'

'You don't know that,' Cassie cried. 'This entire expedition was risky enough, without putting a bloody typhoon in the mix.'

'Hats sent me the links for the JustGiving page before he left. I thought the boat looked very professional and high-tech.'

Cassie cried harder. Her mother's idea of high-tech was an ice dispenser on the fridge. 'God, poor Hattie,' she wept, pressing her palms against her eyes, but the tears just overflowed through her fingers. Her son was missing at sea and Cassie knew her well enough to know that behind the brisk Pollyanna demeanour was the heart of a bunny. She looked up. 'Where is she?'

'Upstairs, resting. I was giving her half of one of my Valiums when you arrived. It's all too much. She has to try to relax. She's no good to anyone if she's exhausted. The poor old girl's running on fumes.'

'What about Suzy?'

'Arch is with her. I think they've taken Velvet in with them for the night.'

'Right,' Cassie nodded, trying to swallow down the tears, to calm down.

'We should get you up to bed too. Kelly and Nooks said you were up early, running around like the proverbial fly all day, and then a seven-hour drive on top of it all? It's no wonder you were giddy.'

'I'm fine, Mum, really. I think I'll just . . . I'm just going to sit here for a bit. But you should go and check on Hats. Make sure she's OK on your medication. I bet it's super-strength, isn't it?'

Her mother smiled, but her eyes were sad. 'It's you I should be looking after. You're my baby girl.'

'But you must be jet-lagged out of your mind.'

Her mother squeezed her hands again. They both knew Cassie was trying to say that she wanted to be alone.

'Well,' she said finally, 'I suppose I am a little all over the place.' She rose to standing. 'But I'm in the blue room, if you need me, OK?'

Cassie nodded, sniffing as she watched her walk to the door.

'Mum?'

Her mother turned.

'I'm so pleased you're here.'

'Me too, darling. We'll face this together. We will.'

'I know.'

Cassie listened numbly to the sound of her mother's footsteps retreating down the hall, fading into silence as she climbed the carpeted stairs. Cassie slumped back on the sofa, the words *'typhoon . . . lost contact . . . missing . . .'* buffeting her from the inside. She tried not to imagine the waves; she tried not to think of the bottles drifting off one by one, of Beau grabbing the last life jacket, of Henry being a hero to the others stuck in a cabin . . .

He wasn't even supposed to have been there! If he'd just had that meeting after the race, he'd be safe in the Arctic by now. If he hadn't run into Beau, he never would have known about this damned trip. *'Beau was doing a favour for a friend . . .'* Amy's words floated through her mind again, snagging somehow.

Her face crumpled, sobs wracking her in spite of her best efforts. How could she only know about his torment now? Why hadn't she *felt* it, somehow – a fear in the pit of her stomach, that something, something was wrong?

How many rings of hell had he been to while she had debated whether or not to leave him? What furies had he battled while she kissed another man and indulged herself in fantasies of reviving a long-lost love affair? Had he shouted her name in the waves even as she insisted that losing her freedom was too high a price to pay for love?

She retched, feeling sick to her core, sick with herself. She had been a fool to think she ever deserved him, that *she* would ever be the one doing the leaving. He was too good for her. She'd been lucky to get away with keeping him for as long as she had. The glint of gold caught her eye and she grabbed at the bangle with her right hand, desperately pulling at it, trying to get it off as though it scorched her skin; but no matter how hard she tugged and yanked, trying to force the precious metal past skin and bone, it remained fixed round her wrist like, Kelly had said, a handcuff, shackling her to her own ugly delusions, mocking her falseness.

She cried again, her eyes falling to a photograph on the side table: Henry aged eleven, in an Aran jumper, his bright blond hair shaggy and unkempt and falling into his eyes so that all that could really be seen of his face was his exuberant smile, Rover's paws resting on his forearm as the two of them grinned for the camera.

Cassie reached for it with her treacherous, cuffed arm, tears splashing onto the glass as she stared at the little boy who'd become the man in whose eyes she had glimpsed forever, the man she had loved, the man she had now lost.

Breakfast was a ghost of itself. Tea grew cold in the pot, croissants stale on the plates, smoke from the toaster allowed to drift, unnoticed, to the open windows.

Cassie hadn't slept – in fact, she hadn't even been up to her room. Her overnight bag was still in the hall, and her clothes were so rumpled from a night on the sofa, her body so inert, it was like she'd been trampled by cows. It didn't appear anyone had slept, except for Velvet, and they all sat round the kitchen table, staring into the woodgrain like it held answers that would unlock the riddle of where, quite literally, in the world Henry was now.

Sighs issued from Archie like gales as he stood boiling the kettle for the sixth time without ever remembering to pour, much less to drink. Suzy was trying, in a tiny voice, to cajole Velvet into eating mango with a bib on; Hattie and Edie were still upstairs.

'Please try to have some tea,' Kelly said, setting a fresh, steaming cup in front of her. (Archie had wandered into the garden and was standing staring out to sea, the kettle forgotten again.)

Cassie blinked a 'no', her eyelids so puffy and raw they barely needed to move at all.

'Maybe coffee?' Anouk tried, earning herself an arched eyebrow from Kelly.

'I . . . can't.' She felt sick, wretched, disgusted. She felt more things than she could consciously process.

The room fell silent again, Kelly and Anouk uncomfortably aware of the frozen sea that separated Cassie and Suzy as they sat, oblivious to each other across the table, each wrapped up in their own pain.

'How about a walk?' Kelly tried. 'Some fresh air would do you all good.'

This time, no one bothered to answer and Kelly got up, a pained expression on her face, as she gave Anouk a tiny, imperceptible shrug.

'Well, have a shower at least,' Anouk implored, doubtless being driven to the edge of reason that Cassie wasn't in fresh, matching lingerie. 'Put on some clean clothes.' She reached for Cassie's hand, tugging at it gently until Cassie got up wordlessly and followed after like an obedient puppy.

She stood under the water that Anouk got running for her, only coming out when Anouk turned it off and wrapped her in a towel, drying her hair lightly before laying out clean clothes on the bed.

When she came back downstairs forty minutes later, she

was clean, but not revived. Nothing had changed. They were still waiting.

Archie was no longer in the garden. There was a void where he'd been standing by the hedge and she went to fill it, her eyes on the thin stretch of blue that ran across the horizon like a ribbon on a birthday cake. What had it done with him, that malevolent body of water? Was it tossing him like a cork on the froth of its waves? Had it pulled him down to the murky depths where blue turned to black?

Her gaze swung round the ellipse until it came to the tiny church's steeple, which punctured the sky like a nail, a sudden blip of activity on a heart monitor that was flat-lining. Her feet began to move towards it, one in front of the other over the grass. She climbed over the stile as if on automatic, her hand trailing over the prickles and thorns of the brambly hedgerow, welcoming the pinpricks of pain, grateful she could feel that, at least.

Ahead, she could see two figures rushing up the path, back towards the house. The smaller one was faltering, stumbling, arms outstretched as if to break a fall.

Cassie stopped, waiting for them to reach her.

'I just . . .' Gem's eyes were as red as her own, her face as pale as a moon. 'It's off. I've told the vicar.'

'I'm sorry,' Cassie said quietly. In truth, the wedding had completely slipped her mind, but of course, how could it have gone ahead in these circumstances? She remembered, too, another wedding that had slipped her mind as she realized that, right now, hundreds of miles north of here, Gil was moving on. Just like that, their marriage was being erased, overwritten by a new one, a new hope, as if it had never existed at all.

Her eyes slid over to Luke, silent as a shadow, behind Gem.

'It's because of the timing,' Gem said.

'Yes.'

Gem stared at her shivering in the warmth. 'I have to see Aunt Hats.'

Cassie watched her go.

'I'd better stay with her. She's in pieces,' Luke murmured. 'She didn't want this. It was Laird's decision.'

'Oh.' She didn't know what to say. Speaking felt like an effort too far. It was almost more than she could manage just to breathe and move when all her efforts were going into trying not to feel. 'Where's Amber?'

'Sleeping.'

Cassie didn't reply. Wasn't Amber supposed to be Gem's friend? Her bridesmaid?

'She needs a lot of sleep,' he added, his voice an apologetic mumble.

Cassie bit her lip. She felt a sudden wave of anger to think that Amber could be so peacefully, so indulgently sleeping her way through this living nightmare.

'It's not just the timing,' Luke said, bringing her back to the moment, back to him. 'He thinks she's not ready.' He looked at her closely as he said it, as though the statement was also a question. For her.

She ignored it. 'Where is he now?'

'Laird? Giving her space. His brother landed in Newquay this morning, so he went to pick him up and I think they're spending the day over there. I wouldn't like to be him, having to explain that the journey was for nothing.'

When Cassie didn't reply, he carried on. 'Anyway, he

reckons it'll be better all round if he's not in the way for a while.'

'Probably,' she murmured, looking back at him, aiming the double meaning at him this time.

'Cass.'

The word was like a red balloon that had escaped a child, bobbing untethered, trying to rise.

She looked at him and saw the same apprehension in his eyes that she had seen last night. She understood it now; she knew he had realized – even before she was told the news last night – that this changed everything. He couldn't know that she had already made her decision anyway, that the very sight, sound and smell of him, intoxicating though he was, wasn't her home. She had known it with utter certainty when she'd walked into the room. He was an interloper in her life, a pleasing and sexy diversion, but distraction was all he offered. Henry was nourishment. He fed her soul. He made her a better version of herself, bigger in every way.

His mouth opened, his speech – pleas – ready, but she shook her head, looking back out to sea. Their silence would have to say it all. Words, actions, chemistry, history – they weren't enough. He wasn't enough; he wasn't Henry. Even if she couldn't have Henry, she didn't want *him*.

'You need to take this off,' she said quietly, holding up her arm. The bangle dangled from her wrist – beautiful but dead.

He stared at it. 'But it's yours.'

'I don't want it.' Her words were flat, the rejection absolute.

He recoiled as though she'd slapped him. 'Well, I can't. I

don't have the screwdriver here. On me.' He patted his jeans pockets as if to show her.

She forced herself to hold his gaze, even though the look in his eyes sliced at her like a swinging scythe. She knew she had to do this. 'Later, then. Bring it to the house before you leave.'

His mouth parted at the order that, strictly speaking, wasn't hers to give.

'Cass, look, I know you're hurt – it's terrible not knowing about Henry – but don't you think you—'

'No.' She blinked at him, knowing exactly what he was saying – that the news coming her way might be the worst, that Henry was never coming back. Why throw away everything they could have for something she might never be able to have? He didn't see that she could never forgive herself for what they had done in these past hours. That they may have had a complicated past, but even if she *had* still wanted him, their future was already too tainted to navigate, bound as it was now in the jet threads of this nightmare. She would choose to be alone over ever being with him. 'It's not going to work, Luke.'

'But the other night, you felt it too – I know you did; you said so yourself.'

'You said what I wanted to hear. You want me to just ignore my fears, to run away from my life, from *myself*. But I have to face up to my past. There's no way around it. I can't keep pretending it didn't happen or it didn't matter, I am who I am because of it.'

'And I love you just the way you are, Cass. I always have.' He took a step towards her, desperation in his movements. 'The girl in front of me – that's all I've ever wanted.'

But Cassie took a step back, holding up her arm so that

the bangle glinted in the sun. 'This isn't love, Luke. This isn't freedom. It's denial, it's possession. You just want back what you lost – your ego needs—'

'No.' He shook his head, his jaw clenched. 'You're upset; you're not thinking straight. See, I *knew* this would happen. I knew it'd send you off spinning back to him, that you'd feel some kind of . . . duty.'

She laughed suddenly, like he'd told a joke. 'Duty? Being with *him*?' The smile faded from her face as a vision of Henry – windswept and tanned, his roguish smile lopsided, his grey-blue eyes soft as he stared at her – swam before her eyes. 'I should be so lucky ever to stand by his side again,' she murmured. 'To say that I was his . . .' Her fingers found the Tiffany solitaire and she brought the ring to her lips, her eyes closing as she kissed it with almost reverential tenderness. She had to believe . . .

Cassie opened her eyes and met Luke's gaze with sombre certainty. 'Please, Luke. Please believe me when I say I never want to see you again.' She knew the words were like knives. She regretted their savagery, but there was nothing else to be done when he wouldn't give up. He just wouldn't let her go.

She watched as his eyes roamed her for the last time, his idea of love – possession – hardening in front of her into something cold and brittle before he turned and marched away. Cassie watched him go, catching sight of a familiar figure standing on the balcony, hair blowing in the breeze, her child on her hip.

Cassie raised her hand, like a boat signalling to the light-house, but Suzy simply turned and disappeared back into the bedroom, leaving her to crash upon the rocks. Alone.

Chapter Twenty-Nine

Her mother was sitting on the bed unpacking when Cassie knocked and put her head round the door. 'Hi.'

Edie straightened up. 'Oh, darling. How are you? Did you get any sleep?' She wrapped her arms around her daughter as Cassie sank onto the mattress beside her and bent to put her head on her shoulder.

'A bit,' she mumbled, trying not to cry again. Being with her mother lowered all her adult defences and they sat in silence for a while, Edie rubbing her back in large, soothing circles, just as she had done when Cassie was a little girl.

'You had gone out when I came down earlier,' Edie said, as Cassie finally pulled away.

'Yeah, I needed a bit of fresh air.'

'Where did you go? To the beach?'

Cassie shook her head. She hadn't been able to bear the thought of going somewhere that celebrated the sea, a joyful place where people played and relaxed on the sand, and swam in the still shallows. 'To the church.'

'Oh. Have they taken down the flowers yet?'

'Not yet,' Cassie said flatly, picking at the bedspread as she idly looked around the room, comforted somewhat by the sight of her mother's possessions on the surfaces – her old Mason Pearson hairbrush, her silver Asprey travel clock, identical to the one Cassie's father had given her too.

'Such a shame. They were so pretty,' Edie said. 'Still, it provided a good distraction for Hats yesterday if nothing else. We were doing the flowers for most of the afternoon. We found some lovely blossoms in the hedgerows, which Hats somehow fashioned into pew-end pieces.'

'How could she think about a wedding when her son's missing?' Cassie asked with disbelief.

'Oh, I don't think she thought for one minute that the wedding would actually go ahead today. Even Gem isn't that headstrong. No, it just gave her something to do with her hands. Far better than moping around the house, just waiting. Hats isn't very good at being a spectator.'

'No.' Cassie remembered Henry's frustrated helplessness when Archie had been in the hospital. 'I saw the roses in the hall last night.'

'Yes, they were for the bouquet.' Edie sighed. 'Poor Hats – she'd give up her objections to the wedding in a moment, now, if she could just get her boy back.' She paused, bringing her fist to her mouth for a moment, as though stopping a sneeze. 'Oh well, we can get them into some water anyway. They'll brighten the place up a little.'

Cassie didn't say anything. Even roses as beautiful as the Maiden's Blush couldn't distract from the horror being played out in all their lives.

'How is Gem?' Edie asked.

Cassie shrugged, getting up and wandering over to the dressing table. An orange suede jewellery travel bag was unrolled on the glass surface and her fingers tripped lightly over the strings of pearls, gold knot earrings and delicate chain necklaces that she remembered her mother wearing all her life. 'I've barely seen her. Not great, I don't think.'

435

'No, she wasn't taking it too well when I saw her in the kitchen earlier, although I do believe it's the right decision, even though Laird seems like a lovely chap. He was very decent when we sat them down on Thursday and explained about the letter of wishes. I felt almost bad about it, as it really does cast so many aspersions on him, poor fellow.'

Cassie turned round, resting her bottom on the dressing table. 'Sorry, you've lost me. What's the "letter of wishes"?'

'Hasn't Suzy told you? It's why I came over in the first place, darling. Hats took advice from her solicitor about the trust and apparently it came with a separate letter of wishes, which acts like a directive, if you like, stipulating how and when the estate should be given over – or *not*. And a young, rushed marriage like this, which is opposed by the trustees, is sufficient grounds to delay the transfer of the trust.'

'But . . .' Cassie was still confused. 'I don't get why you . . .'

'You were very young when all this was arranged but your father was one of the trustees, darling. He and Pip had become very good friends over the years and, well, when Daddy died the trusteeship passed over to me. Naturally I didn't really think there'd ever be anything I had to do, but of course when Hats told me about the letter, well . . . I had to back her up on it.' She gave a small shrug. 'We told Gem and Laird almost as soon as I arrived on Thursday.'

'Told them what exactly?'

'That the inheritance was being pushed back till she was thirty. The poor girl's got a *lot* of issues. Hattie firmly believes, and I do agree with her, that coming into that kind of money could very well be detrimental to her well-being. It's going to be some time before she's really standing on her own two feet.' Her mouth pursed thoughtfully. 'They took it very well, I thought. Maybe he really wasn't interested in her money after all.' She sighed. 'Anyway, then Archie came back with the dreadful news about Henry and all thoughts of weddings fled.'

'Yes, right.' Cassie looked down, reaching for the dressing-table stool and sitting on it carefully. She felt giddy again and realized she hadn't eaten anything since yesterday afternoon. 'I remember these.' She picked up a pair of silver cufflinks and rolled them in her palm. 'Dad always wore these.'

'They were his favourites,' Edie said, watching her from the bed. 'I bought them for him when I was pregnant with you. I think he'd have worn them with his pyjamas if he could.' She chuckled softly, enlivened and saddened at the same time by the memory.

They were quiet for a little while.

'While I've got you all to myself for a bit, tell me why you and Suzy aren't speaking.' Edie held up her hand quickly. 'And don't bother trying to deny it. It was as obvious as a punch in the face, last night.'

Cassie put the cufflinks back in the travel bag, feeling her hands begin to tremble. 'I've been an idiot.' Her voice was quiet, her eyes glued to the faded green carpet.

Edie waited for her to explain.

'You remember Luke?'

Edie frowned. 'You mean the American you went out with before Henry?'

Cassie nodded, biting her lip, waiting for the penny to drop. Her mother had been here with their group for two days now. Sure enough, her frown gradually deepened again. 'You don't mean the one—'

Cassie nodded. 'Going out with Gem's bridesmaid.'

'That's *him*?' Edie asked in astonishment, before her expression changed. 'Oh, Cass, no.'

Cassie bit her lip, her hand inadvertently tugging against the bangle again. 'Henry and I were having problems. Well, just one, actually, but it's a big one. He wanted to get married and I . . . just didn't.'

'Oh, darling.' Edie's hands fluttered and folded above her heart.

'He basically issued me with an ultimatum before he left: we get married or we split up.' Cassie looked at her pleadingly. 'I wasn't trying to make things worse, but Luke just—'

Edie sighed. 'Luke just turned up, saying all the things you wanted to hear, I imagine.'

Cassie nodded miserably. 'But it was true, some of it. Our relationship *hadn't* run its course. I was off on a year-long adventure back then, running my life to a timetable that took no notice of the fact that we were happy together. I left him behind simply because we ran out of time, and I told myself that he was just a rebound. But then when he came back and everything felt the same between us, I started thinking, What if he wasn't?'

Edie shook her head patiently. 'That's just the fear talking, darling. No one who's ever seen you and Henry together could doubt that what you and he share is the real thing.' She shrugged. 'I'm not saying what you and Luke shared wasn't wonderful too, and no doubt just what you needed to start moving on from Gil, but, darling, he's not Mr Right. He was – and will only ever be – Mr Right Now.'

'And Gil's getting married today as well,' Cassie said quickly, a sob punctuating the end of the sentence before she could stop it. Her eyes shone suddenly with tears. 'Mum. I think I panicked.' Her hand covered her mouth, as though the very words were dirty.

'I think you did too,' her mother agreed, her eyes soft. 'Does Henry know about any of this?'

Cassie's mouth turned down. 'No.'

Edie nodded. 'Well, do you know what I've always believed is the best thing about your past?'

Cassie shook her head.

'It shows you what *not* to bring into your future.' She smiled, leaning forwards and resting her elbows on her lap. 'You can learn from this, Cassie. It doesn't have to have been for nothing.'

Cassie sniffed. 'You think so?'

'Of course! After what you went through? I think it's only to be expected that you'd get a case of cold feet.'

'Nooks thinks I should steer well clear of marrying again.'

Edie rolled her eyes. 'Well, with the greatest respect, she would say that.'

Cassie frowned. 'What do you mean?'

'Henri – her father – was a *terrible* rogue. Just terrible! He cheated on poor Camille more times than any of us could count. I mean, I know the French believe in turning a blind eye to that sort of thing, but everyone's got their limits. He humiliated her, flaunting his girlfriends in her face.' Edie tutted. 'No, it was beyond any of us why she stayed with him, and now look – Anouk's got commitment issues of her own. *Quelle surprise!*'

Cassie was quiet. She had never known any of this

before. Hers and Suzy's, Kelly and Anouk's parents had all been friends – it was how the girls had met in the first place – but she had been a child, oblivious to the under-currents and sexual politics at play in their parents' social set. To her mind, Anouk's father had simply been the sharpest-suited man in the group, who made them laugh by blowing the smoke from his Gitanes out through his nose like a dragon and always carried a pack of cards in his pocket.

'I suppose—' Cassie began.

A sudden scream downstairs made them both gasp, their faces turned towards the door, ears pricked as the sound of raised voices in the kitchen were muffled by the thick carpets.

'Oh God, what the hell's happened now?' Cassie whispered, running to the door and looking out into the hallway.

'Cassie!'

She froze as she heard Suzy holler her name, stood motionless on the landing as the sound of heavy footsteps drew closer, quickly, on the stairs, almost dropped on the spot as a rangy, long-legged figure in a navy-and-red sailing jacket cleared the top step.

Henry stopped, like he'd run into a glass wall, at the sight of her. His face was bearded and sunburnt, but that only served to make his eyes brighter, his teeth whiter . . . He looked more alive than she had ever seen him; he seemed to glow, almost, like an angel.

She gasped. Was that what this was? Was this a trick of her mind? Was this what happened when sleeplessness and fear combined?

He seemed to read her panic. 'Cass.' The word was as real as a touch.

'You're here,' she quailed, scarcely able to believe what her eyes were showing her, one hand to her mouth, the other held out to touch him, still half expecting it to pass through him like a mirage. But he took her hand and placed it to his chest; she could feel his heart pounding – almost as quickly as hers – beneath her palm.

'If not duffer ... won't drown,' he said, stepping in closer and cocooning her face with his rough hands, kissing her tenderly, feeling how she shook as the adrenalin took charge, disbelief morphing into relief.

'You're not a duffer!' she laughed, tears splashing from her eyes.

'Didn't I tell you?' he laughed back, looping his arms around her and twirling her on the spot, both of them laughing, faces nuzzled into the other's neck as they revelled in their touch and smell all over again.

He lowered her feet to the ground, his eyes boring into hers. 'But, Cass, you were right about the rest of it. I will never not listen to you again, oh, She Who Must Be Obeyed.'

A sound behind her made him look up – stiffen up, straighten up. 'What's *he* doing here?' His voice was suddenly cold and hostile, all levity gone.

Cassie turned to see Luke standing outside her bedroom, his hand still on the handle as he closed the door behind him.

She saw how Luke froze too, as he took in the sight of Henry – action man, adventurer, hero returned – his arms around her. Cassie noticed he was wearing his linen flak jacket – the one with the big pockets that he always wore on jobs – his jeans, his charcoal suede Prada trainers. For someone who had spent the past two weeks in a wetsuit or T-shirt and shorts, he looked suddenly overdressed. And very urban.

'H-his girlfriend, Amber, is Gem's bridesmaid,' she said quickly, fear thinning her voice as she kept her eyes upon Luke in a silent plea. Would he spill their secret? Was it going to be a case of if he couldn't have her, no one could? Would he try to ruin their relationship out of spite? Because if their history was anything to go by, she wouldn't put it past him. 'Well . . . was going to be,' she mumbled into the vacuum when neither man spoke.

Henry looked from Cassie back to Luke, back to Cassie again. 'Cass, what's going on?'

'It's nothing, honestly. His girlfriend's Gem's brides-maid.' She put a hand to her heart as if trying to stop her heart from leaping out. She needed to get away from here, away from Luke. This was all too much to deal with at once and she felt dizzy again. 'Can we talk about it down-stairs? I need to sit down and eat. If I don't eat, I'm going to pass out.'

Henry looked back at Luke, his body battle-ready.

'Please,' she insisted. 'Let me just enjoy the fact that you're back.'

Reluctantly, Henry dragged his eyes off Luke. 'Come on, then,' he mumbled, leading her towards the stairs, but she could tell from the feel of the tension in his body that his hackles were up. She knew he was on the scent.

Twenty minutes later she had eaten a sausage sandwich and drunk two large mugs of tea and felt thoroughly sick. But she didn't care. Henry was back. He was safe and he was here and they had *all* come alive again – even Gem.

The noise in the kitchen was rowdy, the windows steamed up, and the hob extractor was on max to cope with the kettle being boiled repeatedly and the smoke coming from the bacon and sausages that everyone kept forgetting to turn. Poor Bas had been almost overlooked in all the excitement. After a night's stopover at the Pimlico flat, he had unwittingly travelled down on the same train as Henry, but not knowing which carriage opened exactly opposite the exits (unlike Henry) had meant he'd been last, not first in the taxi rank, arriving at the house amid screams and cheers more suited to Halloween night. Cassie knew she needed to have some time alone with him too – he had already transmitted his latest heartache to her with a sad face – but he'd have to join the queue. She had Kelly to connect with too. And as for Suzy . . .

Henry was sitting at the table beside Cassie, his hand over hers and Velvet on his knee. Edie and Hattie were sitting on the other side, with Suzy and Archie at opposing ends of the table, Suzy surreptitiously letting Rollo sit in her lap and thinking no one could see as she stroked him. Anouk and Kelly were supposedly busy tidying away the dirty dishes, but they had been wiping the same spot of worktop for five minutes now, their eyes glued to Henry as his energy radiated around the room like a comet, bouncing off the walls. Gem was sitting on the arm of the small armchair by the window, eyes closed like a basking cat's as Bas undid her cornrows and treated her to one of his special head massages. Cassie didn't know where Luke and Amber were, but she thought she could guess. She hoped, anyway . . .

Henry was in full flight about the travesty that was the trip, things really coming to a head when Henry had caught Beau tossing his beer cans overboard. 'The whole thing was just a beard. He never gave a toss about pollution in the oceans; his old man had disinherited him till he did something "worthwhile" and "gave something back",' Henry said, shaking his head. 'Bringing me in – the pro-explorer – at the last minute, gave it all the whiff of respectability. Did you know he even tried to get off at the Solomon Islands when we stopped to get more water and supplies, saying he'd *catch us up* in Hawaii!'

'Unbelievable,' Archie muttered. 'What a pillock.'

'You'd have killed him, Arch. I honestly think you would.'

Archie drew himself up and puffed his chest out a little 'Probably, mate,' he nodded earnestly. 'But that's enough about him. What about the typhoon? You must have been bricking it, weren't you? What happened to the boat?'

Henry looked puzzled. 'Mate, what are you talking about?'

'The big, wet, windy thing that tossed you about four days ago?' Archie prompted with a laugh.

Henry laughed too, but he still looked confused. 'Well, yeah, but . . . I'd already left the boat by then. You know that.'

'We didn't know that.' There was a long silence. 'How would we have known that?' Suzy asked.

'Because Beau spoke to Inmarsat and got them to email you saying I was coming back. I heard him doing it myself. For all his uselessness, he did do that.' Henry looked around at the faces intent on him, their most hysterical reaction to his homecoming seeming disproportionate now that he thought about it. 'Are you saying you *didn't* get the message? You thought I . . .?' His eyes fell to Hats, Suzy, Cass – their darkly shadowed eyes his silent answer.

Archie looked uncharacteristically stern. 'So when was this?' he frowned.

Henry thought. 'What's it now? Saturday? Wednesday, then. We'd docked at the Marshall Islands because we'd been warned the typhoon was coming, and that's when I told Beau I wasn't getting back on board. The whole thing was a farce. I didn't want my name attached to it. I just got the next flight back to San Fran and then back here.'

'But we never got any email, did we, Arch?' Suzy said, reiterating the point.

Archie shook his head. 'Absolutely not. No gadgets down here. I'm de-stressing, doctor's orders. No emails.'

'But hang on!' said Suzy suddenly, remembering the very thing Cassie had been meaning – and persistently forgetting – to ask Arch herself. 'Henry's list. You got that from the little internet cafe in the back of the village store.'

Henry looked surprised. 'Are they doing Wi-Fi up there now?'

Cassie watched the panic rise in Archie's face. She knew as well as he did that there was no internet cafe in the village store.

'Uh . . .' Archie stammered.

'Did *you* get my emails?' Henry asked Cassie, leaning in to her.

Plural? Cassie's stomach lurched as she shook her head. 'Why? How many did you send?'

'Every other day . . . ?' He frowned, his expression darkening. 'Inmarsat were supposed to be forwarding everything on.'

'Well, Arch has been checking in at the store every other

day to get our personal emails and there was never anything, and certainly nothing that suggested you were disembarking, was there?' Suzy asked her husband.

He shook his head vehemently. That, at least, wasn't a lie. 'Absolutely not. God knows, it would have saved us all a *lot* of heartache if we had known.' He squeezed Suzy's hand tightly, reaching over to kiss her cheek.

'Christ, I can't believe you all thought I was caught up in that typhoon. If I'd had any idea . . .' he murmured, pulling Cassie closer to him and kissing the top of her head. 'But I don't understand it. I heard Cooper do it. There's no way Inmarsat wouldn't have forwarded the information. All hell will break loose when I report this back.' Henry's eyes were distant, his mouth set in a flat line.

He didn't notice that Cassie was stiff in his arms. She thought she might understand it. An ugly truth was beginning to form in her mind: '*Beau was doing a favour for a friend . . .*' Cassie had thought Amy was referring to Henry, giving him a job when he was on his uppers; but what if that friend had been someone else entirely, someone who would benefit from having Henry out of the picture for a while? Someone she knew from personal experience had a souped-up laptop with super-boosted Wi-Fi . . . someone who wouldn't want her to hear from her fiancé and might benefit from destabilizing them further?

She placed her hand across her mouth as a wave of nausea rose up inside her. Luke had planned it all from the start. There had been nothing 'fated' about their reunion after all; he had played her, manipulated her. She had been a damned fool to think he could ever change. Part of her wanted to think the best of him, to think he couldn't possibly have wilfully kept something like this from her, from them all.

But instinct told her he had. He had known Henry was on his way back; he'd realized he had only a tiny window of opportunity and he'd taken it. And when the news of the typhoon had come through on the news the next day, he'd chosen to keep quiet, to let them all suffer and weep as he held his nerve, trusting she would get back before Henry, that he'd snatch her away with hours to spare.

'Are you OK, Cass?'

She turned to find Henry's eyes upon her, concerned, attentive.

'Too much sausage, darling?' Edie asked, handing over a napkin.

'Or is it the nausea?' Henry winked, his tone instantly more playful as he picked up her hand and kissed the back of it tenderly.

She gave a wan smile. 'Just too much high emotion, that's all. I haven't slept properly either.'

'I guess it's to be *expected*?' He squeezed her fingers, his eyes bright, that dazzling smile plastered all over his weather-beaten, handsome face.

She smiled back at him, perplexed as she sensed he was talking in riddles.

'Is there . . . something you're trying to tell me?' she asked.

'The other way round, more like,' he grinned, leaning in to kiss her on the lips.

She shook her head, aware of a murmur rustling around the table. 'Huh? Sorry, you've lost me.'

He swallowed, his eyes burning with emotion. 'The baby?'

'What?' she echoed, thunderstruck.

'We're having a baby!' he laughed.

'We are?' she asked in astonishment.

'Oh, darling!' Edie shrieked, jumping up and almost sending the teapot flying.

'Oh good God!' Hattie cried at the same time, both women throwing their arms round each other and spontaneously bursting into tears. 'Happy dance, Edes! We're going to be grandmothers!'

Everybody laughed, Henry louder than everyone else. 'Well, you're *supposed* to be the first to know, darling, not the . . . not the . . .' His smile disappeared as he registered her blank expression. 'Wait, are you saying we're *not* having a baby?'

Cassie blinked, horrified and stunned. *What was going on?* 'Henry, what on earth made you ever think we were?' she asked.

A rush of emotions clouded Henry's fine-boned features – shock, disbelief, confusion, humiliation, anger . . . 'Because it's in your diary!' he stormed, desperately willing her to remember, to know what he was talking about, as though it was something she could possibly have forgotten! 'It was in red pen. "Nine weeks." "Twelve weeks." "Baby due."' He counted the entries off on his fingers.

Cassie retched. No.

'Why would you put that in your diary if it wasn't true?' he demanded.

She looked at Kelly in panic. Her friend was bone-white and holding on to the worktop for support. She looked as ill as Cassie felt.

'W-what were you even doing with my diary?' Cassie countered, trying to buy time, to think faster.

'I packed it in error – what do you think?! It wasn't like I had a burning desire to know your business commitments for September!'

She hid her face in her hands, wanting to hide. How had this all gone so wrong? What could she say? What possible excuse could she have for writing that a baby was due, in her own diary?

'It's mine.' Kelly's voice was thin, as hollowed out as a piccolo as she put a voice to her secret and sent it out into the world, like a message in a bottle. 'The due date is mine.'

Cassie stared at the table miserably, her heart breaking as she waited for Kelly to explain, to tell them all about the terrible brutality she had been subjected to by her own body over the past year. How she was carrying the burden alone, protecting the man she loved from needless suffering . . . Cassie had failed her. All she'd had to do was buy lemons, call, keep quiet.

Wait . . . Cassie's head whipped up. *Is* mine?

Kelly's eyes were already upon her, as though waiting for the realization to dawn. 'I'm ten, nearly eleven weeks now.'

'You mean . . .' Cassie whispered.

Kelly nodded. 'It didn't happen. Hasn't happened *yet*, anyway. I'm still, you know . . . waiting . . .' Her voice split as Cassie pushed back her chair, throwing her arms around her. 'Even as I got on the plane I thought . . . I was so convinced, you know? Any minute now I kept saying to myself, even as the seatbelt sign went on . . .'

'I can't believe it,' she squealed.

'Me neither,' Kelly half laughed, half cried into her hair.

It was only a split second later before Suzy and Anouk

double-wrapped them, eight arms overlapping and inter-twined like a wisteria tree, holding each other up; one particularly firm hand found Cassie's arm and squeezed it hard – maybe so hard it would bruise, but when she met Suzy's eye, it was forgiveness that she saw.

'Look,' Kelly said, almost shyly, pulling a black-and-white scan photo from the inside pocket of her bag. 'I know there's not much to see yet. I mean, it's more like a coffee bean than a baby, but—'

'Oh, Kell, she's got your nose!' Suzy cooed.

'It hasn't got a nose,' Anouk frowned, peering closer. 'And who said it's a girl, anyway? Do you know that? Do you know that for certain?'

'I can't believe it. I was so sure that because you were here it meant the worst had happened. I couldn't under-stand how you were able to act so normal! I'm so happy,' Cassie laughed as she saw Archie toss Velvet into the air, Hattie and Edie forehead to forehead, their eyes closed. But she fell still as her gaze came back to Henry. He was the only one in the room without a smile on his face, the only one in the room with desolation in his eyes.

It was the screwdriver on her pillow that was the final nail in the coffin for the prodigal homecoming. It only took Henry a moment to make the connection between Luke closing the bedroom door and Cassie desperately unscrew-ing the expensive-looking bangle as though it was burning her.

'Henry, nothing happened, I swear. One kiss—'

'You *kissed* him?'

'It was a moment of madness,' she cried, watching as he

almost bounced off the walls, red-cheeked and looking for a pillow to punch. 'I was angry with you for pushing me. You kept on pushing when all I wanted was to hold on to what we've got now—'

'Oh no, we don't have anything *now*. You destroyed that when you kissed him! Wrong tense. Past tense. What we *had*.'

She stared at him, trying to stay calm. One of them had to be calm. The cliffs were crumbling beneath their feet.

'OK, then – the life we had, that was the one I trusted. The one I had chosen to lead. I didn't want to go back to something that I had *already failed at*. Why can't you see that?'

'Because it's not about going back to your past; it's about stepping into *our* future. I'm not Gil; you're not even the Cassie that he married. Why can't you see *that*?'

She swallowed. They couldn't keep going round in circles. They had to move forward. One of them had to break. 'Well, I think I do now.'

'Oh, really? So it took you kissing your ex before you could decide you do want to marry me after all?' he asked sarcastically. 'Well, don't do me any favours.'

'Henr—'

'Don't!' The word was like a bullet, stopping her in her tracks, his eyes wild, his warning finger in the air as deadly as a gun.

He paced the room in silence, his shoulders rising and falling heavily as his breath came short and fast, his jaw clenched.

Cassie waited, more scared than she'd ever been.

'What's the fucking point, huh, can you tell me that?' he asked finally with a defeated shake of his head. 'I mean, what really connects us? You don't trust me. You won't place your faith in me. You want to keep your options open, just in case.'

'That's not true,' she pushed back. 'I thought I did. I thought I—'

'Look at yourself, Cassie! I've been gone three weeks and you were straight back to *him*.' Jealousy swelled the words, the whites of his eyes bared like a warrior's.

'It wasn't like that,' she said, her voice beginning to waver.

'It was *exactly* like that,' he seethed, jabbing his finger towards her, continuing to jab the air even as the words ran out. His hand dropped down to his side, his mouth flattening into a bitter line as another silence filled the space between them. It was the silences she dreaded most – the narrative in his head hidden away from her, locking her out of the argument, giving her no space to defend, debate, fight back . . .

She felt despair rush in. Despair and worse, defeat.

'I don't know where we go from here,' he said finally. 'Well, I do, but . . .' His voice cracked and he looked away.

'Henry, please, *look* at me,' she begged. 'Please.'

It was a moment before he complied and she could see his Adam's apple bob in his throat, his jaw thrust forward defiantly. He looked at her and for a moment, when their eyes locked and it was just them again, she felt the sense of home settle around them like a shared aura. Why had it taken her so long to realize that marriage wouldn't trap her? It couldn't. She had worried about losing her freedom, but it was life *without* him that made her a prisoner. He was where her soul resided; he set her mind, body and heart free; she was the opposite of shackled when she was with him.

He could feel it too. She knew it. She saw the softening in his eyes, the give in his cheeks as their eyes explored each other like green shoots reaching into the sky; but outside, the sun slipped out from behind a cloud and the shaft of light that streamed through the window caught the gold bangle – off her wrist now and in her hands – so that it glinted like a flaming wheel.

The brightness made him squint and his gaze fell to it, his expression changing before her eyes.

'You'd better put that back on. It looks expensive,' he said flatly, turning and heading for the door. He stopped, his hand on the frame, his back to her. 'Just do what you want, Cass. I'm done.'

Chapter Thirty

'Listen, I'll speak to him,' Suzy said. 'I saw it all, remember? It's not like you were looking for it to happen. Luke manipulated you from the off. I mean, the very fact that he followed you down here tells you what you were up against.'

Cassie wiped her eyes with the backs of her hands, even though the tears were still coming. 'It won't do any good. The damage has been done, Suze.'

'It was just a kiss, for God's sake. He'll get over it.'

Cassie shook her head. 'It was worse than that. In my head, I . . . I went too far. There's just been too many things recently. We had something that used to be so good and now it's just t-toxic.'

'Nonsense. It's just a rough patch,' Suzy said peremptorily.

'That's what I keep telling her,' Kelly said, cushions plumped around her like she was the Queen of Sheba as the girls insisted she rest.

'But he said he's *d-done*,' Cassie said, beginning to sob again. How many times had she cried in the past twenty-four hours? She felt emotionally wrecked.

'Yeah, right. Like Henry's ever going to get over you. You're the love of his life, doll.'

'You didn't see him,' she protested.

'No, but I heard him – they could have heard him in Padstow, frankly – and that, my dear, is what jealousy sounds like. You kissed your ex? He's probably plotting to murder him right now.'

'Where is he?' she hiccuped.

'Arch has taken him off to calm down. Translation: lunch and a few beers at the Mariner's.'

There was a pause as Cassie brought her hands to her throat. The first aromas of roast lamb were beginning to drift up the stairs, Hattie and Edie having fallen into maternal cooking mode now that the worst of the trials – Henry's disappearance, Gem's wedding – had been dispensed with. 'Oh God, I feel sick.'

'You always feel sick,' Anouk said. 'You're just upset. Try to . . .' She blew out through her cheeks, her lips in a perfect pout; she looked like she was in a Lancôme ad. 'Try to be calm.'

But Cassie's hands had suddenly flown up to her mouth and she scooted off the bed, eyes wide as she ran for the en suite, kicking the door shut behind her.

'God, she's really in a state,' she heard Suzy say, just before she threw up brunch. 'D'you think we should get Edie?'

Cassie slumped against the loo, her eyes closed as the girls consulted in the next room: she wasn't a child . . . what could she do anyway? . . . needed to get Henry back here . . . had to talk calmly . . . would all get sorted out . . .

She heard the bedroom door open and a male voice drifted in under the bathroom door. Cassie stiffened, ever hopeful, but the accent was American – 'Leave it to me . . .' – and a moment later Bas's voice was calling softly through the door to her.

'Cass? Can I come in?'

'If . . . if you want,' she hiccuped, pulling herself up to standing and staggering across to the basin, running cold water over her pulse points and splashing her face. It helped a little.

Bas came in, his head almost brushing the ceiling. His red-toned tan clashed with the 1980s orange pine of the bathroom cabinets, and the pink shagpile carpet didn't do either of them any favours.

'Oh, honey. What a pickle.' He put down the loo seat and sat on it, looking up at her with his hangdog eyes.

She nodded. It was a pickle. Technically, it was way worse than that, actually. But still a pickle.

'The irony is, I'd finally come round to it all, Bas. I'd got my head fixed at last.'

'There was never anything wrong with your head. You were entitled to take your time after what you'd been through,' he said loyally. 'Talking of your head, when did you last wash your hair?'

She shrugged desolately. 'Don't know. Too many other things to worry about.'

He sighed. 'Neglect, neglect, neglect. And you wonder why you get split ends! Come on, I'll give you a double condition, my treat, and maybe some Indian magic too,' he smiled, waggling his fingers. 'You know it always calms you down.' He walked over to the bath and picked up the hand-held shower attachment.

She took off her T-shirt, not in the least bit concerned about him seeing her in her bra, wrapped a towel round her shoulders and positioned herself at the edge of the bath, her hair hanging over.

'What?' she asked, noticing that he'd seemingly frozen

at the sight of her. 'What? *Bas*? Why are you looking at me like that? Oh my God, Bas, you're not . . . you're not *bi*, are you?'

Ten minutes later she opened the door and three curious faces peered back at her.

'Jeez, *what* was going on in there?' Kelly asked, open-mouthed.

'You OK, hon?' Suzy said, looking past her to Bas, who was standing watching them, chewing on his thumbnail. 'What's happened? You look . . . Christ, sit down. What on earth can have happened in a small contained room with a gay hairdresser and us on the other side of the door to make you look like that?'

Cassie swallowed. Where to begin this time? 'I think I've maybe just had the maddest idea. *Ever*.'

'This is the worst idea *ever*,' Cassie wavered, as Kelly handed her another glass of water. 'What if he won't come?'

'Drink.'

'Oh, he will! Arch is under strict instructions,' Suzy said confidently.

Cassie stared out of the window again, her heart banging against her chest like a caged nightingale. She couldn't believe she was actually doing this. If someone had told her this morning that she'd be doing this, she'd have had them committed. Even the girls – her most stalwart allies – had looked at her like she was completely crackers for a full thirty seconds before getting on board and swinging into action.

'I can see them!' Anouk gasped from her perch on the window ledge.

'He's coming?' Cassie croaked. 'He's actually . . . ?'

'Yes!' Anouk squealed, hopping down.

'Oh God, I feel—'

'Don't be sick!' the three of them chorused together.

'I'm fine. I'm fine,' Cassie repeated, taking deep breaths. She could do this.

'You OK?' Suzy was squeezing her hand.

Cassie nodded.

'Come on, then. You don't want him to miss you.'

'Yeah, like there's any chance of that happening,' Kelly laughed, holding the door open.

'I can't believe we're doing this,' Anouk laughed, shaking her head and leading the way.

They got into position, Cassie standing staring at the door, hands trembling, her eyes shining with apprehension and hope. This was it. Her last chance to get it right.

A minute passed. Two. She couldn't stop the shakes. She willed her feet to move, to run – this was a terrible idea; idiotic – but they were rooted to the stone floor.

After the fourth minute, just when she was beginning to think the sight of the two men had been a bad case of wishful thinking, the door opened, a blast of light bursting through like the heavens were shining in. It took her eyes a moment to adjust before she could see him, silhouetted and still in the doorway, as the organ suddenly started up.

She saw the question in his body language as he turned to Archie for explanation. She watched as Archie leaned in and whispered something, as Henry stiffened, looking back.

He could see her now. The avalanche of light had settled,

only a light misting of dust particles hovering in the air between them as he took in the sight of her in the dress – powder-pink rosebuds at her hips, the silk tulle veil pinned in her hair, *their* roses in her hands . . .

It felt like an eternity as she waited for him to understand, to decide. But his feet did finally begin to tread the stone flags – very, very slowly – his eyes wary and disbelieving as he came down the aisle, past the wild flowers pinned so prettily to the pew ends, followed by his best man in every sense of the word; his eyes meeting first her mother's, then his own, sitting together, hands held, the three bridesmaids beaming with unrestrained joy in the matching blue silk dresses Paula had hurriedly swept up in her frantic dash over. Velvet, in a white Monsoon dress with flowers from the hedgerows woven into her hair, made the most enchanting flower girl as she sat on her mother's hip, waving a Sleeping Beauty wand, and Henry stopped to kiss her cheek as he passed.

And then he was in front of her, looking somehow even more heroic in his morning suit – the one Archie had picked up, ready and waiting at Moss Bros, thanks to a call from Paula – than he had in his exploring kit. He hadn't shaved. The call that Archie had taken from his wife, declaring that the wedding was back on and Gem supposedly needed walking down the aisle, meant he hadn't had time. But then Cassie preferred him like that, anyway. That was who he was – her adventurer, rough and ready, still salty from the sea.

His eyes travelled down the length of her, overawed, his Adam's apple bobbing in his throat again as he took in the sight of her, the nerve of her to be doing *this*. 'You look . . .'

His voice was hoarse, his eyes reddened and slightly wild. 'So beautiful.'

She smiled, relieved to have passed that test at least.

He glanced across, as if noticing the vicar for the first time. He remembered himself, remembered his manners, starting slightly as he extended a hand. 'Father Williams, good to see you.'

'Good to see *you*, Henry,' the old vicar smiled. 'Are you ready to make this brave young woman your lawful, wedded wife?'

There was a silence as Henry looked back at her, then at the vicar again. 'But how is it . . . ? I mean, would it be lawful? Don't the banns have to be read?'

'We have submitted a common licence. You were baptised here, Henry, by me, no less. That means you have what we call a "special connection" with this church. If you choose to go ahead, then this young lady will be your wife in both the eyes of God and the law for the rest of your life.'

Henry looked back at her, emotions running over his face like dancing clouds on a spring day, but no words, no answer was forthcoming.

Cassie felt panic spike through her. She had left it too late, pushed him too far. He couldn't forgive her betrayal after all. This wasn't enough. Her, in a wedding dress, standing at the altar before him, wasn't enough.

Tears shone in her eyes. Was this it, then? Was this their end, in the place that was supposed to have been their beginning?

No. She swallowed hard, summoning her courage in one final, desperate burst.

'Henry?' she asked, her voice soft but clear. 'Will you marry me?'

His eyes roamed hers and she hoped he could see beyond the fear in them, to the love behind, that she was willing to do this, again, for him. She had realized it now – she didn't have to break, just bend.

His head turned, as though looking for someone to jump out from behind a pillar and shout, 'Hoax!', but he took a step towards her, one hand reaching apologetically for her elbow, and she felt her breath hitch as she braced herself for the rejection. The flat 'no'.

He blinked down at her, home in his eyes. 'What do you think?' he smiled, bending down to kiss his bride.

Epilogue

Diaphanous pink clouds trailed across the melba sky, the cows in the field tearing at the grass with their powerful teeth and providing a backing soundtrack of sorts as they snorted and groaned, mooed and munched, and the black raven-like Cornish choughs barked their distinctive chirps from the trees.

Archie was asleep on his rug. He had just finished his first bottle of red for weeks – Suzy had relented just for the day – and it had gone to his head; Hattie and Edie were upstairs bathing Velvet; and Gem and the bridesmaids (well, Kelly and Nooks) were inside 'preparing the bridal suite', which had made both Henry and Cassie very nervous. Cassie was quite sure she'd heard something about a collapsible pole Gem had picked up in Argos – she hadn't felt up to the service, but she had felt up to that. Suzy had last been seen on the drive trying to teach Rollo to roll over. Gem had given him to her as a twin 'thank-you' and apology, and peace appeared to have genuinely broken out between them at last.

'Laird's going to have a shock when he gets back to find not only that you're home but that we hijacked his wedding. He only went out for the day,' Cassie laughed softly, picking at the grass. She was still wearing her veil – Henry didn't want her to take it off; he didn't want anything of today to start ending – and it wafted lightly behind her in the breeze.

'Forget Laird. I don't think *I'll* ever get over the shock of what you did today,' Henry said, looking up at her, his head in her lap.

'Well, you've always proved your love. It was time for me to prove mine.' She took his hand and kissed it, right on the finger where his new wedding ring sat.

He grinned. 'I'll bet Suzy loved it when you told her, didn't she?'

'You could say that. She did a cartwheel.'

He laughed. 'Actually a cartwheel?'

'Actually a cartwheel. Almost wiped out your mum's Clarice Cliff crockery.'

He shook his head. 'I just can't believe you pulled it together so quickly.'

'Actually, it was sort of already done without us realizing. I mean, obviously I stole bits of Gem's wedding – the church flowers were already done, and your mum had brought our roses with her. Anouk ran – actually broke into a run, can you believe it?'

'Not really.'

'She ran down to tell the vicar we needed the wedding slot after all. But I'd already done the food – *my* menu. Bizarrely, I'd gone off plan for once – so that was pretty much ready just to pack into the baskets. I'd even tried on the dress when Gem was trying hers. All I had to do was pick up the phone to Paula and she sorted out the rest. She's really been amazing. And even Mum's here!' She shrugged. 'It was serendipity, the whole thing.'

'Serendipity? *That's* what you call the past twelve hours?

I've been to hell and back,' he groaned, his hand automatically going to his face and pulling at his temples.

She reached for his hand again and pulled it away, forcing him to look at her. 'Well, it brought us here, didn't it?' she whispered, leaning down to kiss him once more. His hands reached up, skimming her curves delightedly. They hadn't been alone since he'd come back this morning – the fight in the bedroom earlier did *not* count – and she had a feeling their wedding night was going to feel like their first time.

She laughed as he sat up, already excited by the feel of her, and beginning to nuzzle her neck again, his hands wandering up her back, marvelling at the tiny silk-covered buttons dotted up her spine. He pulled back suddenly, a devilish expression on his face. 'Of course, there was one thing you overlooked.'

'Oh really? And what's that?' She arched a hastily plucked eyebrow. (Anouk had taken charge of that domain.)

'The bridal tradition of having something old, something new, something borrowed, something—'

'Blue?' she finished for him with a sigh. 'Tch, you really must think I'm some kind of amateur. I'll have you know I'm a pro at this gig. It's my second, you know.'

'Hey!' He prodded her in the ribs with a finger and she laughed.

'Well, if you must know . . .' She reached inside the top of the bodice of her dress and carefully pulled out the Tiffany locket that had been pinned on with a satin ribbon. She watched his disbelief as he realized what it was.

'But . . . the key – we threw it away, didn't we?' he frowned, doubting himself.

She nodded, smiling but not offering any explanation.

'So then how did you get it off?'

'*I* didn't. Nooks did. They're clearing the bridges apparently and she couldn't bear to think of it being tossed away. She's got some sort of tool that jimmied it.' She wrinkled her nose. 'I don't thinks Nooks is a jeweller at all. She's a cat burglar.'

He grinned. 'So that's your something . . . ?'

'Old.'

'So what's new?'

She held up her hand, the wedding ring glinting in the red light. 'Lucky for us that Nooks also carries a little inventory of basic pieces for sizing at consultations.'

He couldn't take his eyes off her as she smiled, admiring her wedding ring in the sunlight. It looked so right on her hand, and she knew that if she was to take it off, she would already feel stripped without it.

She indicated to the pearl earrings she was wearing. 'My something borrowed, from your mum.'

He nodded, thoroughly amused. 'And something blue?'

'Ah, now actually, that's for you. It's my wedding present to you.'

She reached into the vintage beaded pink-and-white bag from Paula's personal collection, pulling out a small, old Tiffany's box. She took his hand, turning it over and placing the box in the palm.

He looked down at it for a moment with a baffled smile, so unused to being the one surprised. 'Don't tell me you're proposing to me all over again?'

'You should be so lucky,' she grinned.

'Can I open it now?'

'I insist. It's actually also the last thing I had to do on your list.'

He looked puzzled, his interest piqued as he grasped the lid of the box. 'Last thing?'

'You said I had to give a Cornish gift. Mum didn't need it anymore, so she gave it to me. I don't need it, so . . .'

He looked worried. 'Is this the bit where you tell me you only married me to complete the list?'

She laughed, throwing back her head, and he couldn't resist kissing her neck again. 'Not *quite.*'

He opened the box. Inside glinted her father's old cuff-links. 'They're Elsa Peretti,' she said.

'They're great,' he said, lifting one. 'What are they?'

'Coffee beans. Mum bought them for Dad the year they came out, when she was pregnant with me.'

'Cute.'

She smiled as he rolled them in his palm, and waited, watched as the echo sounded somewhere in his memory.

'Wait, *coffee bean*?' He looked back at her, prompted by her enigmatic smile, his eyes falling to her ripe breasts, which had almost felled Bas earlier, the other clues beginning to fall into place, too. 'Are . . . are you saying . . . ?' he stammered.

Cassie leaned in to him with a radiant laugh, her happiness complete. 'What do you think?'

'Oh, Cass . . .' He kissed her, over and over, gazing into her eyes before clasping her face lovingly in his hands. 'The things you'll do to be done with my lists,' he murmured.

'I know,' she smiled as she saw the wetness in his eyes. 'But I'm home free now, mister. Home free.'

Acknowledgements

It's been a joy revisiting the old gang with this story and I really hope you've enjoyed it. Henry's job as an explorer is such a fascinating one to write about and research, and it was in the course of my investigations into what modern explorers actually do, that I happened upon an expedition undertaken a few years ago which aimed to raise awareness of the amount of plastic floating in the oceans. A high-tech boat called the *Plastiki* was built – yes, from bottles – and successfully sailed from Sydney to San Francisco. It's a fascinating adventure to read about, if you're so inclined, but I would like to stress that although I have used the framework of that expedition for this book, none of my characters or any of the events in the plot are based on real life or true events.

As ever, I want to thank the hugely supportive and encouraging team behind me at Pan – my brilliant and very patient editors Caroline Hogg and Victoria Hughes-Williams, Natasha Harding, Wayne Brookes, Jeremy Trevathan, Katie James, Jodie Mullish, Anna Bond, Daniel Jenkins and Eloise Wood.

My copy editor, Laura Collins, deserves a medal, frankly, for unknotting and working out the timelines that elude me even now. And James Annal is the mastermind behind a cover that is so beautiful that I'm tempted to frame it and hang it on my wall. Thank you so, so much.

To my agent Amanda Preston, thank you for always being so positive and supportive. I can't imagine doing this job without you.

And my family: Mum and Dad, Vic and Lynne, it's only because of you that these books are ever delivered. Thank you so much for the endless tea and glasses of fizz at the end of those long, hard days. For Anders and our babes, I just love you. End of.

It's time to relax with your next good book

THEWINDOWSEAT.CO.UK

If you've enjoyed this book, but don't know what
to read next, then we can help. The Window Seat is
a site that's all about making it easier to discover your
next good book. We feature recommendations,
behind-the-scenes tales from the world of publishing,
creative writing tips, competitions, and, if we're honest,
quite a lot of lists based on our favourite reads.

You'll find stories and features
by authors including Lucinda Riley, Karen Swan,
Diane Chamberlain, Jane Green, Lucy Diamond
and many more. We showcase brand-new talent
as well as classic favourites, so you'll never be
stuck for what to read again.

We'd love to know what you think of the site, our books,
and what you'd like us to feature, so do let us know.

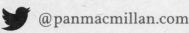

@panmacmillan.com

facebook.com/panmacmillan

WWW.THEWINDOWSEAT.CO.UK

Christmas at TIFFANY'S
by
Karen Swan

Three cities, three seasons, one chance to find the life that fits

Cassie settled down too young, marrying her first serious boyfriend. Now, ten years later, she is betrayed and broken. With her marriage in tatters and no career or home of her own, she needs to work out where she belongs in the world and who she really is.

So begins a year-long trial as Cassie leaves her sheltered life in rural Scotland to stay with each of her best friends in the most glamorous cities in the world: New York, Paris and London. Exchanging grouse moor and mousy hair for low-carb diets and high-end highlights, Cassie tries on each city for size as she attempts to track down the life she was supposed to have been leading, and with it, the man who was supposed to love her all along.

The Perfect
PRESENT
by
Karen Swan

Memories are a gift . . .

Haunted by a past she can't escape, Laura Cunningham
desires nothing more than to keep her world small
and precise – her quiet relationship and growing
jewellery business are all she needs to get by. Until
the day when Rob Blake walks into her studio and
commissions a necklace that will tell his enigmatic
wife Cat's life in charms.

As Laura interviews Cat's family, friends and former
lovers, she steps out of her world and into theirs – a
charmed world where weekends are spent in Verbier
and the air is lavender-scented, where friends are wild,
extravagant and jealous, and a big love has to
compete with grand passions.

Hearts are opened, secrets revealed and as the necklace
begins to fill up with trinkets, Cat's intoxicating life
envelops Laura's own. By the time she has to identify the
final charm, Laura's metamorphosis is almost complete.
But the last story left to tell has the power to change all
of their lives forever, and Laura is forced to choose
between who she really is and who it is she wants to be.

Christmas at CLARIDGE'S
by
Karen Swan

The best presents can't be wrapped . . .

This was where her dreams drifted to if she didn't blot her nights out with drink; this was where her thoughts settled if she didn't fill her days with chat. She remembered this tiny, remote foreign village on a molecular level and the sight of it soaked into her like water into sand, because this was where her old life had ended and her new one had begun.

Portobello – home to the world-famous street market, Notting Hill Carnival and Clem Alderton. She's the queen of the scene, the girl everyone wants to be or be with. But beneath the morning-after make-up, Clem is keeping a secret, and when she goes too far one reckless night she endangers everything – her home, her job and even her adored brother's love.

Portofino – a place of wild beauty and old-school glamour. Clem has been here once before and vowed never to return. But when a handsome stranger asks Clem to restore a neglected villa, it seems like the answer to her problems – if she can just face up to her past.

Claridge's – at Christmas. Clem is back in London working on a special commission for London's grandest hotel. But is this really where her heart lies?

The SUMMER WITHOUT YOU

by
Karen Swan

Everything will change . . .

Rowena Tipton isn't looking for a new life, just a new adventure; something to while away the months as her long-term boyfriend presses pause on their relationship before they become engaged. But when a chance encounter at a New York wedding leads to an audition for a coveted house share in the Hamptons – Manhattan's elite beach scene – suddenly a new life is exactly what she's got.

Stretching before her is a summer with three eclectic housemates, long days on white-sand ocean beaches and parties on gilded tennis courts. But high rewards bring high stakes and Rowena soon finds herself caught in the crossfire of a vicious intimidation campaign. Alone for the first time in her adult life, she has no one to turn to but a stranger who is everything she doesn't want – but possibly everything she needs.

Christmas in
THE SNOW
by
Karen Swan

In London, the snow is falling and Christmas is just around the corner – but Allegra Fisher barely has time to notice. She's pitching for the biggest deal of her career and can't afford to fail. When she meets Sam Kemp on the plane to the meeting, she can't afford to lose her focus. But when Allegra finds herself up against Sam for the bid, their passion quickly turns sour.

In Zermatt in the Swiss Alps, a long-lost mountain hut is discovered in the snow after sixty years. The last person expecting to become involved is Allegra – she hasn't even heard of the woman they found inside. It soon becomes clear the two women are linked and, as she and Isobel travel out to make sense of the mystery, hearts thaw and dark secrets are uncovered . . .